enjoy Compendium.

All the best,

COMPENDIUM

Book One in the Artifacts of Lumin Series

Alia Luria

Willowslip Press
ORLANDO, FLORIDA

Alia Luria/Willowslip Press
P.O. Box 547726
Orlando, FL 32854
www.willowslip.com

This is a work of fiction. Names, characters, places, and incidents are products of the author's imagination. All locales exist on the planet Lumin and are used for atmospheric purposes. Any resemblance to actual people, living or dead, or to businesses, companies, events, institutions, or locales existing on Earth is completely coincidental.

Ordering information:
Special discounts are available on quantity purchases by corporations, associations, and others. For details, contact the "Special Sales Department" at the address above.

Compendium / Alia Luria. -- 1st ed.
ISBN 978-0-99084-030-5

For my family, my love, and my pups.

*Special thanks to Angela Brown, Al Watt,
and Terri Valentine for their guidance and
feedback in the crafting of this novel.*

*I exist in two places,
here and where you are.*

–MARGARET ATWOOD

1 THE CORE   L.C. 9498

"WE CAN NO LONGER IGNORE THIS,"
said Minister SainClair, her voice echoing in
the massive cavern. Its resonance was dampened by
the deeply embedded roots threaded through the foundation of the room.

The encircling vines carried twinkling gourds and
night flowers, all of which threw soft light around the
chamber. Melia Kannon glanced around. The spectacular romance of the atmosphere contrasted sharply with
the tense faces of the assembly. What was filling her
with such deep unease? Was it the tension pressing
down around her or the moist air? The heat of the

chamber, which usually softly enveloped the Central Counsel like a cocoon, nurturing the growth of a civilization, crackled with energy that bordered on oppressive.

Are you getting this?

"Affirmative. I am recording," said a smooth voice directly into her ear.

Good, because Minister SainClair wants a full account of the proceeding.

Melia swallowed hard, her gut a mangled knot. She looked over to the carved elderwood table that arced around the front of the Core's assembly hall. The ministers sat facing the general delegation.

"Lumin grows weaker by the cycle. We've hit a critical degradation threshold. We must act now to immediately implement Gamma Protocol," said SainClair to the frowning faces.

The delegates erupted into frantic chatter that resonated up through the roots of the Core and into its trunks. No doubt the branches high up in the sky above shook from the force. Melia stifled a small smile from her position at the ministers' table. Now wasn't the time.

"Silence!" Minister Draca's voice thundered through the assembly. He banged the gnarled stick in his hands hard against the stone floor.

Melia flinched, but he struck the staff only once.

"Minister SainClair is speaking, and you'll let her finish."

"The ministers already voted, and we're unanimous," SainClair said. She stood up and stepped around the table to approach the assembly.

Minister SainClair had aged much over the last ten cycles but still looked regal in her finely woven teal robes. Her whitening blond hair was intricately plaited back with loose tendrils curling around her ears. Her soft clothes and features belied the ice of her almost colorless eyes. Her look of intense determination made Melia proud to serve with the woman. She swallowed hard, her heart thumping against her ribs; it didn't want to be here any more than she did. She glanced to her right. The other ministers sat stony faced, eyes forward.

SainClair folded her hands in her robes. "Lumin is at a crossroads. To continue down our current path will bring doom. We all know this. We've seen the wilt in the Great Forest. Jefferson has shown us the data on projected electrical use."

Minister Jefferson nodded from his seat.

"Gamma Protocol is too extreme!" a voice interjected. Delegate Rosewater stood from his chair to face SainClair. "Why can't we just institute a more stringent ration? A full-scale Network blackout is madness."

Murmurs of agreement rose from the crowd.

Rosewater moved to stand next to Minister SainClair. "And why five hundred cycles?" he added. "How do we even know it'll work? We're dooming Lumin either way. There'll be no way to restore it, us, anything, if we go forward with Gamma Protocol."

SainClair raised her hand to quell the burgeoning discontent mirrored in Rosewater's words. "The rations aren't working. We need a total reversal. I fear we're almost too late as it is."

"What if we are? You want to throw us into five hundred cycles of blackout, but if it's too late, we should be working harder to find a solution, not sitting on our hands."

"It's not just about us now," she said. "It's about Lumin. The planet needs to rest and regrow. If she doesn't, it won't just be us who'll be doomed. It'll be all life. We have a responsibility greater than the Core."

"So we just burn all our technology?" Rosewater's face grew dark, and his fists clenched at his side. His spring-leaf-green robes swung behind him as he turned to face the other ministers. "I guess we just torch the Network we've spent thousands of cycles building? Fill in the Core with dirt? Is that your proposal?" He glared accusingly at each of the ministers in turn, his eyes flashing. He slammed his hands on the table in front of them.

SainClair suddenly looked very tired. The iron melted from her eyes, and she rested her hands on the table. "Gamma Protocol dictates that we are to cease all use of the Network immediately. The Network will be locked, and access will be revoked for all devices."

"What about the devices that don't rely on Network access?" asked a voice from the general assembly.

"What about preservation of information?" asked another.

The floodgate released, and the room again erupted in a clamor of noise and movement. This time Minister SainClair seemed inclined to let the delegates air their grievances and concerns for a bit.

Melia sat at the ministers' table and took in the spectacle. SainClair nodded to those addressing her and leaned over to speak to the others. Melia mentally retraced the Protocol again, her brain caught in a loop that played the same steps over and over. Everything was in order, and nothing could stop it now.

She fingered the chain around her neck. The key lay against her chest under her robes. SainClair had given it to her for safekeeping. Ministers Draca and SainClair already had set the switch, with Melia there to witness. They knew this proceeding would be rife with discord, but SainClair was right. They no longer could put off the inevitable. Every week the Network grew hotter, and the trees wilted a little more. The Core itself, once a pleasant enclave, had grown uncomfortably warm over the past couple of cycles. Whether the decision was right or wrong, Melia couldn't say, but it was the only viable option. The brightest minds of Lumin had worked on this problem night and day, and now it was too late to do anything but shut it down and hope for the best.

Still, she hadn't expected such a visceral reaction from Rosewater. He was just as passionate as any minister about protecting Lumin, but all the delegates, minister or otherwise, were in this together. *All of Lumin will be looking to us for guidance, to see them through the dark cycles to come*, she thought. Melia's side twitched at the idea of informing the general populace why they no longer had access to the Network, of explaining that all their equipment was dormant. She knew they'd never understand how close Lumin had come to the brink.

She would miss the beauty of the Core. She frowned when a bounce of light caught her eye. Something had glinted just then, and she shook her head to clear the foggy thoughts. In that brief moment, the disordered chaos devolved into terror.

"No!" she screamed, bolting to her feet. She rushed around the elderwood table just as Minister SainClair crumpled on the floor, with Minister Draca on his knees at her side. "What have you done?" she shouted at Rosewater. "Seize him!"

Rosewater held a curved knife that dripped with blood. At her words, his hand loosened, and it clattered to the floor. "Only what I had to do to stop this madness," he said, his face menacing. He held his hands out as two delegates emerged from the mass, each taking one arm.

"You've done nothing," SainClair said weakly from the floor. "Gamma Protocol already has been initiated." Her voice was raspy but gurgled slightly.

Melia shoved past Rosewater and knelt at SainClair's side. She pulled away the minister's hands to find a large bloom of blood spreading quickly across the woman's chest. "Her lung," she muttered to Minister Draca.

The man nodded, his face ashen and hands shaking. "For your deed, we'll all suffer," he told Rosewater. His voice was cold and hard.

Melia focused her attention on SainClair, who was coughing. "You must relax. Coughing will only hasten it."

"Listen to me," SainClair said, her voice sounding hollow. "You have to get out of here. The Network is monitoring my vital signs."

"Hush," she said. "You must preserve your strength."

"No. You have to get the key out and to safety. When I'm gone, the Core will go into lockdown. If the key's here when I die, the dissenters will override the Protocol."

"I can't leave you," Melia said, fear lacing her voice, "any of you. I can't live with that."

"You must."

"But you'll all be trapped," she whispered fervently. She glanced over at the general assembly. The delegates' chairs were in disarray, and the other ministers were trying to calm the delegates.

"There's no time," Minister Draca said. "She's fading." He held two fingers to SainClair's wrist.

"Melia," SainClair whispered. Her skin was tinged with blue.

Melia lowered her head next to the minister's lips.

"Go now. Get the key to my estate. My son will know what to do with it."

"You have only moments now," Draca said through clenched teeth.

"Help me," Melia said, grimacing. She pulled a pin from her robes and stuck it deeply into the pad of her thumb, where a drop of blood welled up.

Minister Draca nodded and pressed SainClair's right thumb into the blood that seeped from her chest.

"Quickly," he said.

Melia pulled a book from her robes and opened it to a random page. She pressed her bleeding thumb into the center of the page while Draca pressed SainClair's bloody thumb onto it as well.

End recording and lock all profiles to these samples, Melia commanded.

"Recording ended and locked," the smooth voice said into her ear.

Activate sleep mode.

"Good-bye," the voice said.

She barely heard the voice in her head as the lights in the Core dimmed.

"Hurry," Draca said, and shoved his walking stick into her hand. "Go!"

Partially in shock, Melia staggered to her feet and rushed away from the crush of delegates as well as the more delicate roots that sprouted up from the earth. The yelling voices of the others followed her as the lights began to fail and a deep throbbing vibrated through the roots. The Core was shutting down. If Melia didn't go now, she would be trapped with the others. In the confusion, Rosewater had broken free from his restraints and was barreling toward her. She swallowed hard, a ball of panic caught in her throat like a bone.

She took a deep breath and yelled, "To the SainClair estate!" then slammed the stick onto the ground twice.

Rosewater's enraged face disappeared behind the swirling vortex that opened up in front of Melia with an enormous crack. It was the sound of something existing where just moments ago nothing had, and it always unnerved her. Turning her head to the side to shield it from the intense winds, she held her breath and leapt into the vortex.

Her knees buckled as she struck a deep snowdrift on the other side. Her stomach churned, threatening to give back her last meal. *So what?* she thought. Nerves had prevented her from having any appetite the last few days. *I call your bluff! Go ahead and vomit. See what it gets you.*

Traveling by baccillum was never pleasant. Still feeling ill, she struggled to her feet. She looked down at the baccillum and the book. They were both inert now; the tiny veins of blue light that shone intermittently on each were dark. She stowed the book in her robes and trudged toward the giant cluster of hearthtrees in the distance.

AFTER A CHANGE OF CLOTHING, a warm fur draped over her knees, and a cup of ginger tea, Melia finally stopped shaking. She wasn't sure whether the tremors were from the cold, from watching Minister SainClair die, or from the knowledge that she had left the rest of the delegation in the Core to die slow, horrendous deaths. The minister's son, Gerard SainClair, sat silently as Melia struggled through her thick-throated recounting of the day's events.

The house around them was dimly lit. The blackout already had reached the Northlands. The main hearthroot of the large home, an alcove of energy carved from one of the large trees comprising the home's central structure, still emanated heat, but the SainClair family was relying on portable gourds that provided temporary light when agitated rather than the vine-enlaced sconces scattered around the rooms. Those were powered by energy from the Network. It was lucky for them that the Northland trees were so hearty. Melia shivered again as she recalled Minister SainClair's charge to go to Gerard. With the terror of the day's events passed, Melia thought now of her husband and children, trapped on Senegast, a large island many thousands of kilometers to the west. An ocean rolled and jostled between them. She sighed deeply and turned her thoughts back to the matter at hand.

"So Mother is dead," he said. "And the others are trapped?"

Melia nodded, her eyes fixed on the smoldering hearthroot before her.

"As a fail-safe, your mother coded the Core to enter Gamma Protocol if her vital signs were no longer detectable by the Network." She stifled a sob with the back of her hand. "We took such precaution, with no real conviction that the situation would get that bad."

Gerard sighed, and Melia looked over. He was slumped over his knees and rubbing his blond temples with his index fingers.

"I could have predicted Rosewater would be the hothead," he said, his face stony. "Well, what did Mother say to tell the others? The blackout reached here right before you did, so chaos must be breaking out all over Lumin."

She winced at the thought. "Yes, well, we anticipated that the delegates would all be returning home to prepare everyone for the changes that would be taking place."

"That's admirable, but now we're looking at total social and economic chaos. Communication is cut off; power is limited; and people's information is trapped. And you say this is going to last five hundred cycles?"

She nodded. "The projections indicate that Lumin needs that much time to heal itself."

Gerard shook his head in disbelief then leaned back in his chair and tapped his cheek with a finger. "So it could be less, it could be more?"

"Yes, but the Core won't reactivate Network access until Lumin is healed."

Gerard unhooked a carved wooden cuff from his wrist. "So this is kindling now?"

Again Melia nodded. She watched him toss the cuff into the hearthroot. It singed and crackled. She swallowed hard and patted the book at her side. She had to guard it with her life. It was her people's only hope for the future advancement of Lumin, a compendium of all knowledge and the only record of what had happened in the Core today.

"What do we do now?" she asked.

Gerard looked over at Melia, his pale-blue eyes so like his mother's, and she felt a pang of loss.

"Mother left you something," he said, and turned to retrieve a letter from a wooden box sitting by the hearthroot.

"My dearest Melia," she read aloud. "If you are reading this, then our efforts to ease Lumin's transition into blackout failed, and I am dead. We had many cycles to prepare for this day, and in that time, we created the Order of Vis Firmitas. Ministers Draca, myself, and the others have each sent similar letters to our families to be opened upon the blackout. The future of Lumin is now up to those we leave behind. Please protect it. You'll find everything you need in the Compound situated in Willowslip. Your faithful friend, Aris SainClair."

Gerard rubbed his face again, as if reliving a deep pain. "She left me a very similar letter," he said. "I am bound for Willowslip as well."

"Willowslip," Melia said. "That's very far south of here. Without a baccillum, it'll take us at least half a cycle."

"Well," said Gerard, a wry, sad grin touching his lips, "we have five hundred cycles. We have all the time in the world."

2 SPORES   L.C. 10152

MIA JAYNE WAS PALE as a ghost birch and dressed in the tropics' garb of gauzy layers. Her wavy auburn hair was plaited down her back, and her bright blue-green eyes reflected the quiet light of the gourds in their gold flecks. She stood outside her hearthwood, the tree house she had called home these past cycles, and stared up at the roiling, colored glow that lit up the night sky. The purples, reds, greens, and oranges showed through the dense forest and formed a vibrant background to the clouds and moon.

A soft woof floated up from the vicinity of her feet. She looked down. Her dog, Hamish, stared intently up at her. His small, foxy face quirked, and a rumble percolated in his barrel chest and through the ruff of his thick neck fur.

"What is it, Hammy? Barking at nothing as usual, are we?"

Thinking about the long hike ahead of her on the morrow, she sighed and opened the door. Hamish scrambled over the threshold ahead of her, almost tripping her. Cursing absently under her breath, Mia entered the warmth of her tree home. The hearthwood was silent inside. She inhaled deeply. *How odd. No supper cooking.* Concerned, she set her foraging basket on the bench by the door.

"Father?" she called. "I know I'm delayed. It was Old Parniff. You know how she gets when she can't steep tea. There was nothing to be done. It took me forever to locate the proper conduit root." The roots of Parniff's hearthwood were damaged badly, and they had sounded like a swarm of bees. It was a tricky job to repair, and Mia's collection of joints, shunts, and conduits had proved inadequate, necessitating a lengthy foraging expedition midday. She was exhausted.

No response. Hamish headed straight for the kitchen at a stubby gallop, his bushy tail down. He made a low keening noise, and the hairs on the back of Mia's arms rose.

"Father!" she called again.

When she turned the corner into the nook that contained the cooking hearth, his crumpled form lay prone on the floor as Hamish whined and pawed at his leg. The makings for a nice vegetable stew were spread out on the counter in various stages of preparation.

"Father!"

Mia skidded onto her knees at his side. She turned him onto his back and felt his chest and mouth. *Is he breathing? Please let him be breathing.* She placed her ear to his broad chest. It emitted a garbled wheeze coupled with a very shallow rise and fall. *Father, what have you done? Why didn't you say something?*

Mia's limbs felt wooden from the shock, but she stood facing the counter and picked through the piles of roots and vegetables. She dropped chopped ginger into a bowl and added boiling water from the cook pot. While it steeped, she managed to heave Father up into a sitting position. *This will have to do.* She set the pungent, steaming bowl below his nose and watched him inhale and exhale shallowly. The strong odor tickled Mia's eyes and chest, but she waved it into his nostrils, hoping it would make its way into his struggling lungs. Hamish whined again then sneezed and panted. He lay down by Father and licked his hand.

Approximately ten minutes later, with a hacking cough, Father regained consciousness. A glob of phosphorescent purple phlegm shot out of his mouth and landed with a splat on the floor. His deep-gray eyes rolled back in his head, and he heaved a long, ragged breath. His olive skin was ashen and clammy, and damp black hairs curled around his ears. Mia mopped his brow with a cloth and waved more of the steam under his nose.

"How long have the spores been polluting your lungs, Father?" she asked quietly.

His eyes were still closed, but his face tightened at the sound of her words. Then it softened. He took the cloth from her hand and blotted his mouth. "A month, perhaps longer. I didn't wish to worry you."

"They're purple," she said. Her throat thickened, and the emotions forgotten in the tense moments of ministration once again surfaced as tears formed at the corners of her eyes and clung to her lashes. "You know what that means."

"I do," he said. His eyes opened, and he looked up at her. He looked so frail and tired and sad. "And so do you." Father took her hand and squeezed it with a strength that reassured her. He wouldn't be dying today at least.

"You have nothing to worry about, daughter." He reached up and rubbed her cheek with his thumb, brushing away the tears. He must have seen the fear in her eyes.

"Come," she said. "Let's get you up and somewhere warm."

Almost plaintive, he tugged the sleeve of her arm. "I'm not long for this world, and I need you to take a message for me."

These weren't the words she'd expected. "To whom? Where?"

Father wasn't a sociable person, and they had no other family than each other.

"We'll talk more on the morrow. It'll be a journey, so you'd best get some rest as well."

LATER THAT NIGHT, Mia sat in the branches of their hearthwood and once again looked out at the night lights as the trees gently hummed around her. Now, however, neither the lights nor sounds comforted her, and fear and sadness usurped her usual awe. Not even the glittering colors in the sky could alleviate the thoughts swirling up from within. She knew no other family. Now, at three and twenty, not a day had passed where the sun didn't rise and set again without her seeing Father's face. Theirs was a simple, solitary, relatively nomadic life. They had inhabited their current hearthwood for the longest period Mia could recall, which she hazarded was about four cycles. And now the life they had built here was crumbling to dust. How fragile their happiness was. Mia hadn't even realized its frailty. And now Father wanted her to leave him and go on a journey. How could she?

She felt the arms of despair drag her down and swallow her whole. Father was all she had. There was no one else. The thought of being set adrift in the world was hard to bear. She stifled a sniffle against the back of her hand. *But I will not cry. I will not cry.*

When she was about eight, she and Father had been traveling between hammocks. He became, as he occasionally did, restless and decided abruptly that it was time for them to move on. Every move they made took them farther into the outer hammocks. Mia rather liked traveling and likewise didn't mind the dearth of people that resulted.

In this instance, their travels had taken them across a channel narrow enough to accommodate an arboreal bridge. These bridges were and remained wondrous marvels to Mia. Even when she was a child, even this short bridge had been nothing less than a spectacular sight that had caused her to suck in her breath sharply, her eyes growing round and full. Large, thick roots wove themselves in an intricate pattern over the channel, knitting together a solid bridge. In the center of the channel, a structure sat solidly on a platform of roots.

"What is that, Father?" Mia had asked.

Partially open to the channel, the structure had an angled roof of planks and fronds. This tiny shack was the first man-made building Mia ever had seen constructed from boards and other finished materials, rather than naturally grown or carved from living plants. Only the clump of heavy roots growing upward in a large lump and carved into a hearth saved the structure from seeming completely alien.

"It's a lodge," Father replied. "The hammocks on either side of this channel are stalker territory." He looked over his shoulder at Mia. "You do remember what I said about stalkers, right?"

She nodded but kept looking forward to the off-kilter little box on the bridge. "Who owns the lodge?"

Father smiled. "No one. It's customary that if we stay a night, we maintain her as payment for her service to us."

Mia looked appraisingly at the lodge and considered his words. "How do we do that?"

"We repair a broken plant, fix the floor, or mend some roots," he replied, and they picked their way through the forest toward the bridge.

Even when Mia was a young child, the trees had hummed around her. One of the root channels that led from the nearby arboreals to the bridge was buzzing strangely. She stopped to listen. Father pulled her along by the rope tied around her waist. It kept her from wandering, as she was wont to do.

"But," she asked, "what about maintaining the other stuff?"

"What other stuff?"

"The stuff that leads to the lodge." She pointed at the buzzing root. "That one needs help."

Father shrugged and continued walking. "Sometimes roots get damaged or broken, and the current is interrupted," he said thoughtfully. "It eventually will grow along another path."

"But what if you need current now?"

"Well, sometimes you just have to abide."

Pushing her bright-red hair from her eyes, Mia frowned at that answer. Her cheeks scrunched up as she thought about the silliness of that statement and followed Father onto the bridge.

When they arrived at the entry to the lodge, Father announced them as the Jaynes. The only other travelers were an old couple setting up camp on the left. They nodded and went on about their preparations with slow, deliberate movements. It would soon be dark, and they were cooking the evening meal.

The hearth in the corner was small for the size of the lodge. It must have taken a very long time for a root to grow large enough to support a hearth at all. Mia walked over to it and put out her hands to warm them. The hearth was pleasant, but the heat that emanated from the alcove was weak. By the hearth, she heard the buzzing again.

"Can you hear that?" she asked the others.

The old couple shook their heads.

"Stop playing around," said Father.

Mia was used to people not understanding. No one seemed to hear broken plants the way she did.

As night fell, the forest and channel dimmed, and the only light around the small group emanated from the hearth, flickery and weak, spilling from gourds growing on vines twined around the ceiling planks and scattered through the forest, and the subtle, pale colors of the night lights of a dark night. Mia and Father ate a meal of dried meat, fruits, and some old crackers. It was meager fare, but she was hungry and tired from the hiking. It wasn't long before she drifted off to sleep to the sound of Father conversing in hushed tones with the elderly couple. Their discussion of the old days failed to hold Mia's attention.

She woke to the buzzing noise. The others were now sleeping soundly. Father snored softly, and the sound of the old man's regular, wheezy breathing carried to her ears. The buzzing remained steady, though. She climbed from her blankets and crept quietly over to the hearth. She touched it, and a buzz vibrated into her fingers. She moved her hand around until the sensations grew strong. She chased the vibration with her hand down the length of the root toward the floor then out of the lodge. Her conscious mind receded, and her thoughts grew indistinct as she followed the vibration along the root in the direction of the shore. At the shore, she continued to walk along the ground where the root partially protruded. About two feet from a large tree, she still heard the buzzing, but it was faint, and the vibration stopped. When she backtracked, the vibration returned, and the buzzing intensified. She looked down at the root where her hands rested. She realized then that she should have brought a gourd from the camp. Unable to see the root, she felt around for it and found a crack in it.

"Here is where you're broken, my friend," Mia said softly.

Maybe I can fix it, she thought. *Patch it with some root paste.*

Overcome with excitement, she turned back toward the lodge when a twig snapped faintly behind her. Mia realized it too late. The owls that were hooting moments before, the insects that were singing, and the rodents that scuttled along the branches all disappeared into the darkness. The forest about her was silent. Her heart stopped momentarily then quickened in her chest as she gasped for a breath. She slowly turned her head to look behind her. The path to the forest was pitch-black. It was there. She knew it was there but couldn't see it. *Where is it? I'm going to die. I can't see it.*

Although her eyes had failed her, her ears didn't. Another subtle snap of a twig and a slight rustle. She threw herself to the ground and screamed as loudly as she could. She rolled onto her side, slightly dazed. Silver fur in silhouette glinted as a black shape sailed over her, momentarily inky against the barely visible night lights. Despite the cat's massive size, it landed with deft grace and circled back on her immediately, claws raking the dirt. It was huge, steely silver with glowing yellow eyes—the largest animal Mia had ever seen. The stories had failed to mention the malice and hunger in those glowing eyes. They spoke to her, mostly saying that she had made a terrible mistake venturing from the safety of the lodge and was about to be dinner. She screamed again, a long, drawn-out howl that tore through her body. Her high voice echoed through the forest, a cacophony of children.

The standoff lasted mere ticks, but Mia felt every moment freeze and then shudder through her. The stalker hissed—a sound deep in its thick neck—and swayed slightly from side to side. A roar and a crash sounded from the direction of the lodge, followed by heavy footfalls. A bright light emerged from the darkness, and the stalker hissed again, this time adding an unearthly yowl, and turned its head toward the oncoming light. It was Father carrying a flaming club. He screamed as he charged the stalker. It hesitated for just a moment at losing its easy prey then crouched and leapt at Father's advancing form.

The mass of the cat drove him back onto the ground. He swung the torch up into the stalker's face, and it roared, digging its claws into his shoulder. Its open mouth displayed an array of large, glistening teeth. The beast snapped its jaws at the flaming stick, breaking it in half. Father whipped the stick's remnants at the cat, aiming for the muzzle, but the beast moved like the wind, and the stick glanced off its temple. The cat shrugged off the blow then raked at Father again, trying to get its face-size paws around his head.

The sounds of struggle ceased suddenly with a howl and a squish. The forest quiet again, Mia looked to see the massive cat slumped over Father, inert. She remained paralyzed with fear as Father, bloody and battered, struggled out from under the cat. When he finally pushed the stalker off himself, Mia saw a thin, supple knife protruding from where the cat's left eye once was. A stream of blood ran down its large head and pooled in the soft dirt floor of the forest. The other yellow eye stared vacantly into the night sky. She whimpered, curled in on herself, and lay there shaking. Bleeding from his shoulder and face, Father rushed to her and wrapped her in his arms. At that moment, Mia felt so very small.

"Are you hurt?" he yelled, then released her from a hug to poke and prod her limbs for injuries. Tongue-tied, she managed to shake her head. He scooped her up and carried her back to the lodge, where the old man was waiting at the entrance. He held a knife, sister to the one lodged in the stalker's eye socket, and was poised to loose it into the darkness. Where he had moved slowly and deliberately before, his movements with the knife were smooth and steady. *How had he even been able to see where to throw it?* Mia shivered again and buried her face into Father's blood-soaked shirt.

"What were you doing out there? Didn't you hear me earlier? We came here for safety, and you wander out into the night alone! Blast it all!" Father yelled.

"I'm sorry," she whispered. "I just wanted to help the tree."

"What in the blazes are you talking about? It's as if there isn't a sensible bone in your whole body."

Father set her on the floor and shook her shoulders. But the rage left his body as quickly as it had come upon him, and he sank onto his bedroll in a heap.

The old woman clucked at him. "Now there, Jayne, ser. We should see to those gashes."

Father nodded sullenly. Mia watched the old woman tend to Father's shoulder and face. He winced but remained silent as she packed his shoulder wounds with ground herbs she had mixed with a thick milky liquid and formed into a paste. Mia didn't recognize it and wanted to ask her what the stuff was and how it worked, but she was still scared, and her timidity won out. Father no longer seemed cross, but his face look haggard and ashy, whereas hours ago it was fierce and tanned.

She'd been so scared that the stalker was going to eat her. And then she was scared it was going to eat Father. It may have too, if the old man hadn't been quick with the knife.

"Can you teach me to use that?" she asked the old man later, after Father had fallen asleep.

"My child," the old man said in his raspy voice, "I can show you how to throw a knife, but this one is much too large for you. You'll have to find a craftsman who can make you a set of your own, balanced just for you. Then you'll never want for food or protection."

The old man was right, and she convinced Father of the idea after they'd settled into their new home. *I should have asked the old woman how to heal people instead*, she thought.

THE NEXT MORNING, Father was up and about as if he hadn't collapsed at all. Mia wanted to believe it had all been a dream, but she knew otherwise. He whistled softly to himself as he prepared some eggs. She smelled roasting sweet onions, lard, and some of the tangy cheese acquired two days before.

"Father, that cheese cost me a rare shunt. Rare indeed." *Might have even been able to use that at Parniff's*, she thought. Still dressed in her rumpled home clothes, she approached the hearthroot quietly and sat at the table.

Father, on the other hand, was dressed as if he were about to go ranging.

"I rather hoped to save it for a special occasion."

"Every dawn faced with vigor is a special occasion for me just now," he said, giving her a pointed look.

"Indeed you have the right of it," Mia replied, her body sagging slightly. They settled into an awkward silence, uncomfortable thoughts boiling inside her head, each clamoring for her anxious attention.

Her eyes slid around the great room of their hearthwood. She recalled their careful selection of the tree, the effort it took to hollow out the center to form their home, and the cycles of living that made it such. Her eyes moved to the lounge, where Father had slept last night. She stood up and walked over to his make-shift bed.

Even in his weakened state, he had managed some-how to pull down one of the heavy furs from the high shelf where they were stored. Those furs had traveled with them to and fro and had remained entirely unused as relics from another time and place. Folks of the tropics had no use for such trappings. The center of the fur retained the shape of a body curled into it. Mia tried not to worry. Perhaps the warm furs were responsible for his current spry state. She couldn't lose hope.

"They remind me of your mother," he used to say when she asked why they burdened themselves with such unnecessary items.

"Tell me more about her," Mia would say.

"She was very beautiful" was all Father would answer to that request.

When she was ten, Father had presented her with a leather bag lined in fur. It was much heavier than the gauzy cloth packs people in Hackberry carried.

"It was your mother's," he said. "I thought you might like it."

It was an aged brown, with scratches and scars here and there marking its adventures. Soft sable-colored fur lined the opening, and the letter *J* was intricately embroidered on the front in soft silk threads of green and blue, matching her eyes. Mia would look at her bag and imagine how it might have gotten a particular mark on its side. Did Mother scale a mountain to look from its peak or traverse an ocean to stand on a foreign shore? Mia had no idea whether she ever had done those things. She must have been a great adventurer, however, to come by these fur items so foreign to the tropics. Mia carried the bag with her always, even though the few hammockers about her always joked at its heft.

"Mia," Father called from the hearth, interrupting her musings, "I've been thinking very long and hard about what my next words will be. I don't say them lightly."

Mia turned back to him. Father had set the table with the morning meal and was taking a seat. She sat across from him, her heart pounding in her chest.

"All right," she said, encouraging him to continue.

"I need you to carry a message to the Order of Vis Firmitas in Willowslip."

Mia recoiled at mention of the Order.

"I know what I've said these cycles past, but the clerics there may be able to render assistance in this matter. They have means not available to the hammock folk here in the backwaters. They're an ancient organization that has retained the ways of old." A viscous cough punctuated his statement.

"But you've always mistrusted their ways," she replied.

"True as that may be, they may have some remedy for the spores, and I have something they may need."

What might he possibly have that Vis Firmitas would want? Despite her reservations, Mia grimly agreed to make the journey and carefully packed her most sacred belongings into her lapin bag, including a small notebook where she kept her thoughts, along with a lock of blond hair from her mother pressed into it. Her mother's locket was Mia's constant talisman, and she placed it into the bag as well. She also packed her collection of the rarer root blocks, shunts, and conduits kept on hand for repair work. A simple tropics gauze wrap contained her clothing and camping gear.

When Father handed her the missive, it was sealed with his sap mark.

"Don't break the seal," he instructed. "We'll be lost if the letter doesn't arrive intact."

Mia thought his request odd, but she obeyed. She was scared for Father and for her own future.

Giving him one last hug and a kiss on the cheek, she leaned close and said, "You'll look after Hamish, won't you?"

3   WILLOWSLIP   L.C. 9499

MELIA KANNON STRUGGLED to put one foot in front of the other. Her feet had ceased to ache many kilometers back. Now she felt only the shock waves that the blocks of numbness connected to her ankles threw up her calves and into her hips. Willowslip stood off in the distance, a speck on the horizon of blowing green stalks, with mountain ranges to either side of the plain. The sight was majestic from a distance, but she had serious misgivings regarding what they would find when they reached the city. It had taken them many months to get this far, and the vastness of Lumin, which had felt to Melia so small before now, appeared as an endless expanse of land and water. From the cold Northlands, with their remote villages and estates, through the mountain pass and its towns carved from the rocks of the surrounding cliffs, they had nearly traversed the open plains. Along the way, they met only chaos, desperation, and frequently despair. Melia regretted not taking a weapon when they had left the SainClair estate.

"I don't think I'll see Senegast again in my lifetime," she said, as she and Gerard walked among the tall grasses swaying in unison, like waves rolling across the ocean. She missed her family, her children, her hearthtree, and she worried for them all.

"I suppose that would indeed be a tall order," replied Gerard.

"I fear all the island towns are already cut off from the main continent," she said after a long pause. "Boats for short travel were always for the common folk, who were unable to afford a trip by baccillum. Now, whether one is poor or rich, common or storied, our tools of travel are the same."

"Mine could use a hot soak," said Gerard, his normally pale skin red and cracking from the merciless wind and lack of shade. He grimaced as he looked down at his travel-weary clothes, dirt caking the fine garments. "It appears my feet aren't the only thing that could use a soak," he added.

Melia smiled at her companion, her white teeth flashing against the brown skin of her face. She didn't burn like Gerard, but her skin wasn't windproof and chapped just the same. She would be glad to get out from the open pass and back to the shade of the trees.

"Perhaps islands like Senegast are better off isolated from the mainland," she said, frowning at a jagged tear in her sleeve, courtesy of a band of distraught citizens. She'd been obliged to hide her status as a former delegate after that incident. "At least for now," she added, deepening her frown.

Gerard nodded as he looked off to the mountain toward their right. If his mother's letter was accurate, they were headed for its base.

"I understand why Mother did what she did," he said finally, "but why not prepare people first? Give them time to develop larger boats and alternate means of land travel." His words were fractured. The fatigue was getting to them both.

Melia shook her head. She pressed her arm against her side, feeling the reassuring warmth of the book against her ribs. "I don't think it would have mattered. We—myself included—were all too attached to our comforts and conveniences. Perhaps Aris understood that a swift wrenching of the bandage was in order."

"I just hope Willowslip is better off than the North-lands," Gerard said, and then his left knee buckled under him.

Melia stepped quickly to his side and supported his elbow as he struggled back to his feet. She shivered against the wind and thought of the Northlands. Somehow she doubted Willowslip would be any better.

MELIA AND GERARD FINALLY WOUND their way down the road into town towards nightfall a few days later. The entry gate was a shambles, but at least it was open. No one paid the two newcomers any mind as they moved along the mossy roads. Melia wasn't surprised. She and Gerard looked wretched; the long journey south hadn't been kind. Gerard favored his left knee with every step, and Melia worried for his health. They needed quarters for the night. It had been weeks, maybe months, since she'd last slept on a mattress. She prayed at least one of the local hospitality hearths was housing folk. They moved through the disordered streets, passing fighters, beggars, vendors, shifty-eyed grifters leaning against the ruins of shops, and every-thing in between.

"Network connection!" yelled a man with a push-cart as they passed. "Get yer adapter conduit here.

Guaranteed to restore yer connection." That trick apparently had worn thin, as the man had no takers.

Some of the shops were boarded up and abandoned. Melia saw signs of rioting come and gone. The early chaos had subsided into hopelessness. Busted shades and bent and torn branches decorated the buildings. Some of the trees were even scorched on the outside. Nothing without a direct hearthroot had power, so all the plank structures had been abandoned and gutted for any useful materials.

Melia and Gerard stayed silent as they traversed the clamor of people and small animals before turning west at a large intersection. The road they had turned from kept north, eventually leading to the Lord's Keep. "Keep" was an inadequate name. It was by any definition a castle and a stronghold at that. Even from their position south, Melia could see the guards standing at every corner tower, keeping careful watch. It was disconcerting, to be sure, but nothing they had time to deal with now.

"Hoy," Gerard said, his voice raspy. "I think I see a hospitality hearth up ahead."

"Let's hope they have a hearth strong enough to heat a good bit of water. I have a mighty need for a bath and a cup of tea." She took Gerard's arm to steady him, and they continued through the ruckus toward the sign that read, HEARTH SHARE INN.

Neither of them noticed the shadow growing long behind them, always twenty paces back.

4 THE VOYAGE   L.C. 10152

M IA JAYNE STARED IN AWE at the large ship before her. It was a sight to behold, with its fantastic metal hull eaten away with age and the ravages of the tropics, a relic from a long-forgotten past. A grove of elder trees grew from the center of the deck. She always traveled by canoe through the channels out among the hammocks, but this ship wouldn't fit through such thin strips of water. It was meant for majestic trips across the straits.

It was Mia's first trip to Willowslip, as Father always had kept them clear of major towns when they'd traveled. "When you've seen how humanity acts during war times, you realize the thin veil of civilization we wear is but a mask we don to be able to continue to live with ourselves," he'd said once, after imbibing a strongly fermented gourd.

When Mia asked what he meant, his demeanor grew surly. "Such matters are in the past and should stay there!"

She never pressed the subject after that. Now, as she stood waiting to embark upon the ship, a small shiver trilled through her. She should have pressed harder for information, paid greater attention to the ramblings of her elders.

"Fare?" said a sailor. His bony face and sunken eyes wore a bored expression as he blocked the embarkation ramp with his body.

"Gourds," she replied, and held up a basket of the squash fruit she'd lugged with her from Hackberry.

"They fresh?" he asked suspiciously. He stared at Mia, as if just noticing something odd about her face. Brushing off his stare, she selected one of the gourds from the basket and rapped it solidly against the rail of the ship's gangway. The gourd pulsed with a soft glow in her hand.

"Freshly picked. They should have at least five uses in them."

He nodded and took the basket from her hands then offered it to a deck hand who'd slunk up by his side. "That'll do," he said, and waved her onto the boat. "Find a place ter set. We'll be off shortly."

Mia boarded and surveyed her surroundings. The deck was built around a large grove of elder trees that occupied a significant portion of the center of the ship. They were a particularly hardy and well-tended bunch. She walked over to the rail that surrounded the dense throng of trees and peeked over it toward the roots below. Their trunks descended into the darkness of the hold, but the smell of moist earth wafted up from the recesses. She reached out a hand to touch one of the branches of the closest elder tree.

"I would refrain," a deep voice said from behind her. She flinched back in surprise and turned her head to locate the source. A tall, lean man stood behind her. He had black hair and dark eyes, not unlike Father's, but his deep skin, although naturally brown and swarthy, appeared ashy and faded. His complexion would be even darker than Father's if he didn't clearly spend nearly every waking moment indoors.

"Why is that?" Mia replied, studying his clothing. He obviously wasn't one of the hammock folk. His heavy garments were devoid of color, as if each piece had been washed one too many times with lye or had been left in the sun to drab.

"The shipmasters are very particular about maintaining their elders. If you were caught molesting one of the trees, you'd be put off the ship."

Mia raised an eyebrow. "Molesting?" She spoke the word as if it were a foreign object discovered in her mouth, shrugged, and dropped her hand back to the banister. "I was merely curious."

He approached the rail to stand beside her and looked at her from the corners of his eyes. "I am called Cedar Kannon," he said casually.

"Mia Jayne," she finally grumbled after some brief deliberation.

"Nice to meet you," he said, and flashed a bright smile at her.

She rolled her eyes in return, but she felt her chest tighten slightly. Something about him disarmed her.

"Quite a pleasant day to set sail," he said, undaunted.

Mia looked up at the bright blue-green sky with its puffy clouds spattered cheerfully about. "Indeed," she muttered, although she didn't feel particularly at ease with the day.

"What takes you to Willowslip?" When Mia didn't reply, he continued. "I was on an errand and am returning to my duties in town. Serving with the Order of Vis Firmitas is important work."

Her ears pricked at his admission. She might be able to learn something of use from this gangly fool. The fact that he was a cleric increased her mistrust, but she had no idea what to expect. *The gangly fool that you know is better than the beast you don't,* she thought.

"I have business with the Order myself," Mia said, still looking up at the sky through the branches of the trees.

"What business is that? Perhaps I can assist."

He was rather getting ahead of himself. They'd only just exchanged names.

"It's a matter of discretion. However, if you wish to be of assistance, I certainly could use direction to reach Dominus Nikola."

Cedar coughed conspicuously, trying to hide his surprise. Mia kept her face impassive despite his almost comical reaction to her request.

"You wish to see the head cleric?" he asked with incredulity. "Seeking an audience with him isn't an easy task."

"Be that as it may, I believe he'll want to speak with me."

As he snorted in repressed laughter, Mia's eyes narrowed. *Granted, my close circle is on the rural side, but are all city folk so disastrously mannered?*

"It's no concern of yours," she replied testily. "The offer of assistance was yours. I'm prepared to proceed with or without it."

Cedar collected himself and nodded. "Oh, I'll be delighted to take you to Dominus Nikola. In fact I'd trade my right eye for a front-row seat."

"That won't be necessary," she said, and leaned against the rail. "It seems I have something the Order needs."

Cedar shrugged and said no more.

After a quiet moment, Mia rummaged through her bag and pulled out a fist-size spiny yellow fruit. She pried off some of the spines then munched on the creamy white flesh underneath. It tasted of mild sweet lemons, and she murmured her approval. "Want some?" she asked, and pulled a second fruit from her bag.

Cedar eyed the spiny fruit as if it would leap out of her hand and attack him. "What is that thing?"

"In Hackberry we call them rollies," Mia said. "They need the moisture and warmth of the tropics."

"Don't you want to save it?" he asked, taking the proffered fruit with hesitation. "It might be a while before you get back here."

"Oh, I doubt that," Mia said. "My business in Willowslip will be quick, and I have no desire to whiffle about."

5 ENTRY L.C. 9499

M ELIA KANNON CAUGHT HER BREATH as she and Gerard approached the cavernous mountain way flanked by imposing hardwoods. The sprawling roots of the elders hugged the rock crevasses that formed the entry to the stronghold within. She stopped and looked upward. The jagged walls of rock slipped into obscurity as they rose steeply into the air, framed by the trees. Green mixed with brown and gray, and curling tendrils of vines caressed the large hole in the mountain toward which they trudged, inviting them to explore. How had Minister SainClair found this place? It was massive yet completely innocuous. Melia continued her trek, taking double steps to catch up with Gerard. He was doing much better after a good night's sleep at the hospitality hearth, but their months of foot travel had taken a toll on both of them.

"What will we find inside, I wonder," Gerard said, more to himself than her.

"Aris said we'd find the future of Lumin," Melia replied, adding, "although personally I think we've carried it with us." She patted her side where the book was nestled, never out of her reach since that day in the Core, a day that had left her with recurring dreams that had her screaming in the night for the ministers, pleading with them to come with her. She quivered at the memory of the blood, the haunted eyes of Minister Draca, and the crazed expression of Rosewater as he flung himself toward her.

"I hope so. Right now it feels like Lumin has no future." He scowled and rubbed his neck.

"An uncertain future, perhaps, but one nonetheless," Melia said, trying to stay positive.

"Look at that door." Gerard squinted into the darkness of the twenty-foot hole in front of them. "It's huge."

Melia slipped a gourd out of the sack slung over her shoulders and knocked it against her palm. The chemical light swirled to life, emanating from the translucent skin of the round knobbed plant. It was too weak to cast light on the distant door, but she held it aloft as they approached, trying to get a better view. The sunlight filtering through the tree branches and down the dark cavern path illuminated the barest outline of the mammoth door. The shadows in the cavern swirled as Gerard and Melia stepped closer, and she grew tenser with each passing moment.

"Do you suppose someone could have made it here before us?" she asked Gerard, clutching at his arm. She felt a niggle in the back of her mind; something worried her. Was it the unnatural silence in the trees, the deep darkness of the entrance, or something else that raised her hackles?

"I don't see how," he said, patting her hand. "Mother's letter said the various families would be notified, but you were the only one that made it out, right?"

Melia nodded, thinking back to the fear and pain of that day. "I'm certain of it. But suppose someone opened their letter first out of curiosity or fear, and they weren't happy with what they read?"

"It's a risk we'll have to take," he said, straightening his back. "We've traveled thousands of kilometers to get here. It's taken many months. I'm sure as the *bloody Core* not turning back now!"

"Poor choice of words," she said weakly.

Gerard looked over at her, his eyes softening. "Sorry." He rested his hand over hers, giving it a gentle squeeze.

The lump that had been building in Melia's throat overcame her voice. She nodded instead of replying, her eyes remaining fastened on the undulating darkness just outside of her vision. As she and Gerard slowly approached, the door resolved itself into focus. The shadows retreated from the gourd's intrusive twinkle, and the bright expanse of polished elderwood jumped forward as the light of Melia's gourd danced on its surface. The gold flecks in the wood shimmered with each step they took, and the intricate carvings— symbols of the old lineages of Lumin—seemed to move with them. She released the long breath she'd been holding, a sigh escaping her throat.

"'Tis quite lovely," he said, his mouth turning up in a bemused smile. "That door is Mother all over."

"It's a beacon of civilization in the grayness," said Melia, smiling as she saw House Kannon, House Draca, House SainClair, and the others, each worked into the smooth wood. Her body softened at the familiar trappings of the Lumin she missed dearly.

They were only a few steps from the mouth of the cavern when Melia heard a noise. Before she could turn, Gerard shrieked beside her, going down on his knees. She screamed reflexively and knelt beside him.

A wicked-looking arrow stuck out behind him, lodged deeply in his right shoulder. She dragged him toward the door as quickly as she could.

"I may have missed my mark on the first shot, but you're trapped now, my friends," a deep voice called out. It echoed inside the cave entrance while Melia frantically tried to stem the blood seeping from Gerard.

"It'll be fine," he muttered. "It's just my shoulder."

"I can't lose another SainClair," she said through clenched teeth, as she pressed her hand to the wound. "How the blast do we get in this door?"

Footsteps rang out on the path as their pursuer advanced at a leisurely pace. "Rosewater sends his regards," said the voice.

Melia paled, her brown skin feeling clammy. He couldn't have escaped. He couldn't have.

"Then why doesn't he tell us himself?" she called back. She pushed Gerard into the corner next to the door and stood before him, shielding his body from further arrows. If this stranger wanted Gerard, he would have to pick her off first.

"I think you know the answer to that. The ministers weren't the only ones to leave instructions. Rosewater was every bit as prepared for this as Draca and SainClair were," he said, coming to a stop right at the entrance to the cave. The sun was at his back, but

Melia held up the gourd to gaze upon their attacker. He was a young man with hatred in his eyes and a sneer on his face.

"Our dear friend Gerard looks like he's losing a bit of blood. What say you hand over the key, and I'll be on my way? Neither of you has to die this day, but I'm leaving with the key one way or the other."

Melia tensed and pushed back against Gerard, shielding him as best she could. She started to slide her hand into her tunic, when the stranger cocked his bow once more.

"I'd think again if I were you."

"Do you want the key or not?" she asked. "Am I supposed to teleport it over to you?"

Sneering, he started toward her, bow taut. "I'll just see to that myself then."

Five, four, three, two... She counted down his approach with each step he took. *One!*

Melia dropped toward the stone floor, kicking her leg to the side and giving his knee a good punch with her foot. He lost his balance, his arrow dislodging and bouncing off harmlessly to the left of the door. The man fell backward onto the ground with a grunt and a curse. He tried to roll to his side, but Melia sprang on top of him, pulling a dagger from her robes. He grabbed for the knife, wrestling her arm. She fought him, thrusting the dagger with both hands toward his heart and kneed him in the groin. He groaned, and his grip spasmed.

"You tiny mongrel," he growled. "You had your chance, but now you'll die."

"Not this day." She leaned down on the knife, the weight of her body overcoming the strength in his arms. The knife was almost to his chest when Gerard came up behind his prone form and smashed a rock into his head. The man went limp. With no resistance to keep Melia's dagger from plunging, it slid into his flesh. She rolled off the man, breathing raggedly, and stared at the ceiling for a moment.

"Is he dead?" she finally asked.

"Surprisingly, no," said Gerard, his voice thin but alert.

"Good. I have some questions for our guest," Melia said, sitting up. "Assuming he continues to breathe. But first let's get you inside, if we can figure out this damnable door."

6 THE COMPOUND L.C. 10152

B *LAST THEM TO THE CORE! How dare they?*
Even though they were balled into tight fists,
Mia Jayne was sure her shaking hands betrayed her
fear and rage. Standing before the Order of Vis
Firmitas, she found no solace in the rough-hewn walls
of the chamber; the dim yellow glow of the gourds
resting in their sconces; the somber, coarse robes; the
craggy faces; and the multitude of inscrutable eyes
that bored into her from the dais at the front of the
room. She felt exposed by those eyes.

One of the clerics, an older man with grizzled blond
hair, pale skin, and hawkish features, openly sneered at

her. Hate emanated from his cold blue eyes. They were pale, almost colorless. She swallowed hard, but the challenge of it lodged in her throat. The silence was large and round in the room.

Mia grimly scanned the crowd of faces in hopes of catching Cedar's eye. She frowned softly; he wasn't there to provide friendly reassurance. She focused the fire in her gut and her gaze back to Dominus Nikola.

"You must be mistaken, sir." Although she attempted to keep her voice calm but firm, she was quite certain she was failing miserably. "My father is gravely ill, to be sure, but such claims as you've asserted just now are entirely outside the realm of possibility."

Dominus Nikola, the oldest of the assembled clerics—a withered, stooped-back man with piercing gray-blue eyes as clear as Mia's favorite pond and disheveled silver hair that jutted at seemingly random angles—turned Father's letter gently in his hands. He stood from his great chair on the dais, his height imposing even given his sloping shoulders and advanced age.

"Miss Jayne," Dominus Nikola said, his voice soft, with the slightest rasp. It was a low voice that weighed each word carefully and deliberately. It was a voice that commanded attention. "I assure you that the contents of the letter as I have described them to you are accurate in all respects."

Mia's eyes narrowed in response. "Then, pray, let me read it myself." She held out her hand.

Father had sealed the letter with a sap mark, and she had respected the mark's intent. It was galling that Dominus Nikola felt he could use the existence of the mark of privacy against her.

"That won't be possible, Miss Jayne. The letter provided specific instruction in that regard."

Mia's composure slipped, and her attempts to collect herself gained no purchase. "So I'm to believe my father traded me for succor, and now I'm yours to do with as the Order commands?" she asked, her voice shrill. "I'm an adult. My service isn't his to give."

The room was silent except for their voices reverberating along the walls. The group of eyes shifted back and forth at their exchange.

"That your service is yours alone to give is certainly the way of it. That your father wishes succor is also the way of it." He paused to scratch his ear thoughtfully. "No person can choose for you. The path is yours alone to take. Be that as it may, it's the Order's choice whether to provide the succor, and the only payment for such that you've brought to our doors is your person."

"What is this organization that it requires payment to assist a dying man who is reaching to you for aid? Perhaps you *are* monsters, as Father led me to believe."

The Dominus smiled softly at her words, his eyes clear as pools yet unreadable. "Ah, but your father would request charity from us where each person among those here serves a role of import. To send one of our own skilled clerics on a journey to your father to administer a speculative treatment when such person is sorely needed among us and to in turn leave you with no ascertainable competencies to fill such a valued role is charity indeed. To expect more is foolhardy, and your father is no fool."

"So I really have no choice then?"

"One always has a choice, Miss Jayne."

IT WAS DONE. Mia's limbs moved woodenly and without input from her brain. A voice on the edge of her consciousness advised her to pay closer attention to the gravelly voice barking nearby. Brother SainClair, the sneering, hawk-faced cleric from the Great Hall, shoved her brusquely along the maze of carved stone passageways. He marched along the dim corridor deep in the depths of the stronghold and pointed gruffly at various doorways, each identical.

Mia was fairly certain the noises he made weren't actually words. SainClair was clearly just as unhappy with their present situation as she, but Mia was under no illusion that this fact created an alliance between them.

As her mind sank down inside itself, Brother SainClair and the featureless caverns faded away.

"Are you even listening at all?"

The demanding bark ripped through the foggy haze of Mia's memories.

"Ah," she said, struggling to retrieve SainClair's words from the ether.

"I thought not," he said. He stopped abruptly and spun on his heels to face her.

Mia almost collided directly into his chest.

His already cold blue eyes narrowed further. "I don't understand what you're doing here."

"Ah," she said again, sliding her eyes downward to look at her belt.

"You were full of grand words earlier," SainClair said, clocking her on the shoulder, "but you have none for me now?"

"I...um...I'm not sure what you're expecting." Mia cringed at the sound of her stuttering.

Brother SainClair smiled slowly and malevolently, his teeth large and wolflike. "I don't understand why you're here among us," he repeated slowly. "This isn't a game, girl. This is no place for frauds or pretenders."

"It's not as if I had a choice..." Mia said. Her voice trailed off as she spoke.

"Were you not privy to your own conversation? You did have a choice. You just weren't thinking. I still don't think you're thinking now. And I fear you aren't much of a thinker at all. You don't belong among us. It was unacceptable for Nikola to even entertain this ridiculous enterprise." He practically spat the last sentence at her, his eyes glittering. "You're a fraud and a pretender and a useless one at that."

"Apparently the Dominus disagrees with you," she replied with as much steel as she could muster.

"Well, unfortunately for you, going forward, I'm the one you'll have to impress," Brother SainClair said. He grimaced through clenched teeth. "The tour's over. I'll see you to your quarters."

Mia stifled a yelp as he grabbed her upper arm and dragged her along. She tried to remain stoic, but she winced when he wrenched her around the final corner to a hallway that looked identical to the one they'd just left. A large wooden door was set into the carved stone of the wall, and it looked like every other door they'd passed.

"Does the Order not believe in signage?" Mia said in a low voice.

"My lady," he said, and opened the door. With an exaggerated, deep bow and withering look, he shoved her through the door into a capacious room.

The low chatter that moments earlier had filled the room ceased immediately, and fifteen pairs of eyes swung around to face in her direction. Uncomfortable, Mia grew self-conscious at the abrupt gazes.

"The newest acolyte," announced SainClair unceremoniously to the group. "Someone find the pretender a bunk."

With that he stalked out.

Mia surveyed the barracks where Brother SainClair had deposited her. It was large and dim and carved of solid stone, much like, as far as she could tell, every other room in the Compound. This particular cavern room—for that was what it was—was carved smoothly at the ground level then rose into a rough-worked dome ceiling that yawned upward into the dimness. It was lined with bunks, ten on each side, with an additional five along the back. The center of the room housed a large wooden table fashioned from elder hardwood.

The fifteen pairs of eyes studied her closely, and her face flushed hot at the scrutiny. *In no time at all, they'll be calling me "red ghost" or something else equally unflattering.* At that glum thought, Mia took the opportunity to return the stares.

The assemblage was a motley collection, composed of males and females. There were children as young as perhaps twelve cycles, ranging to adults older than Mia. Short, tall, skinny, meaty, light, dark, brown...

Cedar! A jolt of surprise then anger at seeing him among the acolytes instead of the clerics coursed through her system when she recognized his face, which shared an equivalent look of shock at seeing her standing before him. From there, their emotions diverged. His large dark eyes softened, their thick lashes crinkling at the corners, and a small smile pulled at this mouth. Mia's eyes narrowed, glowering, but she tried to keep her mouth neutral. Scowling at everyone would make a great first impression.

"Mia," Cedar said, coming forward, apparently unsure what she was doing here. He clearly wasn't the only one. "Joining us, are you?"

She responded with her best contemptuous look, trying to indicate that she didn't much wish to speak of her circumstances at the moment. This gesture was also intended to convey that she didn't much care for his hyperbole or his company.

"Us? I rather thought from your—what was it?— important work, you'd be off doing something important."

His brown cheeks flushed rosy at the implication, and he cleared his throat. "Ah, yes, well, all service to the Order is important, no?" He directed the question to an older acolyte.

While clearly surprised at being addressed, the man nodded solemnly.

Cedar turned back Mia and smiled warmly. "Things went well with Dominus Nikola then?"

It was her turn to be embarrassed. "Where am I to sleep?"

From his vantage at superior height, he surveyed the large room. "It looks like the bunk behind Taryn is free."

"Yes, well, which bunk would that be?" Mia asked, suddenly very tired.

Cedar moved away from her, down the left side of the room. She followed him slowly, lugging her lapin bag and pack, and surveyed each bunk as she passed. By this time, the other acolytes—that thought was still very odd to her—had returned to their chatter, and small groups whispered quietly among themselves. Here and there, she caught some of them glancing at her from the corners of their eyes. Whether it was her Hackberry garb or her translucent skin and bright-red hair that drew their looks, she couldn't tell. It could just as equally have been her newness.

The bunks themselves were constructed of stone. Each had a stone pallet set against the wall at thigh height as well as a raw wooden shelf attached to the wall above each bed—if one could call them that. An alcove designed to house a gourd or some other light source was set into the wall below each shelf. At the head and foot of each pallet was a short wall that stood no taller than Mia's chest and extended maybe three arm lengths past the side of the sleeping pallets.

They were small cubbies, but each acolyte had taken great care to personalize his or her space. One had a colorful quilt made of exotic fabrics Mia had never seen before, cozily laid over the austere mattress. An extra-thick mattress overstuffed with something soft and cushy graced another acolyte's bunk. Some people had pinned up drawings, possibly of family, others letters, still others scraps of colorful cloth.

Most cubbies had books neatly stacked on a narrow shelf. Some had trunks or chests stowed below the bunk or tucked along the sides of the low walls. There was even one alcove with a narrow desk made of a heavy, orange wood oiled to a shine. It was stacked with open books and a quill and paper. Apparently many of her new bunkmates had arrived under markedly difference circumstances than she had. Mia sighed.

After a laborious trek to the back of the large room, they arrived at an empty bunk. It wasn't a particularly well-lit portion of the barracks and abutted the back corner. In both corners, where the clerics couldn't fit bunks, they'd placed a series of bookshelves that rose almost to the ceiling. The shelves towered over the acolytes and required a ladder to reach the top shelf.

"Well, here we are," Cedar said, and made a noise with his throat to signal Mia's attention.

She looked at the referenced alcove then turned back toward the shelving in the corner. Anyone climbing the ladder would be able to see right to her bed. She was about to say something when she realized with a rising sense of panic that anyone could walk past and see her or walk up to either wall and peer directly over, ladder or no. Privacy was no longer a luxury she enjoyed.

Cedar must have caught her staring at the ladder and mistaken her interest for that of the books. "That's just the basic collection for acolyte study," he said. "The Order has quite a large archive, greater than even this room. It's only one level up. I'll take you to see on the morrow."

As it was, Mia had never seen so many books in one place in her entire life and had trouble picturing the archive Cedar had described. Although she was a voracious reader, her access to reading material had always been limited by her circumstances; living in the rural hammock of Hackberry, she hadn't been exposed to a great many books. Over the cycles, however, she had built up a small collection, mostly by trading for them, whether for repair services, manual labor, or whatever she could forage in the wild.

There were also a few books that had traveled with her and Father over the cycles. Father used to read them to her when she was a child. He wasn't overly interested in reading—he was much more concerned with ranging, hunting, and building—but he had taught Mia to read and made sure she had access to books whenever they crossed their path.

She suddenly thought of the time she had come running home one afternoon, waving a heavy volume triumphantly in both hands. Father had squinted skeptically at her acquisition, as if she were brandishing some sort of incendiary or other potentially harmful device.

"Look," Mia had said, opening the book to its center and beaming. "I traded ten gourds for this huge book!"

Father shrugged and peered at the open page, his skepticism holding strong. "What's it about?"

"That's the best part," she replied. "It's filled with words and all their meanings. Every word I've ever read or heard is in here and many more that I've never heard of at all!" Her excitement overflowed, making her bounce on the balls of her feet.

"Well, what use is that?" Father said crossly. "You traded ten gourds for a book about nothing?"

Mia rolled her eyes at him. The traveling merchant had failed to see the value in the book as well. Although he'd hemmed and hawed at her offer of ten gourds, Mia was certain he felt he'd gotten the much better end of the bargain.

She had spent considerable time after that holed up in her secret hiding place, reading through that book, studying all the words and saying them out loud to herself and any fauna that happened to wander past.

Father never understood, but he always supported her. The pain that seared her chest when Dominus Nikola first announced the contents of Father's letter flared up again, and she suddenly felt as if all the air had been sucked from her lungs and there was none to draw from the void surrounding her.

"I'll think on it," Mia said to Cedar as her mind snapped back to the shelves that loomed over her bunk. The archive would definitely interest her. Right now she just wanted to be alone but doubted she'd ever be alone again. "I think I ought to settle in now. Many thanks for the assistance."

She turned away from him and barely heard his retreating footsteps. She set down her pack and bag in the empty stone box that was now her home and sat on the lumpy and simultaneously thin pallet mattress.

What is this thing stuffed with, rocks? She swung her feet, still in their boots, up onto the bare mattress and laid her head down on the equally lumpy pillow. Even as Mia's aching body protested, her consciousness slipped away.

Some time later, she awoke and rolled onto her side. The mattress was still horribly uncomfortable. A deep darkness enveloped the silent barracks. An occasional cough or soft snore emerged from the shapeless lumps settled into their bunks. The air was breezeless, with no rustling of trees and no sounds of nature to calm her nerves.

Just twenty-four hours earlier, she'd been a free woman, camping under the rolling colors of the daily spectacle in the night sky and listening to the soft hum of the forest and its residents. Now she was trapped in the stagnant air of the Order's cavernous Compound.

How in the blazes can they survive with their trees burrowed in the earth like this? In her daze-like state following SainClair through the underground compound, she hadn't seen the elder hardwoods required to power the Order's facilities. It was beyond the scope of any home she'd ever seen. *This place must consume more power than the entirety of Willowslip,* she thought. *Where does it all come from?*

That wasn't the most pressing question, though. Really, how could anyone be happy locked up in a stone box instead of surrounded by the warm, soothing buzz of the forest? In the suffocating darkness and stillness, Mia berated herself for not reading that stupid letter before the Dominus ever saw it. *He must be lying.* There was no way Father would have promised the clerics her service in exchange for some crazy treatment. And yet his behavior had been odd. Perhaps he had been telling her good-bye. With that thought in her head, she fell back into an uneasy sleep.

7 THE OATH L.C. 9515

MELIA KANNON SAT AT A SMALL TABLE, back stiff, eyes fierce. She circled her arms protectively around her chest. The small room was an alcove deep in the Compound, dank and moist with the life-giving detritus that nourished the Crater Grove. It filled the air with its earthy fragrance and their lungs with tiny particles. Hans sat across from her, his face a mask of calm. Melia wasn't deceived. She saw the slight twitch in his right eye. They sat there a long time. The room was like a tomb—neither

one shifted or breathed audibly. The air was completely still. Finally Melia coughed, breaking the silence.

"It's for the good of Lumin," Hans said at last. "We
must protect the key and our records at all cost."

"Don't you think I know that?" Melia snapped.
"For almost twenty cycles, we've been under constant
assault by those…Druids, as they've taken to calling
themselves. They're convinced that the Counsel erred
and that the only way back to civilization is to restore
the Network. Long-term consequences be damned."

Gerard's face flashed into her mind, and she had to
blink it away and fight back tears. Rosewater's people
had finally finished her dear friend just this cycle while
they were on a mission to the South. The Order
already had sent a death notice to the SainClair estate,
but it would be months before they heard anything
back. The more lives the Druids took, the less inclined
the Order was to try for a truce with them.

"I know that as well as you do," said Hans, rubbing
a hand through his spiky hair.

The brown of his hair was threaded with silver, his
eyes severe, his brow low on his forehead. In that
moment he very much reminded Melia of his uncle,
Minister Draca, another dear friend lost to this madness. The list grew longer every cycle.

"It's a burden you've borne with dignity. You've
done a service to us all. But these attacks have been

increasing in recent cycles. It's no longer safe to keep the key and book on your person. They must be secured."

"I made a sacred vow to Aris SainClair when she entrusted these items to me. Besides, the Druids only know about the key."

"That may be true, but you know better than I that they'll need both the key and records if they hope to restore the Network. Our only advantage is that they don't know this, an advantage that could easily disappear if either object fell into the wrong hands. We all have a stake in the protection of the records, especially those of us who've sealed them."

"A stake, yes, but these relics of Lumin's past aren't our birthright. They belong to Gerard's family."

"He's gone," Hans said softly.

"They'll send someone to take his place," Melia said, her voice also soft. "I know it."

"That's irrelevant frankly," Hans said, leaning back in his chair and folding his arms across his robed chest. "Aris SainClair and my uncle set Gamma Protocol in motion. It did what they envisioned. It shut down the Network, and we've been living off individual hearthroots and groves for twenty cycles now. The worst of the chaos is behind us. Would you really jeopardize the ministers' sacrifice? Would you risk reversing Gamma Protocol?"

Melia sat silently, the book clutched against her chest. Its subtle warmth permeated through her robes, reassuring her that it was only sleeping and not dead.

"Individually the key and the records are powerful, but together they can reverse all the work we've done in Lumin's name," said Hans, his eyes pleading with her now.

"Even with them, they wouldn't get into the Core. They don't have the families on their side."

"You don't think Rosewater's murderous brood wouldn't take by force what we won't give willingly? Gerard should be evidence enough of that."

Melia winced and breathed deeply. "What do you propose?"

Hans gestured around them. "This Compound has depths like no other structure I've known. We hide them—separate them and hide them."

"And how will the rest of the Order find them when they need them, when we're gone?"

"Preservation, research, restoration. This is our mission. We'll pass on knowledge of the relics only to the leaders."

"And who decides who the leaders are?" Melia asked. "I myself wasn't even a minister. Who gets to name the great families?"

"It is done," said Hans. "Gamma Protocol has chosen our leaders for us."

Melia closed her eyes, willing time to rewind back before the anguish of the past twenty cycles, back before Gamma Protocol, back to her island home of Senegast, to her happy son and daughter smiling up at her. Yet it persisted in its solemn forward march, dragging her unwillingly into decrepitude. Her children would be grown now. Perhaps they didn't even remember her face. She thrust her arms out and placed the book in Hans's hands.

"Here, take it. Before I change my mind."

"And the key?"

Melia pulled the key from her robes, lifting the long chain that held it over her head and placing it solemnly on top of the book.

"Shall I hide them?" Hans asked.

"No," she said. "Let's do it together."

8 THE BARRACKS L.C. 10152

MIA JAYNE WOKE with the crinkly feel of Father's letter in her hands and a terrible crick in her neck. In the dream she had opened the letter, and it was blank. The letter was a dream, but the crick was real. The dream lifted from her mind, leaving behind both relief and desolation. She wasn't at home in her bed. She was in the Compound of the Order of Vis Firmitas on the most uncomfortable mattress she'd ever had the displeasure meeting. The lack of sunlight was disorienting. Accustomed to glancing out a window or up into the sky to determine the time, she was at a disadvantage here. The gourds along the walls and the overhead lanterns dimly lit the large room. She sat up on the mattress, her joints screaming. They apparently had just gotten used to the hard lumps of the pallet, and now it was asking too much to require movement so quickly. Mia was also parched. *How long did I sleep?* she wondered.

It must still have been morning. The others were busily attending to miscellany in and about their bunks. A tall blond boy, about fifteen or so, was straightening his belt. His gawky hands brushed the robes into place. One of the younger girls was meticulously plaiting her thick brown hair into a neat braid while an older acolyte stood over her, guiding her hand and nodding, her plump cheeks pursed in concentration. An older man, maybe in his thirties, was seated at the center table with a large tome open in front of him. He frowned as he rubbed his temple absently, his hazel eyes narrowing as he studied the volume then flipped farther along in the book.

Mia was surprised that no one had shaken her awake and commanded that she ready herself for the day. However, she was still a complete stranger here, and the other acolytes had their own business. They each wore a variation of the same general uniform, a taupe robe almost colorless in the dim light, blending into the drab stone background. The robe, wrapped in front of the body and belted at the waist, fell almost to the floor. Beneath that was a pair of flowing pants in the same brown-gray color and cinched at the ankles. Over the robe each acolyte wore a wide swath of fabric that circled the body and was pinned at the shoulder. For most acolytes this sash was nearly the same shade as the robe and pants, although some of them looked orangey in the light of the gourds. A gray metal pin sat at the shoulder atop the sash that held it into place. The designs of the pins varied.

Mia felt out of place in her white gauzy pants, undershirt, sheer tunic, wide blue-green belt, and cream-colored overshirt, the entire ensemble somewhat grungy from travel and rumpled from sleep. Her clothes provided inadequate warmth in the cold, dank Compound.

She rubbed her forehead and sighed. She was woefully unprepared for pretty much everything about her current situation. Her stone cubby would remain barren for some time. As she stretched her back gingerly, the fantastically uncomfortable mattress creaked under her legs. *Blast it!* What she wouldn't give for one—who was she kidding?—*all* of those damnable furs they had at home. Father could have at least warned her of the cold.

She stood and stretched her back and arms again. Almost instantaneously, Cedar appeared at the entrance of the cubby.

"Good morn," he said, and smiled cheerfully.

She returned his friendly demeanor with what she hoped was one of her better scowls. "What's in these mattresses?" she asked, rubbing her neck. "I feel like I slept on rocks."

"Escule beans," Cedar replied.

She raised an eyebrow in his direction and squinted.

"I suppose they're essentially small rocks," he continued. "You'll either acclimate, or you'll procure an alternate mattress from somewhere. Many acolytes come prepared, and some even have custom-made robes."

She shouldn't have been surprised but was regardless. It was naïve to assume that all acolytes came into service of the Order by indenture, but why would anyone willingly forsake the sun and trees for this cave?

"Haven't you been paying attention?" Mia asked, her voice laced with sarcasm. "In case you failed to notice, my presence here was entirely unplanned."

"What happened with the Dominus?" Cedar asked.

She huffed and stretched her neck again.

"Well," he continued, ignoring her unpleasant mood, "the Order provides bedding, obviously, for acolytes, as well as meager but clean robes, basic toiletries, and facilities. It's actually not a bad arrangement." He shrugged.

She sighed but decided against commenting. Complaining to Cedar wouldn't change her circumstances.

"I will say," he said, then paused, as if considering his words. "Brother SainClair definitely has it in for you. I've never seen him look at any acolyte the way he was looking at you last night." He squinted at her appraisingly.

What are you looking at? "Well, that makes me feel loads better."

He laughed and clapped her on the back. She lost her balance and stumbled forward, muttering a curse as she fell. The older acolyte studying at the table turned to glare at them. If Cedar registered the attention, he didn't react. Mia righted herself to a standing position and brushed the dust from her hands.

"Well, as Brother SainClair obviously has no intention of properly settling you in, we should at least make sure you don't stick out like a sore thumb," Cedar said, and gestured to her belt.

She doubted it was just her clothing that made her stick out, but perhaps she'd blend in better if dressed head to toe in drab. Making its own demands known, her stomach growled audibly.

"Ah," he added, "you missed the morning meal. I'm sure we can scavenge something, given the circumstances."

"That's quite all right," she said. She reached down to her lapin bag and snagged a rollie. "I still have some of these with me." She took a big bite of the fruit and chewed contentedly.

Cedar looked at the fruit and smiled. At least there would be some remnants of home for the short time she had until she ate them all. Cedar gestured for her to follow him toward the door of the barracks.

"I'll never be able to find my way around this place," Mia muttered half to herself, as they walked.

"Oh, you'll quickly pick it up. I don't suppose you know the first thing about being an acolyte of the Order?"

She detected the slightest pleading tone in his voice. Once they were through the large carved dormitory doors, they made their way to the right down a long, dimly lit corridor.

Grimacing, Mia shook her head. "My attention...wandered last night while Brother SainClair was speaking, but I doubt he said anything useful."

"Well, we aren't allowed to leave the Compound except with permission, so you'll be spending a lot of time in these caverns."

"What! We aren't allowed to leave?" Mia stopped dead, her legs feeling suddenly leaden even as her heart raced. She was trapped here. It never occurred to her that they would lock her in. "But you were outside when I met you."

He cracked a wide grin. "I had permission. I told you it was special business." At that, he noticed she was no longer next to him and turned back. He frowned. "Are you okay? You look kind of pale. Pale for you, I mean," he added hastily, frowning. He grasped her fluttering hand. "Your hands are like ice."

His hand felt warm and brown against Mia's bone-white skin. This contrast barely registered in her mind. She was still too alarmed to resist this small intimacy, and before she could think longer on it, he released her hand.

She breathed deeply, trying to slow her heartbeat. "How long does acolyte service last?" She raised her eyebrows expectantly when Cedar didn't immediately answer.

"Let's go," he said. "I want to get you some proper robes before you freeze."

They continued to walk down the long corridor.

"Service varies depending on the acolyte. We're promoted when the clerics feel we've contributed enough to the mission or if we have some special skills. Some may spend as long as five cycles or even more in service before taking their vows. Others might ascend in a cycle or even two quarter cycles."

Five cycles? Her heart fluttered again, but she continued to walk resolutely. "How long have you been in service?"

"I'm approaching the anniversary of my second cycle. I'm in the final stage as an acolyte," he added with a smile. "You can tell by my pin." He gestured to the metal pin on his sash. It had an elder tree carved in it, and the tree was heavy with fruit. An illegible symbol was engraved on the trunk.

Mia would never get all these details straight, but she nodded anyway. Although the panic was still with her, like a shadow cast behind each step, she tried her best to remain composed.

"Where are the conduits?" she asked, changing the subject. There was plenty of time to learn the rest of the distressing details of her new position later. "Some mighty elders must be powering this place. I've never seen so much energy consumption. I didn't even know it was possible."

A look, relief perhaps, flickered across Cedar's aristocratic face. "The Compound has a central arboretum that houses our elders," he said. He kept glancing over at her as they walked, probably making sure she wasn't going to keel over. His large, dark eyes met hers, and he smiled reassuringly.

Suddenly self-conscious at her distress, her face, her everything, she slid her gaze away.

"How do they stay alive underground?" she asked.

"Well, they're a hardy bunch, to be sure. I've ne'er been to the central arboretum myself, as acolytes are strictly prohibited there. When Brother Quintus is in his cups, he gets really chatty, though. He described to me a large central cavern carved from the core of the mountain with tunnels leading up to the surface in all directions. These tunnels capture the light as the sun crosses the mountain. Some of the branches of the elders are rumored to actually grow up into the tunnels, so when you look at the mountain, some of the trees you see are outgrowths of our elders. Some rooms even have branches traversing them."

"What about the hearthroots? Acolytes have to be able to access hearthroots, or there would be cold baths and no ability to cook."

"Well, the warmth from the hearthroots is harnessed and distributed to the underground bathing springs as well as the kitchens."

The impotence and fear Mia had felt only moments before turned to excitement and curiosity. She'd never heard of such a complex power system. For the first time since she'd arrived the day before, something piqued her interest about this wretched Compound. Such a system would be magnificent to behold.

"Who maintains the elders?" she asked, trying to sound casual.

Cedar scratched his chin as he thought. They had passed a number of tunnels on their straight shot from the barracks, but now they were approaching a stairway on the left, and he gestured that they should descend.

"A select group of clerics is responsible for maintaining the system. We, as members of the Order, are charged with protecting this Compound and the systems and remnants within, so the clerics take the maintenance and enhancement of the elders very, very seriously."

What could possibly be worth protecting in this dusty ball of rock? Honestly, though, her knowledge of the Order was quite limited. Father had given little in the way of actual explanation during his spasmodic fits of oaths sworn against the clerics. He had called them fiends and cowards who only cared about their own necks and were willing to let society hang to preserve their sanctum. It didn't seem much like a sanctum from where she stood.

Despite her reservations and perhaps partly because of Cedar's speculation, she was extremely curious about the workings of the elders and the Compound. Although her chest tightened at the thought of Hackberry and her hearthroot, she nodded politely.

THE SUPPLIER, SISTER VALENCIA, outfitted Mia with three pairs of light pants, three taupe undershirts, two heavy taupe robes, one rope belt, and one sash. She also handed her a dull metal pin adorned with a tiny plant with one leaf engraved on the face.

"'Tis a sapling," she said amiably, as if she had cast the pin herself.

Mia thought about it for a moment and supposed she very well could have cast the pin herself. She smiled grimly. "Many thanks, Sister."

"That is not all," she said in a businesslike tone that seemed to contrast with the lilt in her voice. "We also have slippers, boots, a cold-weather outrobe, hose, smallclothes, quill, ink, parchment, soap, gourds, brush, comb, and what else?" she said, as she pulled items from various shelves.

She appeared to be speaking to herself, so Mia didn't answer.

"Do we have any spare mattresses or pillows stuffed with anything but escule?" Cedar asked.

"Ah." The sister stopped, looking thoughtful. "I canna say we have any mattresses at this time, young man." She turned to Mia. "I can put ye on the list for one and when one comes up see what I can do." She kept rummaging. "Does look as if we have a piller, though."

She handed Mia an only slightly dilapidated pillow. It didn't rival her pillows back in Hackberry, but it also wasn't stuffed with escule. As she sighed with content at the feel of it, Sister Valencia smiled knowingly.

"While we're at it, ye may want a proper blanket. The standard issue is naught but a sheet in me opinion." Sister Valencia pulled down a woolen blanket.

It was colorless and rough to the touch, but Mia was grateful for something more substantial.

Sister Valencia gave another look to Mia's light clothes and pulled down another blanket. "'Ere, perhaps ye could use two then?"

Mia accepted the second blanket gratefully. With a nod, Sister Valencia looked her over. Mia's arms were now laden with newly acquired necessities, and Sister Valencia dismissed them with a cheerful wave.

"Best be off then, m'dears. Ye both must have duties to be attendin' to. I know I do."

"You'd best change into those," Cedar said, gesturing to the robes. "I can show you how prepare the sash, but hop to it. Lunch waits for no one!"

Upon their return, Mia surveyed the barracks. They were the only ones in the large room. "Where do the acolytes change?" she asked.

"What do you mean by 'where'?" he said after a moment's thought.

"Don't we have a designated changing room? What about relieving ourselves?" She was mildly scandalized by the thought of conducting her business with an audience. Even in the close quarters of their hearthtree, she and Father had made provisions for privacy.

"You should see your face," Cedar said, and laughed heartily. "We have a lavatory for relieving ourselves. It's the room right across the hall. I don't think anyone sees the point in privacy for changing clothing. It's not something we haven't all seen. Not sure I would want my billowing robes dragging around the floor of the lavatory anyway," he muttered, wrinkling his nose.

"All right. Whatever," she replied, feeling exasperated. "Will you at least turn your back?"

Cedar shrugged and complied. Mia removed her light tropics clothing and carefully folded each item, placing it in a neat pile on the bean-filled lump of a mattress. She pulled on the undershirt and loose pants. Although the cloth looked rough, it was surprisingly soft to the touch. *They've probably been worn by a hundred people*, she thought.

"Is there any special trick to this robe?" she asked.

Cedar turned and leaned against the wall. "Just pull it on over your shoulders, with the open side to the front, and wrap the right side around your waist and then the left side. Then secure it with the belt."

She tried to follow his verbal instructions.

"No, no, knot it like this. See?" He brushed her hands away and proceeded to reknot the belt in an overly complicated fashion.

His proximity disconcerted her, and she slapped away his hand.

"That's quite enough. What about the sash?"

"That you drape around your person, starting with one edge against the left shoulder. Sling the sash under your right arm, around your back, over your left shoulder, and pin it just so."

Again, Mia was having trouble following his verbal instructions, so Cedar intervened to rearrange the sash and set the pin.

"You'll quickly become accustomed to the process," he reassured her.

How many times has he said that in the last hour?

"Yes, then. I'm positively famished," she responded.

The dining room was one of those rooms with large branches traversing its middle. The faint hum was familiar when Mia entered the hall, and it brought a warm feeling of comfort with it. Her ears had pricked here and there at the occasional hum as she and Cedar had made their way along the tunnels and staircases, but this was the first sustained sound of the forest she had encountered since her arrival yesterday.

Her muscles relaxed a little at the sound, and even that slight reduction in stress was a welcome feeling. In the large branch at the center of the room stood a carved hearth that warmed the space and heated a sizable iron cauldron of something that smelled of meat and spices. The fragrance wafting from the center of the room drew her toward it—a harmony in concert with the humming tree.

"Do they actually cook meals here?" she asked Cedar.

"Oh, no, this hearth is much too weak for that. I expect it's pretty far from the elder roots. We use it to keep the meals warm for serving, though. Someone always brings the provisions up from the kitchen. Only certain trusted clerics even know where the kitchen is located." He gave her a wicked grin. "I expect they want to prevent midnight snacking among the acolytes. Some of us are still growing boys, you know?"

Mia ignored his joke. "Who assigns the duties?"

"Well, the Taskmaster does," he said with a shrug and made his way toward the hearth.

She raised an eyebrow. "They actually have a position called the Taskmaster?"

"What's so odd about that?" he asked.

Mia shook her head, brushing off his remark. "What are your duties then? It doesn't appear as if you do anything but travel off the grounds on special business and act as a tour guide for wretched new recruits." Mia tried to prevent it, but the last word came out sounding sardonic.

"Yes, well, I was the only one who volunteered to show you the ropes, so I got a reprieve from my normal duties," he replied. "I'm usually assigned to an engineering team."

When they reached the center of the room, Cedar grabbed a bowl and spoon from a table to the left of the hearth. He swirled a wooden serving spoon in the cauldron then ladled himself a hearty portion of a brown stew. He topped the stew with a scoop of rice from a wide carved bowl atop a separate table on the right side of the hearth. Mia followed suit.

"I thought you said you didn't know firsthand the exact location of the elder trees," she pressed, as she ladled herself heaping servings.

"I don't," he replied.

Cedar picked out a spot at a table nearby. They sat alone. It didn't appear as if the clerics and acolytes took the midday meal simultaneously, as many of the tables were empty. Mia spotted a small gathering of faces she recognized at a table across from the hearth, all acolytes. They whispered among themselves and averted their eyes when they saw her watching. Mia turned her head and saw Brother SainClair on the other side of the room, taking his meal with some of the other clerics. He sneered derisively when he caught her looking in his direction. She turned her attention back to Cedar.

"So how is it that you work in engineering?" she asked.

"Oh, well, there are many access levels in engineering. I focus on the tunnels primarily. Along our walking corridors, we have a parallel network of tunnels where the roots run. Given the delicacy of stretching the roots as far as we do, they're often in need of repair or support. It's only grown harder to maintain, as our numbers have dwindled and our elders aged."

"I see," Mia said through a mouthful of stew.

"Well, at least you like the food," Cedar said, and chuckled.

"'Tis not half bad," Mia said reluctantly. "And I didn't even have to cook it."

"Well, you might have to yet. You'll have to see where the Taskmaster assigns you."

9   END & BEGIN   L.C. 9551

MELIA KANNON MASSAGED her knuckles against the hard wood of the chair's armrest in an attempt to alleviate the stiffness in her fingers. The Compound of the Order was cold, and time hadn't been kind to her joints. She sat for a long while, looking at the volumes in the Archives, the dim light of the portable gourd throwing the table it sat on into stark relief. The room was a silent refuge from the bustle of the busy Compound. Over the past fifty cycles, Melia had painstakingly collected books from the rubble and decay of Lumin's civilization. From forays into the cities fraught with danger, to ventures far and wide, each book had been excavated carefully and protected from the Druids in a battle for knowledge. Other volumes had come to Melia from the personal collections of the great families and lineages, scraps gleaned from the splendor that once had been her glowing planet, cherished beyond measure.

The Druids had expanded their limited mission of restoring the Network to an entire belief system, one that had them at odds with the Order on more than just the Network. The Druids now styled themselves as preservers of the old ways, keepers of Lumin, and restorers of peace and prosperity. The tune sounded similar to Melia. The Order had equivalent mandates for its membership. Thus, the constant tussle over knowledge, whether in the form of books or in relics of pre-Fall Lumin. It amazed her how cycles of bad blood had further divided those that strived toward the same goal.

If she had anything to say about it, and a glance at the wrinkled, gnarled hands resting on her armrests signaled that perhaps she didn't, Lumin would rise again. Melia had done all she could to protect its future. There was just one thing left. She reached into the sash of her robes, her aching hands fumbling. She pushed aside her white braid of hair and pulled the ornate leather volume from her sash. She gently rubbed a rigid thumb over the medallion on the cover, which was bright as the day Minister SainClair had first thrust the book into her much younger hands.

"I'm sorry," she whispered to the dead. Hans was certainly spinning in his alcove in the Catacombs. "I know this isn't what you want, but I can't, even after fifty cycles, shake the feeling that this is the best place for it. I know you will forgive me."

Melia struggled to her feet, holding on to the table for stability. Everything and everyone she loved was long gone—and with it the oaths she had sworn. She had outlived them all. But this was just the beginning. Lumin had a much longer journey ahead, and all histories started somewhere. She tottered over to the shelves of the Archives and slipped the ornate book into a space between two others. Its binding held no title, and the small tome instantly disappeared among the other volumes, blending into the body of words surrounding it. With that addition, the Archives now held the collected knowledge of pre-Fall Lumin. She leaned over the table and fetched the gourd from its center. With cane in one hand and gourd in the other, she foraged her way to the stairs and gave the dim room a sigh and one backward glance before proceeding back down the narrow stone steps, disappearing into history with the Archives itself.

10 THE ARCHIVES L.C. 10152

O *F ALL THE JOBS.* Mia Jayne looked around the massive, dim room with endless rows of shelves that led back into the darkness and up to the ceiling. Cedar hadn't exaggerated when he'd described the Archives. It was huge. And this chamber was only the ancient texts chamber. The main chamber was down a set of stone steps behind her.

The main chamber was better lit, but the dull amber of the special orange gourds that Brother Cornelius, the Archivemaster, specially cultivated for the Archives was engineered to minimize light damage to the old volumes contained in this room. Mia had been surprised by the agility of the old brother's mind, despite his decrepit body. He looked at first glance to be so frail that a strong breeze could break his leg. His hands were bony, almost claw-like. His beard was long and shaggy and a mottled mix of gray, white and yellow. His hair was long and unruly but tied back with a leather strap. But these trappings of age fell away instantaneously when Brother Cornelius engaged Mia with his hazel eyes that oscillated from gray to green, even if they did so behind delicate silver spectacles slung low on his nose, and infectious enthusiasm for his special inventions.

Brother Cornelius instructed Mia to remove all the spore growth afflicting the ancient texts. The amber gourds did well in preserving the old volumes' paper and ink, but the benefit it provided the tomes was equally advantageous to a low-light spore that conducted itself through the air ducts and settled on the books. Brother Cornelius taught her the laborious process required to kill the spores. She had to remove each book from its shelf, scan the binding and pages for signs of spores, and administer a flash of light from a special gourd. This particular gourd was long and thin and emitted twice the brightness of standard lighting gourds, but it produced a bright light only for a moment when shaken. As soon as the shaking stopped, the light did as well.

"How does this work?" Mia asked him, amazed at the old man's ingenuity.

"'Tis a simple matter of the agitation that causes a chemical reaction," he said simply. "Nodes of separate chemicals are clustered inside each gourd, and the shaking makes them bounce together and release the chemicals, which when mixed, cause the flash of light we see. I created it through a system of iterative breeding. I call them wands."

Awestruck, Mia nodded. "You'll have to show me your garden," she said, giving the wand a shake to produce the sparkling flash of light.

"I don't keep a garden, my child," he said, and chuckled amiably. "I keep a laboratory. When you complete the delicate task of ridding our most treasured historical tomes of the spore infestation, I'll take you to it and show you all my secrets."

His eyes sparkled, and Mia smiled for the first time since arriving at the Order. Savoring the happy thought, she proceeded with him toward the back of the dark room.

"So how far back to do the books go?" she asked.

"The oldest of the tomes in the Archives dates back thousands of cycles. There are precious few from that far back, though. Much was destroyed."

She looked at him quizzically. "Destroyed?"

"My child, you really must sit in on the history lectures that we offer the acolytes." He gave her a reproving look then sighed and continued. "Many hundreds of cycles ago, Lumin was thrown into chaos. Now all that's left are the remnants of what was, and the Order was established more than five hundred cycles ago with the sacred duty to protect those remnants and learn from them what we can to restore our future."

Mia nodded and smiled. "I'll be sure to sit in on some lectures then."

She had no intention of doing any such thing. Most acolyte study was individual. Each of them was allotted private study time that could be conducted in laboratories, reading rooms, the barracks, or the library. Alternatively each acolyte had the option to attend any number of subject lectures held by clerics for the benefit of the others. To date, Mia's study time primarily had been composed of snooping around the Compound and listening carefully for the sounds of trees. As a benefit, her job in the Archives provided ample time to think through her present situation.

She had questioned Cornelius extensively about his methods when he first had described the amber gourds to her, and her attention pleased him. He mistook Mia's enthusiasm for deep interest in the archival process. Of course her fascination was derived entirely from the idea of modifying flora to suit her needs. She'd never before considered the possibility that she could modify the flora around her to accomplish such specific tasks. Most of her skill lay in repurposing existing roots for different ends, such as rerouting power from damaged roots to functional ones or encouraging them to grow in specific ways to establish hearths and the like. The idea of creating entirely new types of roots and gourds completely fascinated her.

"Do the Archives contain books on modifying flora?" Mia asked Brother Cornelius.

"Well, working this job, my child, you'll quickly become familiar with where all the tomes are stored, but there's no harm in showing you around now, I guess."

He ushered her through the vast number of shelves and alcoves, describing all the sections. Mia made note of ones to peruse on her own. All the brothers and sisters apparently referred to the acolytes as their children, regardless of age or prior station in life. The intent was harmless, but their tone and method of address sometimes set Mia's teeth on edge. She over-looked such endearments from old Cornelius, though, because he seemed genuinely pleased to have someone to talk to during the day.

No other acolytes were stationed at the Archives, and it appeared none had been for many cycles. He'd been left alone for decades to tend to the tomes. Mia suspected many clerics of the Order had little patience for his measured speech and economy of movement and thought. They preferred the bustle of the younger clerics, with their heated discussions, physicality, and generally zealous passions. That wasn't Cornelius by a mile.

Cornelius was no longer as sure of foot, however, and he had complained to the Taskmaster that spores were taking over the ancient tomes.

"If I don't receive some sort of assistance, I'll die out of spite, and the Order will be left with no one who knows his or her way among the stacks," he recounted to Mia.

When she had come along unexpectedly, the Taskmaster had brushed aside her plaintive requests to be stationed with the engineering crew or even the maintenance crew and had assigned her here with Cornelius.

"But I have ample experience repairing and maintaining conduits, as well as detailed knowledge of the types of shunts and methods of their insertion," she had insisted. Sister Penelope would hear none of it, though. *I should have told her I can hear them, but she'd have thought I was crazy.* Mia tried to tell her father that once, and he had chucked it up to the wild imaginings of a child.

That is utter poppycock! Mia imagined Sister Penelope's high, squeaky voice. *And for such a ridiculous lie, I'm changing your duties to emptying latrines and chamber pots. You'll wish with your entire being that you had been stationed with kindly Brother Cornelius after two days of that job.*

Something in Mia's gut told her to keep silent about the sounds of the roots. *I'll have time to prove my usefulness, or I'll be gone from here.* Either way, it was best that the Order knew as little about her as possible.

She pulled another book from the shelf and checked it for spores. Although it didn't seem to be badly damaged, she gave it a couple flashes with the wand just to be certain. It had been a fortnight since her arrival. Mia supposed that meant she was settling in, as much as one could settle in where one was not wanted, apparently not needed, and essentially ignored. Other than the occasional companionship of Cedar at meals and during their limited free time, none of the other acolytes spoke to her. A couple of times, she had caught Mallus, a young man with a boyish face and sandy-blond hair, looking at her when he thought she wasn't aware. If she turned to look at him, though, he would avert his eyes and hunch his shoulders. Even Cedar's interactions seemed hesitant and conflicted. When pressed, he had hemmed and hawed and finally admitted that Brother SainClair's loud and continuing insistence that Mia was a fraud had put everyone off a bit.

"Then why do you continue to associate with me?" she asked.

"Well," he replied, weighing his words carefully, "I feel some sense of obligation, I suppose. I kind of feel responsible for you. If I started ignoring you entirely now, what would that make me?"

His response certainly didn't quell Mia's increasing loneliness. If her only companion maintained their acquaintance out of a sense of pity and obligation, she certainly had no confidants or friends among her. She reminded herself that she wasn't here to make friends. Setting yet another book on the shelf, she moved to the next one, methodical in her actions.

Her mind wandered to Father. She was here because he needed her here. She gritted her teeth. *He might already be dead.* Her throat felt dry and scratchy the way it did every time her thoughts turned in his direction. She had drafted a rather angry letter a couple of days after she'd arrived, but since post made its way to Hackberry by messenger, she had yet to find anyone willing to carry it to him.

What if Dominus Nikola lied to me, and Father's letter had asked no such task of me? What if Father's scared for me? What if he thinks I abandoned him to his most hated enemy? Seeking an audience with the Dominus was significantly harder as an acolyte than as a message bearer. No good ever came of these thoughts. Her mind twisted and turned through the labyrinth of questions and potential answers, none of which gave her any peace. She squeezed her eyes shut and rubbed them hard, hoping to brush away the unpleasant thoughts and return to the task at hand.

Mia had worked out quite a rhythm. She examined the binding first, read the title, and checked for signs of spores. If she saw any sign of contamination, she'd set the book out so that the pages were splayed then flash the exterior and interior of the book with the wand. Then she'd check again and replace the book in its spot. These older books were particularly susceptible, and all the books she'd encountered thus far had at least a little bit of spore contamination, although it varied by tome.

She put back a burgundy book titled *A Treatise on the Peoples of the North*, which had been particularly full of spores, and proceeded to the next book on the shelf. It was a smallish brown leather volume with an intricate leafy design in faded gold on its binding and across the cover. Centered on the front was a large golden medallion of an open lotus flower with an owl crouched in the center, wings spread as if to take flight. *That's an odd combination of symbols. What is this?* Mia looked at the binding, but it had no title or text of any kind engraved on it. She opened it and flipped through. On one of the pages, she saw a long list of names. She turned to the title page, and on it was written *An Exhaustive Genealogy of the Families of the Realm.* The book was compact for an exhaustive genealogy.

Something was off about this book. Mia skimmed it again but saw no sign of contamination on the outer binding or any of the pages within. This was the first book in the entire Archives to be entirely clean of contaminants. That wasn't the only odd thing about it. The book felt warm to the touch, like a plant root that pulsed with energy under her hand. She put it up to her ear, but it didn't hum. The warmth was subtle but constant.

Although Mia had no great interest in the genealogies of the families of Lumin, she slipped the book into the large pocket formed by the folds of her sash, suddenly unwilling to part from it.

A gentle, deliberate cough came from behind her. Her body stiffened momentarily in surprise and fear. She turned her head to peer over her shoulder. One of the other acolytes was standing near the entrance. It was the acolyte with the bunk next to Mia's. In two weeks they'd never spoken to each other; she kept to herself mostly. At first Mia thought perhaps she was just shy, but when Cedar confided that SainClair was warning the others about Mia, she assumed the other acolyte was avoiding her on that account. Still, here she stood at the doorway to the dusty, spore-ridden Archives, giving Mia a tight smile. Her short pale hair, peachy skin, and gold eyes emanated an ethereal glow. The acolyte's robes added to the effect. Mia didn't even hear her come up the stone steps or enter the room. Mia blinked her eyes a few times, clearing her mind of random cobwebs.

"Can I assist you?" Mia said, trying to sound polite and not menacing. *This is my chance to engage another acolyte.*

"I hope so," she said in a soft, musical voice. "I was just telling Brother Cornelius that I had interest in some of the ancient texts. He told me we store all historical texts in the Archives up here, and I should come speak to you, as you can tell me which books are safe to take." She smiled again, this time more naturally, and added, "He actually kind of lost me when he started showing me a strange long gourd that made flashes when he shook it."

Mia smiled back. Brother Cornelius was a horrible show-off. Well, those gourds were fantastic, so Mia would probably do the same. She held up a wand as she arched an eyebrow at the other acolyte.

"They're used to remove spores from the books," Mia said.

"Yes, I recall him saying something of the sort," she said, looking around at the many shelves of faded volumes. "I'm Taryn Windbough, by the by. I don't think we've been properly introduced."

"Mia Jayne. I've been rather unpopular among the others." She gave Taryn a wry smile. "Brother SainClair doesn't appreciate my presence among you overmuch."

"Ah, yes, well, he's always been one to stand on formality. One only joins the Order because one is called." She gave Mia a knowing smile. It carved the edges of her lips, and her eyes sparkled. Mia didn't think anyone had smiled at her this much since she'd arrived. "I don't believe he's much impressed with me either. He's told me more than once that he finds my area of concentration useless to the betterment of the Order."

"Why would he say that?"

Taryn glided closer to Mia on her noiseless slippers. Mia noticed that the pin on her sash bore a mature tree on it but one with no fruit. Taryn set down the load of books, parchment, and other accouterments she was carrying and turned one of the wooden chairs at the central reading table around to face where Mia sat on the ratty carpet at the base of the shelves. When it was situated to her liking, she dropped gracefully into a sitting position like a leaf falling from a tree. A slight tinge of jealousy niggled at the nape of Mia's neck; she moved like a boar in the forest, crashing about. She could sneak, but it was never fluid, and she certainly hadn't mastered Taryn's economy of movement.

"Well," Taryn finally said, "as I spend more time with the Order, I'm finding that I've much interest in the history of our realm and the Order's place in that history. I suppose Brother SainClair finds so much focus on what was to be useless." She shrugged, apparently not bothered by his wrath. "It's of no concern to me. I'm of the firm belief that history provides many of the clues we need to secure the future, like following a trail of gourds someone who has come before has left for us to follow and use. Besides," she added, waving a hand at the Archives, "one of our tenets is the protection of the old ways. How can we protect something we don't understand?"

"That makes sense," Mia said, although she could confess no great interest in history herself. She'd been dealing with these volumes for weeks, and although it was certainly interesting to think about history, it wasn't always interesting to read about it. "Personally, though," Mia continued, "I much prefer books that tell me how to do something practical."

Taryn raised a thin eyebrow at that comment. "Like what? Cooking instruction?"

"No," Mia said, "like those books that show you drawings of various types of plants so you can determine which ones can be used for light and how long, and whether they need to remain attached to the root or whether they're portable, and whether they're edible after their electrical function is concluded."

"Ah," said Taryn, "you're much like Brother Cornelius then."

"I suppose I am," Mia said. "I get rather excited when he talks about his inventions, although his study is clearly focused on these volumes." She gestured around. "He lights up like a firefly when he's talking about book preservation and such. I think my interest is more electrochemical. I like to tinker with the trees and roots and augment hearths and such."

"Why are you here in the Archives then?" Taryn asked thoughtfully.

"I suppose I'm needed more here. Brother Cornelius has no one to assist him." *No need for her to know how hard I lobbied with the Taskmaster. It's embarrassing enough remembering it.* "I like it well enough," Mia added.

"Well, it's certainly peaceful up here," Taryn said, and sighed. "I should visit more often so I can get some reading done. My duties fall to assisting Brother Valentine, the Ledgermaster. It's detailed work, which I don't mind, but it can numb the mind. I find being surrounded by these old volumes refreshing. How did I not think to come up here before?"

Mia smiled again, even though Taryn was clearly daft for wanting to spend her time up in the stuffy Archives. "What changed your mind?" she asked.

"Ah." She frowned and slid her eyes away from Mia's. "I suppose I've exhausted all other available resources."

"Well, I'm glad I could be your last resort then."

Taryn's cheeks pinked, so Mia quickly switched to librarian mode. "I'm still removing spores from the volumes up here, but I'm through with all the volumes up to this point." She gestured to her point of demarcation. "Everything from here back has been worked through and should be fine for research. You'll be glad to know the books are in chronological order, so the oldest volumes have been tended to. I've been working as quickly as possible, but if you see something you really must check out, and I haven't gotten to it yet, just let me know, and I can check it for you so you can take it from the Archives."

Taryn stood from the chair in one light, graceful motion. "Excellent," she said. "You don't mind if I get to it while you work?"

"Not at all. I'll be glad for the company, even if it's quiet." And this was the truth. Mia was glad for Taryn's company just then, conversation or not. It was nice just to be regarded and considered rather than ignored.

11 A Friend L.C. 10152

"HEY." A melodious voice floated over the short wall separating Mia Jayne's bunk from Taryn Windbough's.

Mia was staring at the ceiling of the barracks, her thoughts jumping around in her head. She frowned slightly at the interruption.

"Hey," the voice repeated.

"Yeah?" Mia asked after a moment.

Blond hair and a pair of gold eyes peeked up over the wall. "Are you busy?"

Mia sighed as she leaned up on an elbow. "What if I am?"

"I'm bored."

Mia yawned in response and flopped back on what supposedly passed for a mattress. "Blast it, this thing is so uncomfortable."

A gold eyebrow arched upward, and a smirk lifted up the corner of Taryn's mouth.

"What?" Mia said.

"If you entertain me, I'll let you do it from the comfort of my feather mattress."

Mia shot into a sitting position and stared straight into Taryn's eyes.

"If you're lying..." she said in a menacing tone.

"I'm not. Come see for yourself."

Three seconds later, Mia decided that she'd died and was reposing in bliss. "Where did you get this? I need, need, need one."

Taryn surveyed Mia's recumbent form from the chair at her desk. "I brought it from home."

"Figures," Mia said. "Everyone here joined up voluntarily. I'm going to be sleeping on rocks for the foreseeable future."

"What do you mean voluntarily? Did you not hear the calling?" Her voice was tart and hinted at sarcasm.

Mia chuckled and stretched her back as she settled into the mattress. "Ah, no. I didn't. I thought everyone knew my story already. I figured with gossip and all that."

Taryn shrugged and put her feet up on the bed, leaning back in the chair. "I suppose I'm not the most popular acolyte myself."

"Well, in that case," Mia said, then told her about her meeting with the Dominus.

"So you just walked right in and demanded to see Dominus Nikola?" she asked.

"Yep."

Taryn gave her a funny look.

"You know, Cedar thought it was odd too, when I met him on the ship."

"Wait," Taryn said, her eyes glittering. "You met Cedar outside the Compound?"

Mia nodded. "I met him on the ship over here."

"Oh, do tell," she said, bouncing slightly in her chair.

Mia's face grew warm. It wasn't that big of a deal really. Her mind wandered back to the ship, and she told Taryn an abridged version of the story.

"That sounds just like him," Taryn said with a smile, referring to Cedar's warning about touching the boat's trees. "Scoot over," she added, and made a shooing motion with her hands.

Mia shoved toward the wall, and she flopped down next to her. They lay side by side, looking up at the ceiling for a long while, each lost in thought.

"You know," Taryn finally said after a long while. "Getting such an easy audience to the Dominus is rather peculiar. We do have a pecking order here, and acolytes aren't high on it. Potential acolytes even less so. I myself have never been privy to a meeting of the general assembly, and I've been here almost two cycles. Are you sure there's nothing your father may have neglected to tell you?"

"All my life he's been my guidepost, but now I really don't know anymore." When Mia frowned and bit her lip, Taryn grabbed her hand and gave it a reassuring squeeze.

12 THE BRIG   L.C. 10152

"THIS WOULD BE PERFECT to slip inside my pallet at night to keep my feet warm against the deep chill of the Compound," Mia Jayne said, as she handed Brother Cornelius a bowl of stew, a crusty loaf of bread, and a spoon.

She was referring to yet another of the cleric's ingenious gourds that he called cakes. This one was flat and mimicked a miniature hearth. When agitated, it warmed instantly and remained so for hours as the heat slowly dissipated.

More than a month had passed since she had arrived at the Order. She had largely settled into a routine at the Archives, but Brother Cornelius was still able to surprise her with his ingenuity.

"My child, what an excellent idea," he replied, beaming with disproportionate pride. "These old toes are practically numb as it is. How could I not have thought of that myself?"

"Well, I came here from the tropical hammocks," she said with a shrug. "I'm quite unused to this chill, and I fear I won't ever adjust. I cling to every scrap of warmth I can find!"

Brother Cornelius chuckled. "I promise to bring you a cake on the morrow then. We shall both be testers for this new idea of yours. The cakes have only a few good uses in them. The chemical reaction required is quite strong, even though the heat is fairly mild." He patted the cake to gauge its warmth. "This one here is on its last use, I daresay."

"So you'll toss it then?" Mia thought about cutting it open to look inside.

"No, no, cakes are also excellent for eating," he said, his voice taking on a conspiratorial tone. "Under the tough exterior is a tender, spicy meat. If you've been wondering what gives our stew that special kick, I slip all my exhausted cakes to Brother Borus, and he uses them in his recipes."

Mia raised an eyebrow at that confession. She actually had been wondering how they got that deep, hearty flavor into the stew. It settled into her stomach and sank into her bones, warming her from the inside.

"Don't be telling anyone that bit of trivia now." Brother Cornelius's eyes twinkled at her. "Brother Borus likes to pass that off as a secret of his cooking prowess."

She laughed heartily. She certainly enjoyed the old man's company, but her good cheer hinged more on the fact that, for the first time since she'd arrived at the Compound, the acolytes were going to be allowed outside tonight.

"Are you attending the Gathering?" she asked Cornelius. A smile still played at her lips.

He swallowed a bite of the stew he'd been enjoying and shook his head slowly. "Even with the night lights at their apex, it'll be too dark for my old eyes, child. I have some of the other clerics gathering on my behalf, I'm afraid." He spoke with a wistful tone. "I do miss the bountiful variety of foliage, but at least I still enjoy the night lights from my laboratory on clear evenings."

The night lights were magical, but Mia truly missed the forest's dense press of life teeming all around her. That was the true source of her excitement.

"Well, if there's anything else you forgot to instruct the clerics about, I'd be glad to assist," she said, as she tidied the surrounding table, putting away the wands and readying to leave. "If not, I think I'll be off so I can prepare for the festivities. Taryn, Cedar, and I have made plans to attend together."

"You've done enough for one day, my child," Brother Cornelius said, as he scooped up a bit of stew on a piece of crusty bread. He smacked his lips in anticipation but paused. "That said, I'm glad to hear you're getting on with some of the other acolytes."

Mia smiled again at the old brother, nodded in a slight bow, and departed out the great wooden entry to the corridor beyond. As usual the hallway was empty. The Archives were situated in a low-traffic area of the Compound.

She walked slowly along the corridor, as she often did on her way back to the barracks, savoring her last moments of privacy before coming under the scrutiny of her peers. She ran her hand along the cold stone, looking for warm patches. She'd been taking private moments when available to seek out the elder grove.

In the last four weeks, she'd managed to extract a little bit of information from Cedar regarding how the root system conduits functioned. She was certain the major corridors joined ancillary ones accessible by tunnels. The ancillary corridors were well hidden; she supposed it was to preserve the stark aesthetics of the Compound.

She sighed. Aesthetics was subjective, and her tastes differed drastically. The Order wouldn't stand for greenery, though, at least not in any corridors she'd been down. She approached a fork in the corridor. The left fork led to the barracks, and the right led down a dark hallway to a part of the Compound she hadn't yet explored. As she approached the fork, she peered down the right corridor. It was a black hole descending into the earth. After stopping to listen for any footsteps or other telltale noises, she ducked down the right corridor. Now was as good a time as any to have a peek.

She pulled a small, old gourd from the pocket of her sash and tapped it against the corridor wall with a slight thrum. The gourd hummed, the noise thin in the stone hallway. A weak yellow light emanated from the fruit. It would have to do. She urged her eyes to adjust by closing them briefly and felt along the edge of the wall. She stepped carefully down the decline of the tunnel, her eyes slowly acclimating to her surroundings.

With the rhythm of her downward steps, Mia gained confidence and walked quickly toward the bottom, her slippers almost noiseless on the stone floor. The stone walls grew warmer against her hand as she descended into the darkness. The farther she walked, the more the walls took on a sheen not present in the higher levels. Some sort of film covered them. She felt it as well as saw it; it was almost like a fine moss against her fingers. She brushed her hand lightly over it and paused. There it was. A very faint hum. She pressed her ear close to the wall, and the noise grew stronger.

Mia marveled at the texture and fine quality of the moss. It was completely unlike anything she'd seen or felt before. By the time she reached the bottom of the descent, the moss had thickened and now covered the walls and ceiling of the corridor. It hummed ever so slightly in every direction, the sound comforting her.

She continued along the corridor, cautious in her movements, waiting for the tunnel to open into a room or split off, but it continued on as it was for quite some time. Then, suddenly, the hum grew louder. It deepened and reverberated through her body, squeezing her heart gently and relaxing her muscles.

It almost sounds like the forest. Almost.

She stopped and stood with her ear close to the mossy wall. At the point where the hum was the strongest, she rapped her knuckles lightly along the wall, methodically from side to side, starting near her head and moving back and forth and slowly downward along the point of concentration. There was no discernible change in the feel or sound of the stone. She was almost ready to give up in frustration when one of her slippers came in contact with a particularly squishy piece of moss near the ground.

Crouching near the stone floor, careful not to step on her robes, Mia pressed her hand along the mossy bottom of the floor. Where her slipper had given, her hand did as well. It sank into the moss with an odd sensation, and she rooted around among the slick green until she found a hole in the stone wall. She groped urgently and felt out the edge of a square shape in the corridor wall.

It was a bit larger than the width of her shoulders, slightly taller than her crouched figure, and completely disguised by the spongy moss. *Ingenious!* She pushed on the moss at the center of the hole experimentally, tentatively at first then with greater force. She squeezed her eyes closed, expecting to hear a ripping noise. Instead the moss gave way under her fingers. As if burrowing through a thicket, her hand slipped past the moss, and warm air swirled past her elbow on the other side. Mia stared at her arm, which was stuck in the moss, and twisted it back and forth. It moved freely. She pulled it out slowly, expecting to leave a hole. To her surprise, when she'd fully extricated her arm, the hole sucked itself closed. She saw no sign that anything had passed through it at all. She touched the surface of the moss again, and it sprang against her palm just as before.

"Amazing," she uttered quietly. "Just brilliant. This must be one of the access tunnels."

Her heart thumped in her chest at the prospect of getting a peek at the complex system that ran the Compound. She took a deep breath and leaned her head and shoulders into the moss. As with her hand, it stretched against her cheek. It was soft and fresh smelling, like when she had rubbed her face into the grass as a child. The moss gave way, but before she was able to open her eyes on the other side, footsteps resonated along the passage.

Nervous excitement dissolved instantaneously into panic. Mia wasn't sure where the footsteps were coming from or where they were going, but she retreated back into the corridor. She pushed herself with such force that she came out of the moss too far on her heels and lost her balance, collapsing hard on her rear end with a thud. The footsteps quickened, and to Mia's horror, Brother SainClair's face appeared around the corner. She tried to scramble to her feet, but it was too late. He'd already spotted her.

She cringed as the roar emanated from SainClair's lips. His boots slammed on the hard stone as he bored down on her. She braced herself for the impact of a blow. Instead he grabbed her by the neck and dragged her to her feet.

"You! What are you doing snooping around this part of the Compound?" he yelled into her turned face then shook her roughly.

Mia instinctively tried to squirm away from his grip. "I was lost," she said quickly, trying not to stutter. Her eyes were still averted. She had to think quickly. Saying that she was trying to head back to the barracks wouldn't work. Everyone knew where those were. *Think, Mia.*

SainClair sneered, shaking her again. She was already wary of him, already hated him for how he had alienated her from the others, but now she was terrified of him. His eyes held a manic glint, and his hair was wild. There was something not right about him.

"You expect me to believe that, pretender?" he said with another growl, squeezing her neck tighter. "Do you know where you are stumbling about?"

She didn't for certain but had every intention of finding out.

"I was looking for Brother Cornelius's laboratory." The thought popped into her mind with relief. "He sent me to fetch him some additional wands for tomorrow." Her voice wavered, but she pressed on. "I've yet to visit the laboratory, so I got mixed up. Where are we exactly?"

She immediately regretted that last bit, which engendered nothing but additional rage. Brother SainClair's grip on her neck didn't loosen even a fraction of an iota.

"The laboratories are higher in the Compound," he growled. "Are you a half-wit as well as a liar?"

Sweat trickled slowly down her sides under her robes. "I must have gone down instead—" Her voice was cut off as his viselike grip on her throat tightened. She tried to breathe, but nothing filled her lungs.

"You know what I think?" he asked casually, as if he weren't choking the life out of her. "I think you were down here snooping around, trying to figure out a way to bring the Order down. I think you were spying on us." His harsh, sharp face appeared ghostly white in the dim light. His scruffy jaw looked like that of weird bird with blond hairs protruding from around its angular beak, and the cold fire in his pale-blue eyes made it clear that he wasn't jesting. He really thought Mia was a spy.

There was no way for her to contain the quaver that shuddered through her body.

Brother SainClair narrowed his eyes as if he took her shaking as a sign that he was correct. "You know what we do to spies, don't you?"

"Yeh…" She tried to speak but was still unable to draw a breath. His grip loosened only enough to let her lungs fill with air. She took a few ragged gulps but still was unable to form words.

"You'll soon find out." He didn't elaborate.

Mia's dizziness ebbed with each gasp. At least he wasn't going to kill her right here in the hallway.

"The Order required my presence at the Compound," she said through gulps of air, regaining her composure and trying to add a bit of logic to his outlandish claims. "I didn't choose to be here. Whether my father really did write that letter or whether Dominus Nikola made it up, being here wasn't my wish. Why would I be spying?"

At her reference to Nikola, SainClair's face grew darker. "You accuse the Dominus of lying?" He shook Mia again but mercifully didn't tighten his grip on her neck.

"Er, I was making the point that I'm not here of my own accord."

"I grow tired of your lies and excuses." He turned her away from him, his hand still firmly on her neck, and forced her along the hallway. Her feet raced to stay ahead of him and avert any further pain.

Where is he taking me?

He shoved Mia back up the tunnel, and they took the fork toward the barracks. Maybe he was just sending her there. Her optimistic thoughts were dashed when they took a right turn before reaching the dormitory entrance. This turn led down a particularly narrow passage that was exceptionally long and sloped back downward. After a long while, the ground finally leveled out at a slightly wider tunnel. Spaced along this tunnel were gourds that illuminated metal doors set into the stone walls along both sides. Brother SainClair pushed her along past a couple of the doors.

They were cells, she realized, her breath catching in her throat once more. Before she could protest, he tossed her into a cell and bolted the door. It was a small, dank cube with a danker, lumpier version of the bean mattresses the acolytes had in the barracks, situated against the back wall. There was also a chamber pot on the floor and not much else. It was a tiny stone cave that made her cubby in the barracks look spacious and comfortable.

"You can believe Dominus Nikola will hear about this," SainClair said coldly. "If the Gathering wasn't taking place tonight, I'd take you there straightaway, but maybe you could do with a good think." He turned and stalked off.

"Wait!" she called after his retreating footsteps.

His long strides didn't pause or even miss a beat. And like that, his footsteps were gone, and Mia was utterly alone in a mostly dark cell with just the light of the gourd in the corridor. The Gathering. She was supposed to be enjoying a night out with the others.

For the first time since she'd left home some weeks ago, she began to cry.

She held it together for a while, but finally the sobs poured out of Mia with an intensity that surprised her. Father, home, Hackberry, her freedom. Attending the Gathering with Taryn and Cedar was just the last in a long list of what was no longer hers, and she found herself mourning them all simultaneously. She finally allowed her heart to experience the abject pain she'd denied for so long. She collapsed to a kneeling position, gasped from the sobs, and swallowed hard. Her throat was sore from SainClair's bruising touch. She hugged her arms to her body as she let the tears roll freely and her chest quake. She stayed like that, crumpled on the ground, for a good long while. It was hard to say how long, but when she finally rolled onto her back on the dirty floor, she was exhausted from crying. Her eyes were almost puffed closed, and everything felt thick. She wiped her nose on her sleeve. A subtle warmth pulsed softly against her stomach.

It was the small, brown leather book. She had taken it from the Archives more than two weeks ago and carried it with her in her sash. She couldn't say why it was with her now, except she felt compelled to carry it. She pulled it free from her robes, clambered up onto the dirty mattress, and leaned against the cold stone wall at the back of the cell.

"How is this even less comfortable than my barracks bunk?" she said to no one.

Mia held the book in her hands, savoring the warmth it emitted. Although she'd been carrying this book around, she'd never even cracked it open. She breathed in deeply, held it, and breathed out, repeating this process to calm her nerves. She squinted at the volume in her lap and opened it to the index.

Blast that bloody SainClair for leaving her with no light. Numerous family names graced the first page of the index, none of which she recognized. She flipped to the letter *J*. There was a Jaynor but no Jayne. Maybe the Jaynor family was a distant relation. This seemed to be an ancient tome after all. She flipped back to the beginning and noticed Draca. Dominus Nikola's family name was Draca. She turned to the entry for it. The page contained a complex listing of the descendants of the Draca family; it even had a Nikola. *That can't be the Dominus. This book is ancient. Maybe he's named after that ancestor.*

"We Jaynes don't have any such storied history," she murmured. "No seal, no family estate."

Clearly she was alone, and at this point, she wasn't above speaking to herself. The ability to talk openly was actually rather liberating. She flipped again to the index and found another name she recognized: SainClair.

"Figures," she muttered. "I should have guessed that blockhead has a family entry." She opened the book to SainClair. The family crest was an owl sitting on a lotus flower. "That crest looks very familiar." She turned the book over in her hands. "Ha!"

The author must have rather liked the SainClair crest. After flipping back to SainClair, she looked through the list of names. She didn't think anyone had ever told her SainClair's first name. *Could any of these dusty old names be his?* The very last line caught her attention.

"Jayne!" She exhaled sharply.

One of the SainClair ancestors had Jayne as a first name. *How much would that irk SainClair?* Jayne SainClair had a sibling named Thaddeus. That was where the line had left off in the description. It was odd that no dates appeared by any of the names, but there was a lot about this book that was odd.

Between the dank cell, her bout of crying, and her inadequate access to a handkerchief, Mia's nose was running unabated. A tickle hit it just then, and before she was able to cover it with her sleeve, a large sneeze erupted, spraying indelicately across *An Exhaustive Genealogy of the Families of the Realm*.

"Oh, blast me to the Core!" she yelled, and patted at the page with her damp, nasty sleeve.

Brother Cornelius wouldn't be happy if she ruined this archival tome, boring topic or not. Fear gave way to full-on panic when the phlegm of her sneeze soaked into the page and the ink started to fade and change.

"No, no, no!" Mia flipped through the book, but words were fading all over the place. "What in the name of..."

She turned back to the title page and with continuing horror looked at the fading text. The ink shifted, melting into a puddle and reforming before her eyes. She blinked, mouth agape. The title now read *Compendium.*

Below that, she read aloud, "Alpha Level activation coding complete. Please state your name."

As she spoke, the text changed again, and an invisible hand inked in additional words below the ones she'd just read aloud.

"Affirmative," she continued to read. "Please state your name."

She paused for a moment. "Mia Jayne," she said, suddenly embarrassed about speaking aloud.

It was one thing to talk to herself, but it was something entirely different to talk to a book. If she wasn't going daft before, this very well could be proof of an acceleration in her deteriorating mental state.

The book's text updated itself again. *Name acknowledged. Welcome to Compendium, Mia Jayne. Your profile has been created.*

"What is this daffy book?" she asked, still staring at the title page in disbelief.

The text in the book obliged her question. *Compendium at Alpha Level is a voice-activated knowledge acquisition and storage tool coded to your current profile. Please proceed at your convenience.*

"What do you mean by 'knowledge acquisition'?" she asked, dubious.

Compendium has access to a collection of information that can be searched at your command. It is ready to assist at your convenience.

"What kind of knowledge?"

She probably had gone insane, alone in the dark, but even if she could believe her eyes—and if this book really was doing what it appeared to be doing—if it was an ancient volume, how much could it know about anything current? It had to be archaic and full of misinformation.

Compendium has access to information pertaining to history, politics, engineering, botany, literature, genealogy, and many other topics. Please specify your desired criteria at your convenience.

"Can you stop doing that?" she asked.

To what are you referring? the booked wrote back with an elegant flourish in its script.

"That 'at your convenience' thing. It just seems cumbersome. And please stop referring to yourself in the third person. It sounds condescending."

The phrase "at your convenience" is appended to certain responses to create the feeling of politeness and understanding.

"Well, it irks me," Mia said. How embarrassing that her first conversation with a book was to complain about its attitude. Its tone was really bothering her, though.

Please confirm that I am correct when I state that you are requesting that I not be polite, the book wrote.

Mia would be blasted if that book wasn't just a tiny bit snarky. She smirked a little.

"Be polite," she said. "Just don't be overly polite."

Please provide more specific parameters, the book printed out.

Well, it wasn't being polite anymore; she would give it that.

"Never mind," she said. "Tell me the history of the Order." *Trick question!* She congratulated herself mentally. After all, this book predated the Order.

Accessing the Network, Compendium wrote. *This may take a moment.*

Yeah, right. To her shock, the pages began to populate with information, including a timeline, cleric roles, bylaws, branches, major players, and many other subjects related to the Order, the scope of which encompassed surprising detail.

"How is this possible?" she muttered to herself.

Please provide additional detail in your query, Compendium responded.

She rolled her eyes then decided it might not be a bad idea to ask the book.

"How is it possible that you have information about the Order when you're older than the Order?"

Compendium reconfigured its text again, and the information about the Order receded into its pages. *I am Compendium,* the book scribbled out.

Mia rolled her eyes again.

I am an information resource. The timing of such information is irrelevant.

"How do you learn this information?" she asked.

My apologies, Mia Jayne, Compendium jotted in its elegant hand. *You haven't unlocked sufficient access to that information.*

What in the Core did that mean?

"So can you can tell me information that hasn't happened yet?" she asked, her mind reeling with possibilities.

Negative. My data is based entirely on factual information in existence as of this moment. I can provide information of the present, but I cannot foretell the future. I can make projections based on past information, but these are inherently speculative in nature.

"Can you only show me text?" she asked, pondering the cryptic responses the book was giving her.

Negative. I also can provide drawings and schematics.

"Show me a map of Lumin."

Mia expected a tiny ancient map to appear, but instead a grid manifested with numbers running across the top and letters running down the side.

"Where is Willowslip?" she asked.

It spans E4 to E6 on the grid, Compendium replied. *Would you like me to enlarge those tiles?*

"Please do."

The ink blurred against the page as if it had been doused with water, and the image zoomed in. All of Willowslip was mapped out in the small drawings. The alphanumerical system returned as well.

"Please enlarge D1."

Compendium complied, enlarging the image further, until the little hammock islands of her home in the tropics to the southwest resolved in ink before her eyes.

"It's so far away," Mia whispered with longing in her voice.

The location you have designated is precisely 547 kilometers from your present location.

Compendium knew where she was located in relation to other places? Interesting.

"Do you have the schematics of the Compound?" she asked. Those might come in handy. She was still getting lost often, even after a full month as an acolyte.

Do you wish to view a topographical rendering or a planar outline of the level where you are currently located?

"Topographical."

An intricate drawing simulating the elevation inside the mountain was rendered on the first page. Again there was an index allowing her to call out any section she wished to see in greater detail.

"Please provide a greater description of my location," Mia said, instead of bothering with the letters and numbers

Compendium shifted again and sketched out drawings of the cellblocks and the tunnels leading to them. *You are in the upper cellblocks of the brig,* Compendium wrote.

"There are other cellblocks?"

Affirmative. A maximum-security dungeon is located three levels down.

"How many levels are there in the Compound?" Mia had firsthand knowledge of four separate levels but suspected there were more. It was hard to tell because of the way the passages were situated.

The Order's facility has fifteen separate elevations, Compendium replied. It then qualified its response. *Some levels overlap in elevation, so I have elected to respond in terms of elevations rather than levels per se.*

The Compound was much larger than Mia had suspected.

"Show me the schematics for the chamber containing the elders," she said, itching to see how the Order harnessed the power of such massive trees so deep inside a mountain.

A complex diagram drew itself onto the pages of Compendium. A grove of trees stood in the center, their trunks very large and containing many heavy branches heaving skyward. The trees were so large they actually tunneled up through the mountain just as Cedar had speculated in their earlier conversation. A massive cylindrical shape had been cut in the center of the mountain, through which the arboreal elders grew. They stretched right up and out of the top of the mountain. They also branched out into various smaller tunnels like a honeycomb.

"That's amazing," Mia said, in awe of the drawing. "It's like the entire Compound is situated in a volcano with the elders grown up through the crater."

That is precisely correct, Compendium chimed in helpfully. *Thousands of cycles ago, where we sit now, an active volcano existed. It is now dormant, and after the last eruption, it filled with mineral-rich water that seeped into the crater bed and created layers of moss. For 656 cycles, the Order has been cultivating this mountain and the elder trees growing through it. Over hundreds of cycles, the people of Willowslip have for-gotten that the mountain was ever a volcano, and it appears, for all intents and purposes, that the Com-pound is like any other flora-covered mountain in the near vicinity. Its Crater Grove remains a secret, ex-cept to those trusted among the Order.*

And now me, Mia thought. "That's really amazing," she repeated. "I have to see it for myself."

Compendium composed a map from the cells to the Crater Grove's entrance.

"Thank you," Mia said, and yawned. In the excitement of discovering Compendium, she had almost entirely forgotten that she was a prisoner in a cell in the Order's brig and that she not only had missed the Gathering but also likely would be questioned as a spy on the morrow. It was ridiculous, but she took comfort in the stilted words and arcane language of Compendium's text. An ancient artifact gathering dust—or not actually gathering dust at all—on a bookshelf for who knew how long had sprung to life in her hands. Now active, it hummed almost inaudibly and remained soothingly warm to the touch.

"How long has it been since you were last active?" Mia asked, the strain of the day finally catching up to her.

Six hundred fifty-four cycles, replied Compendium.

"Wow, you must have been really bored" was all she could think to say in response.

It was the last thing Mia said, and she promptly fell sound asleep on the cold, smelly cot in the brig with Compendium resting open on her chest.

13 The Network L.C. 10152

"SO IT FINALLY HAPPENED?" asked Dominus Nikola Draca. He rested a hand on the large console and felt the energy pulse through its thick surface. "An unknown device has accessed the Network?"

Nikola and Moritania stood in the bowels of the Compound, below the living quarters, below the kitchens, below the Crater Grove even. The room was dark and damp and warm, with vines curling among the roots that covered the walls and snaked along the ground and up along and under the large console. Its smooth surface was etched with faintly glowing blue lines displaying symbols, text, and numbers, most of which Nikola didn't directly concern himself with. This was Moritania's purview, the Deep Compound.

"Yes," said Moritania. She frowned and rubbed a finger across the surface of the console, as if lost in thought. "But we don't know what it is. Its identification signature is locked. See here? Something is drawing energy." She gestured to a blinking blue ideogram in a line of identical but darker ones. Nikola could almost see it sucking energy from the Network as it pulsed steadily.

"How can that be?" he asked. In his many cycles as head cleric, nothing had accessed the Network except the Compound itself and certain other devices known only to a select few clerics, and those few clerics were Moritania's engineers down here in the Deep.

"We really don't know," said Moritania. She rubbed her eyes in frustration. "As you're well aware, nothing has accessed the Network in more than six hundred cycles. How this device was able to do so is a mystery."

"Well, is this good or bad?" he asked. He had his opinion, but he wanted to hear Moritania's.

She laughed oddly, as if he had made some terribly funny jest. "We've waited so long for something to happen, for the Network to show new signs of activity. But now that it has, I'm terrified. What if a hostile device has infiltrated us? Gamma Protocol was supposed to end more than one hundred fifty cycles ago, but we're no closer to understanding why it hasn't ended and what to do if it does. We're severely handicapped without the key!"

"I understand your fears completely, Moritania," he said, and frowned. "We can't rule out any theory at this point, including that Clavis has fallen into the hands of the Druids."

Moritania frowned as well and made as if to speak, but Nikola held up his hand.

"However," he continued, "we must remember that no living person has ever seen the key, and its very description has been locked in the lost Network logs archive for six hundred fifty cycles."

She sighed and nodded, her hands returning to the console before them. The blue light continued to blink in the dank dimness of the Deep Compound. "I'll continue to research the matter," she said. "In the meantime I can't prevent this device from accessing the Network, but I can at least monitor the access logs."

"What has it accessed so far?" Nikola asked.

Her frown deepened, and her brow furrowed. "A history of the Order and maps of the Compound."

Nikola patted Moritania's hand but turned his head away to hide his worry. "We'd best not tell SainClair of these developments. He carries too much guilt and anger as it is."

14 THE DOMINUS L.C. 10152

M IA JAYNE WOKE FROM A SOUND SLEEP to
heavy footfalls advancing toward the door to
her stone cell. Still groggy, she opened her eyes slowly.
The quality of the light was unchanged, and she had
no sense of the time. The footsteps came to a stop, and
the heavy lock to the door unbolted with a hollow
thunk. SainClair stalked in.

"Well, what do we have here?" he sneered. "Have
we been doing a bit of night reading? Enjoying our
leisure time?" His body was rigid, and his eyes glinted
coldly at her prone frame.

Mia sat up quickly, trying to simultaneously close and stow Compendium in her sash. SainClair moved with speed that belied his age. He snatched the book from her and held it away from her grasping fingers. Bile rose in her throat, and she tried not to let him see her panic. He took a step back and leisurely flipped the pages.

"*An Exhaustive Genealogy of the Families of the Realm,*" he said, reading from the title page.

Only after she realized she was holding her breath did she emit a long sigh.

"What are you doing with this?" he asked.

She tried to think of a plausible excuse. Telling him that it was warm to the touch and that she'd felt compelled to take it probably wouldn't elicit a positive reaction. She was initially relieved that Compendium had reverted to the relatively mundane tome on genealogical history, but she quickly panicked once again. What if she had gone daft? What if her entire experience the night before had been a feverish hallucination born from stress? Or worse yet, perhaps she had contracted the purple spores from Father and was now doomed to die a slow, horrible death as a prisoner in this Compound. She almost had worked herself into a full frenzy when her eyes slid back to SainClair's angry, expectant face.

"I never knew my mother," she said. It wasn't a lie. "So I was trying to learn more about my family." That statement also was true, even if not entirely so.

Mia hadn't known her mother, and Father had almost never deigned to talk about her. She had used Compendium to try to look up her family. SainClair didn't need to know that the effort had led nowhere fast. What sounded like a perfectly reasonable explanation, however, only enraged him further. His tall frame towered over her as he shook the book in a meaty fist, his pale face sallow in the backlit glow of the gourds set in the hallway. He laughed then, the sound malicious and cold and not at all jovial. He spat on the ground near the bed. Mia had no idea what had caused this reaction.

"And what did you learn about your family?" His question was more than a little sarcastic.

"Not much," she squeaked. "The Jayne family name apparently isn't all that illustrious."

Her self-deprecating remark did nothing to quell SainClair's rage. His face reddened in anger. "Well, I have my own theory," he said, grabbing the shoulder of her robes and dragging her to her feet.

At least, he doesn't have me by the neck, she thought. As it was, it still hurt to swallow, and she suspected she had some bruising.

SainClair dragged her from the cell into the tunnel that led back to the living quarters. He didn't return Compendium to Mia's possession, instead stashing it in his own sash.

"I think you were learning as much as you could about all of us, hoping to find some weakness that could be used to exploit the Order for whomever you have allegiance to."

"I have no care for the Order either way. I'm here at my father's request, at the pleasure of Dominus Nikola, and out of no desire of my own. Think what you will, but I have no other purposes."

SainClair made a growling noise in his throat and continued to march her along the corridors. "We'll see what the Dominus thinks," he said.

After that, he fell silent, and they proceeded with no further conversation. Mia was more than grateful for an end to the discussion. Eventually SainClair marched her up to a curving staircase set invisibly into the stone wall of the corridor. She walked this passage regularly but hadn't noticed it before. SainClair briefly let go of her robes to stuff a gourd into her hands.

"Up," he said tersely, and pushed her ahead of him. "We are expected."

With only the gourd lighting the path, they climbed the curving staircase for a long while until it ended at a similar alcove that led to an exceptionally brightly lit room, the brightest Mia had seen since she'd arrived at the Compound.

She blinked from the light as she stepped out of the alcove. *By the Core, this room actually has natural light. We must be up high in the volcano.*

She saw a large opening in the side of the room, mostly shaded by foliage growing up and from outside. There also was a thick branch that formed a sizable hearth near the open wall. The humming vibration of the forest resonated through the opening. *This must be the most beautiful room in the Compound*, she thought.

She resisted the urge to ask SainClair where they were, as she rather wanted him not to speak to her, and he'd probably take the question the wrong way anyway. She tried not to look awestruck by the view of the outside world.

Mia was so focused on the window that it took her a moment to notice the desk in the corner of the room. Seated there was Dominus Nikola.

"Lovely view, isn't it?"

His question jolted her from her reverie. It seemed she was in Dominus Nikola's chambers.

Apart from being airy and open to nature, the space was well appointed. The desk was a large, oiled hardwood, gleaming in the sunlight. A thick rug woven in many colored furs covered the floor, damping the sound of slippers and boots alike. Tapestries hung on the stone walls, displaying scenes of worldly beauty. One depicted a grove of massive trees that seemed to grow out of the center of the earth. Another displayed a frozen landscape with a thicket of trees glowing through the frost. Two separate closed doors led to other rooms. The walls on either side of the open window were floor-to-ceiling bookcases stuffed with books, perhaps as many as the volumes that filled the cases in the acolyte barracks. By the hearth there were a couple of overstuffed chairs.

I bet he doesn't sleep on a stone pallet.

"Brother SainClair," Dominus Nikola stated in a calm, clear voice, "I think it's safe to let go of Ms. Jayne." He gestured with a bony hand to the robes twisted about her neck, where SainClair was still gripping them tightly. "I highly doubt she plans to bolt."

He exchanged a knowing look with SainClair that left her feeling confused. SainClair twisted his mouth as if to reply but instead released his hand from the neck of Mia's robes.

"As I informed you earlier, Dominus, I caught this acolyte poking around the corridors on the lower levels. When I asked her what she was doing in an empty passage, she told me Brother Cornelius sent her to his laboratory. We well know that the laboratories are nowhere near that part of the Compound, and I very much doubt Brother Cornelius would send this upstart to fetch something from his private laboratory." SainClair stated all of this in one breath and took another to continue his diatribe.

Dominus Nikola held up his hand to silence him. "Yes, yes, Brother," he said amiably. "Did it not cross your mind that the young Ms. Jayne was telling you the truth?"

Mia tried to hide her surprise.

SainClair's face darkened. "It didn't cross my mind because it clearly wasn't the truth."

"Yes, well," said Dominus Nikola. He then paused as if considering his next words carefully. "Brother Cornelius came to see me this morning. When Ms. Jayne didn't report for her duties at the Archives, he was sufficiently worried to request an audience."

SainClair added a slightly curled lip to his grim expression but remained silent.

"When I explained the situation to him, Brother Cornelius said that he did indeed send Ms. Jayne to his laboratory to retrieve some additional wands for the next day's work. He apologized, saying he must have sent her in the wrong direction when he instructed her regarding where to find his laboratory. It was a very long day, and you know how it is with those of us of advanced age."

Dominus Nikola raised an eyebrow at SainClair, who continued to seethe silently. Mia tried to maintain a nonchalant face, although a slight smile might have escaped her attempt at neutrality. If it did, Dominus Nikola made no comment. SainClair was too focused on the Dominus to look her way. Brother Cornelius had vouched for her.

A warm feeling spread through her chest. Perhaps she actually had a friend among the cleric ranks or at least someone who selfishly didn't want to lose an able-bodied assistant. She would take it even if it were the latter.

"Did he mention any books missing from the Archives or from his laboratory?" SainClair asked casually.

Dominus Nikola's forehead furrowed in thought. "I don't recall him mentioning anything being missing." He looked over at Mia.

She kept her expression passive but took a deep breath. SainClair drew Compendium out from his sash. "Well, she had this on her when I visited her cell this morning. It must have been with her when I caught her snooping in the corridors."

He tossed the book onto Dominus Nikola's desk, where it landed with a clank. The Dominus picked it up and examined the cover. Then he opened it to the title page.

"I'm sure I have no idea what this book has to do with anything, Brother SainClair," he replied. "It's merely a historical archive of families. Where did you get this, Ms. Jayne?" he asked.

There was nothing accusatory in the Dominus's tone, and despite Mia's concerns that he had been less than honest with her regarding Father's letter, she decided that whatever he thought of her, his opinion had to be higher than SainClair's. She would tell him the truth.

"Brother Cornelius has me assisting him with spore removal in the Archives. I came across that book, and something struck me about it, so I decided to borrow it from the library. In my excitement about the Gathering, I did forget to tell Brother Cornelius that I had the book with me. As no particular person was clamoring to borrow an ancient book on families, I suspect it's irrelevant whether or not I mentioned I had it."

An expression passed over Dominus Nikola's face as she spoke, like a statue cast in the momentary shadow of a passing cloud. When she stated that something struck her about the book, he definitely reacted. Was that flicker on his face relief? She couldn't tell. However, he said nothing further on the subject.

"Brother SainClair," he said, turning his attention away from her, "I find that explanation perfectly reasonable. We must not discourage the future of the Order from reading and learning, correct?"

Brother SainClair pursed his lips. He wouldn't be winning today's battle. "If that is all then, Dominus, I will return Ms. Jayne to the barracks."

"If you please," Dominus Nikola said, "I should like to have a moment to speak with Ms. Jayne alone. Do not hold yourself up from your duties on our account."

"Do you think it's wise to let her wander alone—"

Again the Dominus held up his hand and fixed his clear, gray eyes on SainClair, silencing him with the gesture and the look.

Mia dearly wished she could master that one. SainClair sucked air into his lungs, expanding his chest. He looked rather constipated all of a sudden.

"Very well, Dominus." With that, he bowed deeply to the head cleric and retreated back through the alcove.

His boot steps resonated down the spiral staircase, and Mia was relieved to be away from him.

"Ms. Jayne," Dominus Nikola said after the sound of SainClair's feet faded from earshot, "please have a seat." He got up from his desk and came around toward the hearth, gesturing toward one of the overstuffed chairs.

Mia looked down at her rumpled robes. She was dirty and disheveled from her night in the brig. Seeing her face, Dominus Nikola waved a hand in dismissal.

"Never you mind, my child. These chairs have survived worse than a bit of grime. I believe it's high time we had a proper conversation."

She didn't know what he meant by "proper conversation," but she was too weary to protest. His implacable demeanor and concerned face put her at ease, despite her reservations. She made her way to one of the overstuffed chairs and sank down. Her body relaxed into the chair almost against her will. The thick cushions cradled her sore muscles and bones. What on Lumin did they stuff into these chairs? She suspected puppy tails or maybe the feathers of baby chicks. Either way they were blissful.

"What did you want to talk about?" she asked.

"How are you settling in?"

Mia was surprised by the question, but then Taryn had said the Dominus's interest in her was peculiar, and she grew uneasy.

"I'm not sure," she said slowly.

"Not sure? That's rather odd."

"Well," she continued, trying to explain, "I've lived my whole life in the forest, most of it in the hammocks of the tropics, and this place is nothing like my home. I find it foreign in every respect."

"Yes," he said, then paused to consider her words. "I would imagine the Compound is rather different from where you lived with your father. Still, we have much to offer in the way of learning, and I believe as you acclimate you'll find the cool weather refreshing."

"It's not just that," she said, trying not to sound accusatory. "I find that, generally, the other acolytes have no interest in me. I've heard rumors that Brother SainClair has threatened them against befriending me. He hates me with a vehemence I don't understand." *I may as well use the Dominus's personal interest to my benefit. He's going to pry either way.*

"Ah," reflected Dominus Nikola. "Brother SainClair is of the opinion that there's only one correct way. He looks at a mountain before him, and to him there is one path to the top. It's so clearly emblazoned in his mind that he doesn't understand why others might see one or many directions to the same place. It isn't that the path he sees doesn't exist. It does. He's just incapable of recognizing the many different ways one can achieve the same goal."

"And you believe many paths lead to the same place?"

"My child, there aren't just many—there are an infinite number. We each travel our own path, no two exactly alike, and yet we're often capable at arriving at our destination together. It's a remarkable thing."

"I take your meaning," Mia said, then added, in a somewhat terser tone, "Then why not just tell Brother SainClair that he's wrong and shortsighted?"

Dominus Nikola smiled softly at her. "Does he strike you as the type to take suggestions?"

She shook her head glumly. The Dominus reached over and patted her hand in a conciliatory fashion. "Just as he sees his own path," he said, "he must walk along it and learn from its experiences on his own. Just as you must walk along yours and learn from your experiences. No one can tell Brother SainClair how to be, and no one can tell you how to be. You must both learn through your own actions and decisions." He looked at her pointedly, his eyes sliding down to her neck and his mouth turning down in a slight frown. "Still, though, whatever emotions your presence may bring to light in him, it's no justification for his actions."

Mia reached up to touch her throat. It was warm and swollen under her hand. She had to know whether this ordeal was worth it. "Dominus," she said, "have you any word about my father? I should very much like to know if he's recovering."

The Dominus shook his head as he looked at her gravely. "My child, we haven't yet received news. The clerics attending to him are surely busy with their treatments and will send word when there is news one way or the other."

Questions bubbled up in Mia's mind, one after another. Had Father really sent the letter Dominus Nikola claimed? How many clerics had the Order sent to Father? What was this treatment supposed to be? What were the chances of it working? How long must she stay here? Would they be willing to apply the treatment to her if it turned out she also was infected? Her mind raced with all that she wanted to know, but what came tumbling from her lips in one long rambling mass of confusion was none of that.

"Brother SainClair says I'm a pretender, that I didn't feel the call to the Order. This isn't wrong. In fact, Father always taught me to mistrust the Order and the work it does. You must have known this. The letter was addressed to you, so he must know you. How? And why would he mistrust this place so greatly? Further, if you know he feels that way, why would you accept his daughter into your ranks? I don't understand." She shook her head slowly, still mulling over the questions herself.

Dominus Nikola smiled as her questions tumbled forth. "It is true that your father bears little love for the Order. It's a very long story, one you deserve to know, but it must be reserved for another time. Trust me when I tell you that your father had very good reasons for sending you to us and that I have every confidence that your unique skills and spirit are greatly needed as we prepare for certain coming trials." Suddenly his smile faded to a grim line, and his gray eyes appeared troubled.

Mia wanted to press him for further explanation, but he stood abruptly from his chair and turned to face the window.

"Ms. Jayne, this has been a good conversation. We'll talk more when the time is right. I trust you can see your way back to your barracks without getting lost. I'm sure Brother Cornelius will be much relieved to find you intact."

"Yes, Dominus," she said. "Thank you for taking the time to speak with me, and thank you for intervening on my behalf with Brother SainClair."

"He will eventually come around." He turned back to look at her once again, his composure restored. His face resumed its serene smile.

Still disconcerted and very discombobulated, Mia smiled back and turned toward the alcove. She was almost to the stairs when Dominus Nikola stopped her.

"Ms. Jayne," he called, "I believe you've forgotten your book on the families of the realm."

Compendium! I almost left it behind without a second thought. Her mind was still a jumble between Father and her conversation with the Dominus. She hurried back toward him as he held out the book to her.

"Best take good care of this," he said.

Could he...? She frowned, observing the glint in his eyes. She slid her fingers along the pages casually and peeked inside. It was still just a book of family trees.

"I shall," she said. "Brother Cornelius would take no pleasure in any harm befalling one of the archival books, even if it's an outdated volume on family histories."

Dominus Nikola smiled softly and nodded. That glimpse of relief behind his veiled gray eyes flickered again.

He doesn't believe a single word of what I've just said, but he isn't going to take Compendium from me. Mia stashed the book in her sash, bowed again, and departed down the stairs in haste before he changed his mind.

15 Retreat

"**B**LAST IT ALL. I REALLY NEED YOUR HELP." Compendium stubbornly continued to display genealogical charts instead of Compound maps. Mia Jayne stuffed it back into her sash. No question she had been awake when Compendium had presented itself to her. It wasn't just some crazed dream born of incarceration. She was sure of it.

"I'll figure that damnable book out later," she muttered, as she hurried along yet another identical corridor.

"Mia, is that you?" a soft voice asked, floating from behind her.

She stopped and turned on her heels. Taryn took double steps to catch up with her.

Where had she come from? And how was it that she never seemed to make any noise? It was unnerving.

"I'm lost per usual," Mia said, flustered.

As Taryn approached closer, her eyes roamed over Mia's dirt-covered clothing, her bruised neck, and what was probably a haggard face. Taryn drew a hand up to her chest in surprise.

"By the sacred elders, what happened? We waited for you last night. Finally we had to leave or risk missing it all. When we all returned, your bed was empty. No one knew where you were." Taryn reached out, placed a hand on Mia's upper arm, and squeezed it gently. "You look as if you lost a fight."

"I did, and I didn't," she said, and grimaced. "Do you know where we are?"

Taryn looked at her oddly then nodded.

"I suspect I'm frightfully late for my duties, and I can't go like this."

"You are, and you can't. When was the last time you ate? You look like you need some nourishment." Taryn guided her along by the elbow.

Mia was relieved to no longer have to concentrate on directions. Eventually she would learn her way around here. *Then I'll get the heck out!*

"Now, please." Taryn paused, and her eyes settled on Mia's face. "Please tell me what happened."

Mia felt an indescribable ease when she was with Taryn. The other acolyte emanated a deep calmness. It was like being with Dominus Nikola, only relaxing. She could talk to Taryn, who would listen without judgment.

"It was Brother SainClair." Her jaw tightened as she recalled the experience.

"He did this to you?" Taryn's gold eyes grew into round orbs lit within, and she shook her head slowly. "Even with all his gruff, I never would've thought him capable of that."

"I was running an errand for Brother Cornelius, and I found myself lost in the lower corridors. Plainly directions aren't my strength. I'm much better navigating a forest than a stone fortress."

"I also feel most at home in the forest," Taryn said. She patted Mia's elbow again. "You'll adjust to this place eventually. We all do."

"Everyone says that," she muttered, and told Taryn about Brother SainClair discovering her in the lower corridors. "The whole business was very weird. He was acting completely paranoid."

Taryn's eyes narrowed slightly. "What could have made him think you're a spy? I mean, are you?"

"No!" She uttered her response with unnecessary and probably damning force.

Taryn cleared her throat and gave Mia a pointed look before returning her gaze straight ahead. "We all have our reasons for being here. Some different from others."

"Everyone knows I didn't come here for the love of it. I only serve the Order so that my father can receive medical treatment."

Taryn acknowledged her statement with a nod but didn't speak.

"So Brother SainClair believes I must be spying for some other group." She lowered her voice. "Who would even bother spying on the Order? It's an out-of-touch, dusty, old fortress."

"I suppose he could think you're a Druid."

"A Druid?" Mia mulled that over. "Aren't Druids some sort of fairy story?"

Taryn laughed, producing a light tinkling sound, and slipped her arm into Mia's, hooking it so they were elbow to elbow. Her grasp was surprisingly strong and equally unyielding, and its proximity suddenly felt a little intimidating. Mia fought the urge to wriggle free.

"Mia, you're so wonderfully silly."

Mia hardly thought so, but there was no point in trying to contradict the statement. It was just a fact that people in Willowslip assumed she was a total bumpkin. And she supposed she was about some things.

"So what did he do after he caught you?"

"I thought he was going to kill me, but he hauled me off to the brig for the night. It was filthy and horribly uncomfortable. This morning he marched me up to Dominus Nikola to plead his case."

"Well, the Dominus must've believed you," Taryn said, tilting her head. "Else you'd be in the dungeon now."

"Apparently I'm not the only one who thinks Brother SainClair is prone to paranoid flights of fancy. Although I suspect it would have been a close call if Brother Cornelius hadn't vouched for me."

"I knew I liked Brother Cornelius," Taryn said with a bright smile, and steered Mia down a corridor that she would have missed otherwise.

"I like him too," she said. "Quite a lot actually." She was surprised to hear herself say it and even more so to know it was true.

MIA WAS MORE THAN A LITTLE EMBARRASSED by the state of her appearance in the looking glass and was glad Taryn had found her in the hallway and not Cedar. She never put too much stock in formalities, but she looked a fright, even by her standards. After bathing and combing out her hair, she put on a fresh set of smallclothes and her only spare robes. She would have to go sashless until she made it to the laundry. Perhaps a maintenance detail in the brig every once in a while would be a good idea. She donned her lapin bag and stuffed Compendium inside. She plaited her fiery hair into a long braid down her back. Strands here and there glinted in the dim light of the wash chamber, but the mass of it looked like wet blood. She took a deep breath and fought back the shiver that crept up her spine.

That's appetizing.

Her face was pale and reflected a bluish cast, and the cold whiteness of her skin caused her blue-green eyes to pop more than usual. Dark smudges hugged the hollows under those eyes. She looked even less a person than usual, like a scrawny, pale creature dredged up from the bottom of the sea.

"Well, there's no help for it," she said, and hastened out of the room.

When she finally burst through the door of the Archives, Taryn was there, and the dear girl had brought her food. Brother Cornelius had placed the stew on a cake to keep it warm, and it was steaming gently, smelling fantastic, and waking Mia's stomach from the deep slumber that had allowed her to get through the last eighteen hours.

"There she is," he announced, beaming his usual smile in her direction. "I was overwrought."

He clucked and fussed, and Mia smiled softly.

"I'm totally fine," she said, brushing aside his concern. "Famished but fine."

She sank into a chair at the reading table with Taryn and Brother Cornelius, filling the empty seat in front of the bowl of stew.

"You'll pardon my less-than-exemplary manners," she said through a mouthful of stew.

It was hearty and spicy and warmed her bones like it always did. Taryn watched serenely as Mia shoveled stew into her mouth and mopped drippings up with a piece of crusty bread.

"I was just telling Brother Cornelius about your awful night," the girl said, and patted one of Brother Cornelius's gnarled hands.

Apparently she wasn't the only one Taryn was grabby with.

"Yes, yes. Ms. Windbough here was giving me the full details. Most perplexing that Brother SainClair would make such accusations. I should almost think a visit to the medical corridor might do him some good. If nothing else, perhaps he needs to rest up." He looked at Mia's neck and tilted her head up with a long finger. Disapproval flickered in his hazel eyes, which looked a pale green at that moment, as his throat clicked.

"I bruise easily," Mia said, trying to minimize his worry. "'Tis been that way since birth. Father says I get it from my mother."

"Still, there is no need for such behavior. We are a unit here. We are a family, and one does not harm one's family."

"I guess he doesn't consider me family then." She twisted her mouth and narrowed her eyes.

As much as she might enjoy being family to Brother Cornelius and maybe even Taryn, this place wasn't her home, and these people weren't her family. Perhaps Brother SainClair understood that better than the rest of them. Maybe he had sensed a truth that clung to her like the reek of sweat, as if he could smell a taint infecting his family, disrupting his quiet enjoyment.

Unsure why, Mia struggled with the thought that SainClair maybe was justified in his reactions. Perhaps it did matter that she didn't care to join the Order, to make them her family. She had a family. No matter how small or how tenuous the link between her and Father grew, she had a family. Mia *was* a pretender, and perhaps that meant something, not just to SainClair but to her as well.

Brother Cornelius made a dismissive noise and waved his hand as if knocking aside the fog of her thoughts. "Poppycock," he said.

"What time is it?" Taryn asked suddenly. "I'm most certainly late for my afternoon duties with Brother Valentine." Her voice held a hint of panic.

"Nonsense," said Brother Cornelius. "Just tell that old coot that you were assisting me with a particularly delicate matter and that if he needs more information, I've said to come speak to me directly. No one wants to bother coming here and having to deal with me. Outliving everyone has its advantages."

"I can't imagine why anyone doesn't find your company utterly enchanting," Taryn said, smiling coyly at Brother Cornelius.

"Don't mock me now, my child," he said, his neck reddening slightly under his voluminous whiskers. "Flattery is wasted on a codger like me." He looked pleased nonetheless.

Mia rolled her eyes at the scene. Taryn bid her farewells and departed the library, leaving Mia and Brother Cornelius alone at last.

"Now," he began, his tone turning serious, "what actually happened? I got the children's fairy-tale version just now."

Mia smiled at his pointed look and swallowed the bite of stew rolling around in her mouth. "First, let me say thank you for covering for me. I think Brother SainClair would have had my head on a stake if it weren't for that."

"'Tis fine," he said, waving a hand to dismiss her thanks. "Do not try to distract me from the question," he added.

"I was just curious about how this place works. I've never been in an electrical system this large before. It was just simple curiosity." She took another bite of stew.

"Ah, well, a little curiosity now and then is a virtue, but I don't suppose Brother SainClair sees it as such."

"There was this amazing moss down there," she said, eager to turn the conversation away from SainClair. "It covered the walls like a springy blanket. Is it used as camouflage?"

Brother Cornelius chuckled at her description. "It's an insulator for the walls that lead toward the elders and has the lucky property of covering openings. 'Tis nothing so special really. Born of necessity, like much else in our world." He rubbed his whiskered chin. "I suspect your poking around in that area would have aroused some suspicion in Brother SainClair, who's mistrustful by nature. But still, his reaction seems entirely out of range, even for him."

"That's not all," Mia said.

She wasn't sure how much she should say about Compendium. She had genuine affection for Brother Cornelius. He was like the grandfather she might have had in another life, kind and doting and full of supremely interesting stories and bits of gossip. Her logical mind told her she was a fool for trusting anyone here, but her longing for someone to confide in and dote on her fought valiantly and ultimately landed the killing blow to caution.

"I'm sorry I didn't say so at the time, but I took a book from the ancient texts." She pulled Compendium from her bag and set it on the table.

Brother Cornelius picked up the book and examined it carefully. "You say you found this in the Archives?"

"Yes, a couple of weeks ago, while I was removing spores. It was one of the books I tested. It struck me at first because it was completely spore free. Something about it made me think I should spend more time with it. So I took it but neglected to say anything. I didn't think you would mind, but I should have said something earlier."

He cracked open the book and examined the pages and the binding, spending more time on the book itself than its contents.

"It's in remarkable shape for a book from the ancient texts," he finally said. "Perhaps it was just misfiled. It certainly is unusual. This scrollwork on the outside isn't something one usually sees. What does this have to do with Brother SainClair and the incident?"

"Well, there are a couple of things," Mia said. "Brother SainClair seemed enraged that I might be researching lineages. I found that reaction completely odd. He was especially derisive about my family name, Jayne."

"Ah, well," Brother Cornelius said, scratching a long bony finger across his chin whiskers in thought. "He himself has lost all his remaining family," he continued. "And if I recall correctly, his sister's name was Jayne. She was killed in the war."

"Really?" Mia picked up Compendium from the table and opened it to the SainClairs. "So his first name is Thaddeus?" she asked.

Even as Compendium hid itself as an ancient volume, its family lineages were accurate up to the current generation. *Poor design, that is. Not much of a disguise.*

"Yes, I believe that's correct. How did you know that?"

She showed him the page and pointed to Thaddeus and Jayne SainClair.

"How is that possible?" he said. "Has someone been updating this? I'll have the head of anyone who's been sneaking into the Archives to deface the texts."

She forced herself not to smile. It was hard to imagine Brother Cornelius having anyone's head for anything.

"There's even more to this book," she said, and told him about activating Compendium.

If Brother Cornelius thought she was unhinged, he didn't betray it in his manner. He pondered Mia's words carefully and scratched his perpetually itchy chin whiskers.

"So you're saying the book altered itself? The ink moved around on the page, and the text changed? And you spent a large amount of time communicating with it, but then in the morning, when Brother SainClair picked it up, it had returned to its previous state?"

"Yes. And I know it sounds positively mad."

"It's certainly unusual, but life is full of strange happenings."

"You mean you believe me?" Mia asked incredulously. She wasn't even sure she believed it herself at this point. As she looked back, it just didn't seem possible.

"Of course," he said. He raised his shaggy silver eyebrows in her direction. "The Order's primary mission is to protect certain ancient artifacts. This may very well be one of those artifacts."

"What exactly do you mean by 'artifacts'?" she asked, curious.

"Well, that's indeed a long story." He rubbed a finger against his temple then scratched his whiskers again.

I should research whisker anti-itch balm, Mia thought.

"Are you familiar with the details of the Great Fall?" he asked.

Mia shrugged. She had heard bits and pieces here and there. The folk in Hackberry weren't much for ancient history. Nothing that couldn't be eaten or traded for provisions or used to warm a body's feet on a frigid evening—not that there were too many of those in the hammocks—was valued.

"I heard there was a before and an after. At home we don't give much consideration to what came before, as it hardly seems to matter at this point, with us being so far removed from it. Taryn would disagree," she added, thinking back on Taryn's admission that history was her favorite subject.

"As would I," said Brother Cornelius. "We have much to learn from our forebears, and there's much that we could do if we could recover even a fraction of what they knew."

"Was it really so great back then?" Mia asked. "I mean, how do we even know?"

"Books of course...those that weren't destroyed in the chaos or lost to the Core. In some ways, it was very similar, but in many others, it was very different. Our ancestors lived off the land the way we do, but they possessed an advanced grasp of biochemistry and biomechanics, and they were able to use it to stunning effect in ways we may never understand." His voice held a sad, wistful note.

Mia supposed she would be sad too if she had some knowledge of what was lost.

"Our forebears were also part of the Central Counsel, which is described in some ancient texts as a counsel of peers comprised of delegates from all over Lumin. We ruled Lumin in peace as one body. After the Great Fall, the Central Counsel was...well, no one is really sure what happened to the counsel," he said, his face marked with concern. "Now no city-state benefits from trade with the others, and there's very little communication among us. Willowslip is essentially on its own."

"What caused the Great Fall?" Mia asked.

"Ah, now that's the real question, is it not?" Brother Cornelius rubbed his chin, but his eyes narrowed. "Alas, whatever was responsible for the Great Fall impacted the record keeping of our forebears. We have some texts from before the Great Fall and many that start perhaps fifty cycles afterward that discuss the political changes that occurred, but we don't have much that describes the loss of technology, what happened to the Counsel, or other questions that remain largely unanswered. The texts we can find that describe those times are generally personal memoirs rather than official historical records and, as such, contain little in the way of definitive answers. It's been a perplexing study for many of the scholars of the Order for some time." His eyes slid down, and he examined a bony finger with interest.

He's not telling me something, she thought.

"So how does all this relate to the artifacts?" Mia asked.

"Well, artifacts are the remnants of society before the Great Fall. They were likely common-day objects in antiquity, but now they're marvels of technical magic and mysteries to be solved and protected. There are clerics who would hide them away from the outside world under the guise of safety, others who would study them and learn their secrets, and yet others outside the Order, like the Druids, who would try to possess them. And still further I suspect there are those who would use them for mischief and trouble."

"Which are you?" she asked.

Brother Cornelius gave her question some thought before responding. "I suppose I'm the type who would use them as they were intended to be used by their makers, to better society."

Mia said gave him a big smile. "I think that's a sound position."

"If," Cornelius said, pushing Compendium back toward Mia, "this book is one of the rare artifacts left from before the Great Fall, it clearly has chosen to reveal itself to you. What reason it might have for that, I cannot say, but perhaps you'll be able to find out."

"So you'll let me hang on to it?" she asked. She was relieved but tried not be too obvious about it.

"I don't see why not," the old cleric continued. "It's of no use to anyone except you. Just take good care of it. And for all our sakes, best keep a wide berth from Brother SainClair in the future. Be more careful where you snoop next time, child!"

16 THE SEED L.C. 10152

THAT EVENING Mia Jayne dragged herself down the dining room to scrounge up some dinner. In penance for her tardiness, she had worked through the afternoon and into the early evening. Her neck was still sore and bruised and her body achy from Brother SainClair's rough handling and the discomfort of the brig cell. If asked before yesterday if she'd ever look forward to climbing into her stone cubby atop her lumpy mattress under her rough-spun blankets, she would've told such person that he or she needed their head examined by a healer or possibly an exorcist. However, with Compendium and a fresh cake from

Brother Cornelius tucked into her sash, she was anticipating the gray barracks and her hard pallet like never before.

Upon feeling her stomach gurgle inside her robes, she patted it and said to herself, "There, there, I suspect tonight will be a nice roast with root vegetables and some rice. I can just tell." Despite everything that had happened, she was in excellent spirits.

"Oh, can you?" a voice said from behind her. "Have you taken up in the kitchen or become precognitive?"

She stopped dead and spun around to face her detractor. Cedar's form was comically lanky as he made an emergency stop to keep from slamming into her. She poked him in the chest.

"My sources are none of your concern," she said lightly, and turned to continue to the dining area.

He took long steps to catch up to her short but rapid footfalls. "I don't suppose your recent absence was a reconnaissance mission to determine our dining-room menu."

"Alas, no," she said. "I had a tangle with the beast." She looked over to Cedar with mock foreboding.

"The beast?" he replied, arching a black eyebrow. The light in his eyes darkened as they slid down to her throat.

Mia was suddenly very conscious of the bruising. She supposed her levity was out of place, but she had too much worth focusing on at the moment to brood over SainClair's misplaced ire. She had a secret weapon now, a means to change her fortune, something she could rely on to see her through this experience.

"Might this beast be a surly cleric who stomps around in boots all the time while the rest of us wear slippers? And might he have some sort of bizarre vendetta against you?"

"Perhaps," she said. "Perhaps he caught me having a look around the lower corridors and assumed I was a Druid spy. And perhaps he threw me into the brig until Dominus Nikola knocked some sense into him, figuratively of course. Although I would rather like to see Dominus Nikola clock a particular someone real good."

Cedar laughed, his voice deep. It resonated down the corridor toward the dining hall. "I suspect you could get a good value in trade for orchestrating a viewing for that match."

They entered the dining hall, the good spirit between them lingering and mixing with the hearty smell of the roast emanating from the hearth.

"Ha-ha!" she exclaimed. "I *am* precognitive!"

Really she had just noticed that every fourth day the kitchen served some sort of roasted meat, probably to keep those who might be less than thrilled with stew every night from lodging complaint.

Cedar rolled his eyes, and they proceeded to pile their bowls high with meat, vegetables, and rice. Mia smiled at the sight of a hunk of cake in her ladle of vegetables and recalled Brother Cornelius's admonition against spilling Borus's secrets.

They surveyed the dining room for an empty seat. Mia spotted Taryn across the hall, and she waved them over with her knife.

"You're looking refreshed," Taryn said as they approached.

"I'm feeling quite a bit better indeed."

Mia and Cedar sat down across from Taryn; it was odd to actually be part of a group. Cedar was friendly with most of the acolytes, and Taryn welcomed his presence with easy jibes back and forth.

"Have you been cooking the books for us?" Cedar asked her, grinning his usual playful smile.

"I suppose we could cook up the three sacks of rice we received today in exchange for that basket of extra-long-lasting gourds Sister Moritania engineered, but I think Brother Cornelius would take issue with us cooking his books."

Mia couldn't decide whether Taryn's response was dry wit or genuine naïveté. She had such an innocent, unassuming way about her that made her hard to read.

Cedar nodded. "I suppose rice would taste better than dusty old books anyway."

"Now, now," Mia chimed in, "I take issue with use of the word *dusty*. I've been working very hard to de-spore every single one of those tomes in the Archives. I won't have my reputation as a librarian tarnished by your defamatory words."

Taryn giggled. "Actually you've been doing quite a thorough job. The books I checked out yesterday were all in tip-top condition."

"Thank you, Taryn. I feel I truly have a calling as a book cleaner."

Taryn giggled again.

"Oh, please," Cedar said with a grin, "we all know you're just using Brother Cornelius because he's easygoing."

"How dare you imply that I'm anything other than devoted to the good Brother Cornelius!" Mia made an exaggerated display of mock insult.

Truth be told, she was rather devoted to him, but it was nice to entertain and be entertained. When the hilarity died down, she weighed her next question.

"What do you know about the artifacts from before the Great Fall?" she asked.

Cedar shrugged. "There are always rumors about which artifacts might be out there. I heard one once about special paper that you write on, and it sucks in your words and stores them for later, almost like a journal. It's only a single page thick but can store much more than a page of writing. I heard another story about a gourd that can boil water without a hearth to make it potable when you travel."

These sounded interesting but nothing as complex as Compendium.

Taryn sighed, and a dreamy expression crossed her face. "In my historical research, I've run across references to an object called the Shillelagh. It's some sort of stick, and you supposedly can use it to travel anywhere in Lumin just by tapping it against a surface and telling it where you want to go. Then a hole will open up and take you there."

Cedar raised an eyebrow. "That sounds like rubbish."

Taryn's face grew even more animated. "Oh, I assure you it isn't. Numerous references are made to it in the ancient texts. It's even depicted in some of the drawings I've seen. The real question is what happened to it after the Great Fall."

"I've never heard of such thing," Cedar said, waving his hand dismissively.

"Still," said Taryn, not dissuaded, "can you imagine how amazing it would be to travel instantaneously anywhere in the realm? You could go home for the day or visit the top of the highest mountain or see the snowy peaks of the Northlands." She rested her chin in her palm, and her eyes lolled upward, as if her whole body were following them up and out of the Compound and far away. "If I had the Shillelagh, I'd use it to visit the whole realm, one town at a time. I would see it all. It would be glorious."

"Do you think something like that really exists?" Cedar said, his voice still holding doubts. "I mean, if the Order had an object with power like that right under its nose, I'd think they'd be making use of it."

"How do you know it isn't here? They could be making use of it as we speak," Taryn shot back. "It's not as if we're privy to every move the senior clerics make. We're among the Order's lowest ranks and certainly wouldn't be trusted to even know about the Shillelagh's existence, let alone whether it's being employed on secret missions."

"Secret missions?" Cedar asked. "Now you're really starting to sound a little bit mad. This is an organization dedicated to study and reflection, not crazy secret missions using ancient technology."

"I don't think Taryn is completely mad," Mia added, trying to be helpful.

"Well, thank you," Taryn said, gesturing her knife at her in salute. "I think...wait, *not completely* mad?"

"Well," Mia continued, "I've heard many stories about the Order from my father, and if he's to be believed—and I think he is—the Order isn't entirely about study and reflection."

Cedar's face darkened slightly. "What do you mean?"

"For instance, Father said that during the last war, the Order refused to get involved even as Willowslip pleaded for help. Certain clerics went against the Order to assist the people and were ejected from its ranks. Many clerics and nonclerics alike died. By the time the Order got involved, the city's losses were great. Father said the Order waited so long that it sacrificed its chance to remain relevant."

Both Cedar and Taryn looked somewhat scandalized by Mia's words.

"Well, even if that's true, what does that have to do with anything? It sounds like perhaps warmongering wasn't the Order's place." Taryn squinted, as if she were mulling over her own words.

Mia lowered her eyes. "I might agree, if Father hadn't also told me of rumblings from the Order of a weapon that could change the tides of the war."

"Well, that's just pure speculation," said Cedar. "There are no records of any cataclysmic weapon being discharged during the last war."

"No records that are public," Taryn corrected, tapping a slender finger against her jaw. "Perhaps in my digging, I can unearth some."

"That's twenty cycles in the past," Cedar said. "How's any of this relevant?"

"Well," Mia said, "one, we don't necessarily know everything there is to know about the Order. And two, I believe artifacts exist. I also believe it's possible the Shillelagh exists."

"Very well," said Cedar. "Suppose it does indeed exist. How does that have any impact on us?"

His question was entirely valid. Supposing the Shillelagh existed, what did that mean for them in real terms? Probably nothing. They were just acolytes, after all. Even if this traveling stick was an artifact under the protection of the Order, it wasn't as if they'd be offered a go with it. *Yeah, sure. Take it to visit the waterfalls of Concordia. Just be sure to bring it back in the morning so we can make that grain delivery.* It was nonsensical speculation, fodder for idle minds.

"I don't know," Taryn said. "Just knowing it exists gives me a sense of optimism." She paused, her voice catching in her throat. "Like I might see Ma and Pa again someday. But I guess it's all just daydreams," she said, smiling a sad smile, the fight and fire leaving her demeanor.

Mia understood completely. Daydreams of home. She supposed they all had them, even those of them here by calling—or at least choice.

"Ah, well," Cedar said, his tone softening, "there's always cause for hope. I mean, one of these days Mia might learn her way from the barracks to the dining hall without getting hopelessly lost."

"Hey," Mia said in mock indignation.

Taryn giggled, and Cedar playfully nudged Mia's arm. She elbowed him back.

"Perhaps Taryn can research me an artifact that gives directions," she said, shaking her head in simulated despair.

Taryn laughed. "Well, that might take more manpower than the entire Order is capable of."

Mia laughed too, although her mind began to wander. She would tell them about Compendium eventually, she supposed. It wasn't as if she didn't trust them, but for now it was her secret, her weapon against the threat of losing herself to this place and its ways. Compendium would see her through the maze. She no longer feared losing her way.

COMPENDIUM

THAT NIGHT and countless nights afterward, Mia spent her free time after dinner tucked under her blankets, her feet nestled up against one of Brother Cornelius's cakes. She whispered questions to Compendium on every topic imaginable until she fell asleep with the tome in her hands. When she was alone, she always opened the book to find Compendium's title staring up at her with a personalized welcome. It was only around others that it appeared as an innocuous listing of family lineages.

Sometimes Taryn peeked over the half wall and asked what she was doing. Mia would invite her over to toast her feet for a bit and listen to her moan about how the Ledgermaster never had any amazing inventions that warmed feet or created different kinds of light. They'd sit in the dim light of the barracks and tell each other stories about their childhoods and their lives before the Order.

Cedar often wandered around as well from his bunk on the opposite wall, if he noticed them engrossed in conversation. Mia learned about his family and his life in the northwest on a large island called Senegast. He had two brothers that were rangers, following after his father. He followed after his mother, who worked as an engineer on Senegast. She would tell him stories about his ancestors who helped found the Order, and it was then that Cedar knew he would serve. She'd been very proud when he'd made the decision to leave Senegast for Willowslip.

It was a generally calm period. Mia slowly worked her way through the ancient texts, removing spores from the books. Although it was an easy task, she finished each day with a concrete feeling that she had at least accomplished something productive. She spent her free time in study, primarily combing through bio-chemical engineering books or schematics provided by Compendium, or socializing with Brother Cornelius or Taryn and Cedar, and she was able to mostly avoid any confrontations with Brother SainClair. She had an odd, morbid sort of curiosity about the man who would sooner throttle her than look at her.

Still, Mia couldn't help feel as if there were some connection between them, some reason she had trig-gered his rage, and it wasn't just because she was a pretender. She was, to be sure, but the circumstances of the acolytes here were so varied, and the more she learned about them, the more she realized that not everyone was here because they had a calling.

Cedar had the calling, but Taryn had grown up in a gypsy forest camp, and her parents had sent her to the Order because they thought she would benefit from the stability of an education there. She missed the freedom of roaming all over the main continent, especially the forests, and talking to her grandfather.

That said, Taryn was constantly amazed by the amount of reading material at the Order. Her family always traveled light, so she had little in the way of a book collection. She'd been at the Compound for a few cycles, but her dedication to history wasn't enough to progress her past the stage of acolyte. Another of the acolytes joined the Order specifically because he'd heard whispers about its feats of engineering. There were as many reasons for coming to the Order as there were acolytes.

Something else had to be driving SainClair's mistrust, and Mia was curious what that might be.

"Compendium," she said, "tell me about Thaddeus SainClair's family."

The results were surprising to say the least.

The SainClair lineage is long and illustrious indeed. The SainClair family served as ministers on the Central Counsel. The very last SainClair to serve on the Central Counsel was Aris SainClair.

"What happened to her?" Mia asked.

Unable to respond. Information locked.

Mia sighed. She sometimes encountered such roadblocks when she asked Compendium questions.

"What happened to the SainClairs after the Great Fall?" she asked, changing the subject.

Gerard SainClair, Aris's son, was among the founding members of the Order. The SainClair family has served in the Order continuously since its inception.

No wonder Brother SainClair was so wrapped up in the idea that the Order was a calling. "He sees it as his sacred familial duty. He probably thinks the purity of the Order's mission is being diluted. Still, that's no reason to be a total arse."

The SainClair family has been decimated in recent generations, Compendium continued. *At least one SainClair from every generation has taken vows to serve the Order. That is the family's sacred pact. In Brother SainClair's generation, two signed up for service, Thaddeus and his sister Jayne. They both served dutifully. Jayne married a cleric, Claude. He had no illustrious bloodline or family of his own, and he took Jayne's family name and was welcomed as a son into their fold. The SainClair family had a sprawling estate in the Northlands that remained peaceful until the family started to divide itself over the increasing political tensions that rippled throughout Lumin.*

"What Father told me was true," Mia said. "The Order had no intention of involving itself in political matters, and it made that position clear to the leaders of Willowslip."

Yes, replied Compendium. *This official response created a fracture within the Order's ranks. Some clerics agreed with the establishment that the Order should not involve itself in political disputes. Another faction in the Order did not believe that remaining neutral would serve the mission. They championed peace and lobbied the Order's leadership to get involved. When the Dominus refused, this faction left and joined the war effort. Jayne and Claude SainClair left the Order, and Thaddeus SainClair remained. This rift tore apart an already fragile family.*

Jayne and Claude were killed in the war. In addition, the SainClair estate was torched to the ground, killing the rest of the SainClair family. Thaddeus SainClair never learned who set the fire, but foul play was suspected. The family had been too vocal politically. Numerous bodies were found in the ashes, but all the remains were unidentifiable, burned beyond recognition.

"How horrible." The story almost made Mia sympathize with SainClair. Almost. He had lost all of his family and was the last in a line that stretched back thousands of cycles. It seemed she and SainClair had more in common than Mia initially had thought. *Still, why take it out on me?* She was just a nobody from Hackberry.

The logical part of her brain said he was just being protective of the only family he had, the Order. *I would do the same. I did do the same. It's why I'm here.* However, the emotional part of her said he could go jump off a cliff.

Mia pressed her lips together in determination. The Order might be Brother SainClair's family, but it wasn't hers. She still had Father. *He may not be perfect. He may even have sold me up the river for a long-shot cure for his spores, but he's still my family.*

Her thoughts turned to the Shillelagh. If it really did exist, she could use it to visit Father. It wouldn't really be leaving if she just popped in to make sure he was recovering then popped back. If it were capable of instantaneous travel, no one would even notice.

She daydreamed about the forest. Instead of the quiet talking and occasional cough of the acolytes, the songs of birds rising from the resonant hum of the trees filled her ears. Instead of the smell of dusty books and sweat, the earthy smell of soil richening at the roots of the trees wafted into her nostrils. Instead of the lumpy bean mattress and flat pillow, the soft soil and grass padded her back as she lay on the ground and took in the visual gymnastics of the night lights rolling across the sky.

She was suddenly so homesick that her breath caught in her chest. As she lay in her bunk, her feet warmed by the cake, her chest tightened, and it took every muscle in her body to keep herself from crying. All this drama and politics had nothing to do with her quiet life in Hackberry. Maybe Compendium could help her find her way back there.

17 THE GROVE L.C. 10152

MIA JAYNE STARED UP IN AWE at the massive trees, the largest she'd ever seen. They fit snugly into the even grander cavern that soared upward to an open volcano crater. It was just as Compendium had described it. After her run-in with SainClair in the tunnels, she had become even more adamant about finding her way here, partly because she missed the sight, smell, and feel of trees and partly because she had to see for herself what was needed to power this place.

The first time she entered the Crater Grove and gazed upon the elders within, she wasn't disappointed.

The trees stretched so high that their tops were out of her view. The roots were enormous and gnarled, snaking out from under the trunks in every direction, popping up like giant worms wriggling in the dirt.

She always came here in the middle of the night, when no one would be about. She hoped to be able to see the night lights through the branches of the trees, but they were so thickly clumped that they formed their own closed roof over the immense crater. The room was so spectacularly huge that she almost couldn't fathom that it was inside at all.

The hum was loud and vibrant. It drew her toward the trees, and she so wanted to reach out and touch the closest elder's trunk, but thus far she had resisted. Before she saw them for herself, she labored under the delusion that perhaps she could climb up one of the elders and be gone, disappearing like a mouse in the night.

Clearly that was a silly idea. She instead contented herself to stare up at them and breathe their fresh air and pretend she was in her forest. Tonight she took her usual spot on the root-disrupted soil, with its springy mosslike grasses, and lay back on the ground, staring up. She inhaled deeply and let the energetic hum sink into her bones until she reached an almost meditative state. She knew it was insanity to lie out here in the open like this, but she needed these trees the way she needed water. They cleared her mind and filled it with calm—comforting, protecting, nourishing her, providing her with a small piece of home in foreign surroundings.

It was an impossible feeling to describe to others, so she'd never bothered to try. She also knew it was far from normal. It had been this way for her since she was a child, and she still didn't understand it. *I'll have to ask Compendium about that.*

Compendium. She had grown to rely on it to the point where she carried it everywhere, even though she couldn't use it in front of others. It was tucked into her sash even now. She patted it at random intervals to reassure herself of its presence. Its weight and warmth had sunk into her body and become a part of her.

Mia was deeply entranced in her meditative state when a muffled crunch snapped behind her. She froze. Whoever or whatever it was must see her, as she lay prone on the ground of the Crater Grove.

"Who is it?" she asked softly, still frozen.

"It's just me" came the whisper of a familiar male voice.

A sheepish-looking Cedar emerged from behind her to stare down at her sprawled figure. He looked as if he had caught her engaged in an embarrassing or perhaps supremely private act.

"Oh," she said, relaxing, her voice also a whisper. "What are you doing here?"

"Um, mind if I sit down?" he asked.

"Suit yourself," she said, and shrugged her shoulders against the grass. "My permission is pretty pointless. Neither of us is allowed in here."

He sat down near her and crossed his legs. "I suppose that's true." His dark, fathomless eyes stared up at the branches in wonder. He eventually uncrossed his legs and lay down next to her, so their heads were near each other, and whispered, "I see why you position yourself like this. It's amazing."

"I've never seen elders this large," she murmured.

"I read that before the Great Fall the Central Counsel used to meet at a grove of ancient elders that were so large that they started deep in the ground and reached so far into the sky that no individual ever climbed them to the top." His voice sounded soft and dreamy.

"You're beginning to sound like Taryn," Mia said, poking him in the rib with an index finger.

He grabbed the offending hand and covered it with his, resting it on his lean chest. His heart beat slowly and rhythmically beneath his breastbone. Her mind wasn't sure how to process this touch. She rather liked the gentle warmth of his hand and the steady beat of his heart, but she was unsure of the meaning. Her social education in this area was sadly lacking. She just left it be and enjoyed the sensation of having her hand held.

"I should very much like to see this grove some-day," she said quietly.

"Me too," he whispered.

"You never answered my question. What are you doing here?"

"I followed you," he said, turning his head to look directly at her.

His features were lit with a bronze glow in the dim light, like a browned butter and sugar combination. Mia marveled at the beauty of the light on his face.

"I've recently noticed you leaving the barracks in the dead of night," he continued, "and then sneaking back some time later. I got so curious that I couldn't get a good night's sleep, because I wondered if you were going to sneak out, then wondered where you went."

His hand was warm, his voice smooth. Mia closed her eyes and let them sink into and melt and mix with the rest of her senses.

"So one night last week, I followed you out of the barracks and into a moss-covered corridor," Cedar continued. "But when I looked around the turn, you were gone. It was the oddest thing. So I waited for you. Finally, after a long while, the moss of the wall began to move, like something was going to punch its way through. I panicked and was going to run, but then a pale, thin arm popped through."

"I never saw you," Mia said quietly.

"Well, I ran off before you could," he said. "Tonight, when you disappeared in the corridor, I followed you through the moss, and here we are."

"So you followed me because you were curious?" she asked, opening her eyes again. Cedar's hand still pressed hers against his chest.

"Essentially. I thought you might have been up to no good," he said with a crooked grin. "I know how nefarious you are."

"Aye, indeed." Mia cracked a smile. "I'm terribly untrustworthy."

"I half expected to find you rerouting power to the library to give Brother Cornelius his own hearth."

"Oh, that's an excellent idea. He would love that. Although he's rather sensitive to humidity and temperature in the library. He even invented a special gourd that absorbs water from the air."

"You don't say?" said Cedar. "That sounds incredibly useful."

"I know. Right?" she exclaimed slightly louder than she'd intended. She lowered her voice again. "You can take one with you when you travel to absorb water from the air and crack it open when you need a drink."

"He should invent one with a hole," Cedar said. "Then it could be emptied and reused."

"I suppose we could just drill a hole, as long as it doesn't damage the gourd. I can't recall how long they're good for."

They mused for a bit on Brother Cornelius's unending ingenuity.

"So you just come here and lie under the trees?" he asked, turning the topic back to Mia's presence in the Crater Grove.

"Thus far," she said. "I do have an interest in the systems, but when I get here, the warmth and the hum of the trees cajoles me into a relaxed state, almost like a trance, I guess." She looked over at Cedar to gauge his reaction.

She'd never mentioned the humming to others, except for Brother Cornelius, who didn't seem to notice, but she felt warm and comfortable, and Cedar's steady heartbeat under her hand reassured her. He looked over at her, his dark, luminous eyes searching hers for something.

"I hear them too," he said. "I thought I was imagining it, but I hear it." He frowned slightly. "They're always like this?"

"All trees and roots hum and vibrate," she said. "Some louder than others. I've heard them since I was a small child."

Cedar looked surprised but not disbelieving. It probably helped her case that he heard them too, at least here, in a room where the trees practically screamed with joy.

"Does it drive you mad?" he asked.

"Not at all. I find it incredibly comforting. It's as if I'm never alone. The trees are always whispering to me."

"That seems kind of creepy," Cedar said softly.

"I suppose it would to someone unused to constant noise. To me, though, the deep quiet of the stone walls of this cavernous Compound seems creepy."

They lapsed into a comfortable silence. Mia succumbed to the sounds of the trees once again, and when she glanced over at Cedar, his eyes were round and absent, as if they were out of focus.

Finally he said softly, "Did your Father make it?"

Mia's body tensed a little at the question. "I don't know," she replied, and bit her lip.

Cedar squeezed her hand reassuringly.

"They haven't told me anything," she continued, her voice trembling like her hand.

"Is he your only family?"

"Yes. For as long as I can remember, it's just been Father and me."

"What about your mother?"

"I never knew her. She died when I was an infant. I have no drawings of her, and Father never described her except to say she was very beautiful. I must resemble her, because I look nothing like him."

"Does he not talk about her?" Cedar asked.

"He avoids talking about her to the extent that over time I conditioned myself to stop asking. Instead I make up fantasies about her in my head. Silly, I know." Her cheeks grew warm from the embarrassment of the admission. "All I have of her are my fur bag and her locket."

"You have a locket?" he asked, perking up. "Is there anything inside?"

"I don't know," she replied, disengaging her hand from his to tug at the long, intricate chain around her neck. She retrieved the chain from deep inside her robes and slowly pulled up the shiny metal egg at the bottom. "I've never been able to get it open, and I don't want to damage it, so I'm hesitant to force it. I like to think it'll open when it's ready."

Cedar took the small golden locket from her hand and ran his thumb over the latch. "It almost looks as if someone jammed it intentionally," he said softly, peering closely at it in the dim light. "It would require some fine tools to work it open. The quality is exceptional, though. How old is it? The details look too fine to be accomplished by just any old country jeweler."

"I really don't know," Mia said, feeling useless. What did she know? Apparently nothing. She admired the way the locket glinted in his long brown fingers as he handled it.

"Well, you're quite a mystery," he whispered solemnly then gently placed the locket in her hands.

Mia gave it one last glance before she propped herself up on her elbow and dropped it down the front of her robes.

"Are you hiding anything else in there?" he asked with a mischievous grin.

"Wouldn't you like to know?" she blurted out, flustered.

"Aye, I would," he said, matter-of-factly, looking over at her carefully.

Mia quickly flattened herself against the grass once more, baffled as to what to say next. A part of her craved the intimacy that Cedar's eyes offered within their shiny depths, but another part said it was madness. Words tumbled through her mind, but nothing witty emerged.

"Oh, don't be daft," she said, again louder than intended. Her voice echoed up among the trees, and she thumped her hand lightly on his chest.

In an instant, he tugged her hand and pulled her over to him. Before she could speak or even think, his soft lips were on hers, and his right hand was caressing her cheek. When she gasped in surprise, he deepened the kiss. Her body relaxed against his, and when Cedar finally released her mouth, she was trembling.

"If you look like your mother, she really was beautiful." With that simple statement, he sprung to his feet gracefully and held out a hand to pull her up.

She let him pull her to her feet, standing much closer to him than she was accustomed. His lanky frame towered over her. She took a small step back, still rather dumfounded by the entire exchange. Her heart pounded in her chest. She reached up to Cedar's chest, but his heart was beating strong and steady and slowly under her palm. Wordlessly he took her hand and led her out of the crater and back toward the barracks.

They walked in silence so as not to draw attention and proceeded into the acolytes' chamber. Before he released her hand, he brought it to his lips and gently kissed her palm. Then he smiled softly and slipped off to his bunk.

That night, Mia lay in her bed a long time before finally falling into a restless sleep. The meditative relaxation of the Crater Grove had been replaced by heart-racing thoughts and fears, some to do with Cedar and others to do with her mother.

18 THE FIGHT L.C. 10152

"I RATHER THOUGHT CEDAR was above thinking with his anatomy," Taryn said, shaking her head at Mia's revelation.

A few days had passed since Cedar kissed her in the Crater Grove, but Mia hadn't had a chance to be alone with Taryn to discuss it. They weren't really alone now, truth be told, but the din of the dining hall and the others speaking animatedly at their respective tables made it unlikely anyone was listening in.

It seemed as if the spell woven between Mia and Cedar by the great elders of the Crater Grove had dissipated after that night, and what was left was a series of awkward interactions. It would have been simpler to pretend nothing had happened and to continue on in their friendship, but Cedar had thrown down the gauntlet, so to speak, when he had made his feelings unequivocally known that night in the dim light of the Crater Grove.

Mia laughed at Taryn's characterization, but it really wasn't as simple as lust. "Well, I didn't get the sense that he was interested in a fling, as it were. I think it runs deeper than anatomy. It wasn't the sort of coarse groping in some hidden backwater that's just for play, if you get my drift. I think he's serious about me."

At least she wanted to think he was serious. But could it really be anything else? He had been determined but gentle, and his touch had been firm yet soft.

"If it was base seduction, I think he would have been more persistent, and I also think there's more tension now than there would be in that case." Mia was rambling, but her own feelings on the matter were hardly settled.

Until that moment in the Crater Grove, she hadn't let herself think of Cedar that way. But once he had touched her and kissed her, she couldn't think about him any other way. It was distracting to say the least.

"It's about time there was a bit of juicy gossip around here," Taryn said, grinning. "I think there hasn't been anything to grab the acolytes' attention in this way since Flora ran off with a boy two Gatherings ago."

Mia raised an eyebrow at the story, which clearly had happened before her time. "Yes, well, eloping together probably isn't on the agenda."

"Not yet." Taryn winked.

"Ha, don't tempt me."

"I don't think I'm the one tempting you at all," Taryn said, keeping the jokes flowing. "Well, what brought on the sudden tidal wave of passion?" she asked, waving her knife in her typical dramatic fashion before spearing a piece of meat and popping it into her mouth.

"We were talking about the trees and my family and my mother's locket, and he reached over and grabbed me."

"A locket is an odd thing to get worked up about. You've never mentioned it before. Didn't you lose your mother when you were young? Maybe it holds some clue about your past."

"Yeah," Mia said. "I actually tend to forget I have it. It's so much a part of my attire that I often don't think of it or notice it. Plus, I wear it under my robes usually, for practical reasons." She pulled it out and over her head and handed it to Taryn to examine.

"Wow, this is fine work," Taryn said appreciatively. "Very detailed." She examined both sides carefully and added, "This design reminds me of some of the scrollwork found in the ancient texts. I wonder if it predates the Great Fall."

"I don't know." Mia bit her lip. "Cedar made similar mention that it must be a very old piece."

"Well, it's brilliant," Taryn said, handing it back to her.

Mia pulled the chain over her neck and was about to stuff the locket back down into her robes when a calloused hand clenched her wrist painfully.

"Have we added stealing to snooping?" came a gravelly voice from behind her.

A lump formed in her throat as Taryn's eyes grew wide. Brother SainClair was standing at their table with his fist clamped around Mia's wrist.

"I will have a look at that," he demanded. "Remove it."

"It's mine. I brought with me when I arrived. It belonged to my mother, and I'll not remove it."

"You will," he said, not letting go of her wrist.

She tried to wrench it free but failed.

"I will not," she replied, iron in her voice.

"If you don't submit to examination, I'll have you flogged," Brother SainClair said through gritted teeth.

"Go ahead," Mia said softly, menace in her voice. "But you'll have to kill me if you want this locket." She transferred it to the hand he wasn't gripping and dropped the gold orb back into her robes. "And I rather doubt Dominus Nikola would be overly pleased," she warned.

It was a bluff but the only one she had. All eyes in the dining hall had fallen on them, but she was beyond caring at that point. She was sick of the constant glares, ill treatment, and odious insults she received from Brother SainClair, and she wasn't going to bear it silently any longer.

He shook her arm violently and tried to pull her from the bench. She bent her head toward his hand and bit his wrist hard. He growled and struck her with the other hand, sending her flying to the floor.

"Such a brave man," she said, practically spitting at his feet. "It must be so hard to brutalize someone half your size. Bully!" She was too angry to be embarrassed.

Brother Valentine, the Ledgermaster, gripped SainClair by the shoulder. "Thaddeus, what is going on here?" Brother Valentine looked from SainClair to Taryn to Mia on the floor, his face kindly and concerned.

His inquiry seemed to snap Brother SainClair out of whatever haze of rage he was functioning in.

"Nothing," he said in a growl, shrugging out of Brother Valentine's grasp. He looked down at Mia with malice in his eyes. "I was just informing Ms. Jayne here that her father is dead. Your father is dead, y'hear? Dead!"

Mia was overcome with rage at his words. "Liar!" she cried. "You filthy liar!" She scrambled to her feet and charged him, punching her bony shoulder into his gut and toppling him to the floor. She stood over him, panting like a dog.

He laughed at her from the floor, a brutal sound that clawed at the back of her neck.

"If you don't believe me, go ask Dominus Nikola." He laughed again, but he clearly was serious. He believed what he said.

Mia turned and fled the dining hall, leaving Taryn, Brother Valentine, and the rest of the diners dumbfounded. SainClair's cruel laughter chased her down the corridor.

MIA RAN THROUGH THE COMPOUND in a state of grief and fury. She wasn't sure which emotion ruled her movements, but she found herself headed straight for the Archives. The barracks hardly offered privacy, and she didn't think she could take questions from the other acolytes just then. As it was, given the spectacle

in the dining hall, gossip was likely flowing freely
among the ranks.

She didn't stop running until long after she was
sure no one was following her. She couldn't seem to
feel or think, only cry. When she finally reached the
Archives, she collapsed, out of breath, into a large
reading chair and curled into a ball. She may have put
on a brave face in front of SainClair, but he had left
her a wrecked mess, and that infuriated her.

His words about Father also infuriated her, and the
thought that they might be true filled her with panic.
The angrier she became, the harder she cried. It was a
vicious circle that continued until a shuffling noise
wandered in from a small side room. *Brother Cornelius
must still be about.* She hastily wiped tears from her
face.

"The library is closed," his voice called from the
side room before he appeared, shuffling along in his
slow, determined way.

"'Tis just me, Brother," Mia said, attempting to
steady her voice. Trying to hide her tears was
probably pointless. Her eyes were almost sealed shut
with puffiness, although that could just be the swelling
from where SainClair had struck her. She tried
anyway.

"You're here late, my child," he said. As he
approached, his eyes moved from her swollen, red eyes

over her cheeks. "Whatever is the matter?" He pulled a chair close to the one where she sat and gave her a sympathetic pat on the shin.

Mia sputtered through the events of the evening, telling Brother Cornelius about her conversation with Taryn and the locket and then the altercation with SainClair, including his claim that her father was dead, and even about her kiss with Cedar. He sat and listened to it all with quiet interest and compassion in his eyes. She saw no scorn or judgment in his face, and when she finally stammered out the last line of her story and admitted that the Archives was the first place her feet had carried her, he smiled softly.

"In truth it is rather the perfect place for quiet reflection on personal matters," he said matter-of-factly.

She smiled at him then. He always had a way of making a situation seem less dire than it had only moments earlier.

"You know, I still haven't shown you my laboratory," he said, instead of tackling her story head on.

"Yes, well, I'm still de-sporing this place," Mia replied, adding, "And at the rate I'm going, I'll have to start again at the beginning just as I finish." Her mouth curved downward glumly.

"Well," Brother Cornelius said, scratching his beard with a bony finger, "it's high time you had a look. I find that, even better than here, I do my best thinking in the laboratory. We shall consider it an emergency." With that, he stood to his full height, stretched his back, settled his walking stick into a comfortable position, and beckoned her to follow him with a crook of his finger.

They ambled along the corridors. Brother Cornelius was never one to hurry anywhere, which suited Mia just fine. He left her to her thoughts for most of the walk. They worked their way past the barracks, up an inclined corridor, then over to what appeared to be a blank wall. Like the entrance to Dominus Nikola's quarters, it was a hidden alcove leading to a staircase that spiraled up into the darkness. Unlike the spiral staircase Dominus Nikola used, a series of gourds were embedded in the walls. It was impossible to see them until Brother Cornelius rapped his walking stick firmly against a section of the stone wall. Then they lit up one after another, leading up the staircase.

Mia's jaw dropped. "How did you do that?" she asked in her usual tone of amazement at Brother Cornelius's ingenuity.

"Ah, well, it's terribly complicated. But feel free to come back and poke around. You may be able to figure it out yourself."

She grinned at him. Cornelius obviously had grown to know her quite well in the short time she'd been his assistant. Her excitement at figuring it out herself and confirming it with him would far outweigh any explanation he could provide. He waggled his whiskery eyebrows at her and winked, and then they ascended the steps. Mia let Brother Cornelius go first. Another difference with this staircase was that it featured a groove along the wall at waist height. Brother Cornelius used it to steady himself as he made his way up the stairs.

"Eventually they'll have to install a wooden landing with a pulley to get me up these stairs," he said, almost to himself.

"I'm surprised such contraptions aren't used throughout the Compound," Mia said, thinking on it.

"Oh, they're used extensively to get supplies down to the kitchen and the laundry, but it is felt among the clerics—and I can't say that I disagree—that the exertion of making one's way up and down the stairs and inclines and declines of the corridors is good for keeping the physical body mobile and flexible."

Mia couldn't disagree with that, even if travel throughout the Compound sometimes seemed laborious. They emerged into the small alcove landing that gave way to Brother Cornelius's laboratory. As the old man moved into the room and Mia's view became unobstructed, she scanned her eyes across its expanse in wonderment. Whereas the staircase had been similar to Dominus Nikola's, the laboratory itself couldn't be more different from the head cleric's quarters.

The room was vast, with large portions of the ceiling open to the sky above. There was a small window on the back wall, although it didn't offer as picturesque a view as the head cleric's window. Still, one could lean out and get a look at the mountains and city below. Books lined every conceivable space on the walls that wasn't open to the air. That in and of itself shocked Mia, given how persnickety Brother Cornelius was with the stacks in the Archives.

One long table, where numerous projects were laid out in various states of completion, spanned almost the whole length of the room. A series of long, deep planters were situated under the sky lamps. This gave the indoor garden light to grow and allowed the planters to catch rain when the skies brought it forth. The planters contained all sorts of gourds on vines and plants, some of which Mia recognized and some of which were totally foreign to her. Near the window, as in Dominus Nikola's quarters, stood a hearth.

Instead of overstuffed chairs providing a cozy sitting area, a collection of roots spread out from the hearth and cascaded up onto a table, where they were fused using shunts to other odd plant life. Mia stepped over to the table and examined some of the connections. One root was fused to a vine with a gourd that gave off perpetual light. Another was fused to a very thin vine. She touched the vine, and it zapped her lightly. She let out a yelp and sucked on the end of her finger.

"So this is my laboratory," Brother Cornelius said, chuckling, his pride obvious.

"It's fantastic," Mia told him, awe in her voice. She walked over to the planter boxes to more closely examine the various gourds. "Are all these gourds your own inventions?"

"Indeed they are." Brother Cornelius followed her to the planters, where he pointed to a dark-purple gourd on a pale vine. "This one produces the most beautiful purple ink. You don't even have to grind it. You just slice the top off and dip a quill in."

Mia looked up into the sky and sucked in her breath. As Brother Cornelius had promised, the night lights shone through the open ceiling. She hadn't seen them since she was on the ship, making her way to the Order. That felt like forever ago.

"So rain is captured by the planter boxes?" she asked.

"Yes, it works out quite well that way, unless there's extreme wind of course." He chuckled softly.

"One cycle we had such a rainy season that I came to the base of my laboratory stairs and found water rolling down the steps. I was most distressed. I lost most of my planter contents to waterlog that cycle. Very sad indeed." He lowered his body onto one of the stools in front of his project table and set his walking stick to the side. "Whenever I feel glum, my child, I come here to my sanctuary, and tending the vines and roots and gourds refreshes my heart and mind."

"I'm so grateful that you felt you could share it with me," she responded, settling herself on a stool across the table from him.

Before them lay a root that was in the process of being dissected. Pins held open the flexible inner parts of the plant's structure. It was all she could do to keep her focus on Brother Cornelius and not touch and examine every little curiosity her eyes settled on.

"How do you keep the books from molding with so much open air?" she asked.

"Ah, I have dehumidifier gourds set on each shelf, as well as shutters if the weather gets particularly violent. I do so adore the elements, so I risk it, I suppose. None of these tomes are delicate archival books in any case. They're all duplicates of common references that are kept in the Archives as well. I just like to have my favorite references on hand when I'm conducting experiments."

Mia didn't question Brother Cornelius as to why he needed hundreds if not thousands of references on hand. She imagined she'd be just the same in his situation, so she could hardly question his methods.

"Do you think my father is really dead?" she asked, her thoughts drawn back to her present situation.

"Who is to say, my child?" he said, resting his temple against a fist, his elbow propped on his project table. "SainClair isn't usually one to present fabrications, but he's been acting most peculiar since you arrived at our threshold. It's most unlike him to lose his temper in such a public fashion."

"He demanded my locket. Why do you think that is? I mean, what would make him think I had stolen it, apart from his general dislike of me?" Mia pulled the locket from inside her robes and handed the globe to Cornelius to examine.

He pushed his spectacles up on his nose and peered intently at the locket, turning it over in his fingers carefully. "This is a very ancient object," he said, "and the clasp appears to be fused."

"Yes, it came to me that way. Father said it was my mother's. It's been with me since I was a small child. I've never tried to force it open for fear of breaking it. I've always been a little curious about it, though, since I know so little about her."

"That's to be expected, I should think. Life is full of these little mysteries." As he scrutinized the locket further, a small frown of concentration crossed his face. Eventually he pointed toward the scrollwork patterns crisscrossing their way across the outside of the small golden globe. "These markings here remind me of the illuminations on some of the ancient scripts we have. This locket could have been created before the Great Fall, or it could have been designed to mimic antiquities. It's hard to say without a more detailed analysis of the symbology on the outside and without viewing the interior."

Mia sighed. "I have a feeling this incident with Brother SainClair isn't over." She swallowed a growing lump in her throat. "I'm afraid the Dominus will tire of this feud, and I suspect I'll be the one to bear the brunt of the blame."

"Ah, well, as to that, there's no saying really," Brother Cornelius continued, hemming and hawing. Still, Mia saw worry in his eyes.

"I couldn't bear it if Father were dead," she said, choking up again. The brother's kindness reminded her how tenuous her grasp on family was. "He's all I have."

"Now, now, child," he consoled her, patting her hand with his. "You aren't nearly as alone in this world as you believe you are."

She buried her face in her hands, the wonders of the laboratory fading into the background as dark shadows of her fear crept forward to encompass her. "If Brother SainClair is right, I have no family now."

LATER THAT NIGHT, AS MIA LAY IN HER BUNK, restless from the stress and the deep, throbbing ache that settled on her head like a vice squeezing at her temples, she thought about Brother Cornelius and Taryn and Cedar. Taryn had asked after her worriedly when she'd finally returned to the barracks. Her friend—for that is truly how she thought of Taryn—consoled her, assuring her Brother SainClair was an oafish brute and everyone in the dining hall had borne witness to his deplorable behavior. Cedar had approached Mia with alarm, having heard about the exchange. He had hovered over her, clearly afraid to touch her and skittish about appearing too concerned. It had made Mia anxious to look at him just then. The slap to her face had blossomed into a fine red welt, which she was certain she'd have to parade around the Order for a few days until it faded, a lovely remembrance of Brother SainClair's hatred and disdain.

"I assure you I'm fine," she had said to her friends, shooing them away. "What I need is a good night's sleep."

Once settled into her bed, despite a fresh cake at her feet and Compendium nestled warmly against her side, she sighed. A good night's sleep wasn't to be had. Thoughts boiled in her mind, a stew of unpleasant odors and flavors wafting into the air. Each pungent breath and burning sip reminded her of everything she'd lost since arriving there. She had gained some friends and a mentor and, most important, Compendium, but she had lost her home and possibly—no, likely—her father and even her beloved Hamish.

If that were the case, then what was she still doing here? She had made this vow for Father's sake. She meant to honor it as long as it would benefit him. If he truly were dead, her vow no longer was of any consequence.

Her lips tightened as her thoughts turned to Brother SainClair. He would be glad to see her go, no doubt, but she didn't think the others, particularly Dominus Nikola, would take kindly to her departure. Alas, she hadn't the heart to confront him either. He was a kindly old man, if somewhat detached from his surroundings. She had little doubt Brother SainClair fed him a steady stream of lies about her.

It would be best to leave without a trace, with no way for them to track her, to disappear and start over in a new hammock somewhere. She made the decision then that she would leave. She would find the Shillelagh, and she would use it to leave this place, to confirm her father's situation, and then disappear to where the Order couldn't find her if what Brother SainClair had claimed was true. She didn't yet know where she would go if that were the case, but with the Shillelagh and Compendium, she would be free like a breeze rustling through the canopy of the Crater Grove.

The throbbing in her head subsided, and she finally relaxed, her body growing leaden against the lumpy mattress. She tightened one hand around the locket still strung around her neck and the other around Compendium and fell into a fitful sleep.

19 THADDEUS L.C. 10152

"THADDEUS, YOU'RE ACTING like a madman," Nikola told Brother SainClair. "The others are becoming concerned." He and Cornelius sat at the hearth in his chambers while Thaddeus paced by the window, his eyes wild and bulging.

"I'm telling you, it doesn't matter what that letter said. She's a pretender!" He raked his hands roughly through his gray hair and continued to pace. "She could have forged it herself. On top of that, I think she's a thief."

Nikola exchanged a glance with Cornelius. The older cleric frowned as he scratched his whiskers. The unexpected appearance of Mia Jayne at the Compound had taken them all by surprise, but the more time that passed, the more Nikola saw that Thaddeus's paranoia was affecting him.

"What makes you say that?" Nikola asked, avoiding the real question on his mind.

"She has this necklace. It looks so familiar. I know I've seen it before." Thaddeus slammed his hands on the windowsill and drew a large breath into his lungs, like a bear preparing to roar.

"So you assaulted an acolyte because she was wearing a piece of jewelry you think looks familiar?"

Thaddeus's eyes darkened, and he turned away from Nikola and Cornelius. "I know what it sounds like. I can hear myself saying the words too," he said finally. "But you must understand how this is for me."

"We do, my son," said Cornelius, "but this situation requires the utmost patience. If you continue down this path with her, we'll all suffer."

Nikola shook his head at Cornelius, but Thaddeus was too distraught to notice.

"Thaddeus," said Nikola, "we have to let this situation run its course naturally. Mia's loyalties will make themselves known in due time. Interfering will only muddy the waters."

Thaddeus turned and leaned against the window-sill, his arms crossed. "I understand," he said, "but I can't sit idly by as my family is mocked."

Cornelius narrowed his eyes at Thaddeus, and his hands tightened the on the armrest of the chair. Nikola patted his friend on the arm.

"You must," Nikola said to Thaddeus.

"HE'S JEOPARDIZING all we are doing here," said Cornelius in a rare show of anger and only after Thaddeus had left the room.

Nikola sighed, suddenly very tired. "He's had a very hard time of it."

"We all know that, but this is greater than just Thaddeus. Moritania says the device has been researching the Shillelagh. You know what that means for us."

"I do," said Nikola, and he did, but that was only part of the equation. "I understand the concerns on all sides, but in one hundred fifty cycles, we've made no direct progress toward restoring Lumin until now. And to think that book was on our shelves all this time."

"Yes, no need to remind me," said Cornelius dourly.

Nikola waved a hand flippantly. "I'm not blaming you, Cornelius, but you and I know she is no pretender."

"Very true, but we still don't know whether she's trustworthy. She's been researching travel by baccillum."

"That is concerning indeed," said Nikola, "but perhaps we can use this area of inquiry to solve more than one question."

"What do you mean?"

"There is the question of loyalty but also the question of ingenuity."

"Perhaps you should speak to her," said Cornelius, concern lighting his soft eyes.

"This is a path she must walk herself," said Nikola, his face grim.

THE PLOT   L.C. 10152

"**A**RE YOU UNHINGED?" Cedar asked incredulously, leaning back in his chair at a table in the ancient texts room of the Archives. "I know your battle with SainClair has been taxing, but you can't possibly be serious." His alarm surprised Mia.

"I'm stone-cold serious," she replied. "I mean to retrieve the Shillelagh."

Taryn's reaction was completely opposite Cedar's. She manifested immediate excitement at the thought. This also surprised Mia, but she was glad for some positive reinforcement. "Oh, what an adventure! But how will you find it?" she said.

"I have the means," Mia said carefully, unsure how much to reveal. She had begun to ask Compendium details about the Shillelagh, and Taryn was correct when she had speculated that it could be somewhere inside the Order. It was in fact hidden in the Order, and Compendium had a map to prove it. A map alone, however, wasn't sufficient; Mia also needed a plan. The Catacombs, where the Shillelagh was hidden, was apparently where the Order housed many of its more keen secrets. Unlike the Crater Grove, it was actually well guarded.

"I'm confused," said Cedar. "The last time we discussed this, we thought the Shillelagh probably was a myth, a legendary artifact, the existence of which we weren't even certain. Now you say you know where it is."

"I do," Mia said simply.

"How?" asked Taryn.

Their curiosity aligned them against her. There was no way around it. She slipped Compendium out of her sash and handed it to Cedar. He looked the book over and opened it, reading aloud the false title with which Mia had become so familiar.

"Have you finally descended into madness?" he asked. "What does this book have to do with anything?"

Taryn peered over his shoulder. "I agree with Cedar. This book would certainly be useful for my historical research, but it has no bearing on the Shillelagh."

"Compendium, reveal yourself," Mia said on a hunch. Cedar almost dropped the book as the text of the pages changed. "Read aloud what it says," she told him.

"Welcome, Mia Jayne," Cedar read. "What can I assist you with today?"

"Compendium, please show me the map you created leading to the artifact Shillelagh," Mia said.

Taryn's eyes grew wide as the ink melded into the pages, replaced with schematic drawings, something as familiar to Mia as her own pulse.

"This is incredible," Taryn breathed. "Incredible." She touched the page, tracing it with her finger and lifting it up to look underneath.

"I assure you it is what it seems," Mia said. "For some reason, it's coded to me. If another person picks it up, it reverts to the book you first saw. Only upon direct command of my voice will it reveal itself." Cedar gave Mia a skeptical look, clearly doubting she was somehow the book's master. "Try to command it," she said. "Ask it anything."

"Compendium," he began hesitantly, "what is today's date?" He paused, and his brows furrowed and eyes squinted. "Access not granted," he read. "What a priggish book!"

Mia laughed. "Compendium," she said, "who am I?"

"Mia Jayne, authorized Alpha Level user." Cedar looked up at her. "Alpha Level? That implies there are additional levels." He ran his hand across his face, as if wiping away cobwebs.

"I don't have total access to the information it contains," Mia said. "I managed to activate it, but sometimes when I ask a question or request information, especially regarding the book's origins, how it was made, or other information regarding activities before the Great Fall, it tells me I haven't been authorized at a sufficient level."

"So this is a real-live artifact?" Taryn asked, her excitement rising along with her voice. "I knew they existed. I just knew it!"

"How did you find it?" Cedar asked.

Mia pointed to the empty spot on the archival shelf where Compendium had resided for who knew how long. "It's been under everyone's noses the whole time.

I'm still not sure how I activated it. I sneezed on it, and it activated."

"You sneezed on it?" Cedar said thoughtfully.

"That's pretty disgusting," Taryn said, giving the book a dubious look.

"Yes, I was terrified at first that I'd ruined the pages or the ink, but the sneeze sunk right into the book, and all the text melted and changed, and then Compendium revealed itself."

"It must have some sort of genetic activation." Cedar examined the book from every angle, shuffling through the pages.

"I don't see how I could have been in its genetic data stores," Mia said, giving Cedar a skeptical look. "I have no family history to speak of."

"That you *know* of," Cedar corrected her. "You told me you never knew your mother or anything about her. Maybe what you don't know about your family is what lets you use Compendium. Have you ever asked Compendium about your family?"

"I haven't," she admitted. "I'm afraid."

"Well," Cedar said, "the book only responds to you, so you'll have to be the one to ask it."

"That's beside the point right now," Mia said. "I want to focus on the Shillelagh. Compendium, show us where the Shillelagh is hidden and describe its security." Right now what she needed was to escape this place. She needed to get away from SainClair and the other clerics who gave her cryptic advice rather than straight answers. She needed to flee the claustrophobic stone walls that threatened to crush her spirit. She also needed to confirm that Father was really gone for herself, that she was alone in the world. If there was any chance SainClair was lying, she needed to know. And if he wasn't lying, there was no reason for her to be here any longer. She'd have plenty of time to consult Compendium about her family history once she was away from the Compound and could breathe again.

Cedar read the text from Compendium in a quiet, serious voice. "The device referred to as the Shillelagh, once commonly called a baccillum when produced in numbers, is hidden deep in the root system of the Order under the Crater Grove, inside the Catacombs. It is currently being used as a conduit shunt to channel energy from one of the central roots to the peripheral security system of the Order. This serves multiple functions, including alerting the Order if someone has taken the device. A broken connection will extinguish security lights throughout the Compound. The Catacombs has locked gateways and monitoring systems. The Catacombs additionally has a detail of clerics who patrol it at random intervals. The schedule is kept strictly confidential." Cedar interrupted his recitation. "Mia, this doesn't seem like a winning proposition for us."

"It'll be a challenge for certain," she said. "I don't expect you to risk yourselves or your stations here at the Order to help me, but I need your help to figure out a plan, even if I have to execute it myself. I can't keep sitting here, not knowing if Father is alive."

She looked at them carefully, her eyes moving from one to the other. Cedar's gaze was locked on her face, his jaw tightened ever so imperceptibly. Mia knew she was causing him significant stress by even mentioning this scheme. He'd been more than willing to sneak into the Crater Grove with her and fraternize in the fresh air of the trees, but what she was discussing now was an entirely different proposition. It would require spying on and deceiving the clerics and also involve stealing from them. Mia had nothing to lose, however. She was already a prisoner there. She wasn't allowed to leave; she knew her activities were monitored; and SainClair was making her life increasingly miserable. Even thinking of the Crater Grove didn't calm her increasingly frayed nerves. Mia's eyes pleaded with Cedar's until he finally looked away, frowning. She knew how he felt about her, and the thought that she might be manipulating him through those feelings shamed her but not enough for her to stop.

Mia looked over to Taryn, whose face held a hint of excitement. She clearly was interested in the prospect. It was horrible of Mia to prey on Taryn's love of the antiquities and historically themed adventure, but she did it anyway. It also helped Mia's cause that Taryn had confided in her that her family had sent her to the Order from their nomadic camp. She hadn't experienced the calling in the way Cedar had. Mia speculated that Taryn's gypsy blood supported these daydreams of wanderlust to which she often succumbed. Whether she was dreaming of traveling physically with the Shillelagh or traveling through time with her books, she was always somewhere else.

"I, for one, am one hundred percent on board," Taryn said with a smile. "This promises to be the greatest adventure yet. Please let me come with you!"

She grasped Mia's hand and squeezed it, desperate to hold on to Mia as though she might walk through a wall and disappear right then, leaving Taryn behind. Mia looked at her friend with some worry in her eyes; Taryn still had a family, after all. Maybe the Order was the best place for her. Still, Mia selfishly smiled inwardly. It was comforting to know she might have a companion, someone willing to leave this place with her.

"Are you sure?" she asked. "'Tis a big commitment to abandon the Order like this. You've been here a lot longer than me."

"And I fear I'll be an acolyte forever," Taryn said, giving Mia's hand another squeeze. "I've been here even longer than Cedar, and he's practically ready to become a full cleric. Perhaps my family was wrong to send me here." Mia met her fervent gaze and knew Taryn already had made up her mind.

Cedar continued to hold Compendium in his hands. "I can't condone this," he said evenly, "but you know how I feel, and I'll do what I can to help you."

MIA AND TARYN MET REGULARLY in the ancient texts room during their free time. Mia pushed aside her guilt at betraying the trust Brother Cornelius had placed in her, focusing instead on the optimism and hope that she would soon be free. Her heart quickened every time she thought about Father and whether he lived or not. Either way, she would know soon. Dominus Nikola never had summoned her to his quarters to discuss the locket. The fear that Brother SainClair might win support for his theories, however, buoyed Mia's desire to make haste.

Plotting a path down to the Catacombs beneath the Crater Grove was relatively simple. Compendium showed them the way. It was the other matters—namely getting through the locked entryways, passing the random patrols, and figuring out how to disable the security monitor—they focused on in these meetings. Even with Compendium, they still lacked crucial information.

"We need to find out the schedule for the guards the night that we decide to go through with it. That'll probably be the last piece of information we gather," Taryn said, tapping a quill against her cheek. She was transcribing their ideas onto parchments. She had an insatiable need to record everything, which made Mia nervous. She preferred to have no written record to haunt them.

"I agree. Our first order of business should be figuring out how to get through the locked doors," Mia said. "Once we figure out how to disable them, we'll be able to get into the Catacombs whenever we choose."

"We'll only have one shot at actually removing the Shillelagh from the Crater Grove root system and no direct access to it until the day of. How are we going to complete the circuit without the clerics noticing?" Taryn's smooth, elfin face creased in consternation.

"Well," Mia said, pacing the room pensively, "we'll have to make the switch quickly and in the dead of night. That way, most of the clerics will be asleep if there's a momentary flicker in the security lights."

"How will we know what kind of conduit we need?" Taryn looked helplessly at her.

Mia smiled. "Leave that to me. The next Gathering is coming up, and we can use the opportunity to forage for a shunt that should work. We have all the specifications we may need through Compendium. The shunt will serve as a facsimile to fool the Catacombs into believing the Shillelagh is still there."

"Capital!" Taryn exclaimed. "That's a great idea. I don't suppose foraging for shunts will arouse any suspicion?"

"Oh, not at all. If anyone asks, which I doubt is likely, I'll just say Brother Cornelius is looking for some shunts of a particular size. He has so many inventions that no one is bound to bat an eyelash."

"Do you think Compendium would have any advice on how to get through those doors?"

They sat and pored over the book, but a number of days passed before they had any type of breakthrough. It happened on a day when Cedar was with them. They were frustrated and crabby from lack of ideas.

He was sitting with his eyes closed, his fingertips at his temples, as he whispered something to himself. At first Mia thought he finally had dived off the cliff they all seemed to be teetering on, the kind brought about by thinking too closely on one topic for too long a period of time. Mia was about to suggest they all go scavenge in the dining hall to see what, if any, leftovers might be available, when he slammed a hand on the table and said loudly, "Auditory!"

"Auditory?" Mia asked.

"Indeed," Cedar said, resolutely pushing back from the table and standing tall. He paced heavily back and forth, speaking quickly. "Compendium hasn't been able to find any locks in the schematics, correct? We know Compendium itself is controlled through auditory commands. What if the entrance to the Catacombs is controlled by a similar system of auditory commands that open the doors and has been coded to only those clerics with access to the Catacombs? I've racked my brain, and I believe it's the only potential explanation."

"But how's that possible?" Taryn asked. "We know Compendium is an artifact. It's older than the Great Fall, older than the Order itself."

Cedar gritted his teeth. "Yes, that's true, but there are certain pieces of the Compound's systems based on technology that predates the Order. Even among those clerics who are in charge of these systems, they aren't well understood. The texts that originate around the building of the Order seem to assume a lot of knowledge that we no longer possess. It's been a source of great frustration and study for the engineers." His face indicated that he hated spilling these trade secrets. Cedar paused to look at their wide eyes. Finally his shoulders slumped slightly, and he sank into one of the chairs. "I've seen some of these systems myself, and they almost seem to work as if by magic, but we know that's not the case. As with Compendium, they were designed by the hands of our forebears, and we've lost the knowledge we once had as a society to fully understand and replicate them. It's been the Order's greatest challenge to recapture what we once knew, to understand our capabilities to the level we once did."

Cedar was becoming passionate on a topic long deliberated. As Mia imagined engineering clerics having heated debates in their labs, a small pang of envy ran through her. Although she immensely enjoyed Brother Cornelius's company and the solitude of the Archives, it was these greater questions that engaged her mind and made her heart quicken.

"But," Taryn said, continuing her protests, "I haven't seen any texts regarding pre-Fall technology employed by the Order, and I've scoured this Compound from top to bottom."

"That's because these types of texts are kept strictly inside the laboratories of the top engineers," Cedar told her. "Even I don't have personal access to them."

Taryn's eyes narrowed. "Those books should be available to anyone with an interest in the topic. How am I supposed to reconstruct a full picture of the history of this place without that kind of information?"

Cedar and Mia exchanged looks at Taryn's obvious anger. They shrugged imperceptibly to each other. Perhaps she was just put out because she had come to some wrong conclusions in her research and now felt like a fool. Still, her spine was stiff, and her usual airy countenance was set upon and engulfed by a heretofore-unseen sternness.

His eyes moving back and forth, Cedar hesitated. "Well, when it comes to the inner workings of the system, the Order limits its information to those who might directly benefit from it. For instance, were someone to borrow the books to research the historical underpinnings of such technology and its relation to the Order, no matter how important such information may be for records purposes, those books wouldn't be available if an emergency required access to them."

"Oh, and I suppose this place is busting with emergencies?" Taryn huffed, crossing her arms over her bosom and leaning back in the library chair.

"Perhaps it is, and perhaps those of us charged with maintaining and enhancing your way of life deal with those emergencies without making dramatic announcements to the entire Order every time they occur. Perhaps if we did that, no one would ever sleep or eat or do anything but worry that the Compound was going to lock up at any moment." A hint of anger rose in Cedar's voice at the implication.

Even Mia was beginning to get a little agitated. "Oh, please," she said. "This place can't be in a constant state of near failure." She waved her hand in dismissal, and Cedar tightened his mouth in response and continued his pacing. "I understand it's a delicate job to maintain these systems," she continued, "and that engineering should be allowed some discretion and access to resources, but now you're just being dramatic."

"Well, I guess you'll never know," he said, "since I'm forbidden to show you the logs." At that point, they all fell into a tense silence that lasted until Cedar finally said, "We're all clearly tired. We should pick this up again another time. I'll look through the texts that I do have access to and try to learn what I can about any voice-controlled systems pieces we might have."

Mia nodded and yawned. Perhaps he was right. It was late, and their nerves were raw. "Cedar, we appreciate anything you can do," she said, yawning again.

"You two go ahead," Taryn said. She had her notebook open and was scribbling notes, probably trying to determine what type of changes she would have to make to her research to accommodate the information she had learned tonight.

"All right," Mia said, "but you'd better not be writing anything that will upset the engineering team. Cedar is helping us as a favor. We must remember to take it as such."

She waved them off with a nod, and Mia and Cedar proceeded down the stairs to the main Archives. Brother Cornelius was gone for the day.

They walked slowly toward the barracks. Cedar was still agitated, but he slowed his gait to match Mia's own shorter one. She covered another yawn with her hand and rubbed her neck as she walked. They hadn't been alone together since the night he'd kissed her, and that moment still silently hung over them even weeks later. Mia caught stolen glances—gazes turned away the moment her head swiveled in his direction—but they had slowly grown further and further apart. She felt both a sense of relief and loss at that thought. She would be leaving soon, in any case, so it was best not to encourage those emotions. She'd never ask Cedar to betray this place or sacrifice his calling. It was bad enough that she had endangered his position by requesting his help with the Shillelagh.

Still, he could have kept his distance entirely, and Mia wouldn't have blamed him for it, but he didn't.

He didn't take her hand, however, or bend to her for a kiss. When her hand accidentally brushed his, he swung his own up and tucked it into the roped belt around his waist. *It's for the best,* she reminded herself glumly. *Cedar and I have no future together.* Still, his rejection of her inadvertent attention pained her. The silence deepened as they continued their slow march back to the barracks, the warmth between them sputtering and threatening to extinguish.

21   GATHERING   L.C. 10152

M IA HAD BEEN WAITING PATIENTLY, and the time of the next Gathering was finally nigh. The research regarding the Shillelagh's specifications was done, and now it was time to locate a suitable shunt. Mia was a bundle of nerves. Tonight, at the Gathering, would be the first time she would leave the Compound since her arrival. She had to remind herself that she wasn't really free; it was an illusion. As she and Taryn headed down the main entryway corridor to the large doors that protected the Compound entrance, the eyes of the those watching her tickled the back of her neck like insects, making the hairs stand on end.

Gatherings were a tradition. For an organization steeped in history and strict conformity to its mission, the Order didn't put much stock in ritual. The Compound wasn't a place of worship, but rather a place of study and reflection, as the clerics liked to emphasize repeatedly in open lectures, during informal gatherings, and any time they thought they had an acolyte listening. Thus, Mia and the others, as acolytes, were subjected to very little in the way of rites or other empty rhetoric. The quarterly Gatherings served as much a functional purpose as a symbolic one.

As Mia understood it, they gathered, hence the name, in a clearing surrounded by mountainous terrain adjacent to the Compound on a night during each of the four quarters when the night lights were at their brightest. There the clerics made an affirmation of the mission of the Order, and then everyone would split off into the surrounding forested area to gather useful materials, especially those that were hard to come by other than on such nights as these, when the night lights shone brightly. At least that was how Cedar and Taryn had explained it to Mia. She had yet to experience one of these evenings herself, as she'd spent the last one in the brig.

So today, when the day finally came, she made every effort to blend into her surroundings, to incite no rage or ire, and to place no foot out of step. She wouldn't risk another incident like last quarter. SainClair glared at her malevolently across the dining hall, but she pretended she didn't see him. She intentionally sat facing away from him, kept her head down, and ate quietly. Sensing her anxiety, Taryn and Cedar likewise had made little noise or distraction during the evening meal. After dinner, Mia took Brother Cornelius his stew and proceeded directly back to the barracks.

Finally the time had come, and Mia followed Taryn along the corridor and outside the main entryway of the Compound, passing underneath two massive trees on either side, both of which were heavy with lit gourds. Even these impressive elders looked so small compared to the massive Crater Grove trees. The chilly night air whipped at Mia's jacket and blew across her forehead. She shivered as the wind hit her face, and pulled her jacket tighter around her neck. The Compound didn't seem so chilly in comparison. Up in the sky, the night lights threw brilliant colors across the dark. Mia followed Taryn as they walked between two walls of stone down the path away from the mountain then arced to the right along a rocky trail that led to a passageway. Whether it was naturally occurring or carved into the mountain, Mia didn't know, but inside the towering stone walls was a clearing that served as a foyer to the forest beyond.

Mia continued to follow the trail of clerics as they formed a circle in the courtyard, elbow to elbow in the night. Everyone waited silently as the wind whipped through the open space and lights boiled in the sky. After they all had stood quietly for a while, a robed figure made its way slowly down the path. When the figure passed the threshold of the stone walls that surrounded the clearing, Mia saw that it was Dominus Nikola, his features illuminated by the night lights. He wore a solemn expression. He kept walking until he reached the center of the circle.

"My fellow brothers and sisters," he addressed the assembled clerics and acolytes, his voice clear and loud, "tonight we remind ourselves of the vows we have taken. It is a time to remember the mission that we've each made a part of ourselves. It is a time to reflect upon what those vows mean to each of us and to the future of Lumin."

I haven't taken any vows, Mia thought, sneaking a glance at Cedar. His eyes were fixed intently on the Dominus; he clearly was taking in every word the man spoke. She peered over at Taryn. Her attention was less raptly engaged by the Dominus, and she fidgeted, wringing her hands and tilting her head and stretching her neck. The variation in attention wasn't confined to Mia's two friends. Some clerics stood with bowed heads, others stroked their chins and looked off in the distance, and still others snuck glances around the group.

Brother SainClair was staring at Dominus Nikola with his usual intensity, his body rigid at attention. Brother Cornelius wasn't present, his excuse being that his old bones wouldn't allow it. Mia could see why he skipped the ritual if he had no plans to forage in the forest afterward. Dominus Nikola continued to expound about their duties to the Order and the great responsibility that lay with each of them to preserve and protect the sacred knowledge of the realm. Her mind started to wander when Dominus Nikola snapped her back to attention by announcing, "And now we shall reaffirm our sacred vows."

She listened as the assembled clerics and those acolytes who were so inclined spoke in unison. "I do solemnly, sincerely, and truly declare and affirm that I shall protect and preserve the knowledge of my forebears; that I shall dedicate my life to the study of and reflection on those ideas lost with the passage of time; and that I shall make it my life's goal that such may flourish again in my lifetime."

It was a short, austere affirmation. And with that, the ritual was completed. Dominus Nikola, apparently not participating in the actual gathering portion of the evening, turned slowly and proceeded back the way he had come. Once he had passed back through the stones that buttressed the entry to the clearing, the clerics and acolytes proceeded in two lines through the entrance to the heavily forested woods.

The orderly procession broke up not far into the thicket of trees. From there the two groups split off, some choosing to disappear alone into the dimly lit forest and others going in pairs or threes. Taryn and Mia stuck together, picking their way along. Being outside exhilarated Mia. She had the urge to scale a tree and lie in it, staring up at the night sky, the way she used to do back in Hackberry. The air was considerably colder here, though, and the intermittent gusts of chilly wind breaking through the trees disrupted the tenuous illusion that she might be home. She scanned the robes disappearing into the thick foliage for signs of Cedar, but he wasn't among them.

Mia listened carefully to the humming of the trees around her. She had no idea what the Shillelagh might sound like ensconced within the roots of the Crater Grove, but she knew they would need a powerful conduit if they wanted to complete the circuit for the security system. She stopped periodically and closed her eyes, blocking out everything but the sound, then headed in the direction of the loudest buzzing she could. She and Taryn continued this way, otherwise silent, for some time. If Taryn thought Mia was unhinged, she kept such musings to herself. After a few rounds of walking, pausing, listening, changing course, and walking again, something pricked against Mia's ear. She motioned Taryn to follow her as she ducked around the side of a massive tree. Mia quickened her pace as the sound grew louder and she became surer of its origin. She honed in on it like a bat on a glow bug. It was coming from a particularly massive hardwood tree with thick, woody bark and sprawling branches. The branches were of no concern, however. It was the tender but powerful roots at the base of the tree where Mia focused her energy.

It had been months since she had extracted a conduit. She pulled her tool kit from her fur-trimmed bag and unrolled the soft cloth to display a series of chisels, a small hammer, some carving knives, a prying tool, and other implements. She set them out on top of a large root in a patch lit by the churning night lights above. She pulled out a small mortar and pestle and set it next to the other tools.

"You weren't kidding about being into this stuff," Taryn muttered under her breath.

Mia smiled and picked up a chisel and hammer. Slowly she chipped away at the outer bark of a thick portion of root, carefully peeling off long strips and setting them aside. Her goal was to try to preserve the bark to some extent. This tree would never notice if they harvested some for a conduit. Once Mia had carefully removed the bark, she asked Taryn to refresh her on the exact specifications of the Shillelagh. Taryn pulled her notebook from her bag and read the measurements out loud. Mia traced the measurements carefully along the root using a measuring tool and scored gently. Then she chiseled around the scored outline, making sure to dig deeply enough to obtain the proper thickness. The extraction went smoothly, and soon she had what she hoped approximated a good conduit to replace the Shillelagh. It was rather large and wouldn't fit in her bag, so she handed it to Taryn for safekeeping. The next step was to carefully pack the hole in the root with a compound that would allow it to heal while providing a temporary connection.

Mia took some snippets of smaller roots that were no longer connected to a tree, some meat from a nearby gourd, and some herbs she had brought with her from Brother Cornelius's laboratory and used the mortar and pestle to create a thick paste. As soon as a batch was ready, she spread it into the hole left by the extracted root and prepared another batch. This took a significant amount of time, and Taryn became antsy, looking about in worry. "'Tis all right," Mia reassured her. "This is a standard practice for getting a nice conduit. It should arouse no suspicion should anyone see us foraging in this manner."

"Yes, but this root is huge. Its size will arouse suspicion," Taryn whispered tersely.

"We'll encircle it with some long clippings that Brother Cornelius requested," Mia said. "He's attempt ting to graft a new kind of gourd onto an old stem, and he needs some lanky vines. This root is perfect to transport them." Mia was sure Taryn couldn't give two hoots about Brother Cornelius's request for vines, but she at least seemed to relax.

Once the hole was filled with the fragrant paste, Mia carefully replaced the strips of bark onto the root in a rough semblance of where they originally had resided. It wasn't necessary to get them perfect, but she never liked to take from a tree unless she needed to, and she never liked to leave that tree any worse for wear if possible. This root was too large to bind, but if it had been possible, she would have done that as well. With their Shillelagh approximation in hand, they quickly foraged for Brother Cornelius's vines and secured them in a coil around the root.

Time was running low. There was so much vegetation Mia wanted to explore, and Taryn had to drag her back in the direction of the Compound. "We shouldn't make them come looking for us," she hissed at Mia.

"I can't help it," Mia said, looking longingly at a glittering purple gourd hanging high up in a tree. She was thinking of how she could connect that vine somehow to the passage of conduits that ran behind their walls in the barracks. How amazing her cubby would look with purple gourds.

"What are those gourds?" Mia asked. "I've not seen anything like them."

"I'll be blasted to the center of the Core if I know," Taryn said, irritated. Despite her words to the contrary, Mia suspected that adventure wasn't actually Taryn's favorite pastime. She clearly found it stressful. Dainty beads of sweat dotted her forehead, and short blond hairs had come loose from her plait and were sticking up in odd directions. Taryn pulled on them in her anxiety. Her forehead wrinkled, her slim limbs stiff.

"All right, all right," Mia said with more than a hint of sadness. What was the point of this lollygagging anyway? Once she had the Shillelagh, she could explore any forest in the realm to her heart's content. This was just a distraction from the task at hand.

Mia was sure they must be close to the Compound when suddenly a low growl came from nearby. She and Taryn froze like stone columns. The growl deepened. It was moving closer, but Mia couldn't tell exactly which direction it was coming from. It sounded like it was coming from everywhere. She looked over at Taryn, who gave Mia a pleading look, as if she were about to bolt. Mia pulled one of her knives from her belt with her left hand and grabbed Taryn's hand with her right, squeezing it tightly. Their slight rustle caused whatever the animal was to let out a howl, and they bolted back toward the Compound. They had run only maybe twenty feet when something tall leapt out in front of them, a robe billowing. Taryn and Mia recoiled simultaneously. Mia tripped backward, taking Taryn with her, and they landed in a jumble on the root-covered forest floor. Taryn scrambled backward in fear, her eyes wildly veering this way and that, looking for an escape.

"Careful of the root," Mia chided her.

The mass before them howled a great howl and turned to confront them. Mia brandished the knife, holding it by the tip, ready to loose it. Cedar took one look at their faces and busted out in hysterical laughter. Breathing hard, Mia dropped the knife and raked her hand through her hair and over her face, wiping the sweat away. *I could have killed him. The idiot.*

"I totally got you," he managed through guffaws.

Taryn quickly recovered her wits and charged him, pummeling his back with her fist. "What in the Great Forest is wrong with you? Have you absolutely lost your mind?" Her fists appeared to have the opposite of the intended reaction, and Cedar laughed harder.

"You should have seen your faces," he gasped between chuckles. "I mean, Mia is already an electric-white beacon in the night, but if she'd gotten any paler, she might have been translucent!"

Mia frowned. "Well, that would be a handy skill to have, wouldn't it?" She picked her knife up from the ground and stowed it in her belt. She then vaulted to her feet, not bothering to dust herself off, and stalked past Cedar and Taryn, continuing toward the Compound.

"Hey, now," he said, looking somewhat remorseful. "It was just a joke, ya know?"

Mia turned around, but her eyes looked through his and out the back of his head. She was too livid to speak, so she just kept walking.

"WHERE ARE WE GOING TO STORE THIS?" Taryn asked, fingering the rough outer layer of the conduit. Mia had already removed the vines, which were piled on a table in the Archives waiting for Brother Cornelius.

"Do you have a trunk under your bunk? I don't have one," Mia said.

Taryn nodded. "Yes, it should fit in there, although I'll have to move some belongings around."

"Now the pressure is on. We only have a limited time before this root dries out so much that its conductivity will be permanently impacted."

"But the Shillelagh must be dried out already," Taryn said, a look of worry shadowing her face.

"Oh, I'm sure it's quite dry, " Mia replied, focusing her concentration. "Compendium is dry too, yet it has a power source, even if we'd be damned to know what that source is. The same is true for the Shillelagh. It's dry, but its conductivity comes from something else. Our replacement root isn't an artifact. Compendium and the Shillelagh can conduct energy even though they're dead. This shunt doesn't have that power. We'll have to coat it with a paste and keep it moist so the cells don't die while we figure out what to do about the doors."

Cedar had been looking into the door security for weeks. Mia thought back to their last discussion on the topic.

"Do you think that could be it?" she'd asked him. "Could the clerics have some tone they play to open the door?"

"There's no way to know," he'd said.

The mounting frustration increased the already burgeoning tension between them. Their once easy conversation was now stymied by lapses into uncomfortable silence.

"If there's no way to know from the books," Mia said carefully, "then I'll need to watch and listen to the clerics entering the Catacombs to see what actually happens. It's all academic currently, and there's no further progress to be made using study alone."

"That's too dangerous," Cedar replied, shaking his head. "All it takes is one cleric seeing you, and this entire enterprise will unwind. It wouldn't even have to be SainClair."

Cedar was right. It was a standard warning that the Catacombs were off limits. A sign posted above the corridor that led into the bowels of the mountain read, RESTRICTED. NO ENTRY PAST THIS POINT. If anyone ever caught her walking down there, she could expect punishment.

"Is one of the punishments expulsion?" Mia asked Cedar hopefully.

"Alas, not for you," he said, his face stony. They were sitting in Brother Cornelius's laboratory with the night lights shining above. A large storm cloud was rolling in, and inclement weather would soon follow. Cedar stared at Mia's face intently, the usual warmth in his dark eyes shrouded in clouds, opaque. It was as if he mirrored the night sky.

"Given your relatively unusual arrival here and Brother SainClair's existing suspicions, I think it's more likely they'll lock you up down below while they try to figure out if you're working for someone else." He blinked then, and the hairs on Mia's arms rose as his stare grew long. It wasn't a pleasant stare, though; it was filled with scrutiny. Perhaps Cedar himself thought she was a spy. The idea was preposterous.

"I don't know who they think I could possibly be working with," she said sullenly, resting her palm on the side of her head. She turned her head to look up into the night sky at the gathering clouds. The air was becoming heavy and pregnant with moisture. It wouldn't be long now.

"The Druids probably," Cedar said, his eyes boring into her. He likely hoped for some reaction to that statement, but Mia had none for him.

"Everyone here speaks about the Druids as if they're some menacing threat," Mia told him. "Frankly I always thought they would be a benign collective of nature worshipers flitting through the forests and dancing around trees with flowers in their hair."

She kept her gaze focused on the gathering storm. A jagged blue bolt of light streaked out of the clouds, temporarily scarring the air above. Cedar sighed, and she turned to face him. His expression remained serious, his hands threaded together in a knot upon which he rested his chin.

"Maybe you should look up the Druids in Compendium instead of spouting off nonsense based on inane assumptions," he said. "Such ridiculousness is beneath you."

Mia quirked an eyebrow at him. He ran his well-formed hands through his dark hair in exasperation at her apparent lack of interest in the topic. Her thoughts dwelled on his hand covering hers then his lips pressing against hers. Her face grew warm, and she forced herself to shake off the feeling. This nonsense about the Druids and these idle thoughts about Cedar were irrelevant. His mouth set in a tight expression, Cedar was disinclined to let Mia stumble on in ignorance.

"The Druids are a sect as old as the Order itself. Some say they were once the same organization before a divergence of philosophy emerged."

Mia thought she might be able to see where this was going, but she kept silent. The air coming from above Brother Cornelius's planters chilled markedly, and the wind blowing in through the open roof quickened. Her body convulsed in a slight shiver, and she rubbed her hands together.

"Whereas our mission is to protect that fragile link with our forebears through careful study of artifacts and other sources of knowledge," Cedar continued, "the Druids believe such knowledge and any remaining objects that contain it should be used as means to achieve a social ideal."

"So they want to take the knowledge of the artifacts to the masses?" Mia asked. "That hardly seems sinister."

"The sentiment isn't sinister at all," Cedar said, "but the corruption of the idea and the methods to obtain the desired end are quite. The Druids have allied themselves with those who would retain power at the expense of all of our freedom and at the expense of the very nature that they worship."

"That seems rather vague and a bit melodramatic," Mia offered. "Not to offend," she added hastily.

"It's this sanguine attitude by the common folk that has allowed the Druids to flourish and insinuate themselves into government and society. They aren't nearly so harmless as that."

"I just don't understand your position," Mia replied. "If they're interested in using the artifacts to better humanity, how is that any different from the Order?"

Cedar's frustration level wasn't easing as their conversation continued down this path. He sighed heavily and rubbed his dark eyes. When he pulled his hands away, his face was drawn into frown lines. Mia was sorry for being so argumentative when he was clearly stressed out, but it was her opinion that he didn't approach the Order, or the Druids for that matter, with the proper amount of skepticism. Her question hung in the air between them, and with a heavy pop, a flood of rain began to pour into the open ceiling, dousing the flora in the planters and filling the room with a light spray.

P ROTESTS, THREATS, AND BEGGING ASIDE, Mia decided she would get close enough to the Catacombs to determine how the clerics entered. Her hope that she could hide in the auxiliary corridor was short-lived. Compendium pointed out that, in an abundance of caution, such access tunnels terminated well away from the entrance to the Catacombs. She racked her brain, spent hours pacing the Archives fitfully, and rejected one idea after another.

"Why can't I just have you sneak in there for me and listen to how they open the door, since you seem to know everything else?" she yelled at Compendium in frustration.

I am not capable of independent transport, but I am capable of recording auditory information, typed Compendium glibly.

"What?" she asked. "Please explain that second part."

I am capable of receiving auditory input and storing it for later retrieval.

"You mean you can listen to a conversation and recount it?"

I am capable of accessing any auditory input and recounting it, not just conversation.

"But you can't play it back for me, right? If it's a beep or a tone, I'll have no way of knowing from your typing what it actually sounds like."

"Correct. Alpha Level is not capable of direct recording."

Mia rolled her eyes. Compendium was so persnickety sometimes that she wanted to throw it against a wall. She never would, though. When she wasn't yelling at it, she treated it gently, packing it away carefully in her sash or stowing it for safekeeping in her mattress. It was her comfort and her strength of late, and the more she thought about the Shillelagh and what would happen if she and Taryn failed, the more it became her courage itself.

"Well," Mia said, "if I can get you close enough to the entrance, it might just be our only shot at getting any information about the security door. Is there any other information you can collect?"

If connected to a conduit, I am also able to read information that flows through the conduit and store such information for later retrieval.

"You don't say?" Mia said, tapping her chin with a finger, a mannerism she had to stop, lest she begin to grow whiskers like Brother Cornelius.

I did just say, typed Compendium, and Mia laughed.

"Compendium, you really are funny sometimes," she said, patting the book.

I hardly think so, replied the book.

Caught up in her thoughts, Mia indelicately slammed the book shut and replaced it in her sash. She had to find Cedar and Taryn and tell them the plan. They were running out of time.

"I STILL THINK THIS IS UTTER MADNESS," Cedar whispered, as they crept along the corridors.

"Shh," Mia hissed back, moving quietly. Tracking and silent movement never had been her strong suit, but she'd been honing these skills at the Order. Everyone seemed to move as if they were made of air.

"This is my last chance to talk you out of this crazed plan," he whispered back, "so I'm not wasting it."

Mia rolled her eyes at him. "You didn't have to come with me," she whispered. "In fact I wish you hadn't. This task doesn't require two people."

"Your sense of direction is deplorable," Cedar replied. "You'll risk all of our necks if you get lost and caught in the act. I don't know how you ever survived in the forest without falling into sucking sand or over the edge of a cliff."

"The forest has discernible landmarks, and each tree looks different. This place is a winding set of cavernous and identical corridors," she whispered grumpily.

They proceeded in the direction of the Catacomb doors. Mia had mentally reviewed every possible contingency over the past twenty-four hours. They knew when the shift would change. In addition, Compendium provided directions. It located a crevice under the moss where it could be stowed discreetly and which was within its audio-recording range. Cedar contributed the knowledge that the moss itself was conductive and may be transmitting some information from the door. Compendium instructed Mia regarding how to hook it up to the moss. She had nothing to worry herself over. Everything was planned to the nth degree. And yet she had a cold feeling in the pit of her stomach that she couldn't shake. Her hands trembled slightly, so she kept them tucked into her robes as they walked. She couldn't remember being this scared, not even with the stalker.

Even then she had known Father would reach her. As scared as she was then, she was more scared now. She had Cedar with her, but their relations were strained. She sensed from him some suspicion after their talk in the laboratory. Some sense of chivalry or maybe watchfulness kept him at her side tonight, though, as they crept along the empty corridors that led into the bowels of the Compound. The watch wouldn't change for another hour. They'd left themselves ample time to get down and hide Compendium. *Totally simple*, Mia thought, trying to regulate her rapid breathing. *This is just reconnaissance.* She had to get it together, or she'd never be able to go through with the rest of the plan. As they moved down the final corridor sloping downward into a black abyss, their steps slowed. There was no lighting anywhere in this corridor, and the mossy walls were thick and spongy under Mia's hand as she reached out to steady herself.

"Should we use a gourd?" she whispered to Cedar. She could barely see his outline in the darkness, and his features were totally obscured.

"Best not to, I think," he whispered softly, his voice right by her ear.

She shivered from the unexpected feeling of breath against her cheek and gritted her teeth. Placing Compendium and finding the access corridor would be that much harder in pitch-darkness, but Cedar was right. They would be able to see a light coming a mile away in this darkness, and so would anyone else.

"Well, let's get to it then," she whispered back. His hand came up and touched her back, which stiffened. The hand moved up her back to her shoulder and down her shoulder to her trembling hand.

"We need to stick together," he said. "This is the easiest way. I know it's awkward."

It was. The last time he had held her hand, it had been a comforting warmth. But now their hands were clammy. It wasn't so much reassuring as emphasizing the cold fear she was feeling.

"It's all right," Mia said, but it wasn't at all.

With her right hand on the wall of the corridor, and her left gripping Cedar's tightly, she inched along the downward-sloping corridor, careful not to make a sound. She hoped she wasn't cutting off Cedar's circulation, but there was nothing to do for it. Her hand had grown a mind of its own. They proceeded along as fast as Mia dared, with her patting the wall as they went, until it ended abruptly. She snaked her hand along the wall at the back of the hallway until it touched the bare stone of the archway to the door. Suddenly she drew her hand away, as if touching the stone of the door itself might set off the security alarm. She sucked in a breath and let it out slowly. Cedar, as if reading her mind, squeezed her hand reassuringly.

Mia squeezed back, and they steadily inched their way across the threshold to the left of the door. The schematics showed a divot near the base of the door on the left. Once they were past the door, she shuffled her hand down the moss toward the ground, dragging Cedar down with her. Now came the tricky part, especially in the pitch black. She would just have to hope she did this next bit correctly. She disengaged her hand from Cedar's, but he remained crouched so close to her that she felt the warmth of his body nearby. He was stone silent. Gritting her teeth and trying not to make any noise or let her hand tremble too badly, she pulled Compendium gingerly from her sash. She already had instructed it to record everything it heard from the time she gave the instruction until the time she told it to stop. She didn't want to risk speaking in front of the door, having an incorrect voice or command being recorded in its presence, and possibly setting of a security alarm.

Mia patted along the mossy wall, the moss cool and springy under her hand, until she found the divot. She pushed her hand into the moss and was able to wiggle a finger through to the other side. *So at least that'll work*. Her heartbeat quickened in urgency. This entire process was taking far too long. *Concentrate! Stop wasting time clamming up. Just go!*

Her fingers felt around for an individual thread. She found a nice thick vine at the back of the moss matt and pulled it forward gently and carefully so as not to disturb the remaining thicket. Once she had the thread separated, she groped for Cedar's hand and placed it around the vine. He took hold of it and held it in place. She reached into her sash with both hands for her small snipping tool. She also pulled out some small sticky leaf patches sometimes used for binding conduit edges. The tape had been precut into two small squares for precisely this reason. She stuck them to the side of Cedar's arm for safekeeping.

With the cutting tool in her left hand, Mia carefully snipped the vine so that Cedar was holding one side and she was holding the other. After replacing the cutting tool in her sash, she balanced Compendium on her knee and pulled one piece of sticky leaf from Cedar's arm and used it to secure one edge of the cut vine to the binding of the Compendium. She did the same with the other side of the vine and the other piece of tape. When the second vine was in place, a faint but distinct blue light traveled along the patterned design on the outside of the Compendium then faded back into blackness. She almost dropped the book in surprise. She hoped the light was a good sign and not a bad one.

The entire arrangement was precarious in any case, but Mia gently placed the rigged Compendium into Cedar's hands. This next part was delicate work. She wiggled her finger back into the moss near the divot until it was all the way through. Then she added another finger and another until all five fingers were through. Next she widened the hole. Once she had one hand stretching open the moss, she gently took Compendium from Cedar and balanced it on her knees again. With her other hand, she guided his hand to the moss hole and placed it in to hold open the hole. Then she gently pulled the hole with one of her hands while very carefully inserting Compendium into the small pocket in the wall.

They fumbled through the process. Mia was sure the moment a guard walked up, he would notice something amiss. It was the best they could do, though. Once Compendium was in, she felt around the mossy divot for any misplaced vines. It appeared everything was in place. Taking a deep breath, she groped for Cedar's hand again and gave it a quick squeeze. He squeezed back, and they proceeded directly back the way they had come, first up the wall until they were standing, then past the doorway, then along the corridor.

We're almost there, she thought, but then something way off in the distance made her stomach flop. It was the dim glow of a gourd. *Someone's coming!* Cedar apparently saw it too, because he immediately squeezed her hand hard. They picked up their pace. They had to get to the auxiliary corridor before that light came close enough to see them. Mia's arms trembled. Cedar apparently sensed her burgeoning distress and took the lead. He tapped silently along the wall with his slipper as he moved quickly and carefully. Mia followed, almost numb with fear, trying not to make a peep or even breathe.

It took five eternities, but the light drew nearer and nearer. She couldn't see who was carrying the gourd and hoped upon hope that whoever it was couldn't see Cedar or her. Finally Cedar squeezed her hand to indicate they had reached the entrance to the auxiliary corridor. They crouched quickly, and Mia groped around with her free hand. It pushed into the moss just as it had when she had entered the Crater Grove. Cedar took her free hand, and together they pushed their hands through the moss, arms flailing silently out the other side. He pressed against her body as he shoved her silently through the moss into the stone of the auxiliary corridor. They huddled and scooted themselves along the bottom of the corridor so that the moss wasn't directly in front of them. Only moments later, footsteps approached the mossy hole in the stone. Mia waited for them to stop, but they didn't.

"Do you smell something funny?" said a familiar gravelly voice. Mia's body seized up at the sound. It felt like all the blood in her body had drained into the stone floor. Her limbs were stiff and unmoving but rubbery to the touch.

"If you're accusing me of flatulence, I'll not have it," another voice replied.

For the first time ever, Mia heard SainClair laugh with genuine mirth. "No, Brother, I need not accuse. That's just your natural state." The unknown brother chuckled back, and the footsteps receded out of Mia's hearing. Cedar's arm came around Mia's shoulder then, hugging her to his body. They huddled like that, not speaking, not moving, and barely breathing as the moments ticked by. But the tension wouldn't leave her. She did everything in her power to calm her breathing, but it kept coming shallow and ragged. After a while, Cedar gathered her closer in his long limbs, almost tenderly, although she suspected he was just trying to keep her calm so as to not blow their cover.

They had no timepiece, but time slowly ground to a halt as they waited. All Mia knew was that the extreme agitation she felt eventually subsided as the warmth of Cedar's body sank into hers and exhaustion set in, deeper and more powerfully than she'd ever known. She must have fallen asleep like that, because the next thing she knew, he was shaking her gently as the sounds of footsteps approached from the opposite direction. They were slow and deliberate steps. Feeling disoriented, Mia wriggled slightly, but Cedar held her firmly as the steps drew nearer. His frame was slim and hard and his grip like iron. There was no speaking coming from the corridor, but a yawn that was practically a roar for its volume and length echoed along the shaft as the steps diminished into the distance. They waited for a good long while after the sounds of the footsteps departed before trying to wriggle free from the cramped auxiliary corridor.

Returning to the cold, dank hallway with its mossy walls reinvigorated Mia's nerves, and she and Cedar repeated the entire procedure to retrieve Compendium from its alcove. A part of her feared SainClair had discovered it on his way into the Catacombs and had confiscated it, and she didn't take a full, deep breath until it was safely back in her sash. Hand in hand,

Cedar and Mia walked back down the hallway and up the inclined corridor that led out of the restricted level. Once they were back in the relatively dim light of the standard corridors, they continued on, carefully and quietly, Mia's body relaxing and her light steps hastening as they approached the corridor that led to the barracks. At the entrance, Mia pulled at Cedar's robes and stopped him. He turned to look at her quizzically, and she pulled him into her arms and hugged him fiercely.

"Thank you," she whispered into the ear brought close to her face by the hug, and kissed his brown cheek. He pulled away, flushed, and mumbled, "'Tis all right."

Mia had no idea whether all that effort had yielded any results whatsoever. She was excited to find out but also exhausted beyond capacity to think any longer. "Stop recording," she whispered to Compendium, and within moments she was out cold, asleep on her bunk, still wearing her robes.

23 AN IDEA L.C. 10152

I T WASN'T UNTIL THE NEXT EVENING that
Mia, Taryn, and Cedar were able to meet to
review what Compendium had learned about the
security system of the Catacombs. For Mia, the entire
day had passed in a haze of anxiety and excitement—
mostly anxiety.

*What if it was all for naught? What if Compendium
didn't learn anything, or what if I hooked it up wrong?
Worse yet, what if I damaged Compendium when I
hooked it up wrong?* The insecurities rolled through
Mia in waves. But the day's work was finally finished,

and the three friends were gathered around the reading table of the ancient texts room in the Archives. The amber light took on a sinister glow to Mia. She needed to calm down.

"I don't know if I can do this," she said, feeling ill.

"What do you mean?" Cedar snapped. Despite his silent affection last night, he had woken this morning with apparent renewed determination to remain terse in her presence.

"I'm too nervous."

"Well, get over it," Taryn chimed in. "You're the only one who can access the record."

Mia suspected this attitude was manifesting because Taryn considered herself deprived for missing out on yesterday's adventure. Perhaps Mia had misjudged her during the Gathering; Taryn's sense of adventure and hers were very different indeed. Mia wouldn't be jealous of a near miss with Brother SainClair if their situations were reversed.

She swallowed the lump in her throat as she tried not to think of the tension in her shoulders and the ache forming behind her eyes.

"Compendium," she said finally, "did you make a record of all audio sounds captured yesterday during the times I specified?"

Yes, Compendium typed. *Would you like a transcript?*

"Yes," Mia said. She let out the breath she'd been holding as the book's ink melded back into its pages and transformed into a written transcript. Mia was shocked by how sensitive the audio capture was as she skimmed through the opening lines. The book had recorded rustling noises of clothing, hard swallowing sounds, their whispers. Of course it had been on her person at that time, not stuffed in a divot in the stone wall of the entrance to the Catacombs. She kept skimming through the text, past the rustle and the whir of the book as she'd taped the conduction points to it and past the soft sounds of their slippers retreating down the corridor. The next sets of lines were the ones they concerned themselves with. Compendium recounted approaching footfalls, probably SainClair's heavy boots. Then the book recorded some random words. As the clerics approached, conversation formed in the transcript.

Voice one: Nikola...thinks...the heir...compromised, typed Compendium, the dots indicating garbled language.

Voice two: How can...certain?

Voice one: He believes the letter...also thinks...evidence.

What in the blazes are they talking about? Mia wondered.

Voice two: And you don't...

Voice one: To masquerade as...so serious...can't say...

Voice two: If Nikola is so sure, why hasn't he confronted her with it?

Voice one: He's apparently waiting to see what she'll do.

Voice two: Like a test?

Compendium indicated that the footsteps had ceased. *They were at the door*, Mia thought.

Voice one: I suppose, although in my opinion, it's a silly way to go about it. These games only agitate the situation.

Voice two: Well, Nikola would know best.

Voice one: Aye, he would.

Compendium described a heavy scraping noise. Then it indicated that the footsteps resumed.

Voice one: Well, I for one don't intend to wait around forever at Nikola's whim.

Voice two: You'd best consider...such a thing as this...situation could be volatile...

The voices broke up again as the scraping noise resumed, indicating the door had closed behind them. Mia was confounded.

"Compendium didn't indicate any special code word or tone used to open the door. It just seemed to open at their presence," she said, shaking her head.

"Keep reading," Cedar said. "Maybe there's something else."

She continued to read the transcript. Not long after the doors closed, Compendium registered another scraping noise. The doors reopened.

"This must be the watch coming off duty," she said.

Compendium indicated that two new voices were speaking in the transcript.

Voice three: SainClair is in a perpetual bad mood these days.

Voice four: Alas, I think he hasn't been getting on well with Nikola. They don't see eye to eye on certain matters.

Voice three: I suppose, but Nikola always wins these battles.

Voice four: True, true. Hey, do you want to swing by the kitchen on our way up? I'm famished.

Voice three: Absolutely. I could use a...and some nice...

The conversation broke up as the brothers continued their exit from the Catacombs. The rest of the transcript described the rustling noises of Mia and Cedar retrieving Compendium and making their way back to the barracks. She ended her reading there, dropping her head to the table and cradling it in her arm.

"Blast it, there wasn't anything helpful in that!" she practically yelled. She pressed her eyes into her arm, trying to relieve the pressure building behind them.

"Who do you suppose they were talking about in the corridor?" Taryn asked, curious.

"Oh, who cares?" Mia's exasperation was growing. "SainClair probably has a vendetta against half the Order."

She looked up to see Taryn and Cedar exchange pointed looks. "What? You can't possibly think they were referring to me?"

"Mia," said Cedar, speaking carefully, "you're the only one SainClair has a vendetta against. I know you think he bullies everyone, but the dour moods we've all grown accustomed to never have mounted into violence with anyone but you."

"Well, even if that's the case, and Dominus Nikola has some secret he's keeping, it probably has to do with my father. If I can just get the Shillelagh and get out of here, I can visit Father and confirm whatever it is Dominus Nikola is hiding. Either way, their conversation isn't nearly as important as how they got through the blasted door!"

"Why don't you ask Compendium what it collected from the grid of vines?" asked Cedar, his manner implacable.

Of course. Mia rubbed her face.

"Compendium," she asked, "were you able to collect any information from the door or about the door via the hardwired connection?"

Compendium's text shifted away from the transcript, and it typed out a response. *Yes, I was able to retrieve information from the door. Displaying now. The door is activated through a proximity voice sensor. Certain voices are logged for admittance, and when such voices approach, the door responds automatically to their presence. The door will not open for any voice not logged for admittance, and the process for entering a new voice pattern requires authorization by two currently logged voices.*

"So the only way we could add a new voice to the system would be to have two clerics authorize our voices?"

That is correct, Compendium typed.

"Compendium, does the door store records of voices that haven't been authorized for admittance?"

Yes, Compendium stated. *These unauthorized voices are stored in access records. If the voice is accompanied by an authorized voice, no alarm sounds, but if the door detects only unauthorized voices, it will alert the interior of the Catacombs as well as the security office.*

"We have a security office?" Mia asked absent-mindedly.

Correct, Compendium replied in its usual helpful manner.

"Well," Mia said to Cedar and Taryn, "this doesn't seem promising. How are we going to get into the Catacombs if any unrecognized voice sets off an alarm?"

Cedar had been staring downward with a pensive expression during Mia's exchange with Compendium. He looked up at her question and said, "Ask it if it can override the security."

"That seems unlikely," Mia said. "The door is pretty sophisticated."

"If Compendium was able to retrieve information from the door, it may be able to send information to the door, including our voice patterns."

Mia gave him a skeptical look but turned to Compendium. "Did you hear that request, Compendium?" she asked.

Yes, Compendium responded. *I am capable of sending information to the door but only while I am hooked up to it. I would not be able to plant a voice code into its system that remained perpetually after I have disconnected, but I would be able to send the door a voice while I was connected.*

Mia frowned. "That's pretty limiting."

"It's perfect," said Taryn, finally chiming in. "We don't need our voices to be in there forever, and we wouldn't want them to be anyway. If our voices were stored in there, the brothers might find out. If Compendium just sends a temporary voice authorization, then it would be gone once Compendium was disconnected, and no one would ever be the wiser."

"Compendium," Mia asked, "would there be any log of us having entered through the door?"

Not if you don't want there to be, Compendium typed.

"Confident little bugger, isn't it?" Taryn said, smiling broadly.

"Well, one thing's for sure," Mia said, her face drawn, "this will be a one-way trip into the Catacombs. If we don't find the Shillelagh, we won't be able to get out."

ONCE THEY HAD A BASIC PLAN IN PLACE, Mia became single-minded in her mission, planning every moment up until she and Taryn would have the Shillelagh in hand. It was an obsession; she relentlessly questioned Compendium about every detail between the door to the Catacombs and her departure. She grew mentally haggard as the days passed slowly in a haze of plotting and anxiety. She was short with Taryn and Cedar, dour with Brother Cornelius, and openly defiant before Brother SainClair. The strain of constant mental exertion and tension not only drained Mia but also made her reckless.

She also dwelled on the snippet of conversation recorded in the corridor. Something didn't set right with her. Cedar thought SainClair was talking about her. This seemed unlikely, but something about the conversation nagged her. If they were talking about Mia, what could Dominus Nikola have to confront her with? What was this evidence they had referred to and why were they waiting to see what she would do? If Dominus Nikola knew something about Mia that he wasn't telling her, she wanted to know what it was before she disappeared from the Order, never to return.

She told herself over and over that these thoughts were useless. It didn't matter. They probably weren't even talking about her, and if they were, how did it really change anything? Even so, she couldn't discard the feelings; they kept eating at her. As much as Mia didn't want to care about the lot of them, she did, and her curiosity did nothing to discourage her ruminations.

She had the idea that she should place Compendium somewhere in Dominus Nikola's study. If she slipped Compendium onto a bookshelf or under a seat cushion, she could possibly learn what SainClair had been going on about. She fingered the book as she lay in her bunk and chewed on her lower lip, planning where she would stash it and when. Dominus Nikola took his meals in his study, but if she went in there while he was sleeping, she could silently make her way into the study portion of his chambers, and he would be none the wiser. She was deep in thought when something moved at the corner of her vision. It was Taryn's forehead, and it slowly popped up over the wall that divided their bunks until her golden-brown eyes were peering at Mia. Her peachy skin and wheat-colored hair glowed in the dim lights of the gourds.

"You have that look on your face," she said, raising her head up so her chin was resting on the low wall.

"What look is that?"

"Like you're plotting something."

"Aren't I always plotting something?"

"Perhaps," Taryn said, squinting, as if mulling over every time she'd ever looked at Mia's face to determine whether she was in fact always plotting something. "What are you plotting?" she asked. She raised herself up higher so her elbows were propped up on the wall.

"Oh," Mia said, unsure whether she should spill her thoughts out in the barracks, where other acolytes might overhear them, or even at all. A distance was growing between Mia and Taryn and Cedar, and Mia didn't know why. Perhaps she had abused their willingness to do her favors, or perhaps they were having second thoughts about how much—if at all— they should be involved in Mia's crazy schemes. She knew it was more than that, but she couldn't pinpoint the source of the distraction or tension that had infiltrated their group.

She decided to play it vague. "I was just thinking about that conversation in the corridor. I was wondering who SainClair was talking about."

"Cedar thinks it's you."

"Yes. I'm not sure I agree with him, but I don't have any better ideas, which is why I was thinking about it."

"I suppose we'll never know," Taryn said, lifting one narrow shoulder in a shrug.

"Well, there might be a way to know."

"Ah," Taryn said, an air of triumph in her voice. "See? I knew you were plotting."

Mia sighed. "I suppose I was, but I was just curious is all."

"You know what they say about curiosity," she said, as if she thought Mia already knew.

"What?" Mia asked.

"It's bloody bad for your health." She slammed a hand down on the wall and let out a small snort.

Mia couldn't help crack a smile. "Is that so? That's what they say?"

"'Tis." Taryn nodded solemnly. "Now are you going to share that warming cake or what? My feet feel like they're carved of marble."

Mia beckoned her over, and they sat on the lumpy pallet, face-to-face, each with her back against the opposite wall, the cake between them, their knees up, their feet sharing the warmth.

"This is positively heavenly," Taryn said. She lowered her voice, and they talked a little more freely. The evening was still young enough that the acolytes were milling about in groups, chatting softly, and the noise mostly obfuscated their own.

"So, really, what was your plan?"

Mia picked at a thread on the scratchy blanket covering her lap. "I thought I might try to sneak Compendium into Dominus Nikola's study and see what I can learn."

"You what?" Her question was really more of an expletive, and the look on Taryn's face told her that she had in fact heard and processed what Mia had said but didn't believe it was even remotely a wise idea.

"Well, it seems like it would be a relatively simple matter."

"Oh, it does, does it?" Taryn rolled her eyes. "You are daft, daft, daft."

Mia frowned. "That's uncalled for."

"Is it? Do you think you're untouchable? I mean, Compendium is great, and it tells us all sorts of things we'd never know, and it's the entire reason we're going to be able to make it away from this place, but it doesn't afford you total protection from risk."

"I know that," Mia said, snapping in anger.

"I don't think you do," she said. Taryn usually wasn't one to lecture Mia, so she found herself taken aback by the force of her friend's disagreement. "Do you think the Dominus just keeps his door open for everyone to come on in and have a sit-down and a cup of bark tea?"

"Well, no," she said, "but he has no locks on his doors. Actually he has no doors."

"Yes, well, everything is as it seems of course," Taryn replied sarcastically. "If there's no door, there must be no way to know if someone's sneaking into the room. I mean, the Dominus is only a million cycles old. He's not old enough or wise enough to think someone might invade his personal space without his invitation."

"All right, I catch your drift," Mia said sullenly. "No need to overstate it. You really think he has some hidden way of monitoring who enters his study?"

"I don't doubt it," said Taryn, giving her a serious look. "And honestly what would happen if he found the book? If it were to get confiscated or someone else picked it up?"

"I hadn't thought of that," Mia said.

"I know," Taryn said emphatically. "You're getting cocky. Compendium is a huge advantage only while you have it. If you lose it, what will you do then? We need that book to make our escape."

She's right. Why would I jeopardize the chance to leave just to satisfy my curiosity? Maybe she *had* become too cocky and assumed that with Compendium, she was invincible. She pulled her braid over her shoulder and tugged at it, twisting the strands in her fingers. "I just need to get this whole thing over with. I think this entire enterprise is making me paranoid."

Taryn giggled. "You might be right, but then again, you may just need a break from it all, an idle distraction."

"Like what?" Mia asked, cocking her head.

"Oh, well, there's a certain someone I'm sure would be more than obliged to distract you."

"Well," Mia said, studying her hands as if there were something incredibly important about the veins on the back of them showing through her pale skin, "that gourd may have extinguished."

"He doesn't seem like the type to give up so easily," Taryn replied.

"Perhaps not, but he also has his dignity, and I've abused it one too many times already." Mia frowned. "Besides, how can I in good conscience start something when I know I'll be leaving, and I know he won't be coming with me?" she added after a moment.

"Perhaps if you *had* started something already, his mind could have been swayed in that regard."

"I couldn't live with myself if I thought he might regret being with me and forsaking his calling," Mia said. "I may not have the same feelings about this place that he does, but I'd never ask him to give up what he's fully dedicated himself to."

Taryn stretched her arms over her head as she arched her back to get the kinks out. "Well," she said languidly, striking a pose for Mia's benefit, "I suppose *I* could distract you." She puckered her lips and blew Mia a kiss in the air and followed it with a wink.

"Aye, that you could," Mia said, grinning, and threw her pillow right at Taryn's pouting mouth. Her surprised face froze in a pucker, and they both laughed.

"See, it's working already!" she said.

24 THE PARTY L.C. 10152

"WHERE ARE WE GOING?" Mia asked in an insistent whisper.

"Hush," said Taryn in her ear. "'Tis a surprise, as we've already told you umpteen times."

She held one of Mia's hands, and Cedar held the other as they walked along. Mia was already hopelessly lost within a few steps after having the strip of cloth tied over her eyes.

"This is very impractical," Mia retorted. "I could break a leg, and then where would we be?"

"We could always make Cedar carry you," Taryn replied, a hint of playful warning in her voice.

Mia made a rather indelicate noise not unlike a snort, and a hand lightly slapped the back of her head. "Don't think I couldn't do it," Cedar's voice whispered in her ear. Her toes curled inside her shoes at the warm breath on her neck and ear.

"All right, all right," Mia whispered back. "Lead on."

It was the dead of night. They had started in Brother Cornelius's laboratory, where Mia had, with some anxiety, attempted to decipher the perfect concoction with which to coat their false Shillelagh so the Crater Grove roots would accept it. She'd been working herself ragged trying to get everything ready. Tomorrow was the night, and attempting to account for every possible contingency was taking a toll on her body and sanity. Even now she was pulled into thoughts about the composite for the conduit root and where precisely she would need to connect Compendium to get the their recorded voices coded into the door, not to mention she was worried that the door wouldn't recognize the voices for long enough or not at all or that somehow a log of their activity would be recorded. Her stomach and throat burned as these thoughts percolated in her head.

Mia was drawn back to the moment by the realization that they must be headed downward now. The air around them had grown a little cooler, and the floor began to decline under her feet. When they finally leveled out again, the faint smell of greenery tickled her nose, and a very subtle hum of vines pulsed with life. Her shoulders relaxed a tiny amount, and she squeezed Taryn's and Cedar's hands when she realized what they intended. They came to an abrupt halt where the humming noise was the loudest, and Cedar's hand dragged her body toward the floor. His hand let go and guided her head forward until the springy moss was against her face. She was pushed through an opening and emerged on the other side, her vision still obscured but the humming sound of trees even louder. Mia was shuffled along a very tight corridor, one that was very familiar to her, for a long while until they emerged into the cool air and fresh scent of the forest.

They walked forward slowly, the roots popping up here and there under her slippers, forcing cautious steps. The ground was unsteady, and Cedar had to support Mia's elbow as they trundled along. Finally they stopped her, and one of them fiddled with the cloth that covered her eyes. When it came away from her face, she inhaled sharply in wonder. Mia had guessed their destination, but she had remained ignorant of the actual surprise. Spread out before them was a thick blanket beneath the trees of the Crater Grove. Colored gourds of every shade sat among the roots, and some even hung from the sparse lower branches of the massive trees. Set out on the blanket were sweet cider, hunks of bread, berries, cakes (real ones), and some nice cheeses that never seemed to make their way into their nightly meals in the dining hall. Mia's jaw must have been agape, because Taryn smiled mischievously.

"We told the kitchen that it was your birthday and that we wanted to surprise you with a special treat. They were kind enough to pluck some choice morsels from the clerics' private reserves."

Mia was still at a loss and stood mute and unresponsive.

"You really needed a break," Cedar chimed in. "You're exhausted and cranky and incorrigible to be around. I remember how calm this place makes you, and Taryn had never been to see it, so we arranged this." He gestured toward the spread.

"It's amazing," she finally got out in a small strangled voice, trying not to get emotional. No one ever had planned a party for her before, even if it was just a party for three and even if it wasn't her birthday. She gave each of them a tight hug in turn. The muscles in her neck and back already were relaxing from the fresh air and the comforting sounds of the trees. Taryn moved toward the blanket, and they sat.

Mia poured a mug of the spicy, warm cider and took a sip. The fire of the alcohol and heat warmed her body from the inside. "Nothing better," she said softly, sighing contentedly and plucking a bit of cheese off a platter. Cedar and Taryn sat on either side of her, all three of them facing the immense wall of trees in the center of the room. They sipped cider, ate cheese and berries, and admired the trees for a while, enjoying one another's company in a way they hadn't for what seemed like many weeks.

"How could you have known this was just what I needed?" Mia said, breaking the silence. All her nervous jumbled thoughts from earlier had fled at the sight of the Crater Grove. The elder arboreals were truly a sight to behold, and she sighed again, this time with sadness. "Although this will be the one place here I'll miss the most. Well, this place and Brother Cornelius's laboratory," she added hastily. "And perhaps the Archives."

Cedar grinned. "You're not having second thoughts, are you?" His voice sounded hopeful to her ears.

Hating to disappoint him, Mia nevertheless shook her head. "No, I have to do this. I have to find out the truth about Father and get back where I belong. That doesn't mean that I won't miss some things about this place." She looked at him through the corners of her eyes. He was sprawled on his back on the blanket, legs akimbo and chest propped up on his elbows, a picture of relaxation. But his casual posture and easy expression didn't quite reach his eyes. The dark depths appeared troubled. A slight crease furrowed the spot between his elegant eyebrows, and his mouth was set just a fraction too tightly. He clearly was trying very hard not to let her know his feelings, so she pretended she didn't notice the uneasiness underneath the calm visage. She had thought at one time or another, when lost in idle daydream, that perhaps she could return to the Order after everything with Father had been settled and she had regained her life to do with as she chose. *Perhaps I could visit Cedar,* she thought. *But no, when I take that Shillelagh, in that moment I'll never be able to return here. I'll forever be an enemy of the Order.* That thought saddened Mia in a way that it shouldn't have.

She certainly would miss Cedar and Brother Cornelius. She would miss their company and the laughter they shared and the memories. A shiver ran down her spine despite the warmth of the cider and the radiant heat of the trees.

"Well, at least write me from wherever you end up," he said, his voice sad. "You can use a pen name, like 'Melia.'"

"Melia?" she asked.

"It was my mother's name," he said simply. "She's dead, so she won't be needing it anymore." Mia patted his hand, which rested on the thick blanket.

"That's morbid, Cedar," Taryn interjected. "Your melancholia is out of place at a party." She sipped her cider and plucked a berry from the tray.

"Yes, well, it is a going-away party," he grumbled.

"Speaking of 'away,'" Taryn said, changing the subject. "Did Compendium tell you how to use the Shillelagh once you have it?"

"I didn't think to ask," Mia said, worry suddenly creeping into her voice. "It never crossed my mind with all the planning. My head is filled with sawdust!" she exclaimed, exasperated.

Taryn giggled. "Well, you'd better pull it out and ask it then."

Mia retrieved Compendium from her sash. "Compendium, how do I work the Shillelagh? Does it require a keyword or some sort of activation?"

Compendium typed a response in its usual dry but helpful manner. *The Shillelagh can be used by any person. It is activated simply by holding it aloft, speaking*

clearly the specific place you wish to visit, then tapping
the stick assertively on the ground twice.

"That seems pretty straightforward," Taryn said,
biting her lip in concentration.

"Yes, it does. Compendium, how specific do I have
to be in my description of the place?"

You need not have traveled to the place before, but
you must be able to picture it or picture a written
description of the place. A proper name also may
work, but such a method is less reliable, given the
propensity for differing populations to rename certain
landmarks. Additionally you may picture a person and
his or her face, and the Shillelagh will take you to that
person, if that person can be determined.

"Really?" said Taryn in amazement. "How does it
know where people are?"

"Really?" Mia asked, sarcasm lacing her voice.
"That's the big mystery to you? It transports people
to a completely different place; it knows where every
spot in Lumin is just from a picture in the speaker's
head or a written description. Those properties are
totally believable, but your brain stumbles on it being
able to tell where people are located?" She rolled her
eyes a bit, and Taryn giggled.

"Well, when you put it that way," Taryn said,
somewhat dourly, "I suppose 'tis no more crazy than a
know-it-all book that can change its text on a whim."

They all shared a small laugh at that remark. "It's truly a remarkable object," Mia said. "I can't imagine having such power and capability at my fingertips and squandering it so that the whole of society falls and its greatness remains unknown to all but a few."

"Well, how do we really know what happened?" said Cedar. "Our forebears may have acted totally rationally under the circumstances. It may have been their only option. Who's to know? There's no one left to tell us."

"That's true," Taryn interjected, "and the Order spends a lot more time researching the technology itself than worrying about the political and social circumstances that brought us to our current place. 'Tis shortsighted, if you ask me."

"Yes, we know." Cedar sighed. Mia assumed, like her, that he was growing agitated with Taryn's repetitive claims that the Order didn't care enough about history. "We can't all be history aficionados like you."

"Ah, let's not quibble," Mia said. "'Tis our last night together and likely the last time I'll set eyes on the Crater Grove, so let's enjoy the scenery and the company."

Mia relaxed onto her back and closed her eyes, absorbing the sounds of the trees and the feeling of the roots against her spine and head. Taryn and Cedar lay back as well, and the three spent silent time basking in one another's presence. Mia was almost lolled into a quiet sleep when Taryn said softly, "The trees here are rather beautiful."

THE DAY THAT THEY HAD BEEN PLANNING FOR in infinite detail finally came. It had felt to Mia as if it would never arrive, yet the inexorable march of time had carried her here just as it had carried her ever forward since she had first drawn breath. Now, however, she was ready for it. She was no longer being carried forward by another's will; her own will was driving her feet along the path. She had packed all her meager belongings and stowed her large, full pack under her bed. Mia wore her thin, gauzy clothes of the tropics under her heavy acolyte robes.

She left behind some of the cakes Brother Cornelius had provided—as much as she would love to take them—as well as the bedsheets and additional robes allotted to her and the various books from the Archives cluttering her space. She did have Compendium. Even if she didn't need it to get into the Catacombs, she didn't have the resolve to leave it behind. It was too much a part of her now. She wore her slippers but would change into her soft leather boots before they departed, after the other acolytes were all asleep.

Taryn had a harder time with packing. She had arrived with more baggage and had been there longer, accumulating quite a collection of historical texts and other knickknacks. Even if she could pack it all up and take it with her, Mia warned her that they couldn't afford the weight or the sound or the suspicion that an empty cubby might arouse in the others. So Taryn was left to decide what she would take from among her many belongings. She had pulled out the trunk stored under her bunk, the one in which they'd been hiding the Shillelagh substitute, and rummaged through the other items contained within. She pulled out a green hooded cloak of thick yet softly spun wool. It had a delicate metallic thread worked along the edge of the hood and collar that formed small intricate vines. She laid it flat on the bed, fussing over it.

"That's gorgeous," Mia said, fingering the fine wool in her hand.

"Isn't it?" She beamed. "Mother made it for me. See the clasp?"

Mia looked for the clasp along the edge of the wool. It was a silvery rose, curled at the edges as if it had just blown off a stem and landed on the cloak.

"The work is exceptional," Mia said. "Your family must have access to some special mills."

"Oh, yes, well, we mill all our own fabric."

"Gypsies mill their own fabric?" Mia said, not thinking that was possible.

"Oh, aye," Taryn said, a little flustered. "We borrow the equipment when we come across it, but we do the milling ourselves."

Mia shrugged. "However it came to be, it's fantastic."

"It's my prized possession," Taryn said, smiling. "I'm not allowed to wear it here, but I'll put it on tonight once we reach our destination." She folded it carefully and laid it on the bed. Then she carefully compared the volumes of books stacked around her cubby, electing to choose just a couple of slim volumes, one being her notebook in which she was constantly scribbling and the other titled *A Comprehensive History of the Order*.

"Why bring that one?" Mia asked. "There are so many useful histories about Lumin here."

"Memories," Taryn said quickly, patting the book and smiling again.

Mia left her to finish her packing and went to see Brother Cornelius one last time. She searched for him in the Archives, but he wasn't there. It wasn't that late past dinner, so she expected him to still be about. From there she proceeded down the corridors that led to his laboratory; they were more silent than usual.

Perhaps there was a late seminar of interest. Mia had been rather preoccupied with her own ventures of late. She tapped on the stone wall of the alcove that led up to Brother Cornelius's laboratory, and the lights came on as always. She proceeded up the staircase and paused on the landing. It was her habit to knock against the wall of the alcove first then call his name to alert him to her presence.

"Brother Cornelius," she called, "are you about?" There was no response. Mia proceeded in. The hearth was warm and cheery and the night sky clear and full of stars. The night lights streaked magnificent colors across the sky above the planters. Populating his desk was the usual disorderly shuffle of papers and beakers and tools of a person constantly in deep thought about some great idea, but she didn't see Brother Cornelius. Mia stood and looked around the empty laboratory. The door leading off to his quarters was ajar, but she never entered there. She walked over to the door, rapped on the frame, and called out again, "Brother Cornelius, are you in?" The room's silence was the only response.

"Alas," she said, sad that she might never see him again. *Perhaps 'tis for the best*, she thought, not trusting herself to keep her emotions in check anyway. With that, she left to begin the tense wait.

CATACOMBS   L.C. 10152

T ARYN AND MIA STOOD IN THE HALLWAY
outside the barracks. They had timed their
departure so there would be no chance the guard was
changing when they arrived at the door to the
Catacombs. They had just one order of business left,
and that was Cedar. He stood with his hands thumbed
through the belt around his waist, his head hanging,
his dark hair brushing into his shrouded eyes.

"Well, I suppose this is good-bye," he said. His
voice sounded low and calm, but there was a slight
crack on the last word.

"Give 'er a hug," said Taryn, opening her arms to Cedar. He embraced her and patted her shoulder.

"Take care of yourself," he said. Mia saw his eyes linger on the rose pin of Taryn's cape, which was draped over her arm. Taryn pulled back from him and gave him a bright smile. "That I shall."

It was Mia's turn then, and her heart beat quickly. The calming effects of the Crater Grove had lasted with her most of the day, but the serene feeling was wearing off and the tension rising. She hoped she could get through this last trial without Cedar. Despite his disagreement with their entire—in his words, daft—scheme, he had helped them through the whole process. It was just these last few steps that they had to walk alone.

He gathered Mia into his arms for a hug, pressing her against him. "I hope you find what you're looking for," he whispered in her ear. "I hope you find what you need." She squeezed him tightly and released him.

"You take care of Brother Cornelius," Mia said, her voice hoarse. He nodded, although he had averted his eyes and was staring at his hands. "I'm serious. I think he'll be devastated to lose an assistant, and I can't bear to hurt him after all he's done for me."

Then don't! her inner voice yelled. *It's not too late to call off this insanity.*

But it was too late. *You're just scared. Stop being a coward and get on with it.*

Cedar pulled her toward him again and planted a kiss on her forehead. "Take care, and write me, Melia," he whispered. He smiled softly, but his eyes were still far away.

Mia gave his hand one last squeeze then released it. She and Taryn turned and walked down the corridor, leaving him standing there. Part of Mia wanted to look back, but the rest of her recognized that to do so would bring no comfort. They walked along silently, too nervous to engage in idle conversation and too worried about who might be up and about to talk seriously.

When they finally reached the pitch-black corridor where Cedar and Mia had hidden Compendium, she pulled out two gourds from her bag and handed one to Taryn. She had attached strings to them so they might be hung around their necks as a hands-free light source. Taryn took her green cloak from over her arm and fastened it around her neck, where it hung dashingly down her shoulders.

"You cut a striking figure," Mia said softly, and Taryn grabbed her hand.

They walked slowly, hand in hand, toward the door. Taryn always moved with animal grace, but Mia held her natural clumsiness in check with marked concentration so as to proceed absolutely noiselessly down the dark corridor. For a long time, it looked as if they were heading into a black hole of nothing. Their hands gripped each other's tightly, white-knuckled. They barely breathed. The sweat ran down Mia's cheeks and her back, but she made no move to wipe her brow. Economy of movement and silence were tantamount.

When they finally reached the door, Mia gestured to Taryn to raise a gourd above her head, lighting a spot with which to work. The process for hooking up Compendium to send data to the door of the Catacombs was similar to the process for recording, but Mia had to find a particular set of vines. She was looking for a thick vine that ran down the side of the door, well hidden by the moss. It controlled the door's inputs, whereas the ones she had tapped into previously merely received general information from the door. She picked through the moss carefully and silently until she located the proper one. It was heavy, and snipping it in half wouldn't be possible. She took a very small, sharp knife from her tool kit and slipped it along the vine, pulling up a fibrous area and exposing a humming center. Careful not to disturb the connection, Mia retrieved a small flexible connector she had prepped with a very sticky paste perfected in Cornelius's laboratory. His tools for making concoctions were superior, but Mia held her breath until she secured one side of the connector to the door and the other to the binding of Compendium.

As with the last time, the book lit up in blue along the metallic work on the cover for a short while before fading back to its normal gold. Mia and Taryn had prerecorded their voices into Compendium, and Mia had instructed it to automatically send their voices to the door once the book was connected. The voices would remain with the door only as long as Compendium was connected, but Mia could instruct the door to stay open for up to thirty seconds. Apparently this was one of the standard commands the clerics had encoded, likely so they could move items back and forth from the Catacombs.

It was the moment of truth. Mia tried to keep her voice from wavering as she said clearly into the dark corridor, "What do you say we head in then?"

"That sounds like a fabulous idea," Taryn replied. There was some mild tension in her voice, but it still sounded like her. The door slid open at the sound of their voices. Mia breathed a heavy sigh of relief and stooped to Compendium.

"Door, please remain open for thirty ticks," she said. With that, she quickly removed the sticky vine from Compendium's binding and used some of the paste to tack down the split part of the vine then tucked it back into position behind the moss. They had just enough time to step through the door before it closed to their backs. They smiled at each other tenuously, but there was no time to celebrate. If Compendium was wrong, someone already would be alerted to their unauthorized presence. The Catacombs were dimly lit by a series of almost extinguished orangey gourds. Mia motioned to tuck theirs into their robes. This wasn't the time to draw attention to themselves with additional light.

She grabbed Taryn's hand again, and they proceeded forward. They'd both memorized the path from the door to where the Shillelagh resided. With her hopeless sense of direction, however, Mia tended to let Taryn lead the way. The corridors were dark and enclosed, and mixed in with the dirt and stone of the walls were massive woody roots writhing within. These were the roots of the Crater Grove, and each was larger than the trunk of one of the trees in Hackberry. They hummed with thunder that could wake the dead. Ironic, since this was where the Order stored its "dead" items. They continued to thread their way around the massive roots along the memorized path, the noise growing louder around them. Although there was no sign of the clerics on the watch, the numerous alcoves created by the roots entering the earth frayed Mia's nerves. She had a miniature attack every time she and Taryn turned a blind corner, and she struggled to keep her heart rate under control.

When they finally reached the junction, her hand was shaking in Taryn's. Given Taryn's excitable nature, Mia was surprised that hers wasn't as well; on the contrary it was strong and reassuring. Mia pulled her gourd out of her bag and shone it directly on the spot where the Shillelagh should be. She held her breath, hoping Compendium hadn't led her astray. The roots were thick in this spot, bending back in on one another, almost like those trees that dropped roots down to the earth. Mia took her time examining each root in turn, looking for the hidden artifact. Taryn's calm began to crack a little, and she shuffled her feet quietly. Mia's own calm was fading quickly as well. Each root examined wasted a little time and caused her heart to push higher into her throat with the failure.

When she finally found what she was looking for, she sighed in relief and motioned for Taryn to come closer. Taryn bent down and peered at the spot where she pointed, squinting. Mia gestured with her finger to where the Shillelagh was connected, and Taryn's eyes widened. She hadn't even seen it. In truth, neither had Mia. She had gone by sound and touch. That whole clump of root sounded differently, and as she explored each one, she finally had found the Shillelagh when her rapping knuckles cracked against the hard wood rather than a wet root. It blended perfectly into the many roots, though; it was a nondescript brown stick with a knob near the top. Careful not to break any connections, Mia outlined it with her finger. She motioned for Taryn to hand her the package containing their facsimile. Taryn gingerly passed Mia the cloth-wrapped root extraction, and she set it on the ground, opening the flaps of cloth to reveal the root, which was covered in a thick, conductive goo. Mia had engaged in some educated guessing when she had formulated the paste, so she wasn't entirely sure it would work. Still, she hoped it would give them enough time to make a clean retreat. She grimaced, though, because visually, it was a far cry from the aged wood staff that currently was nestled in the roots. It wouldn't fool anyone looking upon it. There was nothing to be done, though.

Mia gestured for Taryn to pick up the substitute and hold it precisely where she was pointing. Then, biting her lip in concentration, sweat running down her brow, she inserted her small knife along the top of the connection and pried the knob of the Shillelagh out of its burrow. It made a terrible cracking noise, and her heart hammered against her rib cage until she realized it was just the sound of the old connections being severed. The Shillelagh briefly glowed blue along its wood grain in the same way Compendium's cover had glowed when it was connected to the Catacomb doors. She quickly handed the Shillelagh to Taryn and took from her the substitute, immediately pressing it into the hole left by the artifact. She nestled it tightly into the recently vacated space and made sure there was enough goo between the fake staff and the connectors. Once she was sure it was the best she could do, she wiped her brow and let out a ragged breath. They had it.

Mia turned to Taryn so she might get a better look at it. Taryn had stepped back from her and was still holding the Shillelagh tightly. A look of sheer joy lit her face, and her eyes were almost wild with emotion. She held the Shillelagh gently, almost reverently.

"Finally," Taryn whispered. "I finally have you."

"Taryn," Mia said, trying to rouse her from her reverie, "we have to go now. There isn't any time."

She looked up from the staff and took another step away from Mia. "I'm sorry," she said softly.

"What for?" Mia asked, standing to her full height and advancing a step.

"For what I'm about to do," she said. "This should explain everything." She tossed something at Mia, who caught it in her sticky hand and peered at it, confused. It was a small stone. On the stone was carved a rose. In the center of the rose was an open eye.

"Halt!" a gravelly voice called from behind Mia. "Halt right there."

"You're too late," Taryn said, laughing gleefully. She held the Shillelagh up in her right hand and yelled, "Take me to Rosewater." She banged the staff on the hard earthen floor of the Catacombs twice.

Then the world exploded. A tremendous flash of light issued around them, like a lightning bolt striking the earth itself. The force picked Mia up from the ground and hurled her backward, and the impact of her return to earth knocked the breath out of her. She coughed as a hail of dirt and root bits rained down around her, her limbs incapable of moving to shield herself. The voices behind her were silenced. The last thing she saw before she slipped into unconsciousness was an empty place where Taryn and the Shillelagh had just stood, dirt and debris still swirling in the air.

26 THE DUNGEON L.C. 10152

MIA AWOKE COMPLETELY DISORIENTED. The smell of mold assaulted her nostrils when she tried to suck in a deep breath. A sharp pain in her side further curtailed her breathing. She groaned, although she couldn't say how she made the noise. She struggled to shift her body, but every muscle touched by movement screamed in defiant pain, so she resigned herself to lying still, even as she shivered from the chill of the stone seeping through her thin clothing. Mia had yet to open her eyes, and a fear settled into her stomach at the thought of what she would see when she did. Her head throbbed with each mangled thought that surfaced.

The scene in the Catacombs rushed back to her as she lay there, and she choked on a cry. Taryn had betrayed her. Taryn had taken the Shillelagh and left her. She couldn't process that still. Why? Mia remembered her telling the Shillelagh to take her to Rosewater. Was that a place? Mia never had heard of it. Why would Taryn do such a thing? *I'll never be able to ask her. She's gone. And the explosion!* Mia hadn't expected such a rocketing surge of power. The force that had catapulted her off her feet and the clouds of debris dancing around her as she had lost consciousness returned as a sick lump in the pit of her stomach. She winced as a hot tear rolled down her cheek. The Crater Grove was a gorgeous spectacle of nature, and Mia had surely damaged it. That thought she could not abide. Imagining the Crater Grove in shambles, its roots dying, she slipped back into unconsciousness, this time filled with nightmares.

She woke again some time later—how much later she had no idea. This time she wasn't alone in the dank room. She groaned and tried to roll onto her side, her head still throbbing and muscles aching. Her body still wasn't overly cooperative, but she was able to at least prop herself up on one elbow. She finally opened her eyes. The light was incredibly dim, her vision blurred. She blinked a few times, and when her vision finally came into focus, Dominus Nikola was standing near the side of the room. She was in a cell, larger than the one in the brig. The room was stone on all six sides and had no cot. It was entirely empty except for a chamber pot and a wooden chair, which Dominus Nikola seated himself on. She gingerly pulled herself into a sitting position and leaned against the far wall.

They sat there in silence for a while. Mia had no idea what to say, and the Dominus didn't seem in any great hurry. Finally he cleared his throat. "Ms. Jayne, do you understand where you are?"

"Am I in the dungeon?" she asked. When she spoke, the voice that emerged from her throat sounded hoarse and foreign.

"That is correct," the Dominus replied. "Do you know why?"

"I stole the Shillelagh from the Catacombs," she said, her voice cracking.

"That is certainly part of it," he said. "You and Taryn Windbough conspired to steal the Shillelagh. In the process you significantly damaged the Crater Grove and allowed an artifact of the Order to be usurped." His voice was devoid of emotion. Given the Dominus's usual warmth, Mia found it unsettling.

"I didn't know she was going to take it," Mia said. "I just wanted to see Father, to confirm that he was dead. I just wanted to be free."

She lay back down on her back, not trusting herself to speak any more at that moment.

"Ms. Jayne, I can't help feel that these actions were extreme. Did it never occur to you to just ask us about your father?"

Mia narrowed her eyes. "You provided me with no answers when I asked. Brother Cornelius claimed not to know one way or the other, and Brother SainClair said he was dead. I didn't feel the Order was giving me the answers to which I was entitled."

"Entitled?" Dominus Nikola asked, leaning forward in his chair. His eyes flashed steely in the dim light. "Might I remind you that you chose to join the Order as an acolyte? That was the arrangement. This organization is responsible for the safekeeping of the artifacts of Lumin, as you are well aware. You may be able to use that artifact, Compendium, and that makes you valuable to the Order, but don't think that such value makes you better than your peers."

Mia scowled at the Dominus. "No one treats me as if I'm better than anyone else," she said. "No one tells me anything."

"Why should they? Have you earned this knowledge? Or special treatment?" He pointed a long finger at her. "You treat yourself as if you're better than everyone else," Nikola said, his face stern. "You flout the rules of our institution. You put your own needs and desires above those of the Order, of your friends, and even your father. Do you think he would be proud of his grown daughter acting like a petulant child?"

Mia's frown deepened. She crossed her arms across her chest but didn't speak.

"If Mr. Kannon hadn't put two and two together"—he shook his head—"I hesitate to think on it."

Mia's stomach lurched sharply to the left. If she looked over, she was sure she'd see it lying outside of her body. Cedar had informed on her. He had looked her in the eye all those times, had pretended to be helping her, and actually had helped her even. *Had it been a farce all along?* She recalled his good-bye in the hallway outside the barracks, when he had whispered that he hoped she found what she needed. It had all been lies, all of it, from both him and Taryn. They both had betrayed her, one for the Order and the other for herself. Mia was apparently just a pawn in everyone's stratagem. Her eyes welled with tears. Father was right; she shouldn't have trusted anyone there. She was a fool to think she had found companions and friendship in a place like the Order. In the dim light she doubted Dominus Nikola could see her tears, but she would be blasted to the Core before he would hear her cry. Unable to speak without betraying her emotions, she just lay there.

"This isn't the end of this," Nikola said eventually, "but that can wait. I can see you're still exhausted. The explosion rendered you unconscious for almost a week. Brother SainClair is still in the hospital." He rose then, and another cleric retrieved the chair from the room. Nikola paused in the doorway and looked back at Mia. "Please think on what you have done," the Dominus said simply, his voice remaining even but tinged with sadness. "We took you in and trusted you with Compendium, and you betrayed us." With that, he left the room, the heavy door shutting behind him. The loud grind of a metal bolt sliding into a stone groove sounded on the other side of the door, and Mia was alone with her thoughts once again.

What did he mean by "trusted you"? Did Brother Cornelius tell the Dominus about Compendium? She couldn't think about that just yet. She needed to assess the damage. Her head and body still aching, she looked down and surveyed herself. She had been stripped of her acolyte robes and sash, with only her gauzy tropics clothing remaining. At least they had left her boots. Even with them, her feet were blocks of ice. They had confiscated her bag, her tools,

Compendium, and even her mother's locket. She gingerly touched parts of her body and face, wincing here and there, feeling bruises and cuts as her hand explored. A bandage was wrapped around her forehead. As she patted her legs, she felt something small tucked into a pocket. She carefully pulled it free and looked at it. She had expected her hands to be dirty and sticky, but they'd been cleaned at some point.

I've been out a week? She recalled the wall of hot electric air hitting her in the chest and forcing her backward with great intensity. It was powerful indeed. In her palm sat the small stone Taryn had tossed at her as she had made her escape. She clenched it in her hand before dropping it to the floor of the cell with a clink. *How did that get into my pocket?*

She drew her knees up to her chest, hoping that curling up would help warm her frigid extremities. *I don't merit a bed,* she thought. Despite her anger at Taryn and Cedar, Nikola was right. She had betrayed the Order. She had been betrayed, just as surely, by those she had considered friends—her best friends—but she also had been the betrayer. Instead of airing her grievances with the Dominus, she had set upon her own solution. She cradled her head in her knees as she contemplated this mess of her own design. The image of Taryn's apologetic expression as she tossed her the stone and called for Rosewater was etched in her mind behind her closed eyes, doomed to be repeated over and over. *Why was I such a fool? Such an obvious fool.* Mia pictured the clerics' faces in her mind, looking at her derisively. It was as if they all had SainClair's face. Brother Cornelius, Dominus Nikola, the other acolytes, even Sister Valencia—they all surely hated her now. They had believed she was one of them, just as surely as Mia had believed Taryn was her friend. No apologetic look could calm her rage when she thought about Taryn's betrayal, yet she knew the others must feel the same about her.

Cedar was a separate matter altogether. Mia didn't know what to make of his actions. He had set her up to be discovered as—and proved—a traitor. Perhaps even the warm feelings he had displayed were just a farce. That thought made her angry. She had warmed to him as well, confided in him, and shared parts of herself that she reserved entirely from others. She didn't understand. If the Order had known all along, why did they let them take it as far as they did? Why not just imprison them when the first treacherous words had been uttered from their mouths? Why help them instigate a theft? Mia should have asked Dominus Nikola these questions. She had frozen up when he had mentioned Cedar's betrayal, but she should have demanded some answers.

Yet Taryn had still escaped with the Shillelagh.
How had the Order allowed that to come to pass? Mia
recalled hearing words right as the world exploded.
And Dominus Nikola had said Brother SainClair was
still in the hospital, so he must have been there to stop
them. Perhaps the clerics hadn't anticipated the
Shillelagh's powerful blast, just as she and Taryn
hadn't, or they hadn't thought one of them would
betray the other. Still, they were a moment too late,
and now Taryn had the Shillelagh. What she intended
to do with it, Mia didn't know. Taryn had played her
for a fool. Was she even a gypsy? Was everything
about her a lie? Mia recalled her cloak and the fact
that she had taken only a history of the Order with
her when she had left. She pursed her lips.

Taryn clearly had a genuine interest in the history of the Order, although likely not for the
reasons she'd previously expressed. Mia squeezed her
knees closer to her body as she recalled all the times
she had pointed Taryn to an ancient text on some
topic or another and smiled when the other acolyte
furiously scribbled notes into her ever-present notebook. Mia had aided her in every way possible as she
gathered intelligence on this place and these people.
She buried her head deeper into her knees and lay
there, reliving every moment of her friendships with

Taryn and Cedar until she couldn't bear to think of them anymore.

MIA AWOKE AGAIN, this time to the sound of the door bolt being thrown back. The door creaked open, and she looked over to see a robed figure, one of the clerics, though she couldn't tell who, place a tray on the ground near the door. The figure left without saying a word, and the bolt returned to its resting place. She had fallen asleep with her knees to her chest and now tried to stretch out her legs again. The persistent pain shot through her cold-numbed flesh, and she gritted her teeth with the exertion.

The dank, moldy smell of her cell was improved by a warm, spicy odor wafting from near the door. Suddenly she was ravenously hungry, as if she hadn't eaten for a week. And perhaps she hadn't. Pushing her protesting muscles and joints aside, she half crawled, half scrambled to the tray. It was visible in the dim light of the single gourd fixed outside the cell door. The tray contained a bowl of stew and a hunk of bread. There was also a gourd of water. She drank a few gulps of the water first, quenching a thirst she barely recognized. In her haste, she swallowed some water into her lungs and coughed repeatedly to clear them, the exertion of the cough renewing the pain in her ribs. She wheezed, cradling her ribs for a moment until the lightheadedness passed.

She wanted to wolf down the stew in a single huge bite, but she made herself take a small bite, chew thoroughly, swallow, sit and wait, then take another bite. She probably hadn't had solid food in at least a week, and she loathed the thought of bringing any of the precious stew back up. After a few bites, her stomach grew queasy, and she paused for even longer, desperate not to lose the nourishment. When she could stand it no longer, her stomach loudly protesting her decision to discontinue eating, she took another couple of bites, balancing the stew with small pieces of bread. She went like that, slowly, until every last speck of food was consumed and every last drop of water imbibed. Her stomach churned, but it was worth the pain. She lay back against the wall near the door, her raw bones and muscles pushing up against the stone walls, and longed for her lumpy cot in the barracks, or better yet, her soft bed in Hackberry, with Hamish warming her feet and snoring loudly. She smiled to herself. Hamish reminded her of Father.

It was easier to think of her life with Father and Hamish in the abstract. Memories made everything too real, too palpable. They brought to the surface the unconditional love that she so desperately missed. Even if Father had betrayed her, she certainly knew

Hamish's love had been real. That ridiculous mutt with his stubby limbs and lolling tongue, always ready to pounce inelegantly after some small creature he could never quite catch.

That clumsy canine would die if left to catch food on his own—that or he would have to turn herbivorous. Mia laughed at the thought of Hamish nibbling on a root or leaf, a wary look on his face as he first took a bite, then a horrified expression when he realized that this leafy green thing was nothing like a hearty chunk of meat and that he likely never would taste meat again. The image made her laugh, but when she rubbed her face, she realized she was crying hot tears as well. She missed Hamish so badly. She wanted to rub her face in the thick fur coat that shot hairs up her nose and have him lick away her tears. If she could just look into his eyes one more time, she knew she would see love and forgiveness.

Mia fell asleep again, thinking of Hamish and Father and trying to quiet her thoughts and tears. Life continued on this way—for how long, she had no idea. She had no visitors, save a cleric who dropped trays at her door and came to pick them up while she was unconscious. She used the chamber pot when she had to, slept, wore herself out thinking hard about everything, slept some more, ate again, and eventually, once her mobility started to return, paced slowly around her cell, running her hands along the walls. The boredom was torturous. She decided at some point, after maybe six or seven more days, that she didn't really like herself at all. She had no desire to talk to herself right now, but she was forced into company with her insecurities and vagaries and betrayals and humors. And she had nothing left to tell herself that she hadn't already confided. There was no one to apologize for, no one to make amends to—just her—and she hated the very sound of her voice rattling away inside her head. When she was almost on the brink of madness, with only her own mind to pick at, multiple sets of footsteps echoed outside her cell.

INFIRMARY C.L. 10152

T HE DOOR SWUNG OPEN, and several figures entered. Mia's heart caught in her throat. One of them was Cedar. He no longer was dressed in the robes of an acolyte. He had taken his cleric vows. Mia was seated in the far corner of the cell with her knees up. She quickly averted her eyes from the three clerics, not wanting to look at them just then.

Brother Valentine stepped forward. "Ms. Jayne, please rise. We need to secure you."

There was a clink, and she looked up to see him holding a wicked pair of leg shackles. *He can't get his hands on Taryn, so he's going to make an example of me.*

"You can't mean for me to wear those," she said. She hadn't intended her statement to sound rude, but that was how her words were received.

"You've been accused of stealing from the Order that took you in, betraying it, damaging the Crater Grove, and injuring others in the process. Do you deny these charges?"

Mortified, she shook her head. Those statements put the embarrassment of leg shackles in perspective. She climbed gingerly to her feet while the small group of clerics looked on. Cedar bent down to snap the shackles around her wasted ankles. She always had been on the scrawny side, but she had diminished further in this cell. The shackles looked comical, and she worried whether she would be able to walk without tripping.

"I guess they won't be too tight," Cedar said, standing to his full height and stepping back to retrieve the manacles that Brother Borus was carrying for her arms. Cedar had the good grace to avert his eyes. He hesitated briefly as he secured the manacles to her wrists, but he did his duty regardless, as he always did. It would be a mercy if the weight of the chains would drag her down through the floor and into the earth, never to return.

"You'll be coming with us," Brother Borus said in a perfunctory tone. A frown and cold voice replaced his usual friendly smile and playful banter.

"Where are we going?" Mia asked. She didn't relish the thought of parading past the entire Order, grungy, injured, and disgraced.

"Save your questions for the Dominus," came the curt reply from Brother Valentine.

Valentine and Borus each took one of her arms, and they proceeded forward, clinking slowly along. As Cedar fell in line behind them, his eyes seared a hole in the back of Mia's grimy neck. Mercifully the clerics didn't hasten her along, as she doubted she could have moved much faster. If the shackles hadn't made walking difficult, her own deteriorated muscles would have. They plodded along through the corridors, turning here and there. Mia kept her eyes on her feet and moved as silently as possible without speaking a word. It was all in vain; the hefty chains clanked, and the sound echoed around the hallways with every step she took.

The occasional whisper reached her ears; other acolytes darted from their path at the edge of her vision; and heat rose in her cheeks. She wanted to raise her head and stare back at them defiantly, but as she had been left to rot in the dark, the fire had died in her veins. Now she possessed just self-loathing, shame, and a good deal of fear regarding what would become of her. It wasn't the way of the Order to execute people, but she probably had challenged a lot of their standard practices of late. They wouldn't keep her here forever. They could banish her, but given the severity of her crimes, she expected they would turn her over to the authorities of Willowslip for criminal proceedings. She hadn't thought through the possibility of being jailed when she had devised her plan to steal the Shillelagh.

Underneath all her stress and anxiety, she was just as egotistical as any common criminal, assuming she would never get caught. She had no one to blame but herself. Just as Taryn had warned, she had let herself believe Compendium made her invincible. It solved problems for her, including some very complex ones. It never talked back, never told her she was wrong, never called her names. It never turned its back on her or betrayed her. It wasn't human. It wasn't her family. And yet she herself was just a human and had betrayed others and been betrayed by them.

Compendium didn't change her life. Its companionship was an illusion that she had allowed herself to see as the truth. She bit the inside of her lip as she walked, thinking about how she had used it as a crutch, a means to avoid truly finding a place here, a way to avoid being direct with Dominus Nikola about her feelings and concerns, a way to avoid confronting Brother SainClair about his actions. She took a tool that could have been used wisely to augment her time here or unwisely to dismantle it, and dismantle it she had. Her choices didn't benefit her, her family, or those around her. And now she no longer belonged anywhere. She had no family; she had no friends; and she had no place here in the Order. Mia sighed, the sound lost amid the clang of her steps.

Just as she was working herself into a full frenzy of self-flagellation, they arrived at a nondescript door set into a stone corridor. She didn't recognize either the corridor or the door. It was a terrible and currently inconvenient propensity of hers to tune out her movements through the hallways if someone else was leading her. Brother Borus rapped twice on the very old wooden door. It creaked open a little, and he pushed it open farther. Cedar tapped Mia on the shoulder, and when she turned, he grasped the manacles around her wrists and held them still while he applied the key.

"The leg shackles will have to stay on," he whispered.

She nodded in acknowledgment of his words and turned back toward the open door. Mia pushed it farther open with her now much-lighter arms. The room was barely large enough to contain two beds and a couple of stools. Dominus Nikola sat on one of the stools, a cane clasped in his hand, as if he were going to use it to row himself across the floor. In the bed closest to the door lay Brother SainClair. He was even whiter than usual, which made his angular features look as if they had been carved from marble. Dark blotches stained the skin beneath his eyes. Two pillows that clearly didn't have beans in them cradled his head. *They're bringing me here to show me the damage I wrought with my actions.* Mia's eyes wandered toward the far bed, where she expected to see another injured cleric.

When she saw who was in the far bed, it almost brought her to her knees. She didn't know whether to laugh or cry or scream. She opted to scream.

"Father!" The leg shackles clanged loudly as she stumbled into the room.

"Mia," a muffled voice called from the far bed, "is that you child?"

"It's me," she said.

As she rushed forward, everything else in the room faded away. She grasped Father's hand. Even given her own decrepit state, she was appalled at how much he had wasted away.

"Dominus," Father said, his voice thin and small, "can you and the others leave us?"

"She is a prisoner," said Brother Valentine. "She is not to be left unattended."

"I hardly think she'll get far in those leg shackles," the Dominus replied.

Mia's eyes didn't leave Father, but she heard the others retreat from the room, closing the door with a thunk. Father's eyes were unfocused and meandered toward the ceiling. He wasn't making eye contact with her.

"Mia," he said. "I shall not survive long now. We must talk."

"Don't say that. You're still hanging in here."

Her words were downright lies. He was gaunt from head to toe. Every inch of his strong, dark frame was shriveled and ashen, with bones protruding like twigs from a bundle of sticks. His once-thick black hair had grown gray, lank, and thin, splayed across the hospice pillow as if making to crawl away from the horror of his scalp.

"They told me you were dead," she said, tears welling up in her eyes.

"Who told you that?" he asked, his eyes narrowing. They remained staring upward.

"Brother SainClair."

"Ah," he said, as if those words explained it all. "Well, he exaggerated my departure. If I recall, he's prone to hyperbole."

"Really?" Mia asked. "You know Brother SainClair?"

"Yes, my dear. There's much we need to discuss, and I haven't much time left. Now, now," he said, and patted her hand weakly. "There's no need for tears."

"Father," Mia said, "if there was ever a time for tears, it's now. I've made a complete muck of everything, and it was all for naught. My actions have changed nothing. You're still ill, and I'm a prisoner here."

He gently grasped her hand and gave it the barest squeeze. "Mia, I didn't send you here in exchange for a cure. We both know the purple spores are fatal. In the letter I wrote Dominus Nikola, I instructed him to tell you that, but it was always the intention that you were to serve within the Order."

"Are you delirious, Father?" she asked.

"I suppose it was irresponsible of me, knowing you were destined for this place from the start. My delay in sending you here was my one act of rebellion against the plan that I was to carry out, the plan your mother made. She wanted you here, but your grandparents would never have agreed."

"This makes no sense."

"I promised your mother that, if anything happened to her, I'd make sure you were sent here to serve. It was the last wish she asked of me, and I couldn't go against her on that."

"Why would Mother have wanted me to become a cleric of the Order?"

Every additional sentence from Father's mouth added to her confusion rather than alleviate it. Mia looked into the eyes gazing upward toward the ceiling. They watered slightly, as if he were opening a box inside himself that he had closed a long time ago, a box he'd thought he had lost the key to open. But open it he did, and what he told her then changed her life forever.

"I'm not your father," he said.

Mia's body tensed. They had their differences, physically and otherwise, but shock ripped through her muscles at the statement. It was simultaneously impossible and entirely obvious. *Then who are you?* her mind screamed, even as she sat inert with surprise.

"I'm a childhood friend of your mother's. We came up together in the Northlands. My father was a servant in your mother's household. Unconcerned with—and largely unaware of—the social boundaries between us, your mother, her brother, and I were constant companions. There was nothing I wouldn't do for her."

His hazy eyes softened as he described how he and Mia's mother had played and built forts under the cold forest and stolen furs from the floors to blanket their interior. Words tumbled forth from his strained voice, as if a tidal wave of memories were breaking free from a dam somewhere deep inside his heart. She wanted to ask who her parents were, but she didn't want to interrupt him. She was worried if he stopped talking, he would never start again.

"As a young woman, your mother joined the Order, was expected to by her family. There she met your father, and they fell in love. They hadn't been together long when Willowslip fell into civil unrest. You know this story," Father said, his voice growing hoarser.

"Father, you should drink something," Mia said, and urged him to sip some water from a nearby gourd. He took a few sips but then, losing patience, waved the gourd away.

"As the political turmoil grew, the internal debate among those in the Order escalated as well. Eventually certain clerics—your mother and father included—decided they couldn't sit idly by as Willowslip devolved into chaos. They elected to leave the Order to enter a resistance faction. By this time you had been born, their only child. Not wanting to involve you in the dangers of the war, they sent you to live with your mother's parents while they fought with the resistance. They visited the Northlands when they could, but the civil war in Willowslip intensified. Your parents died in an ambush of their camp. It was a small mercy, because had they lived, they might have been tortured before they were hanged for treason.

"The last time your mother visited her family estate, she came to my cottage and said that if anything should happen to her, I was to ensure that when the time was right, you would be sent to the Order." A pained expression crossed his face as he shook his head slowly. "Even after she was thrust from the Order and her family was divided over the conflict, she still wanted her daughter to take up the family mantle. Your grandparents were firmly against the idea. The family line was dwindling, and you're the only grandchild. After your mother's death, they decided it was time to break ties with the Order."

Mia sat dumbfounded at this information. The words flowed out of Father. It was as if he were rushing to say everything he could before the spores took him from her. She couldn't process all this.

"So to keep the promise I made your mother, I had to leave the Northlands and take you with me. You were still a small babe when we left your family estate. It ended up being an act that saved your life. The entire estate was burned to the ground not long after our departure, and your grandparents were lost in the blaze. Everyone assumed you perished as well. As I was the current groundskeeper, the neighbors of the SainClair estate blamed me for the fire and held me responsible for your death. I didn't burn your family's home, but that fact didn't change much for me. I already had stolen you.

"So we traveled around at first, not staying too long in any one place. But eventually we made a home in Hackberry. I admit I was very satisfied with the life we had built for ourselves. I was loath to send you here. Some of it was perhaps fear that I would be imprisoned for my crime of kidnapping and likely for the murder of your family. That wasn't the only reason, though. Over the cycles, I've grown to love you like the daughter you've been to me. Some days I told myself it didn't matter whether you joined the Order." Father's voice cracked, and tears rolled from his unfocused eyes.

Mia squeezed his frail hand tightly and buried her face in his chest.

"When the spores came, it was a reminder to me that I had forsaken my promise. It was time that I had fulfilled my vow to your mother."

Mia shook her head against his chest. She still held Father's hand, but her fingers were stiff and cold, as if the blood had drained from them and pooled in her chest to keep her lungs pumping and heart beating.

Father coughed, a hacking noise that grated her spine raw, and his body shook with the force. She brought the gourd of water back to his lips and helped him sip from it.

Through all this, she still was in shock from all he had told her. Her father wasn't her father. Her family wasn't her family. Who was she then? When Father's coughing finally subsided, his breathing had grown even shallower. She continued to hold his hand but was very confused. This man she had clung to never was her father. The idea of family had driven her every action as long as she could remember, and it was a farce. At the same time, it wasn't a farce. With every labored breath from him, she was reminded of the times Father had smiled at her, hugged her when she was upset, or had been strict with her when she misbehaved. He was a father to her more than any family she may have out there.

"Father," she said. His eyes were closed, sweat glistening on his forehead from his exertion. She feared his telling the story had taken all his remaining energy. His breathing was growing even slower and more ragged. "Father," she repeated, "I don't care if you aren't my birth father. You're the only father I know. You're the only family I care about." She lowered her cheek back to his chest as tears welled up once again in her eyes. The rattling sound in his chest made them fall faster. His hand moved weakly to rest against her head, his thumb rubbing her jaw.

"My dear, dear child," he said, his voice but a hoarse whisper. "I have to leave you now, but you still have your uncle. He's still here at the Order. They're your family now. You've made some terrible mistakes but nothing that cannot be forgiven. You must work to be forgiven, my dear girl."

A small sobbing noise escaped Mia's throat. She hiccupped, and the caressing thumb fell away from her face.

"Who is my uncle?" she asked softly. Father no longer was conscious, and his chest barely moved under her head. "Father? Who were my parents?" But he never opened his eyes again.

28 THE ORPHAN L.C. 10152

M IA'S MARCH BACK TO HER CELL was a
blur. She was consumed with grief for Father
and anger at Dominus Nikola. How long had they been
hiding Father here right under her nose? Was it
weeks? Moons even? Had he wasted away alone when
she could have been with him? She couldn't stop the
hot tears from streaming down her face, but she
stoically avoided looking at or talking to any of the
clerics. Dominus Nikola uttered some words to her as
she was pulled away from Father's lifeless body, but
they slipped past her mind like a forgotten dream. She

was beyond caring about what he might have to say, her limbs numb and mind broken.

Brothers Valentine and Borus dragged her back through the winding corridors. She kept her face down and focused on her blurry, boot-covered feet. She noted upon reentering the cell that a bunk mattress and dingy blanket had been dumped on the floor. Her throat tightened, and she restrained a cough. After the others were finally gone, anger boiled up inside her and she kicked the mattress repeatedly, until her chest was heaving from the exertion. Finally, she collapsed on it, still furious but simultaneously grateful for something to cushion her sore body, even if its presence gave her a foreboding sense of finality. Father was gone, and this cell was her home now.

MIA AWOKE TO THE SOUND OF FOOTSTEPS approaching the cell door. *Not again. I can't take any more right now.* She was curled up on the pallet, her eyes crusted with tears and sleep, her mouth gummy. Timepieces were suddenly a luxury. She never knew what time it was anymore. Maybe someone was bringing food. Voices murmured on the other side of the door.

"Not food then," she grumbled under her breath. She rolled over so she faced the wall and stayed curled in a ball, pretending to be asleep. The bolt to the door shifted with a clink, and the door opened. She kept her eyes closed and continued to feign sleep. Whoever entered the cell was undeterred. She heard the scrape of a chair being set in the cell, and then Brother Cornelius's voice said, "Thank you, Valentine. You can leave us now."

"Are you sure that's wise?" Brother Valentine's gruff voice replied.

"Oh, completely, my dear boy," Cornelius said, and chuckled softly. Brother Valentine grunted, and then his heavy footsteps retreated through the door. He bolted it from the other side.

Only Brother Cornelius could pull off calling a cleric over five and fifty a boy, Mia thought. She wrestled with her desire to talk to Brother Cornelius, the rage she still felt toward the clerics for hiding her father from her, and the shame of her betrayal to the good brother. In her plotting, she often had felt a niggle of guilt that she was leaving Brother Cornelius, that she was taking advantage of his kindness and confidence in her. She had managed to convince herself that she never would have to face him again. The longer she lay there, pretending to be asleep, the deeper the silence grew.

"I know you're awake," he finally said.

The sound made her body twitch in surprise.

"You might as well turn around and face me. Cowardice isn't becoming to any of us, I'm afraid," he said.

Mia's resolve melted away at his words. His voice was the soft, kind voice she remembered, but his tone was distant, as if she were some casual acquaintance he'd once met. His tone shamed her more than the words ever could. She sat up on the pallet and shifted so her back was against the stone wall, but she couldn't bring herself to meet Brother Cornelius's eyes. There was a rustle and then a thunk as a cake landed on the stone floor in front of her. She suppressed a smile despite herself and reached forward to grab it. The impact of it hitting the floor already had started the heating process. She tucked it under her feet.

"Thank you," she said softly.

Brother Cornelius sighed deeply, and his chair creaked as he shifted in it. If she looked over, she suspected she would see him tapping the whiskers on his chin, as he always did when he was thinking hard. She didn't look over, though. She stared at her hands as they picked at a thread on the worn blanket that covered her knees.

"Yes, well, this is all very disappointing," he started. "Very disappointing indeed."

Mia nodded but didn't say a word. Her throat was heavy, and she didn't trust herself to speak without croaking.

"We all put an awful lot of trust in you," he said. "I especially did. Brother SainClair said you weren't to be trusted, but no one paid much heed to that. You went ahead and proved him right, though." His gentle voice carried a sturdy, grim edge.

Mia bowed her head lower. Nothing she could say could adequately explain her actions. She knew that. Yet the Order had played her for a fool as well. They had pled ignorance to Father's condition, and as a result, his final days had been squandered.

"When you activated Compendium, we were all interested to see how you would use it. We had high hopes for you, high indeed. I personally hoped you'd figure out some interesting new engineering techniques useful in the library. You can imagine our dismay when we learned you planned to use it to break into the Catacombs."

Mia's stomach churned. "It was all a test?" she asked, her curiosity outweighing her shame and anger.

"Oh, heavens no," Brother Cornelius said. "It was your birthright, so how could it be a test? It was merely a subject of interest and speculation followed by great and bitter disappointment."

"If Compendium is my birthright, why has the Order confiscated it?" she asked after some thought.

"My child," Brother Cornelius said, "it's still your birthright, but you've committed a crime and a serious one. Repairs are still underway on the Crater Grove. The damage was extensive. Parts of the Compound are still without power. Brother SainClair only today woke from his unconscious state. These are very much real issues, but frankly they pale in comparison to the fact that you allowed the Shillelagh to fall into the hands of the Druids."

Mia flinched as the words rolled over her. "The Druids?" she said, her voice hollow. "What do you mean? Taryn took the Shillelagh."

"Indeed she did," Cornelius said. He frowned deeply. "You didn't say that she went to Rosewater, though."

"So?" asked Mia. "I assumed Rosewater was a place she'd been wanting to visit."

Brother Cornelius shook his head and rubbed his neck. "My child, Rosewater is the head Druid."

"What?" Mia said, at first uncomprehending. She sprang from the mattress and walked over to the other side of the cell, shuffling her feet along the floor until she found what she was looking for. It lay in the dust in the far corner. She picked up the smooth stone, walked back to Brother Cornelius, and handed it to him. "Taryn tossed this to me right as she departed. She said it would explain everything. I thought she was just mocking me."

Brother Cornelius turned the stone over in his hand. "'Tis the mark of the Druids," he said, frowning. "When Brother SainClair woke today, he told us he heard Ms. Windbough shout to be taken to Rosewater. We hoped it was a mistake, but alas there was no mistake." His fist tightened over the stone.

"Do you understand how serious this is?" he continued. "This goes well beyond your betrayal, which was a betrayal of not just me and those others who put their trust in you, but of your own family and all our forebears who sacrificed themselves to the service of the Order. All of Lumin may suffer because of this now."

"What would the Druids want with the Shillelagh?" Mia asked softly.

"That's certainly something we've all been giving a lot of thought. Ms. Windbough's bunk has been thoroughly searched. She was researching the Great Fall quite extensively. We think she may be researching how to reenter the Core. What she left behind when she departed is mostly nonsensical."

"The Core?" Mia asked. "She wants to enter the center of the planet?"

"The Core isn't just the center of Lumin," Brother Cornelius explained, "although it's that too. It was the meeting place of the Central Counsel, a chamber deep in the earth among the roots of the Central Grove. Since the Great Fall, no one has been able to access it. Entry to the Core has been lost to time. At least, that's what the Order has led the Druids and others to believe. We knew the Shillelagh was capable of taking us there."

"Have you ever been there?" Mia asked. Her curiosity was growing stronger by the moment, and she was having trouble maintaining her dour disposition.

"Oh, goodness no!" Brother Cornelius exclaimed. "No one in the Order has."

"Well, why not?"

"The Shillelagh gets you to the entrance to the Core, but you can't get in without the key."

"Who has the key?"

"We don't know," said Brother Cornelius. We don't even know what the key is. Our knowledge was greatly diminished after the Great Fall, and the Order has been researching these topics for hundreds of cycles, well past the time when we should have resolved these matters." Uncharacteristic frustration crossed his face. "There's a hole in our records, a large one. It's as if history doesn't want itself revealed."

"It would appear the Druids also are researching how to get to the Core," said Mia.

"Aye, they are. We can only hope they don't already have the key."

"Do you think they mean to go interfere with the Core?"

"Oh, they will eventually, but we have no way of knowing when or how."

"I can't believe Taryn spent more than two cycles here just to spy," she said.

"She has as much faith in her calling as I have in mine," Brother Cornelius said.

"Brother?" she asked. "Why did you tell me all this? I betrayed the Order for selfish reasons, almost killed a brother, and damaged the Compound."

"Oh, believe me, I haven't told you everything," Cornelius said grimly. There was no humor in his eyes. "The Order isn't happy with you right now, hence this," he added, gesturing to the cell walls. "This can't go on forever, though. You must make amends to the clerics. The Order is going to need you."

Mia pursed her lips and gritted her teeth. "Well, how do I do that?" she asked. "Nothing can change my betrayal."

"You can start by apologizing!" Brother Cornelius snapped.

She never had heard him raise his voice before. She looked at him for a moment, her eyes wide.

"I'm sorry," she said finally, her eyes lowered and head bowed.

"It's not me you have to convince," he said with a sigh, "and that wasn't very convincing to me either. After you apologize properly, you'll have to earn back Nikola's trust."

"Earn back the Dominus's trust?"

"You'll have to retrieve the Shillelagh," he said finally, his voice low and eyes piercing. His face held a slight gray cast, and black smudges rested comfortably under his eyes. "Let's hope it isn't too late."

"How am I supposed to do that?" she asked, incredulous. "You just got done telling me it was with the Druids now! Believe me, I'll not be able to waltz in there the way Taryn waltzed into the Order."

Brother Cornelius gave her an uncharacteristically dark look at that dig, pausing momentarily, as if deciding something. Maybe she had gone too far.

"Well, perhaps this will give you some ideas," he said finally. He leaned forward in his chair and pulled a small volume from his sash.

Mia's heartbeat quickened. It was Compendium.

29 THE LOCKET L.C. 10152

MIA'S MIND WAS STILL REELING from her conversation with Brother Cornelius. Compendium was safely tucked between the mattress and the wall of the cell. There it would stay until she could reason through everything he had revealed. She lay on her pallet, trying to make sense of it all in her head.

She'd barely mourned Father. She was too numb from the shock of recent blows to weep for him now. Her own identity was in a shambles. She was not a Jayne. She was not an acolyte. Father was the family of her heart, but who was the family of her blood?

And if they were truly all gone, save an uncle, was she substituting one loneliness for another? Father said the Order was her family now. She could brook no argument that there weren't some here that she felt immense affection for, especially Brother Cornelius. And her feelings for Cedar still remained, even though he had chosen his calling over their friendship. Even as she let the thoughts of those she cared for in the Order fill her, she remembered her home in Hackberry, her forest, and her Hamish.

Hamish! She panicked then. Father hadn't mentioned Hamish, and she hadn't thought to ask after him. *Oh, he must be safe. He must be.* A thrum ran through Mia's chest at the thought of poor, furry Hamish waiting patiently for them to come, waiting and waiting for something that never would happen. She couldn't bear the thought of him starving to death, waiting. Father wouldn't let anything bad come to him. *He probably left Hamish with Old Parniff. I'm sure he's happily chasing lizards and glow bugs through the forest this very moment.* She closed her eyes and pictured Hamish tailing along after Old Parniff as she hiked through the forest. His tail wagged as he stopped here and there to sniff a particularly pungent fungus or bit of detritus. Old Parniff shouted at him to keep up, and he bolted after her and nipped at her walking stick. The images calmed Mia, and her thoughts turned once again to her conversations with Father and Brother Cornelius.

Brother Cornelius said Compendium was her birthright. That hardly explained much at all, however, and he had provided no additional details. Even still, to Brother Cornelius, it was more important to consider the Shillelagh and how to retrieve it from the Druids. *I have to make that my priority as well. I can't sit here endlessly brooding.* Both Brother Cornelius and Father were right. She had to make amends; she had to find a way to apologize. She had been so selfish. She had fancied herself a prisoner here, a victim. And now that she really was a prisoner—and rightly, based on her actions—how could she think that before?

She had made a series of choices, and those choices had led her here, to this dungeon. It was no one's fault but her own. She couldn't blame Father for sending her here; she in fact had chosen to come. She couldn't blame Dominus Nikola for her choice; it was hers. She couldn't blame Brother SainClair for his rage; she had chosen to be here but hadn't accepted it fully. He had every right to be a little upset with her. Granted, he was much more than a little upset. She couldn't blame Taryn. Mia was the one who had chosen to steal the Shillelagh. She couldn't blame Cedar. She had chosen to involve him in her plotting. She stared up at the ceiling, her head swimming. Thought after thought tumbled around her mind in a jumble.

Her own actions had led her here. Her excuse was that she needed to know whether Father was really dead. But she was lying to herself. *I did it for me. I did it because I was afraid I was losing my identity here, and in the process of running from my fear, I destroyed my identity. No one took my honor from me but me.* She cleared her throat, although there was no one to talk to, and rolled onto her side facing the wall. She had trusted Taryn and Cedar, but she had trusted them for the wrong reasons, for selfish reasons. And by doing so, she had betrayed the trust placed in her by Father, Brother Cornelius, and others of the Order. The longer she thought, the more discouraged she became. Her actions and her motives for those actions stood in stark relief to the reality that had built itself up in her mind. Each decision played out over and over, and she was forced to acknowledge that she deserved everything that had come to her and more.

Mia remained lost in her thoughts until footsteps sounded on the stone floor outside her cell. *For a pariah, I sure have a lot of visitors all of a sudden.* This time she didn't bother trying to pretend that she was asleep. The door opened, and the familiar wooden chair was placed inside the cell. She sat up on the pallet and swung her back toward the cell wall, knees up. A tall, thin figure entered through the doorway and shut the door behind him. The bolt slid into place.

The muscles in her neck and shoulders tensed—it was Cedar. She cleared her throat and sat looking at him. He bypassed the wooden chair and walked back and forth a bit. His eyes wandered here and there. He looked nervous. Perhaps they had sent him to inform her that Brother Cornelius had been sanctioned for giving her Compendium and spilling secrets of the Order and that she was to be exiled or something. His pacing wasn't at all calming, and she found herself growing even tenser by the moment.

"Well, out with it," Mia finally said, the exasperation in her voice harsh. Her outburst was out of place, but she realized just then that she was still angry at Cedar. Her logical mind knew she had no right to be angry. Cedar had just been acting in the way he believed was right. And objectively he had been right. But she still couldn't help feeling hurt and betrayed. Whether or not it had been a good idea, she had trusted Cedar with her secrets, and now she felt angry and embarrassed.

He stopped and turned to face her. She looked into the dark eyes made darker by the dim light of the cell. "I just wanted to say I'm sorry," he said.

Shock coursed through Mia's body like an electric jolt. Her anger deflated as quickly as a punctured waterskin. She sighed softly and patted the lumpy spot next to her on the pallet, inviting him to sit. After a flicker of hesitation crossed his face, he approached and settled himself next to her, his cleric's robes bunching around him. Where his tin pin used to sit was a shiny gold one.

"I see they've made you a full cleric," Mia said carefully. "They must have valued your information."

"It's not like that," Cedar said, his eyes clouding. "Listen, I had to say something. The artifacts in safekeeping of the Order are special and rare and are to be guarded and protected."

"Did you think I was a Druid?" Mia asked, looking at him closely. His expression remained stoic as he slowly shook his head.

"No. Honestly I didn't believe either of you were Druids," he said, pursing his lips as he considered that statement. "But when I saw that rose pin on Taryn's cloak, I panicked. It was a rose, but it wasn't—"

"This?" Mia asked, and held out the stone.

He took it from her and turned it over, his mouth tensing. "Yes, this." His eyes blazed. "Like I said, I had to say something. It was too much of a coincidence."

"Did you know who I am then? That my father wasn't my father? That I have an uncle here?"

Cedar shook his head again. "The clerics never discussed any of that with me. They wanted me to keep an eye on you, but they never said why or what they were looking for. All I know about your family is what you've told me."

Mia sighed and yawned and leaned farther back against the rough stone of the wall. "I don't suppose they've decided what they're going to do with me," she said, her question awkward to her own ears. She didn't mention that Brother Cornelius had returned Compendium to her. Perhaps she didn't entirely trust Cedar again, even though he had apologized.

"It's been a subject of some argument. There isn't yet a consensus among the clerics."

"Brother Cornelius told me I'll have to retrieve the Shillelagh," Mia replied.

"Aye, there are those who want to send you on that mission, and others say you'll just run away if we give you the opportunity. There's been a breach of trust within our ranks. Many of those previously on your side have reconsidered their positions." He looked at her pointedly.

Mia bit the inside of her lip and wrinkled her nose. She had no one to blame for such feelings but herself. She had been on the giving end of betrayal as well as the receiving end.

"I'm not sure how I can apologize and earn back the clerics' trust," Mia said. "Perhaps we can call it even since they kept my father here while he wasted away and didn't bother to tell me." Anger flashed in her eyes.

Cedar ignored her sarcasm. "Just do what I did," he said. "Say you're sorry."

"I am sorry. I was callous and thoughtless."

"Well, tell that to the clerics then."

She turned her body toward him. "I'm telling that to you," she replied. "I'm apologizing to you. I put you in an untenable position for months while I plotted to betray the Order. For that, I'm truly sorry. My selfish desire to find my father convinced me that it was acceptable to betray everyone here and make you complicit in such betrayal." When she reached out and placed a hand over his, it flinched slightly. Cedar's eyes stared deeply into hers, and she blushed. She tried to pull her hand back, but he turned his hand palm up and grasped hers as it attempted to snake away.

"When we said good-bye before, I told you I hoped you'd find what you were looking for."

"I recall that," Mia said. "I guess I thought I was looking for a way home and to the security of my old life, but now it turns out my family wasn't my family—not really anyway—and I wouldn't have had safety or security or even my father if I'd gone back.

And now that he's dead, all I have is an uncle I don't even know."

"Perhaps," Cedar said gently, placing an object in her hand, "this will give you some answers."

She looked down. In her hand was her mother's locket.

"Where did you get this?" she asked.

"You were unconscious for a number of days."

Mia nodded.

"Well, given your deep state of coma, you originally were being looked after in the medical center, and I visited you there as soon as I heard the situation. You still had the locket at the time, so I snuck it off your neck before the clerics could confiscate it with the rest of your belongings."

"But why?" she asked.

"Take another look."

Mia examined the locket. It looked like it always did until she got to the tip of the egg at the bottom, where the clasp was. The familiar thin line of fused metal was gone.

"You fixed it?" she asked, looking over at him. Cedar was still staring at her face, his eyes and mouth serious. Then he smiled and excitedly told her about his experiments.

"Yes, Brother Cornelius has been developing a new gourd. This gourd, instead of warming, cools. He's been aiming to use the gourd to chill foods and other items—such as water—just enough to be enjoyed, but by luck, he had a batch that produced exceptionally cold temperatures. I used the cold temperatures of his rogue gourds to freeze off the fused metal!"

"Thank you. That's amazing," Mia said, examining the end. "So how does it open?"

"I figured out that too," he said.

His hands brushed against hers as he fumbled to position the locket so she could see. He turned the ornamental panel at the top that connected it to its chain. Mia always had thought it merely served as a connector for the chain and to give the design a little flair, but it functioned like the knob of a door. Turning the head caused the egg to split open. What looked like a smooth egg on the outside with discreet etchings opened up to look like leaves on the inside. Nestled inside the leaves was a three-dimensional depiction of a lotus flower, and emerging from the lotus flower was a large horned owl.

"It's the same sigil that's on Compendium," Mia said, peering carefully at the owl from every direction. "It's gorgeous."

"Indeed," Cedar said, "the work is quite detailed. I have no idea how old it is, but I still hold to my original opinion that it looks to be from before the Great Fall."

"Well, that makes sense, since Compendium is pre-Great Fall as well. I guess the real question is how my mother came by it and why it was fused closed in the first place."

"Well, I suspect you have family ties to whoever created both the locket and Compendium," Cedar said. "I noticed something else. If you look inside, you'll see the words *Clavis Aurea* inscribed around the base of the flower. That's usually used to indicate that an object has some ability to translate text or solve some sort of mystery. Although I really have no idea what's intended by that phrase here." His dark eyes sparkled as he continued. "Also, there's one more thing I noted. The metal of your locket doesn't seem to tarnish, but the metal used to fuse it did, and it looks like it was only maybe twenty or so cycles old, so it was fused fairly recently."

"That's so odd," Mia said, almost speaking to herself. "Perhaps Father fused it before he gave it to me to keep me from opening it. He did hide me from my true family." Her heart beat quickly, and she couldn't catch her breath. *Father, why didn't you tell me sooner? I would have loved you anyway.* Her mouth turned downward in a frown. "He passed before I could get any information from him about my blood family. All I know is that I have an uncle here in the Order."

"Do you have any idea who it could be?" Cedar asked.

"None. If Brother Cornelius weren't so advanced in age, I'd say perhaps him, but I know he can't be my uncle."

"If you still had Compendium, you could ask it perhaps," he said, shrugging a shoulder.

Mia still wasn't ready to reveal that Brother Cornelius had returned the book to her. "Perhaps," she said, "although there are limits on what I can ask it. Certain information is access restricted."

She turned the locket around in her hand. The owl shimmered in the dim light of the cell. It was so detailed in craftsmanship that it almost looked as if it could flap its unfurling wings and take flight around the dank room like a small golden insect. The outside of the locket held a little forest at the open edges that had been parted when the locket opened. The jaggy ruffled edges of what made up the open leaves contained a very discreet pattern on the outside. Mia turned the knob at the top, and the leaves slid quickly back into place, forming a perfect, solid egg.

"Ouch," she yelped. She had caught the index finger of her right hand in the closing edge of the locket. The precise edges sliced her finger, and a droplet of blood formed on the tip. "It bit me," she said, wincing with pain.

"Let me see," Cedar said, his face darkened and eyes concerned. He took hold of her hand and turned it over. He pulled a scrap of cloth from his robes and blotted the blood away. "That's a pretty nice slice. Your clumsiness never ceases to amaze me." He grinned at her and peered closer at the wound. "Well, you got yourself good, so it may take a bit for it to stop bleeding, but I don't think it needs to be sewn."

"Well, that's a relief, Doctor," Mia said, rolling her eyes.

Cedar laughed and wrapped the piece of cloth around her finger, securing it with a knot.

"Just be careful, all right?" he said. He threaded his fingers into hers and pulled her toward him to gently kiss her lips. Her stomach churned slowly, as if a swarm of butterflies or glow bugs were trying to wiggle out, but she smiled against his lips.

AFTER CEDAR LEFT, Mia paced a bit around her cell to work off the nervous energy threatening to consume her. Between Brother Cornelius's visit and Cedar's, she had much to consider. She waited until after her next meal was served before pulling out Compendium. She rubbed her fingers over the pebbled leather cover before opening the book. She flipped to the title page, which read the familiar title, *An Exhaustive Genealogy of the Families of the Realm.*

"Compendium," she said, "how come you never tell me about yourself?"

The ink shifted in a familiar fashion.

What would you like to know? Compendium typed.

"Do you know who I am?" she asked.

You have identified yourself to me as Mia Jayne.

"What is the symbol on your cover?"

It is an owl emerging from a lotus flower, Compendium typed.

"I know that," she said, exasperated.

Then why did you ask?

"Snarky book," she muttered, slamming it closed. "Blast it!"

The edge of a page of Compendium slid under the makeshift bandage that wrapped the finger of her right hand. The book fell open in her lap, momentarily forgotten. Mia's eyes watered as her finger stung bitterly. She pulled the loosened fabric away, and a single drop of blood oozed out of the slice in her finger and fell onto Compendium. It landed in a bright scarlet dollop on the aged ivory of the open page. She hastily blotted at it with the bit of cloth, but the cloth was already bloody and exacerbated the mess. She scavenged for another piece of cloth, but by the time she turned back, the blood spot had vanished.

"What the—" she started to say.

Beta Level activation coding complete.

Of course. She originally had activated Compendium by sneezing on it. Brother Cornelius had said it was her birthright, but she didn't think he had meant it so literally.

"Compendium," she asked. "Are there any other levels?"

Affirmative, wrote Compendium.

"What could you possibly want from me next, a tooth?"

A tooth will not activate Zeta Level, scrawled Compendium.

"Good to know," said Mia sarcastically. "What's the difference between Alpha Level and Beta Level activation?"

"Direct link established," said a calm voice directly in her ear. She yelled in surprise and dropped the book.

"Who's there?" she asked. She sprang to her feet and looked around.

"Do not be alarmed. Our direct link has been established," repeated the smooth voice. "Auditory communication is now possible."

"Are you telling me the voice I hear is Compendium?" Mia asked.

"Affirmative," said the voice. "Auditory interface is available for Beta Level access."

She covered hers ears and said, "This is very unsettling." She paced around the room with her hands plastered over her ears.

"Auditory communication is more efficient and convenient for most tasks. Please explain what you mean by 'unsettling.'"

Even with her footsteps echoing through the chamber, Compendium's voice was clear as a pond on a sunny day.

"Never mind," Mia said, taking her hands from her ears. It didn't seem to make a difference anyway. "So now you can talk directly to me. That's lovely. Can everyone hear our conversation?"

"Negative," said Compendium.

Well, that's a relief, she thought. It was short-lived, however.

"Others hear only you speaking."

"Oh, excellent. So for all intents and purposes, I'll sound like I've descended into madness. That'll convince the clerics to free me, certainly. What else does Beta Level offer?" Mia asked, almost afraid to know.

"The wireless interface also has been activated," said the voice. It was so calm and neutral that it was hard to discern a gender. Mia always had imagined that residing inside Compendium was a tiny, snarky old man.

"Voice modulation complete," said the calm voice of an old man in her ear.

"You can read my mind?" she shouted. "Could you do that all along?"

"I can access your thought patterns now that you have completed Beta Level activation. I could not always do so."

"Mind asking permission first?" she said out loud, although clearly that wasn't necessary.

"Why?" asked Compendium in her ear. "That would be most inefficient. Additionally now you don't have to walk around sounding mad, and you're free to utilize me while using both hands for other tasks."

Mia realized she was pacing around while the book was still on the mattress. *How far away can I be and still establish communication?*

"I am capable of unlimited range," said the old man in her head.

All right, all right. Change your voice back, please.

"As you wish," said Compendium in its original neutral voice. The tone was emotionless yet comfortingly calm.

Really, though, you do seem snarkier in writing.

"I apologize," said the voice in her ear.

Now that I've activated Beta Level access, can you tell me anything additional about my family?

"What would you like to know?" Compendium replied.

She took a deep breath and wrung her hands in her tunic. *What is my full name?*

"Mia Jayne SainClair," said the voice.

"What?" she exclaimed out loud. She felt the blood drain from her head and her limbs grow shaky. She stumbled over to the mattress and sat down hard before her knees buckled. The breath left her lungs with a whoosh, and she had trouble regaining it. When she finally was able to speak again, she said, "SainClair? That can't be right." She picked up Compendium. "Show me my family tree."

The book presented a vaguely familiar diagram. It was from the exhaustive list of lineages she recalled. She had looked up Brother SainClair the night she had activated Compendium. There was his family tree again. She swallowed hard when her eyes found the sigil of the owl and the lotus flower near the top of the page. And it came rushing back to her. This was the first place she had seen that design. *How could I be so thick? And his sister was named Jayne.* "Compendium, was Jayne SainClair my mother?" she asked, already knowing the answer.

"Affirmative," said Compendium in her ear.

Compendium inked in the name Claude next to Jayne and drew a line below to Mia Jayne. That made her uncle Thaddeus SainClair. She felt as if she'd been punched in the gut.

Pretender, rasped his raw, hate-filled voice in her head. *You're not my niece. You're an impostor. You dishonor my sister's memory with your presence.*

His intense hatred for her made sense now. He thought his niece was dead and she was an impostor. *Father should have warned him,* she thought, *or at least warned me.*

30   GREAT HALL   L.C. 10152

A FTER HER DELUGE OF VISITORS, Mia was largely left to her own devices. At first she counted the days by scratching marks into the stone wall but quickly shifted to asking Compendium the date and time and how long it had been since she'd last asked. Time passed painfully slowly. Minutes felt like hours and hours like days. She tried to keep it in perspective, but too much time to think and not enough physical activity muddled her mind. She paced and exercised, trying to strengthen her increasingly frail body. She had the occasional visitor, usually after the midday meal, and spent time exploring

Compendium further, practicing communicating with it using her mind and testing the limits of its capabilities.

It wasn't able to, for instance, unlatch the bolt on the other side of the door, as it was a purely mechanical lock with no current. It could, however, access the gourds on the vines and snuff them by redirecting the current. It also could light them. At first these explorations and challenges occupied her mind and body, but she grew increasingly restless and uneasy.

"You have to retrieve the Shillelagh," Brother Cornelius had instructed her. "You have to make amends."

But the clerics had presented her with an opportunity to do neither. While she sat there rotting, the Druids had the Shillelagh, and Mia hesitated to think what use they were making of it.

After a full week of near solitude, her routine was finally interrupted. Brother Borus came to her cell and poked his head in. His voice held little of the earlier gruff anger, and she was relieved. "Yer to present yerself before an assembly of the clerics in the main hall," he said. "But first the Dominus has suggested ye might do with a bath an' change of clothes. That right there might have to be burned frankly." He poked a finger at her tropics garb, which had gone from dingy to filthy in recent weeks.

"But it's my only clothing left from home," she said sadly.

"Och," he scoffed. "Is that yer concern then?" He waved his hands flippantly in her direction. "Yer things have all been brought from Hackberry. Is that what ye call it?"

Mia nodded, surprised. All her belongings had been transported to the Order? She pictured her empty hearthtree, and a quiet sorrow settled over her. Her life with Father no longer had any physical representation. She likely never would see Old Parniff and the others of Hackberry again.

"What about Hamish?" she asked, suddenly thinking of her poor pup.

"Eh?" he grunted, looking at her funny.

"Hamish," she repeated, "my dog."

"Oh, that mangy bucket of fur an' teeth?" he said, scowling deeply. "That mutt of yers is here too. Right foul beast, 'tis," he said, holding up a muslin-wrapped hand. "That creature has as much sense as ye, I reckon, biting the hand 'at cooks its supper. I've a mind to cook it fer supper if it don't watch its step, ye hear?"

Mia suppressed a smile at Brother Borus's words. *Hamish is alive!* "I apologize, Brother Borus," she said, covering her mirth with contrition. "He really is terribly good. He is, I'm sure, feeling scared and alone just now."

"Aye," he replied gruffly and nodded. "Well, then, let's be off. I'll take ye to the sisters to sort ye out then and be back to see ye to the assembly."

"No shackles?" she asked.

"Dinna even try me, missy," he said, directing her through the door. She hesitated for a moment, throwing a glance back at the pallet where Compendium was hidden among the folds of the blanket.

"Can I take the blanket?" she asked. "It's rather cold in these clothes."

Brother Borus rolled his eyes at her. "Just grab the book if that's what yer about," he said, and turned toward the door. Her jaw slackened as she gaped at his retreating figure. Snapping to her senses, she quickly threw back the blanket and retrieved Compendium, stuffing it into the belt that secured her tunic, and followed Brother Borus out the door and down the hall.

"How did you know?" she asked when she caught up to the old brother. Despite his age, he moved with quick, resolute purpose. Mia had to take double steps to keep up.

"Oh, so ye thought no one noticed ye suddenly talking to yerself in there, missy? We ain't got lead in our ears, ye ken?"

She smiled. Well, she supposed it was an improvement over their assuming she was daft. Brother Borus escorted her to the laundry, where Sister Valencia was waiting with Iris, one of the other acolytes. Borus left Mia there and told Sister Valencia he would be back to collect her in exactly forty-five minutes.

"Well, then we'd best be quick," said Sister Valencia, giving Mia a once-over and wrinkling her nose. She picked up Mia's matted braid and held it out as if it were diseased. Perhaps it was. "This," she said, gesturing to the tangled lump in her hand, "is goin' ter take some time."

"Snap to it, ladies," Borus offered over his shoulder as he departed.

"All right, all right," Sister Valencia said. "Out er those rags. I see no point in even launderin' them. They'll go straight ter the solvent and be added ter the scrap pile. Hurry now. We have ter get ye inter some water and start workin' on that hair."

Mia reluctantly shrugged out of her clothing, stripping down to her smallclothes.

"Those too," Sister Valencia snapped. "*Especially* those. How unhygienic."

Even in the barracks, where changing was commonplace, Mia had managed to avoid this level of display with the others. Still, the temptation of the steaming tub of water was excellent motivation, and she soon was settling herself into the hot bath wearing nothing but her mother's locket. Every muscle in her body tensed then slowly melted with relaxation as the heat penetrated her skin and muscles, all the way to her bones.

"All right." Sister Valencia clucked. "Ye need ter dunk under now. We have ter soap up that hair and see if we can work out those tangles." Mia submerged herself under the hot water and raked her face with her fingers. She surfaced for a breath with a splash and sighed loudly, sputtering.

"I feel as if I haven't been clean for ages," Mia said. "'Tis glorious."

Iris giggled, but Sister Valencia frowned. "Now there, we donna have time fer shenanigans." She pulled Mia's braid from the bathwater, which was quickly growing murky. "Yer filth is truly impressive," she said. Her lips formed a severe slash on her plain face as she set upon the task of unbraiding and detangling Mia's hair while Mia scrubbed herself clean. In between yelps and squeals as the comb tore through the matted hair, Iris chatted.

"Where have you been, Mia?" she asked shyly.

"Ah, I assumed everyone knew what happened," Mia said, shooting a glance at Sister Valencia. She gave Mia a pointed look then returned to her task. "Well, I've been locked up in the dungeon."

"What?" said Iris, stammering. "You've been…"

"Yes," Mia said in response to Iris's trailing words. "I've been locked up in the dungeon. And now I have a feeling I'm on my way to plead my case to the clerics and beg their forgiveness."

Sister Valencia nodded curtly and continued raking the comb through her hair. "It may not be possible ter save all this hair," the sister said, a frown crossing her face. "How attached ter it are ye?"

Apart from it growing out of her head in a color that turned heads and embarrassed her, Mia'd never given it much thought. It grew, and she braided it to keep it out of the way. "It's just hair," she said. "It keeps growing."

"Blast it all! Yer shoulda said so from the get-go. We can just cut it off!"

Mia shrugged. "Do what you will, as long it's not in my face."

Iris's eyes grew round. "Are you certain?" She fingered her own brown curls. "I'd be devastated if someone lopped off my hair."

"Oy," Sister Valencia said with a scowl. "I'll not be taking an ax to her. 'Tis just a haircut. You, Iris, would do well ter give a ken ter what's important." She got up from where she knelt and left the room for a moment, returning with a pair of shiny shears. "These are fer sewing," she said. "They're nice and sharp, and I shall only take what's needed."

Mia sat as still as a garden statue in the tub of dark, cloudy water while Sister Valencia worked with her hair. The shears made a slicing sound, and scraps of tangled hair plopped down around her. The sister stopped every few snips and combed through various sections. She worked like that until the comb ran from Mia's scalp all the way down through her hair.

"There now," she said, wiping her brow. "That'll do. Given the ample quantity of hair ye trudged in here with, ye still have a bounty left. Plenty ter tie back. Mind you, 'tis not all the same length now. Dip down again. Time ter give it all a good wash and get you dressed. I suspect Brother Borus will be back any moment."

Mia dunked her head in the water one last time. Sister Valencia scrubbed her soapy hands across Mia's scalp with impressive determination, and when it was all finished, she had Mia stand and commanded that Iris dump a bucket of cold water over her head. Mia howled and shivered and grasped urgently for the heavy cloth proffered by Sister Valencia. She wrapped herself tightly and stepped from the basin, dancing as her feet touched the cold stone floor. With haste the ladies handed her clothes and helped her plait her hair back. When Sister Valencia placed the looking glass in front of Mia, she was clean and pink. Her hair was wet but braided and fell to her shoulder blades rather than her waist. Even with the dampness, it felt much lighter. She was robed once again as an acolyte.

"Could you hand me that book?" Mia asked Iris, who stood off to her side. She gestured toward a low stool where Compendium lay.

Iris picked it up, turning it over. "What is it?" she asked.

"It is my birthright," Mia said, plucking Compendium from Iris's hands. She tucked it into her sash and felt the familiar weight and balance of it and its warmth against her belly. "Ah, this feels much better," she said, smiling into the glass. "And much lighter," she added, shaking her head back and forth.

MIA HADN'T BEEN BACK to the Great Hall since her initial audience with Dominus Nikola. Today it appeared that every cleric in the Order was assembled for the proceeding. She steadied her shaking hands in the folds of her sash and stood facing the dais with her back rigid and upper body locked into place. Dominus Nikola was seated in his seat of prominence, centered on the dais at the front of the room. He was flanked by Brother Cornelius on one side and Brother SainClair on the other. All three men sat silently, although Brother Cornelius gave Mia an almost imperceptible wink. Or perhaps he just had something in his eye. Her eyes moved over to SainClair, who wore his usual stony expression, his eyes holding no hint of a smile.

For some reason, she hoped that his just knowing he was her uncle would change something between them. Looking at him now, she held little hope for such a miracle. His time in the hospital clearly had worn on him. His face appeared even more bloodless than usual, and his features looked exaggerated in their sharpness. Mia tried to keep her expression neutral as her eyes slid over the general congregation. She spotted Cedar among the assemblage, as well as Sister Valencia and Brother Valentine. It appeared as if everyone's duties were to be put on hold for this public...reprimand? Denunciation? Sentencing? Mia was remarkably fuzzy on the details, although she knew Brother Borus and Sister Valencia expected some sort of apology and possibly begging to occur. Mia rather suspected that such was the collective sentiment of the Order just then. She would try not to disappoint.

When everyone was gathered, Dominus Nikola cleared his throat. When that action failed to quell the chatter among the group, he thumped his staff against the stone floor of the dais. The sound echoed through the cavernous chamber.

"All right," he said in a loud, clear voice, "now that we're all assembled, let us get to the business at hand. Ms. Jayne, before we continue any further, do you have something you wish to say to the group?"

"Yes," she said. "And you may call me Ms. SainClair." She echoed Dominus Nikola's tone and amplitude. She would be blasted to the Core before she would let herself sound meek today. Brother SainClair twitched slightly at the use of her newly revealed family name. It sounded foreign to her as well.

"Indeed," he said, a small glint in his eye. "Well, then, do you, Ms. SainClair, have something you wish to say to the clerics assembled today?"

"Yes," said Mia. "I wish to ask for the forgiveness from all those assembled here today. I have no explanation that can justify my actions. I can only say I betrayed those here who placed their trust in me, and the Order has suffered a great loss because of my actions. All I ask is that you provide me the opportunity to make amends for my transgressions."

A low murmur rippled through the crowd as she spoke, and when she fell silent, the volume of the conversations increased again. Dominus Nikola sat silently for a moment before raising a withered hand and sternly saying, "Silence!" The voices immediately died down.

"So," he continued, "you stand before us and give a brief apology, and all is to be forgiven? Why should the Order accept you back into its ranks? You wear those robes, but you haven't given any explanation as to why you deserve their honor. You haven't told us what meaning the Order holds for you."

"Would you have me bare a vein and open it for you?" Mia asked, feeling slightly defensive. If her apology wasn't sufficient, what did they want from her?

Dominus Nikola sprang to his feet and pounded his staff against the stone floor once again. Her eyes widened at the display.

"No," he said, his tone serious and, despite the quick movements, his voice calm. "I would have your honesty and your sincerity. It isn't your body or blood the Order requires. It's your heart and your mind. You've been here almost a cycle, and in all that time, you've held yourself aloof. You haven't given of your heart or your mind. You swore to serve this Order. You've asked for the trust of the people in this room, but you haven't given it yourself." With a flourish of his staff, Dominus Nikola seated himself back in his chair. Mia had to applaud his finesse. The room waited raptly for her response.

She swallowed hard. She had spent a lot of time in the dungeon thinking about her actions and their consequences. But standing here now, she only just comprehended what she'd been afraid to admit to herself in so many words. She paused, because what she was about to say could never be unsaid. She'd never be able to reshield her heart or rebottle her vulnerability. Dominus Nikola looked at her, his eyes sparkling slightly. She thought perhaps a shadow of a smile crossed his lips. *That wily old bandicoot*, she thought.

"My father always acted with love," Mia said, her words a hint shaky at first but then gathering strength like a storm taking up water in preparation for a final deluge, "but he did me a disservice when he sent me here. He wasn't honest with me about the mission of the Order, not honest about its foundation, and not even honest about the people I would meet while I was here. I came here on a mission. My mission was to help my father, plain and simple. My goal was to gain my freedom as soon as possible and return to my family. I had little care for you and this organization, even as it attempted to foster me. I focused only on physical freedom—neglecting the freedoms that were given to me here. I focused only on blood family—neglecting to give weight to the bonds established here. It wasn't until after I experienced betrayal against myself and learned the truth from the man who called himself my father that I came to truly understand that this place is the home I so desperately wanted and you're the family I so very much need."

Mia paused to look at SainClair. His gaze was steady but veiled. She breathed deeply and continued, looking straight into his eyes. "And you, Uncle, are my only blood relative. I had no idea what you were thinking or why you hated me, but I can see now why you detest me so." Her voice cracked. "I must be a bitter disappointment to you now. And my actions almost cost you your life. I can never make up for what I have done. I'm so sorry." Her words had grown raspy as she neared the end of her oration, and SainClair rose as she spoke to him.

Despite his recent head injury, Brother SainClair moved like a cat, leaping off the platform in a smooth motion and striding purposefully toward her. The only indication that he had been ill at all was the pallor in his complexion and the dark smudges under his eyes. He reached her in a few long strides, and she recoiled in anticipation of his assault. He grabbed her by the shoulders and shook them hard, his grip solid as a metal vice.

And then his arms were around her, enclosing her in an equally firm hug, crushing her breath from her body. He clung to her like that for a moment, and his chest shuddered against her. A muffled sob escaped onto her shoulder.

"My niece," came words into her neck. "My dear child. I couldn't bear to believe it was you. I'm so sorry. So sorry." Mia's mind was in a state of shock, but her arms came up to circle his back, and she squeezed him back, holding back tears of her own. They clung to each other like that for a long moment, until one of the clerics made a whooping noise. Thinking back, Mia could swear it was Brother Borus. And with that, the whole hall erupted in shouts and claps and hoots. When the din died down, SainClair released the embrace but kept his arm around Mia's shoulder.

"Dominus," he said, "if my niece must face judgment, know that I shall stand by her side." Mia smiled tremulously. This was going wildly different than she'd even considered possible.

Dominus Nikola smiled at both of them. "That may indeed be necessary," he said, "for we have a dire problem that must in fact be resolved." He looked around the room, meeting a number of eyes in his perusal. "I'm speaking, of course, of the matter of the Shillelagh. It must be retrieved." Fervent whispers threatened to overtake the Dominus's voice. "Yes, yes," he said, "to some of you, this sounds like a myth or some old children's story. For many generations, however, the Order has maintained secrecy regarding some of our more important artifacts. Times inevitably change, and we no longer can afford to segregate such knowledge among our ranks. Ms. SainClair's activities, while regarded with reproach by the Order, were highly resourceful. We must use every able-minded person at our disposal in the coming battles, and that starts now—with the retrieval of the Shillelagh." He turned to Mia. "Ms. SainClair, the Order has decided that as your amends, you will be required to lead the party assembling to retrieve the Shillelagh."

"Had you not required it, I would have volunteered," she said.

Nikola smiled and nodded at that statement.

"Do we have any other volunteers to join her?" the Dominus asked.

"I volunteer," said Brother SainClair, squeezing her shoulder.

"I do as well," another familiar voice called out. Cedar's lanky form stepped forward through the crowd and came to flank her other side. After a moment, another recognized voice rang out.

"Och, dinna think ye'll be leaving me behind on this adventure." Brother Borus approached their small group from somewhere behind Mia. Slowly, others stepped up to answer the call, and when all was said and done, they had a party of fifteen ready and willing to accept the risk of infiltrating the Druid Village.

31 THE REUNION L.C. 10152

T HE CLERICS SPRANG INTO ACTION in a way
Mia had never witnessed before. She was still on
a probation of sorts, but her belongings had all been
deposited at her bunk in the barracks. What couldn't
fit in her cubby was taken to storage. Suddenly she
was surrounded by all the trappings of home. It was
surreal and happy and sad simultaneously. Her
comings and goings were limited, however, and her
movements watched. Brother SainClair did manage to
arrange a treat for her, though.

"Hamish!" she yelled across the courtyard, hopping
up and down in glee. The dog turned at the sound of

Mia's voice, let out a delighted bark, and bolted over to her on his stubby little legs, his barrel chest advancing with disproportionate speed, foxy ears back. He leapt at her and clambered at her shins, and she knelt to accept his affection. "Oh, I've missed you, you silly thing," she said, and hugged him tightly. He squirmed away, deciding he should look for a stick to play with. "We haven't time for that," she said in a scolding tone. "Circumstances are much too busy now." SainClair looked on their exchange with some amusement. "Where is he staying?" Mia asked.

"He's been housed in the kennels with the hunting dogs," SainClair replied. "However, since he's house trained and not much good for hunting, the Gamemaster has suggested we find him more suitable quarters."

"Do you hear that?" Mia said to Hamish. He sat at her feet, a large doggy grin on his face, tongue lolling, eyes expectant. "You're being kicked out of the dog quarters because you can't hunt," she said, hands on her hips. Hamish blinked at her and tilted his head.

SainClair laughed. "If you don't mind, I was thinking he could come stay with me in my chambers for a bit," he said. His face wore a strained expression. "I know I haven't been much of an uncle, but I could at least look out for Hamish here while you're still in the barracks."

"That's very kind of you," Mia beamed. He shifted uncomfortably at her gaze of affection. This was new to both of them.

"Then you can visit him any time you like," he said.

"Do you hear that, Hamish? You'd better be on your best behavior or Uncle Thaddeus will turn you into fur boots!" SainClair flushed when she called him "Uncle." They played with Hamish in the courtyard for a little while and made awkward conversation. After much hesitation on Mia's part, she finally asked the question that had been on her mind since her final conversation with Father.

"What were my parents like?"

"Well," said SainClair, thinking on his words carefully, "I obviously knew Jayne better than Claude, but he was a good man. He was infinitely calm and patient. I have such a temper, and his unwavering calm used to confound me and frequently only served to increase my agitation." SainClair chuckled, and Mia smiled. "Your mother was stubborn and headstrong and decisive. She was an advocate for justice above all else. It still tears me up that we fought about her leaving. My last words to her were unkind. And looking at you, such a convincing imposter," he added, his voice sarcastic, "was a constant reminder of my pain. If only I had trusted my eyes from the get-go."

"I always thought I must look like her, since I knew I didn't look like Father. But then, for a while, I didn't really know who I looked like."

"Well, as you may have noticed," he said, "you've got the SainClair coloring." He gestured to his own white complexion. "Rain or shine, we never seem to soak in the sun."

Mia laughed. "I noticed that."

"Your bones and features are also very much Jayne."

"What about my eye and hair color?" she asked. It was always her opinion that they were unseemly and drew entirely too much comment.

"Ah, that's entirely Claude. As he was an orphan himself, no one was really quite sure how he came by such odd coloring, but it certainly drew Jayne in." He chuckled. "You're unmistakably their offspring. I wish we'd all had the opportunity to grow old together," he said, raking back his steely hair from his almost colorless eyes.

"Me too," Mia said. She patted his arm, and he put it around her shoulder.

"Hamish," he called out. The dog was busy nosing about a bush in the corner of the courtyard, no doubt looking for something to chase. Mia reckoned he'd likely be disappointed. "Let's go in, ya mutt," he called again, and the dog emerged from the bush covered in tiny brambles. "Blast me to the Core," SainClair said, and Mia snickered.

"WE SHOULD JUST CHARGE IN THERE," Brother Borus's voice called out. Shouts of "aye" resonated from some of the assembled clerics.

"Don't be a fool, Borus," SainClair snapped back at him. "We must have a plan."

"And so we shall," Dominus Nikola said, attempting to calm the two clerics.

"Perhaps we should wait for the rangers to come back," said Brother Mallus, the young cleric with sandy hair and soft brown eyes. "Sister Aja's the best scout we have."

"There isn't time," said SainClair. "We've already wasted too much as it is. The rangers aren't scheduled back for three months at least."

Mia sat quietly, taking in the argument and thinking through the problem as the others continued their discussion around her. *Compendium, do you have schematics for the Druid stronghold?*

"I have certain fundamental knowledge but not detailed information," Compendium replied.

And here I thought you knew everything.

"I try," its neutral voice replied in her ear.

If we got you close enough, could you attempt to access their systems?

"I can always attempt. I cannot say if I will succeed."

It wasn't a lot to rely on. Mia switched strategies. *Can you locate the Shillelagh?*

"I cannot locate the exact coordinates of the Shillelagh, but it is currently located within the confines of the Druid Village."

So if you had access to their systems, you would be able to map a course there?

"Affirmative," said Compendium.

Why are you always so calm? She had gotten used to hearing the soft lilt of the book talking directly into her ear. When it had started talking directly to her, it somehow had ceased to be just an object in her mind.

"What you are interpreting as calm is merely a total lack of emotion," the voice said. She laughed out loud at that remark. Everyone in the room stopped to look at her. "I sense they in fact think you are daft," the voice said. She stifled another giggle, and Dominus Nikola scowled.

"Ms. SainClair, do you have something amusing you wish to share with the group?" he asked.

She looked around at all the strained expressions and stony eyes. "I don't know if it's all that funny, but I might have a plan."

32 THE VILLAGE L.C. 10152

"ARE WE CLOSE ENOUGH?" Cedar whispered into Mia's ear. She waved her hand at him in a signal to remain quiet. She squinted and tried to focus on the entrance in the distance. It was relatively quiet, but her heart thumped hard in her chest every time a green-robed figure emerged from the stronghold. She actually hesitated to use the word *stronghold* to describe the Druid enclave. If presented with two drawings—the first featuring the cluster of tree structures set into the forest that made up the Druid Village, and the second featuring the austere volcanic fortress of the Order's Compound—Mia would have picked the Druid Village to make her home.

The Village was situated in a vast forest, nestled among the trees, and built high up off the ground. Compendium had directed the clerics to the Village's location, but they'd had to travel almost a month on foot to reach it. The clerics were camped two kilometers away to avoid detection by Druid patrols and had spent the last week rotating scouting parties to try to determine the best way to get Mia down to the base of the Village where she could hook up Compendium to the Village's electrical system and download the location of the Shillelagh.

That day, a scouting party composed of Mia, Cedar, SainClair, Borus, and Mallus had been watching the Druids' comings and goings all morning from a particularly thick patch of forest to the north of the Village. The open quality of the aerial conglomeration of rooms made it harder to sneak up on than Mia had expected. The Druids brazenly had situated the Village in a clearing, which gave their watch an easy job of it. If she could just get close to the base of one of the trees, it would be a snap to get Compendium connected, but that was the rub. She signaled to Cedar and SainClair that they should back off.

"I need to get to the base of those trees," said Mia. "But I don't think that'll be possible without a change of costume. We're going to need to obtain Druid capes at the very least."

"How do you suggest we do that?" Cedar asked. He didn't at all look convinced that such a thing was possible.

"Well, I don't suppose they have laundry and plumbing up in the trees," Mia said.

"You want us to wait around for someone to do laundry?" SainClair said incredulously.

"Well, I hadn't really thought of it like that. I more thought that we should post someone by the nearest running water. Then, when a Druid comes by to wash, we'll make off with their garments."

SainClair chuckled. "I suppose it would be worth an attempt." He signaled to Brother Mallus and told him the plan.

"What? Me?" Mallus asked. His soft, brown eyes shifted uneasily as he looked at the rest of the scouting party.

"The closest body of running water is a stream to the east, which is a five-minute walk in that direction," Mia said, gesturing to a map in Compendium and pointing toward a particularly nasty-looking thicket.

"This had better work," Brother Mallus grumbled as he departed.

"I don't see why he's upset," she said. "I honestly think it's going to be necessary for us all to secure capes. Anyone coming or going will be easy for the Druids to spot."

SainClair grunted in response, which Mia took as a sign of agreement. The rest of the party waited, largely in silence. Eventually a robed Druid emerged from the central ring of the Village. Mia still wasn't sure how they actually got down from the trees, but Compendium could answer all these questions if she could just get it attached to the Village's system. The Druid ambled along the path toward the thicket then took a sharp left before reaching it. Cedar, SainClair, and Mia released a collective sigh. The tension gripped them like an iron hand tightening on their small group. The second Druid also took a path away from the river.

Finally the third Druid to emerge from the trees made his way to the thicket where Brother Mallus was hiding. They all watched, barely blinking, straining to hear any noise. Finally a faint voice carried along the breeze but was silenced. Mia shot Cedar and SainClair furtive looks, and they waited tensely for a scream for help or some other alert to sound. Some minutes later, Brother Mallus reappeared holding a green cape.

"It's not ideal," he said. "He spotted me hiding." He shook his head.

"Is he dead?" SainClair asked.

"No, he's just knocked out," Brother Mallus replied. "I wasn't sure if it would be worse to kill him and have them know or if it would be better to try to get some information out of him."

"Either way they'll eventually notice he's missing," Mia said, her face strained.

"Aye," said SainClair. "We'll have to be quick with this entire misadventure."

She pulled the cloak from Mallus's hands, dropped it over herself, and pulled the hood down over her features. She gestured to the thicket. "I'm going to enter the clearing where the Druid left, in case anyone is watching." The others nodded, and taking a deep breath, Mia picked her way through the foliage toward the thicket. She made sure the cloak was wrapped tightly around her and obscured all her features. Heart beating against her rib cage, she stepped into the clearing and tried to match the ambling pace of the Druid whose place she had taken. She didn't see or hear any caped figures in the trees above her as she walked in among the trunks. Once she found cover below the trees, she quickly scanned the area for signs of movement. Seeing none, she crouched silently behind a massive trunk, hands trembling.

Compendium, can you access their systems now?

"Wireless is too weak from this vantage. I need a direct link." Its normal low voice sounded impossibly loud in her ears.

She cursed silently, and Compendium, reading her thoughts, responded, "I can do nothing about my current range."

I know. She retrieved her tool roll, laid it out on the ground next to the trunk, and foraged the ground for a suitable root. Then she pulled a paring knife from the roll and shaved a strip of bark off a promising-looking root. She carefully attached Compendium to the root with some prepared strips.

"Connection established. Retrieving schematics. Retrieved. Would you like any other information?"

Get any other information about the Druid Village you can grab. I'll tell you when to stop.

"Affirmative. Retrieving access manifest. Retrieved. Retrieving Druid personnel manifest. Retrieved. Retrieving artifact list and descriptions. Retrieved. Retrieving the personal data of Head Druid Augustin Rosewater. Access denied."

Did that set off an alarm?

"Unknown. Retrieving security schematics. Retrieved. No alarm activated. Attempting to retrieve Rosewater's personal data. Access denied. Access denied. Access granted. Retrieved. Alarm. Alarm."

By the Core! Have they discovered you?

"Negative. Alarm indicates that Druid security has spotted movement on the Village perimeter. I believe the others in your scouting party have been revealed."

Mia debated for a moment whether she should try to warn them or whether she should stay hidden. *Can you send a message to any of them?*

"I can connect to Thaddeus SainClair or Cedar Kannon, as both meet minimum requirements."

Connect me to SainClair now.

"Transmission initiated. Patching in Thaddeus SainClair."

"What is this?" SainClair's voice said in her ear.

Uncle, it's me. I'm contacting you through Compendium. Your position is compromised. The Druids are aware of your presence. You have to retreat.

"It's too late," his voice said in her ear. "They have arrows pointed at us already."

Damn. Mia unhooked Compendium from the tree and used the joining paste to seal off the scrape in the bark. She looked around hastily, unsure which way to go. She tried to hold back the rising bile in her throat.

"They will be entering the tree line from your right. There is one main entrance in that direction, so you will have to head in the opposite direction to evade them."

Compendium's calm voice reassured her. She listened carefully, and with each step, Compendium guided her farther from the entrance and from the others. She stood near the edge of the Village on the opposite side, her body frozen, waiting for Compendium's instructions.

"They are distracted by the commotion. You are clear to reenter the forest."

Mia inched toward the edge of the tree line, intending to follow Compendium's advice, but stopped and looked directly up to the massive thick of treetops above her. Tucked between the trunk she was standing next to and the one she had just passed was a bridge composed of branches tied together to form a platform. The branches had grown together over time and melded into a solid surface. Rails had been fashioned from rope suspended along the sides of the plank. Mia's eyes traced a path down the tree to where she stood. *I can climb this.*

"That is not advised," Compendium said.

She gritted her teeth. *I have to do something.* She felt around for handholds in the large, rough trunk behind her.

"It is advised that you retreat and formulate a plan. You are entering the Village alone and unarmed."

Nonsense. I have my throwing knives, my tools, and you.

"You are risking this operation. This is reckless," the voice said. Its tone remained emotionless as usual, but Mia grew irritated.

They're distracted, and any perimeter breach I make won't be detected. I can't wait around any longer. The time is nigh. She had to stop herself from speaking the words aloud. The book continued talking into her ear, warning her of the dangers. She ignored it and picked her way carefully and slowly up the trunk. *You can assist me or be silent. I'm trying to concentrate.* The bridge was still approximately fifty feet above her when she glanced upward. She was a skilled climber, but she'd been cooped up for almost a cycle. Her muscles already were tiring. She took a deep breath and renewed her efforts, scaling the large tree in small increments. The sweat formed a sheen on her skin, affecting her grip. She muttered quiet curses and plodded along. Just as she had lulled herself into a rhythm, her toe slipped, and her feet gave way, leaving her clutching the trunk with just her hands. Her feet scrambled against the rough surface of the tree as she tried to gain purchase with her boots. Her palms dampened further with sweat, and she tightened her grip on the handholds to which she clung. Her heart raced, and it took all her concentration to slow her breathing. She finally regained her footing after a few tries. She stilled herself for a moment, steadied her breathing further, and let her heart rate slow. Once recovered, she began the sluggish ascent once again.

Mia tossed all thoughts from her cluttered mind, emptying a bucket into the void below her, and focused solely on moving her body upward. When she finally reached the lowest branch on the tree, she pulled herself atop it to rest her limbs briefly. She brushed the dampness from her forehead with her sleeve and wished she had packed a gourd of water. She gave herself a brief respite to recover and resumed her climb. She worked like this for approximately an hour, until she was finally right under the bridge. She listened intently for signs of voices or footfalls. Compendium had been silent since she had told it to quiet itself, and she rather thought it was acting a bit petulant at this point or at least as much as an inanimate object could.

Compendium, can you sense anyone nearby?

"Negative," the book replied. "This area appears to be deserted at the moment."

Are my uncle and the others still alive? Mia held her breath as she waited for a response.

"Affirmative. They were taken up a lift into the Village on the north side. They have been deposited in holding cells on the third level." She didn't want to risk communicating with SainClair or Cedar if she could avoid it, not until she could spend some time learning about the Village's sensors and security systems from Compendium.

How do I get to the holding cells?

"You will have to travel across a series of bridges to the center of the trees. The Druids keep prisoners in cells scattered around a central guard tree, which is always manned. Attempting to walk right up to the cells is impossible and thus unadvisable."

Thanks, she thought sourly. *Let me decide what's impossible.* She remained silent on the "unadvisable" part, because she sensed any plan would be deemed unadvisable by a sensible person. *Where is the Shillelagh kept?*

"Higher up in the trees," the book said in her ear. She peeked over the side of the bridge and up.

By the sacred groves! She saw another level of bridges and rooms above. *How many levels are there?*

"Five," said Compendium.

Let me guess, the Shillelagh's on the top level?

"Affirmative."

Ah, how did I know? Her mind was racing, and tension wracked her whole body. *Where should I go first?* If she freed the others, the Druids would sound the alarm. Also, how would a group of them get to the fifth level? The Shillelagh was probably equally well guarded, if not more so. She hoisted herself onto the bridge, trying desperately to be noiseless. The branches creaked subtly under her weight. Once she was on solid footing, she curled herself up into a ball against the trunk of the tree and tried to stay as still as possible. *Compendium, alert me if you sense anyone approaching.*

"Of course," the book replied. Was she mistaken, or did the voice sound just a tiny bit affronted, as if her request were so obvious it shouldn't even have been given form? Mia rolled her eyes and settled the green cloak around her with the dual intent of blending in as much as possible among the leaves and appearing as a Druid who'd just slipped away for some time alone.

She rested her body, but her mind wouldn't quiet down. It was consumed with thoughts of SainClair and Cedar and even Borus. She wriggled Compendium free from her sash and opened it while keeping it largely shielded inside the cloak.

Show me the Village schematics. She studied the plans to the fortress in the trees and peppered Compendium with questions. The entrances were vertical lift conveyances hidden inside the trunks of the trees. *Genius. Why didn't the Order have those?* The conveyances were guarded on the first level to prevent strangers from entering the Village. They weren't guarded from the second level to higher levels.

Mia needed to get to the second level and didn't relish the thought of continuing her climb. She racked her brain; there had to be a way up. It wasn't a pleasant thought, but she asked Compendium how the Druids expelled waste from the village.

"They have a pump that brings water from the nearby river and pumps it up into the trees. This is used for drinking water and waste disposal."

But you can't hear it?

"It is pumped through dead, hollow trees," Compendium replied.

Interesting. Are there other hollow trees? I don't much fancy getting you wet.

"That would not be advised," it agreed.

Apparently not much is advised today.

"There are other trees that are hollow that comprise access tunnels around the Village."

Are they all guarded?

"Negative," said Compendium. "They are sealed off but not watched. From the outside, they are indistinguishable from the other trees, and thus it is not anticipated that anyone knows about them."

Well, perhaps we can unseal one. A plan began to take root in her mind.

33 JAILBREAK   L.C. 10152

M IA FELT THE HOLLOWNESS of the tree the moment her chisel bit into its bark. Where the wood beneath should have been thick and slightly soft, the blunt plane instead met a hard, unyielding surface. Methodically she worked the small tool farther into the trunk with each muffled thunk of her hammer. She damped the noise with the Druid cloak, which was still around her shoulders. It was slowgoing, and blisters formed on her already abused hands. Finally the tool broke into the hollow center, the plane sliding easily to the hilt. Next she worked the small chisel out from the trunk and replaced it with an equally small saw. She moved the saw back and forth along the trunk and alternated tools while her arms ached and body sweated until she was able to pop out a portion of the trunk.

Are you sure there's an access hatch above? Mia gritted her teeth. She had no desire to repeat this process from inside the trunk, suspended far above solid ground.

"Yes," Compendium said.

She rested for a moment to regather her strength then felt around inside the black, hollow trunk for some sort of grip or step or ledge. To her surprise, she found a rudimentary series of ledges carved inside the trunk. She pulled a small gourd from inside her bag and tapped it to ignite the chemical light within. Then she set it to hang around her neck from a lanyard and pulled herself into the pitch black of the hollow tree. Once inside, she braced herself against the curve of the trunk and struggled to maneuver the slab of bark back over the carved hole. "That will have to do," she muttered, and began the slow ascent upward.

Mia'd never climbed inside a tree before, and the entire process unsettled her. With only the flicker of the gourd around her neck to guide her, she climbed up the inside of the tree, silently instructing

Compendium to alert her to the nearest hatch on the next level up.

She was just beginning to contemplate the relief that letting go of the ledges and falling to her death would bring when Compendium's voice broke through her thoughts.

"The hatch is approximately five rungs above on your right," the voice said in its usual calm manner.

And can you determine whether the room is empty?

"My sensors indicate that the outpost currently is unoccupied, but they have not been calibrated for this environment, and interaction with the Druid system data could be glitchy."

Mia grunted. *So you're saying you don't really know.*

"My data indicates that the room should be empty, but I cannot be certain."

She rolled her eyes, bit her lip, and frowned. *Well, I guess it'll be a surprise then.* Trying to stifle any noise her body might make as it knocked around inside the tree, she felt around the wall for the seam to the hatch. *You don't per chance know how this actually opens, do you?*

"Negative."

I thought as much.

"Then why did you ask?" said Compendium's voice in what Mia suspected was its attempt at sounding earnest.

As if it were possible for an artificial consciousness to be earnest. The heat and exhaustion are just getting to me.

"My sensors indicate that your body temperature and readings are within normal ranges," Compendium said in response.

Mia had to bite her lip to keep from shouting a response. *You scan me?* The possibility alarmed her a bit.

"It is a function of my sensors. I automatically scan all beings in my vicinity."

Why didn't you tell me? She was scandalized for her person but also annoyed since it was such a useful function.

"You did not request to know such information."

Well, if something is useful, you should say something. Mia wanted to continue this line of discussion, but she needed to get out of this hatch to solid footing. She could feel the seam but not a means to open the hatch. She knocked softly around the edges but couldn't find a hinge. *Does this door pop off completely, or is it hinged?*

"It has a hinge."

I may have to force it. Bracing herself against the ledges and the opposite wall of the trunk, she positioned her shoulder against the small door then pushed against it. There was no give at all. Grunting, she flexed her leg and applied increased pressure. A small sigh escaped from the wood as it flexed ever so slightly, but still the door didn't yield. Taking a deep breath and holding it, she shoved against the door, applying as much pressure as possible. With a creak and a cracking noise, the door finally swung open. With her shoulder no longer wedged against a solid wall and a relative lack of forward momentum due to her energy being transferred to the wooden door, there was no longer anything holding her up against the shaft wall. She sunk like a stone. It was only her reflexes that saved her from falling back down the shaft of the trunk.

Mia gripped the edge of the doorway into the outpost as her feet flailed uselessly below her, scrabbling for purchase. Grunting again, she urged her foot to the left until a ledge registered under her toe then used the leverage to slowly pull herself up. *If the outpost isn't empty, I'd probably know by now.* Any Druids present had ample time to haul her from the shaft or just kill her right there.

Finally she lay sprawled against the trunk of the hollow tree, attempting to regain her breath and slow the rapid beat of her heart.

"You would do well to make haste," Compendium said.

Unable to string her thoughts together or form words, she merely grunted in response and focused her attention on breathing. As she recovered from the physical exertion, she surveyed her surroundings. Built around the hollow tree was a wooden room constructed of planks and thatch. It appeared largely empty except for the hollow tree to her back, although it did contain a doorway and large windows looking out at the forest. From her vantage point, sprawled out on the floor, she was unable to see anything but sky through a tangle of branches. The light was quickly draining away, and she noted it would soon be dark outside. She had to make it to the proper lift and find the others, but she had urgent business to attend to first.

Compendium, find me a place to rest.

MIA AWOKE WITH A START to the sound of a nearby owl hooting. Darkness had fully settled on the Village. The flicker of the night lights swirling behind the branches above her danced and mixed with the pinpoint lights of the gourds and the glow bugs spattered among the forest, much like in Hackberry. Once, the quiet stillness of the nocturnal fauna and muted lights in the sky and among the trees would have bought her comfort and joy. Tonight, however, a cold fear settled deep in her spine, running itself back and forth from her neck to her bowels. She tried to brush aside the burgeoning feelings of panic and concentrate on the task at hand.

When the owl launched into a particularly intricate series of hoots, Mia used the opportunity to mask her rustling noises as she dropped down from the tangle of trees in which she had been sleeping and onto a wooden walkway. She situated the green cloak close about her body and moved slowly but purposefully toward the center of the Village. Compendium guided her along, whispering instructions into her ear. She found it difficult to hear them over the sound of her own heart, but she proceeded steadily, her face the best facsimile of impassive that she could offer.

Her thoughts were filled with the others. No doubt they would have told her to abandon them and make straight for the Shillelagh. *Certainly not!* she argued in her head, her own responses to the pleading requests to do her duty to the Order. Her companions had supported her on this journey. They had placed their lives and reputations within the Order in her hands, and she wouldn't let them down. They would all leave together or not at all. Her hands clenched in the cloak, and she took a slow breath. She filled her mind with thoughts of Cedar and the Crater Grove, of that night they had kissed. His dark eyes and brown skin floated across her senses. She sighed lightly and tried to remain in the feeling. It was a retreat for her, almost a dream rather than a memory. It was her only one. She shouldn't have squandered their time together. *I knew how I felt, even before that night, and yet why? Why had I persisted in my folly that it was otherwise?* It was always him. Since that first awkward conversation on the ship, she had felt drawn into his vortex. *I really must be related to SainClair. My stubbornness mirrors his so completely.*

Perhaps this wasn't the time to consider the details of her relationship with Cedar. Nevertheless she felt the shake of her hands subside and the beat of her heart slow. *I can still confess my feelings to him. There will still be time for us. I just need to get him and Uncle Thaddeus and the others out of those cells and safely back to the Compound.* That was the pledge she made to herself, the thought that carried her down the winding walkways strung between the giant trunks—bridges through the aerial forest—to the transport room, into the lift, and up to the level where the detention cells resided. Each minute that passed where no one called out for her to halt or placed a weapon in her path bolstered her confidence. She quickened her pace slightly and held her head higher. She didn't pass a great many Druids on her way to the cellblock. A couple of men deep in conversation, their faces old but their strides strong, walked past her with not so much as a glance in her direction. She didn't pick up any of their conversation, so hushed were the tones. *Compendium, could you hear those Druids talking?*

"I did retrieve some audio from them," the book replied.

Could you replay it for me?

"They were from the Order of Vis Firmitas?" asked an older, hushed voice in Mia's ear. "Are we certain?"

"Yes," said another unfamiliar voice, worry present in his tone. "We aren't prepared to travel, but if they're sending clerics to retrieve it, we're no longer safe holding it here."

"I agree," said the first voice. "It will have to be moved."

"Do we suspect any assistance from within?" asked the second voice.

"No, Rosewater doesn't believe we've been infiltrated. Nevertheless it will have to be moved to a more secure location."

"When?"

"Tonight," said the first voice. "Before those clerics are missed."

"I can't believe Rosewater left his granddaughter in charge while he's in Willowslip. There's no telling how long he'll be gone."

"Perhaps a reward for giving up two cycles of her life?" the first said, lowering his voice.

The conversation cut out there. Mia's heart quickened. They were going to move the Shillelagh tonight. *Is that all you got?*

"They walked out of range. Do you want to pursue them?"

No. She gritted her teeth. *But we have even less time than I thought.*

UNCLE, CAN YOU HEAR ME? Mia silently asked SainClair. The time for discretion had passed. They needed to hurry.

Compendium was attempting to establish a connection for her. She looked down through an open sky light from above the room that contained her uncle, Cedar, Borus and Mallus, still not certain of her next step. Below, a single Druid was posted to guard them. He was young, with barely a bristly beard painting his pale face. His head lolled back in a gentle rhythm as he repeatedly drifted off into unconsciousness, snored gently, and awoke with a small snort to adjust his position. His desk wasn't outfitted for a comfortable nap. Its hard wood equally matched the hard wood of the chair in which he was slouched over. Even though every round of nodding brought him deeper into repose, Mia still didn't wish to risk his sounding the alarm and bringing others down upon them.

The clerics were held in separate pens, formed from thick vines gnarled together into cages. They were quite beautiful, in fact, but their purpose left Mia cold inside. Each pen was secured by an arched door with a metal lock. Cedar, Borus, and the others were sprawled out in tiny cells, without even room to lie fully down. It was rather barbaric actually. Mia suspected these were just temporary quarters.

"Mia?" a voice finally sounded into her ear.

Yes, Uncle, she replied, careful not to state any of her thoughts aloud. *I'm directly above you. We need to get you out of here and fast. We need to incapacitate the guard.*

"He already looks rather incapacitated to me." Her uncle's dry, wry voice echoed in her mind, and she stifled a chuckle into a small smirk.

I take your meaning, but I was hoping for something that would give us some time to get a head start on the guards. Do you think you could cause a distraction?

"I'll see what I can do," he said. Very faint whispers came from below, the minute sounds of her uncle and the others engaged in halting conversations through the walls of their individual pens. Mia suspected Brother Borus, as he was never without an opinion on their circumstances of the moment and certainly not afraid to share such opinions. Then a great loud moan erupted from one of the pens below, promptly followed by a bellow. Mia stifled another chuckle. SainClair was going for drama indeed. The young Druid snapped awake at the yell, nearly displacing himself from his precarious spot in his chair. He looked about furtively for signs of danger, confusion, and alarm, which mixed with the sleep that still clung to him like a warm blanket.

"What? What?" he yelled, clamoring to his feet and moving toward the holding cells, still a bit confused.

"'Tis my gut," yelled SainClair. He was doubled over, holding his midsection. "It came upon me fiercely, with demon's fire. My bowels." The others looked on in surprise, their faces pressed up against their respective cages. A look passed between them, but none looked up to see Mia peering down from above. The guard moved toward SainClair and fumbled among his robes. Positioned as she was, Mia was unable to see what was happening, but SainClair helpfully clarified.

"Good god man. I canna hold it much longer. We shall all suffer if you canna get me to the facilities. By all that is holy, why is there no chamber pot?"

Keys jingled in the Druid's hands, but he paused. "I'm, er, not supposed to, er, open the door with no one else present," he stammered.

SainClair must have sensed him wavering. "This is a medical emergency, man," he fairly yelled. "The pain, 'tis unbearable. I'm going to shit right here if you don't get me to a chamber pot." He groaned again and dropped to his knees. The Druid fumbled with the keys again, but then Mia heard the clink of the key settling into the lock. It was time to move.

The skylight was angled down the sloped ceiling. It let the light in and was open to the elements. She thought the Druids must get rather soggy, given the very open nature of their windows. Then again, with so much tree cover, maybe the rains never made it down to this level. As the ruckus reached its crescendo, she dropped a thick length of vine out from one of the trees and down through the ceiling. It already was secured tightly to a higher branch so as not to obstruct the night lights through the skylight. Within moments the vine was down, and Mia hastily slid down it. Her leather boots landed on the plank floor of the detention room with a soft thud. The Druid had just gotten the pen door open and was trying to drag SainClair out of the cell when he spotted her from the corner of his eye. She immediately grabbed a metal pitcher from the desk and flung it at the guard.

"Hey!" he said, ducking and bringing his arms up to shield his face. Behind him SainClair plucked the pitcher, which was still spewing water, from the air and swung it in an arc, bashing the Druid across the back of the head. The young man crumpled to the ground, unconscious. Mia gave herself a moment to take a deep breath and grin before she quickly grabbed the keys and freed the others. SainClair dragged the guard's inert body into the pen. Once they were all assembled, and hugs and thumps on the back had been exchanged, everyone began to speak at once, and even though their voices were low, Mia found herself shushing the others.

"We have to remain quiet," she said. "There isn't much time. I know where the Shillelagh is, but they're moving it tonight, so we need to act quickly. When are the guards set to change over?"

"This fool was to be on duty until dawn, although it's possible that someone could come to check on him before then. Hand me those keys, my dear," SainClair said, and grabbed the keys from her hands. He walked back behind the desk and inserted a key into a tiny hole in a panel of wood. It didn't turn, so he tried another, and another, and another. Finally the fifth key opened a panel flush to the wall, and behind the panel was stowed the clerics' weapons and gear. SainClair pulled a scrap of cloth from his bag and gagged and bound the unconscious Druid. Then he locked him in the pen.

"It's late, and there aren't many Druids about, but we'd best get moving," Mia said. She was still nervous, but she felt considerably better now that she was with the others. She looked over to Cedar, who was buckling a knife onto his belt and fixing his sash over it. He looked up just then, and their eyes locked. Mia felt herself blush slightly. Her heart didn't seem care that it wasn't the right time to express her feelings, and her flesh reddened as the blood rushed to her face. He gave her a crooked smile and stepped forward, pulling a leaf from her hair.

"You're positively filthy," he said.

"Yes, well, I've been crawling around inside hollow trees like a beetle," she replied, arching her brow. "It tends to make one a bit dusty. If you require me to rescue you perfectly scrubbed and in formal attire, your cell is still there if you'd like to wait. It may be a while, though," she said, twisting her mouth in a grimace.

Cedar smiled. "Filthy is fine," he said, and gave her a mock salute. Mia resisted the urge to thump him on the shoulder. They didn't have time for banter.

One by one, they made their way quietly up the vine, with Cedar, Mallus, and SainClair pulling Borus up.

"You need to serve more of your stew, Brother Borus, and eat less of it," Mallus said with a gasp as he leaned over with his hand on his side, breathing heavily.

"If ye'd like to partake of me special recipies going forward, son, you'll do well ter shut yer trap," said Brother Borus, but he smiled at the young cleric.

They made away from the central guard station as quickly as their tired bodies would allow. "Where are we headed?" SainClair whispered to Mia, as she led the way.

"There's only one lift to the level where the Druids are holding the Shillelagh. There shouldn't be any guards, as, according to Compendium, they focus most of their manpower near the lower levels, but it only takes one to sound an alarm."

SainClair nodded.

"They must be trying to mask its signature by embedding it in a powerful elder, but they got spooked by your presence and now want to move it."

"How did you find it if the elder masks the signature?" her uncle asked.

"We got it directly by hooking Compendium up to their system. It didn't need to rely on a sensor to find the Shillelagh."

"Lucky we have Compendium then," SainClair said, his eyes clouded and distant.

Lucky indeed. She lost herself in her own thoughts as the group crept along quietly, all of them tense and alert. Mia was a little unnerved. Compendium was certainly powerful enough to obtain the information, but she was certain Taryn would have warned the other Druids about Compendium.

They reached the transport room with little fanfare, and her uneasiness grew. "I'm going to scout the lift," she said.

"Don't you think someone else should do that?" Cedar asked. "You're the only one who can speak to Compendium, and that bloody book is the only thing that can locate the Shillelagh."

"You've all risked plenty coming here already," she said grimly. "I should be the one to scout."

"Nonsense," said SainClair, in a tone that brooked no argument. "Cedar will scout up ahead. He moves more silently awake than you do dead asleep."

"Aye," said Brother Borus, "and we'd best get movin'."

Mia frowned deeply but could find no fault with their words; Cedar was by far the stealthiest of the group. He stepped into the lift and looked up nervously. Mia unclasped the green cloak from her shoulders and swung it around his. "At least take this," she said.

She squeezed in next to him to show him the controls. "Push the lever for the level you want, which is this one," she said, gently tapping the fifth lever. "When you're coming back down, push this lever," she said, gesturing to the second one. Cedar nodded, his dark eyes focused on her hands. Mia swallowed hard, resisting the urge to make a scene. She was successful, but she openly stared at him as she gently closed the door on the lift. From the other side, she heard him flip the lever, followed by the faint whir of the mechanism that drew the car upward and away from her. Mia took a step back and held her breath.

34 THE FURY L.C. 10152

S AINCLAIR GRABBED MIA'S ARM at the elbow to still her pacing. Brother Borus stood near the entrance to the transport room, keeping careful watch for any Druids approaching from either direction.

"It's been too long," she muttered, mostly to herself. SainClair patted her elbow in what was intended to be a reassuring manner, but the frown lines around his mouth, the slight squint in his eyes, and the furrow of his brows belied the gesture.

"We must wait a bit longer," he said, but his voice sounded soft and unconvincing.

"He may have been discovered," she hissed. The thought caused a shooting pain to radiate up her side. "If they've found him, it may have accelerated the plan to move the Shillelagh. We're risking the mission as well as Cedar," she snapped.

Right after the lift mechanism had begun to churn itself upward, Mia had charged Compendium with the task of following Cedar's movements and instructing him where to go. The lift had stopped, and he had been moving in the direction of the Shillelagh. Then suddenly Compendium no longer had been able to sense his presence. It was as if Cedar had winked from existence.

"It is possible that the shielding that keeps me from directly sensing the Shillelagh without hardwired access to the system also prevents me from taking any readings in that portion of the Village," it said.

Even if that were true, Mia didn't relish the thought of Cedar creeping about with no means of communication deep in enemy territory.

"All right," she said finally. "This waiting is madness. Time is running out."

SainClair sighed deeply and scratched his bristly chin with his grimy fingers. Then he nodded. "I suppose we have no choice," he finally said.

The lift was only big enough to hold two of them at a time, so it took two trips to get them all assembled on the proper level. The night had grown even cooler, and Mia shivered. Whether from the cold or the fear settling in her stomach like a once-fine cheese now green, the electric jolt ran down her spine, through her legs, and into the floor. Following Compendium's instructions, she led the group along the walkways. Her heart thumped in her chest as she pictured Cedar's mangled form in a number of gruesome scenarios. She tried to push those thoughts out of her mind and concentrate on not getting the rest of them killed or captured.

"There is no logic in pursuing such thinking," said Compendium's calm voice, breaking through the fog in her mind.

Certainly not, but sometimes people can't help it. It's involuntary.

"I have spent a lot of time interacting with the minds of people, and it is always fear that is your downfall."

Well, some people are just proud, or greedy, or mean.

"Ah, but deep down so many of those negative traits can be linked to fear. Desire for power is a fear of impotence and rejection. Greed is born from fear of poverty or insufficiency."

Well, what about those who are just mean?

"They fear rejection. If they give others cause to hate and fear them, then they will have risked no emotions of their own."

Are you trying to distract me with philosophical discussion?

"Perhaps," said Compendium. "I was merely expressing my observation that many human problems can be avoided by not letting yourselves be consumed by fear."

It's not that easy. Mia sighed. *How does a book know what fear is anyway?*

"Just because I am incapable of experiencing fear does not mean I am incapable of understanding it and recognizing it when I see it," Compendium replied.

And I suppose you think I'm letting fear cloud my judgment?

"I certainly can read your fear. As for whether it is clouding your judgment, I suppose that remains to be seen. I believe you were correct when you insisted that we press on or risk the mission."

At least you're on my side.

"I don't take sides," said the book.

I don't suppose you can really, but I like to pretend that you're loyal to me.

"Well, in that case," said Compendium, "we should turn right at the next intersection in the path. Around the next bend is where I lost contact with Cedar. The elders housing the Shillelagh should be straight down that pathway. You'll find an entrance to a massive structure built around the elder grove."

As they approached the elder grove of the Druids, Mia signaled for the clerics to stop behind her. Even from a distance, she saw that the trees stretched skyward in an impressive arc. SainClair pulled a small looking glass from his robe and scanned the path and across the massive trees.

"I don't see him," he whispered to Mia.

"Compendium can't sense him either," she said. "I think we'd best make for the Shillelagh and hope we find him along the way. We don't have time to mount a search right now." Her heart ached to say those words, but they had to retrieve the Shillelagh foremost.

"If something is blocking Compendium's sensors and transmitters, I'd best confirm its location now," Mia continued. She pulled Compendium from her robes, and the others huddled around her. She instructed it to show her the schematics it had downloaded from the Village that included the Shillelagh. Compendium marked their location on the map so they could get a clear picture of the direction in which to proceed. Once everyone had a chance to study the details, they brainstormed.

"I expect we'll meet resistance," Mia said. "All we need is to get in, grab it, and get out."

Brother Borus clenched his hands on the massive axes strapped to his waist. "Och, I'm ready for the bastards," he said, a menacing glint in his eye.

"Me too," said Mallus. He pulled a metal rod from his belt and extended it into a staff.

"That's ingenious," said Mia, nodding her approval.

"I made it myself," he whispered and winked at her.

Most of them wore armor beneath their robes, varying between finely wrought mail, plate, or some sort of leather cuirass. It wasn't a side of the Order Mia had seen until this retrieval mission. She had forgone the heavy armor and was glad she did. She never would have survived the climbs and other contortions with a chest plate strapped to her. She gripped the throwing knives that rested along her belt. She had strapped them on before her descent into the detention room, and they were still securely attached to her waist.

"All right," SainClair said, unsheathing his long sword. "Let's move in. Stay together. Cover each other, and don't get killed."

Mia frowned and nodded at her uncle. It seemed like suicide to proceed directly toward the elder grove, but there were no other entrances, and the trees were much too thick to burrow through in some indirect fashion, as she previously had done. As they walked slowly and quietly, she was struck by the eerie silence of the forest. The drone of the trees' energy was loud to Mia, but even in such instances, she usually could hear birds, insects, and other manner of fauna.

The dense hum of the trees couldn't be blocking out the other noises, she thought. *Compendium, is something blocking the forest noises here?*

For the first time since she had activated the auditory communication with Compendium, it didn't respond. She thought the question once more but again received no response. Compendium's calm voice was gone. Stifling a slightly greater than small wave of panic rising from her guts, Mia pulled the book from her robes and opened the cover. It still displayed the map, but the interface didn't change with her thoughts. She whispered at the book, but still nothing. Whatever blocked Compendium from sensing the Shillelagh and Cedar had blocked its entire interface when they had passed into the grove. She tried not to panic any further and kept her thoughts on the task at hand. *At least we still have the map.*

She tucked the book back into her sash and continued the cautious advance toward the entrance to the thickest group of trees. As they moved close, the odd silence grew deeper, even as the vibrating hum coursing through Mia's extremities grew more pronounced. The power of the trees in the Druid elder grove matched the Order's, as did their beauty. Mia saw no sign of wildlife among the sprawling giants, but the night lights still flickered through the tree branches, and sporadic gourds released a soft glow here and there from their vines, which curled gently around the delicate smaller branches of the surrounding trees. Visually it was a stunning display of tranquility and peace, which made Mia's knowledge of their job that much more disconcerting. They crept along for five eternities. With each step, her apprehension grew, raising the tiny hairs on the back of her neck.

At some distance out, they began to pass under the massive branches that sprawled well out from the central trunks, and Mia took a moment to look up, peering into their thick masses. The trunks of the branches were larger than the trunks of many trees in the tropics. Unlike the smaller trees of the Village, however, no structures were settled into the high branches of these elder trees except for the stronghold nestled between them, the entry to which they were headed directly toward.

"How is it that we've seen no Druids yet?" Mia asked SainClair, her voice the barest of whispers.

"It's most certainly a trap," he said through tight lips, his words reinforcing her own nagging fears.

"Then why are we bothering to skulk about?" she said, her voice slightly louder.

"I'm not sure," he added, "but this deep silence compels me to keep my voice low."

Mia chuckled ever so slightly at his quirked eyebrows and his look of confusion as he said those words. "Compendium is frozen," she said. "Something is blocking it."

"The Druids must have an artifact or some other method of dampening the transmissions."

"I don't understand how they can dampen Compendium here, in the center of their own grove. It makes no sense."

SainClair shrugged. "I'm not the one to ask," he said softly.

They approached the entrance to the structure. No Druids jumped out at them brandishing weapons. No trapdoor dropped them down to the earth in one massive fall. Mia grew cold on the inside as they passed through the immense threshold carved with runes and intricately delicate designs in a language she didn't understand. The wood of the structure nestled among the elder trees looked to her eyes as if it had been crafted from elderwood itself. She considered this likely and shook her head lightly at the thought of the possibility; it seemed such a tremendous waste and a tragedy. She couldn't fathom the desire to dismantle an entire elder just to make a fortress. She supposed they could have just found one that had come to the natural end of its life, but Mia never had heard of an elder dying. It was lore that their sprouting had marked the beginning of Lumin and their death would mark the end. *Perhaps it's just stained and manipulated to look like elderwood.* Her body shivered beneath her robes, as if she had entered a structure made of human bones.

The smell of wet earth and wood assaulted her nostrils as they passed through the arched doorway. A long, massive tunnel stretched out before them. Mia scanned the interior of the tunnel, but she was unable to gauge its size. The ceilings were high and curved gracefully above their heads with an eerie life that made her think perhaps the bones had ghosts. The Order tended to light its structures with carefully concealed vines running through the walls in hidden channels, supporting gourds invisibly and making it appear as if they were simply set into sconces. Here vines openly crawled along the walls and up toward the ceiling around them, with gourds dotted among the curling nests and bathing the tunnel in a greenish glow. Mia found the effect at once peaceful and intimidating.

The silence persisted, even as she would expect the thrum of the elder trees surrounding them. It lent an unnatural feeling to overtly natural scenery and did nothing to calm her burgeoning nerves. She grasped at Compendium through her sash. Despite its nonresponsive interface, the book still felt reassuringly warm against her stomach. They proceeded in total silence, the only sounds being the careful footfalls of the clerics on the hardwood floors echoing in the dense silence. According to her recollection of the map, the chamber housing the Shillelagh was all the way at the center of this fortress. It wasn't a straight shot, however, as the tunnel curved around elder trunks, leaving some corners blind.

Mia pulled Compendium from her sash and examined the map again as they continued down the curving hall toward the center of the grove. Though the clerics' location was no longer marked among the lines composing the map's diagrams, Mia could guess it for the most part. Eventually this hallway would give way to a forked set of passages. She grappled with asking someone to man the fork as they proceeded but thought better of it. They likely would have only one chance to escape, so they would need to stick together.

As they approached the fork, she gestured to the others to take the right passage. She was momentarily relieved that the right passageway also was empty, but this feeling mixed with the increasing sense that she and her companions were fodder. They weaved along like this, burrowing deeper into the bowels of the Druid's elder grove like beetles seeking refuge from a deluge. At last they reached the open doorway that led to the chamber that contained the Shillelagh. As they stood silently, Mia peered quickly around the edge of the entranceway, still holding Compendium in her right hand.

A sudden strangled cry caught in her throat. Cedar was hanging aloft above the ground, secured to the back wall of the chamber like a ragdoll. He was strung up by his arms, and his head hanging limply against his chest, his body completely inert. His face was a ruin of blood and gore. Regaining her voice, Mia let out a roar of fury that sounded foreign and animalistic to her ears. Her mind ceased to function, and her body took over. She leapt into the room, racing toward Cedar's immobile frame. She thought of nothing but him. She whipped one of the knives from her belt with her left hand and continued her charge forward. From the corner of her vision, she sensed movement and flung the knife in her hand toward a cloaked figure emerging from the shadows. The figure cried out and sunk to the ground. She didn't even bother to look for the Shillelagh, so consumed was she with fear for Cedar.

Weapons clashed behind her as she charged on, pulling another of her knives from her belt. The room was large, with a domed ceiling of carved wood. The walls were disrupted, as parts of the trunks of several massive elder trees grew up and through the sides of the room. Still, Cedar's prone form was clearly visible, lit by hanging gourds and the lights of the night sky overhead. He was strung up with vines encircling his wrists and snaking down his arms and around his torso. Whether he was breathing, Mia didn't know, but she operated as if he were.

Ignoring the sounds of fighting behind her, she leapt at the back wall of the room, hastily shoving Compendium into her sash. After placing a second knife between her teeth and gripping the vines before her, she heaved herself upward and climbed up the back wall. The vines were thick and hot under her hands and almost spongy in a way she hadn't expected. She hastily pulled herself up. The sounds of weapons

clashing and angry shouts were now distant. *We're quickly going to be outnumbered.* She shook her head. She had to concentrate.

As Mia clung to the rubbery vines and pulled herself higher, she tried to determine whether she was coming up on Cedar in the correct position. He remained unresponsive despite the cacophony below and her occasional shouts of his name. Just as her head passed his feet, something hard struck her from behind. Her breath was briefly knocked out of her as she slammed against the wall. The disorientation of extreme pressure was quickly replaced by a burning, throbbing sensation that seared through her right shoulder. She looked down to see crimson spreading down the right side of her robe. Repressing a scream lest she lose her knife clenched between her teeth, she fought through the burning ache in her shoulder and accelerated her climbing speed.

An arrow whizzed past her head and lodged itself to her left in the wall. Taking a deep breath, she heaved herself around, straining to see to her right. Cedar's limp form hung directly next to her. She twisted her torso and hooked her right arm through a hanging vine to steady herself. After taking the knife from her mouth with her left hand, she hacked at the vines that were restraining Cedar and holding him aloft.

"It's just me," she said reassuringly, as if addressing a child. "I'm going to cut you free now. I don't know if you can hear me, but I'm here for you." The vine around her arm started to clench tighter—these vines were mobile. As she worked to release Cedar, one of them wormed its way around her ankle.

"The vines don't want me to fall either," she said to Cedar, not at all certain he heard her. "Perhaps they should tell the others to stop shooting arrows at us." Under normal circumstances, she'd be utterly enthralled with the prospect of experimenting with and learning the properties of these vines, which seemed capable of growing and moving at what seemed to be breakneck speed. However, the harder they gripped, the more Mia wanted to be let go. She slit vine after vine that pressed along Cedar's torso. Finally a snap came from somewhere near his left arm.

"I hope that was the vine and not your arm," she said with no response. "Although I suppose it's the least of our problems at the moment." She'd already sliced open all the vines along his torso and up his right arm. Now he hung by just his left arm. She grimaced and looked down at the floor of the chamber. Hopefully cutting him loose wouldn't injure him further; she really had no other choice, though. She wrapped her right arm tightly around his torso and sliced the last of the vines that secured his left arm.

"Don't worry," she whispered, "I have you. We'll make it out of here. I won't let you go no matter what." For an instant, she was relieved to feel his heart beating under her hand. It wasn't the strong, steady beat to which she was accustomed, but it reassured her that at least she wasn't retrieving a corpse. Cedar didn't regain consciousness at her touch—though she supposed she shouldn't have been surprised—as her voice had elicited no response. Up close she still had a hard time making out the specifics of his injuries, although his head clearly was covered in blood. She cringed as she looked at him, a meaty pulp where his right eye should be.

"We'll get you fixed up," she said to him, although her voice sounded frail to her own ears. Their bodies began to fall as if in slow motion. They both hurtled toward the ground, the force of Mia's falling body weight ripping her free from the vines that had begun to cling to her arms and legs. She went limp, trying to absorb the impact and shield Cedar from additional harm. As she slammed into the ground, her consciousness slipped away in a haze of pain and slick blood, her arm still wrapped tightly around Cedar and her left hand gripping her throwing knife.

35 SHILLELAGH   L.C. 10152

M IA AWOKE TO A STABBING PAIN in her shoulder. Colors swam dimly in front of her eyes, and a familiar voice carried through the fog in her head.

"There she is," it said maliciously. The voice was accompanied by a sharp, needlelike pain that dug into the depths of her shoulder. A choked moan erupted nearby, startling her. The froggy voice was her own. When her eyesight cleared, a vine-covered wall materialized above her. Obstructing it was the familiar face of Taryn frowning down on her. She held the Shillelagh in her right hand, its pointed tip pressed deeply into Mia's injured shoulder. When she squirmed slightly under the pressure, Taryn pushed the stick deeper into her wound.

Mia had no idea how long she had been unconscious. Her mouth felt gummy, and she was lying in a tangled ball on the floor of the great room. Mia's her arm entwined around Cedar, who remained blissfully unaware of their current situation. Behind Taryn, Mia saw the others—battered, bloody, and bruised—their arms secured behind their backs by a complement of Druids. Mia noticed then what Taryn held in her left hand. It was Compendium.

"I suspected, hoped really, that I hadn't seen the last of you," Taryn said, fingering Compendium's leather cover with her thumb. "Or this." She held the book out to Mia, her expression no warmer than before. "Although, as I'm sure you're aware, Compendium doesn't work in our elder grove."

Mia's head swam, and she tried to control her tongue enough to form words. Instead she just blinked and stared.

Taryn, undaunted, gestured to Cedar's prone form. "I certainly didn't expect you to send Cedar in to do your dirty work. After all, it is your fault that we have the Shillelagh, isn't it?"

Mia's eyes narrowed, and a frown crossed her lips. Taryn smiled, clearly elated that she had hit a nerve.

"Oh, I'm sorry. Did you think that I actually wanted to run off with you?" she sneered.

Mia's cheeks grew warm with embarrassment. It wasn't just the mocking in Taryn's voice but the fact that her uncle and the others could hear her taunts and recall the way in which Mia had betrayed them. The betrayal was her source of embarrassment, not anything Taryn could say to her.

"I thought you were a friend, but I suppose it's my fault for being a poor judge of character." Mia's voice sounded hoarse when it finally erupted from her throat.

"I did fancy you my friend," Taryn said, "but unfortunately, I have no place for friendship right now. My grandfather is counting on me to protect our lovely Shillelagh here and to bring honor to our name." She dug the Shillelagh deeper into Mia's shoulder.

A wave of dizziness caused her cruel features to spin before Mia's eyes.

"Unfortunately, my friend," she continued, although there was suddenly a faraway look in her eyes, "you *have* been proven to be quite the gullible fool." A blond eyebrow raised into a knowing arch, as if they shared some secret regarding Mia's deficient intellect.

"I suppose you need to tell yourself that," said Mia, forcing her words through the pain spidering across her upper body. "It's much more convenient for me to be gullible than for you to have feelings, after all."

Mia may have underestimated Taryn, and she certainly had misjudged her, naïvely perhaps. In Mia's mind, they had shared a bond that transcended politics. And if that was naïve, so be it. She couldn't give up on trust or friendship; Taryn wouldn't ruin those for her. Perhaps Taryn also misjudged and underestimated her. If she thought Mia an insipid fool, all the better for Mia.

"I still don't know what I did to you, Taryn, to make you hate me so." The words sounded whiny and weak, but if Mia could put Taryn her off guard, perhaps they all had a chance. She quelled her struggle against the Shillelagh pinning her to the ground and let herself relax and regroup.

"Oh, you're a prime fool," Taryn continued, not even skipping a beat. Her eyes gleamed as she stared down at Mia's prone form. "Can't you even see that I used you the whole time?" Again, something flickered in Taryn's eyes, and Mia latched onto that hesitation.

"I'm sorry, but I don't believe you. We shared too much for that friendship to be a complete pretense." Mia did her best to look hurt, although frankly there wasn't much pretending in her expressions. While Taryn had talked, Mia had surveyed their situation from the corners of her eyes. Her left arm was trapped underneath Cedar's body. Her hand tingled with disrupted sensations, and she gently flexed her fingers to restore the circulation. It still held the knife, and it was out of Taryn's sight but also trapped beneath Cedar's weight. The others were bloody and battered but alert and on their feet. They were held clumped in a group, surrounded by Druids with swords aloft and ready to pierce. Mia saw her companions watching her, their faces largely appearing emotionless—except for perhaps Borus, who always did a poor job of masking his emotions. His brown eyes were narrowed, his teeth bared inside his dark, heavy beard in a wide sneer that bordered on a grimace.

"Yes, you fool," Taryn was saying in the background, her eyes darting to the other Druids who were listening keenly to their conversation. "I was sent there—really I volunteered to go and immerse myself in the Order to learn its secrets and uncover the artifacts hidden within. We Druids have believed in the existence of a powerful artifact that could allow instantaneous travel, but I was the one who took the rumors and speculations and made them into something real and tangible."

"You're welcome," Mia replied after Taryn finally finished her diatribe regarding how she was able to integrate and live among their group of heathens and secure the most valuable artifact the Druids ever had known. Mia tried to keep the animosity from her voice, but she was growing weary of Taryn's magnanimous talk and couldn't help herself.

"Oh, please," Taryn replied. "You were merely a means to an end, a puppet to pull the strings on."

"Oh, really?" Mia asked, trying to keep her voice casual. She had mostly regained the sensation in her left hand, the tingles giving way to a burning and finally a warm feeling. Slowly, so as not to draw notice to the movement, she slid her arm down, dragging the knife along under Cedar's clothes, hoping she would snag neither cloth nor flesh. Simultaneously she made a show of grasping ineffectually at the tip of the Shillelagh. Her intention was to appear as if she were trying to prevent it from digging farther into her shoulder as well as help Taryn to assume Mia had no strength remaining.

She twitched her head slightly toward SainClair, and his chin moved downward ever so slightly in response.

Borus coughed then, and the others looked over. "Gah, all this chattering is gonna do me in afore one of yer staffs does," he said in a loud voice.

Mia stifled a smile and watched closely as Taryn's head swiveled toward Brother Borus. "You were always a moron," she snapped at him, her voice hard and clipped. All signs of syrupy sweetness had drained away.

"Aye?" he said, his eyebrows rising comically. "Well, if I recall, ye liked my cooking nonetheless. Yer no different than any of us, lassie."

"Fine, have it your way," Taryn said. "Kill them," she snapped at the Druids who were restraining Brother Borus. When she turned back to face Mia, she could see Taryn's face had gone from flushed to wan.

"I'd like to see 'im try ta kill me with that sodding stick," he scoffed at the nearest Druid, who was holding a wooden quarterstaff.

While Taryn recovered her composure, Mia wriggled her arm completely free and lunged toward Taryn's foot with the knife. Taryn's right hand was still wrapped around the Shillelagh, and as Mia forced herself up, it dug even more painfully into her shoulder. Mia thrust her shoulder into the stick and pushed while wrenching the Shillelagh simultaneously with her right hand. Taryn let out a grunt of surprise and toppled backward, landing hard on the floor, one hand still clutching the handle of the Shillelagh and the other clasped around Compendium. Pain thrummed through Mia's body like a bolt of lightning that struck every finger and toe on her right side. The cry that erupted from her throat didn't sound human. It was the roar of an enraged animal. She twisted herself toward Taryn's prone form and swiped at her with the knife. Taryn disengaged from the Shillelagh and kicked at the knife with a boot.

"You," she hissed through clenched teeth, her voice growing shrill.

She reached for the Shillelagh again, but Mia deftly moved it from Taryn's reach and pulled it toward her body as she tried to rocket to her feet. Mia's movements were much more elegant in her mind, but then, her movements were frequently more elegant in her mind. Nevertheless she was on her feet, the Shillelagh held weakly in her right hand and the knife in the other. She wanted so badly to shift some weight against the Shillelagh, but she doubted her shoulder would take it. She was still dizzy from the pain. Taryn was quick to her feet as well but possessed no weapon. And yet she still had all the leverage. Shouts rang out around the cavernous room. The clerics wouldn't be killed without a fight. Mia caught Borus charging a group of Druids with his bare hands before her focus returned to Taryn.

Taryn handled Compendium carefully, her mouth twisted into a wicked grimace. "It appears I'm still at a bit of an advantage," she said, taking a small step forward. She fingered the spine of the book with one hand and ruffled the pages with her other, a look of envy clouding her golden eyes. Compendium was still frozen on the map of the Druid fortress. "I know how much you rely on it. If you'd done a little more talking to those around you and a little less to this ancient stack of paper, maybe your boyfriend over there would still be whole."

Mia flinched at her reference to Cedar. She kept silent, though, unsure what to say. Compendium was useless to Taryn, but it was everything to Mia.

"You thought you were so special when you activated this thing," said Taryn. Her face appeared flushed. She took another small step toward Mia.

Mia wanted to lunge at her and grab Compendium from her hands.

"The illustrious bloodlines," Taryn said, fingering Compendium's pages and opening it to the center. "Perhaps you're worried I'll do this?" she questioned. She spat into the center of the book then wiped a dirty hand around in the saliva. "Aw, it doesn't like me." She held the book out for Mia to see. The page was marred but blank. "I guess the Rosewaters aren't *illustrious* enough."

"You know very well Compendium is blocked in this room," Mia replied.

Taryn smiled. "Perhaps, then, I should make my point differently. Now that this page is ruined, I suppose I should tidy things up a bit." She pulled downward on the page she had defiled and tugged hard at it. Mia flinched, expecting the thin, ancient page to rip from the book. Her heart pounded.

My friend. She willed Compendium to respond. The book really was like a friend to her. It had been there during her toughest moments. It had led her into the darkness and back out again. And now it was going to remain silent as Taryn tore it apart, piece by piece, before Mia's eyes.

"It doesn't matter what you do to Compendium," Mia said. "The Shillelagh is coming with us. It wasn't yours to take, just like Compendium isn't yours to deface. You'll regret interfering in the Order, and you'll regret anything you do to that book." Mia pointed the knife clenched in her hand at Taryn.

She only sneered.

Despite Mia's tough words, she flinched as Taryn tore at the page she held in her fingers. The paper bent in her hand but didn't rend.

That's it. Fight, my friend. Perhaps you can still hear my thoughts. If so, fight.

Taryn's hand tugged sharply again at the page, but still it didn't tear. Mia glanced quickly around the room. Cedar was still unconscious on the ground. SainClair and Borus had disarmed a couple of the Druids of their quarterstaffs and were in a melee with the remaining Druids. The Druid bowmen had been dispensed of first and lay motionless on the floor. Mia couldn't tell if they still lived. Young Brother Mallus lay in a crumpled heap, blood seeping from his crushed skull, an injury that would have been impossible to survive. She forced down the bile rising in her throat.

"We have to go!" Mia shouted.

"Aye," Borus exclaimed.

SainClair grunted and dodged a staff aimed at his head. He rolled to the left and came back to his feet. Mia's eyes returned to Taryn. She had given up trying to tear Compendium and was now moving away from Mia toward the nearest hearth in the room.

"I'll burn it!" she yelled, her voice carrying over the sounds of exertion and clacks of fighting. "Give me the Shillelagh, or I'll burn it."

"Oh, and you'll let us go on our merry way if I do?" Mia asked.

She smiled coldly and tossed Compendium into the hearth. Mia watched, frozen, as the book settled into the orange glow, darkening slowly, its pages curling gently from the heat. She fought the urge to push Taryn aside and retrieve it from the flames. Instead she threw the knife in her hand. It landed in Taryn's right shoulder, forcing her back a step. She screamed in pain. Mia's own shoulder ached from its injury and the exertion.

"That makes us twins," Mia said.

Taryn clutched at the knife, but her hands slipped on the blood. "I'll see you burn in the Core!" she yelled.

"Not without this," Mia said, shaking the Shillelagh at her. "Now! We have to go now!" she called to her companions. Mia carried the Shillelagh over to Cedar and gently grasped his inert hand. It was cool to the touch but still held a faint pulse. Borus and SainClair were at her side in an instant, each grasping on to one of them in a chain formation.

"One, two, three!" Mia brought the Shillelagh up. "Take us to the outer courtyard of the Compound of the Order of Vis Firmitas," she yelled, and knocked the stick twice against the hardwood floor. A howling vortex opened up around them the moment the staff stuck the solid wood beneath Mia's feet.

She felt rather than saw the crack of the explosion, and a wave of nausea washed over her. The bile rose up from her gut and threatened to burst forth from her throat as the world spun and churned around them. She tried desperately to close her eyes, but they were frozen open in her head, her body rigidly locked into position. A moment later, the movement ground to a halt, and they were outside among the trees, the forest silent except for the echoing of the crack of the Shillelagh. The rigidity in Mia's body subsided, and they all collapsed to the ground, groaning.

"That was awful," Mia said, her voice cracking and gasping. She willed herself not to be sick.

"Cedar had the right idea traveling with his eyes closed," said SainClair, and promptly vomited.

Mia's vision was a blur. *Did the traveling do something to my eyes?* She rubbed them and realized tears were streaming down her face. After that, all she could manage was a sob. A sob for Compendium, a sob for Brother Mallus, and a sob for Cedar, who lay broken and bruised beside her—all of it a product of her carelessness. The sobs wracked her body, and she curled into a ball, face pressed into her knees.

"There, there," said SainClair's voice near her ear. "We're home now," he added, but Mia could no more stop the tears than dam an ocean. SainClair lifted her body off the ground, and she let herself be carried in a way that she hadn't since she was a small girl cowering after that stalker attack. Her carelessness had been at fault there as well. With Mia weeping in SainClair's arms and still clutching the Shillelagh, and Cedar unconscious and slung over Borus's shoulder, they made for home.

Through hiccups and tears, all Mia could say was, "I saw it burn."

36 CLERIC   L.C. 10153

M IA SAT ALONE IN HER CHAMBERS looking
out over the mountainside visible between the
thicket of trees shading her open window. Upon their
return with the Shillelagh, she was removed from the
barracks and settled in her own rooms. She wasn't
quite sure whether she was a prisoner, but she hadn't
felt much like leaving her chambers and rarely
ventured forth. A full month had elapsed since their
confrontation with the Druids. Since then, time had
passed in a haze. She spent some time recovering from
her arrow wound. The medics had to remove a number
of Shillelagh splinters from it. This caused the others

to joke that her arm might go off on adventures by itself while she slept.

"Perhaps they missed one," Brother Cornelius said to her after she woke in the medical ward, his eyes sparkling. "You'd best keep an eye on that appendage," he added with a chuckle and patted her face gently. She smiled weakly but couldn't muster a laugh. Not much was funny these days. As far as she was aware, Cedar was still in recovery. It took two weeks for him to regain consciousness, and Brother Borus told Mia the ruined right eye couldn't be saved. This didn't surprise her, given the pulp that haunted her memory when she thought of it. She visited him as much as she could at first, held his hand, stroked his hair, and talked to him, but she couldn't bring herself to go back once she had learned he was awake. She never had shared with him her feelings, but what was the point now? It was all ruined. She couldn't bear to have him look at her, supposing he still wanted to. She wasn't sure what she would say to him when she finally saw him again, but she never let her mind dwell on it for long.

Compendium, also, was never far from her thoughts. She had watched it singe, its pages browning and wrinkling. Her legacy, her family, her history. All gone in a spark. She wanted to vomit every time the image of the book charring to ash in the hearth flashed into her mind. She grieved for Compendium and the companionship it had provided. False or real, it didn't matter. It had become an extension of her; Taryn could have cut a lung from Mia's body with the same effect. SainClair tried to console her, but his gentle words and concern only compounded her guilt, for it was his family and legacy lost as well as hers. And so she hid from the Order and told herself they didn't deserve the pain her face would visit on them.

Lost in her piteous musings, Mia didn't hear the first knock at the entryway to her sitting room. A loud throat clearing followed by a stern but steady knock alerted her that she had company. Normally Hamish would have signaled her long before anyone bothered to knock, but the silly fluff face was off having a romp with SainClair. She sighed and looked back to the doorway from her chair by the window. Dominus Nikola was standing inside the entrance.

"May we discuss something?" he asked in his calm, firm voice. It reminded Mia of Compendium, and she swallowed hard.

Silly, for there was emotion behind Nikola's words.

"Certainly, sir," she replied, gesturing to the chair by the hearth. She pulled her own chair to sit next to the one already hearthside and sat down. Dominus Nikola crossed the room in his deliberate, slow manner. She sometimes wondered whether he had to think through every step before he took it. That, or perhaps he had a touch of arthritis. In either case, she found herself absently rubbing her neck as she waited for him to take a seat.

"Are you still suffering some ill effects from your wounds?" he asked politely, his eyes following the motion of her hand.

"Ah, no," she said after a moment's thought. "At least I don't suppose I do."

He nodded at her response and gave her his usual smile. Although it was warm, Mia couldn't tell what he was thinking deep within. "Is there anything in particular you wanted to discuss, sir?" she asked, adopting a cordial but distant tone.

His eyebrows rose slightly at that statement. "Are you trying to rid yourself of me so expeditiously? I just seated myself. And you have yet to even offer me any tea."

Mia's eyes grew round, and she frowned softly. "Ah, yes, my manners apparently suffered more than my shoulder did," she replied, her sentence trailing off in a mumble. She stood to move toward the stones warming in the hearth. "Would you like some tea, Dominus?"

"Oh, no, I'm quite fine," he said with a chuckle. "I was just having a bit of fun at your expense, my child."

Mia wanted so much to smile and chuckle along with the Dominus, but she couldn't muster the energy or mirth for it. With a tight grimace she fervently hoped didn't look ungrateful, she settled back into her chair.

"To the matter at hand then?" she asked, rubbing the back of her neck again.

"Ah, yes," Dominus Nikola said, clearing his throat and settling back into the chair. His gray eyes held hers in a steady gaze. "I wished to discuss with you your continued role with the Order."

At the Dominus's words, Mia lowered her head and fastidiously examined a thread dangling from the wrist of her robes. Since her return, she had been wearing her acolyte robes and sash every day, but she hadn't participated in life at the Order. She stayed away from Brother Cornelius and the Archives. She ventured down to the dining hall only at odd hours, and she rarely stopped to talk to anyone when she did. She had made so many promises. She had stood before the Order and asked them to take a chance on redeeming her, and she had let them down. They may have succeeded in bringing the Shillelagh back, but at what cost? There was no unkindness or pity in the eyes that tried to meet hers in the halls. There were no broken conversations as she passed. And yet she knew she hadn't earned her place among them. She had worried

that this day was nearing. After all, they had moved
her away from the other acolytes into these beautiful
but remote chambers. She told herself that perhaps it
was to aid in her recovery, but deep down she sensed
it was because she was no longer welcome.

"I'm so sorry, Dominus," she said, her voice low
and words struggling to emerge. "I tried, but I failed.
Just say the words, and I'll pack myself and Hamish
and be off."

"Why would you do that, my child?" the Dominus
asked. He folded his hands one over the other as he
rested his elbows on the arms of the overstuffed chair
in which he sat. He had asked Mia the question, but
his eyes held no surprise or concern at her words. If
anything, he looked slightly amused.

"Why do you ask questions that you already know
the answer to?" she asked in response, evading him.

Another soft chuckle erupted from the depths of his
throat. "If you're going to try my patience and my
nerves, I suppose you'd best offer me that tea again,"
he said plainly, a white eyebrow rising up toward his
close-cropped head. His light, jovial manner wasn't
improving Mia's foul one. She moved to the hearth
and busied herself taking two cups from the shelf
above and filling them with water from a pitcher. She
plucked two red, hot stones from the hearth with a
tong and dropped them into the cups of water.

"Ginger or black?" she asked.

"Oh, ginger," the Dominus replied with a smile, anticipation gleaming in his eyes. "I do so love the spice."

The water in the cups was steaming from the hot stone resting at the bottom of each, and Mia dropped in a small cage of dried leaves and gingerroot to steep in each of the cups. She brought them over on a small tray with tiny carafes of honey sap, milk sap, and cream. Dominus Nikola took his cup and stirred the seeping leaves and gingerroot around. They sat in silence as he tended to his tea, eventually adding a dollop of cream and some of the honey sap before taking a sip.

"Ah, yes, that is quite fortifying," he said with a satisfied sigh. "We'd best begin this conversation anew." He paused in thought, and Mia sat silently, allowing him the moment to ruminate. He took another sip of tea and cleared his throat. "Do you remember how you came to us, my child?"

"I was destined to serve with the Order, like my parents before me."

The Dominus looked at her, his teacup perched below his mouth. "Ah, but that isn't the whole of it, correct?"

"Well, when I first arrived, I thought Father had bargained my freedom for his life," Mia said, "but that wasn't really the way of it."

"Was it not?" he said after a moment's deliberation and took another sip of his tea, breathing deeply of the ginger-spiced aroma that floated around them.

Mia considered his words carefully before she spoke. It had all been a ruse to fulfill her mother's wishes. There had been no bargain struck. And yet she truly had felt betrayed, used, and abandoned. And she supposed she had been all of those things. Father had made no effort to try to explain the situation to her. He hadn't treated her as the independent adult she was but had tricked her as one does a child into eating a bitter root. And then she thought about Dominus Nikola's words that cold morning upon her arrival. She recalled his piercing gaze and her own rage. It had seemed at the time to be a false decision presented her, one in name only.

"If I had turned and walked out the way I had arrived that first morning, would the Order have let me leave?" she asked.

"One always has a choice," the Dominus said, smiling at her and taking another enthusiastic sip of his tea.

She sighed and sipped her own tea in response. "And what is my choice now?" she asked finally, sensing this conversation might finally get to the point the Dominus was dancing around.

"You can either take up your entitled position as a full cleric of the Order and the obligations and rights that are assumed and bestowed with that position, or you can watch from a withering tree branch as Lumin and the elders and fauna so precious to it are endangered by the Druids."

Whatever Mia had been expecting Dominus Nikola to say, this wasn't it. She sucked in a breath, her brow wrinkling.

"That's rather dramatic and not much of a choice, if I do say."

"Extinction is naturally a dramatic topic, I am afraid," the Dominus said.

"Extinction?" she parroted the word, her brain not fully comprehending the Dominus's meaning. For the first time since meeting Dominus Nikola, she considered whether he was going mad.

"There is much you still don't understand about the Order and its inception. We were formed not only to protect the artifacts but also to restore society. Something, however, has gone terribly wrong. Gamma Protocol was supposed to terminate more than one hundred fifty cycles ago, but we can't get into the Core."

"Gamma Protocol?" Mia asked, raising her eyebrows.

"A great deal about the Great Fall remains unknown," he continued, "but you'll have to trust me on this. The Shillelagh has much more than just historical significance. It is the means to get to the Core."

"Yes, I knew that," she said. "Brother Cornelius mentioned it while I was…" *In the dungeon.* She finished the sentence in her head. "But what is Gamma Protocol specifically?"

"Gamma Protocol saved Lumin from extinction once," Nikola said. His tea finished, he leaned back in the armchair and scratched his chin thoughtfully. "But now we know for certain that the Druids are trying to get into the Core, and Rosewater will stop at nothing to put us back on the path."

"To extinction?" she asked, her limbs growing numb and cold.

The Dominus nodded slowly and clasped his hands again. For a moment, he and Mia sat together in silence, each lost in thought. Mia's mind roiled with many unanswered questions, but the gravity of the revelation left her thoughts watery and insubstantial.

"Why don't we just go to the Core first?" Mia asked.

"Because we can't find the key," he said. He smiled ruefully. "So you see, the Order needs your skills and resourcefulness. Your abilities are integral to our survival."

"But I let Compendium be destroyed," she said. "I let Mallus die and the others be injured so we could get the Shillelagh back. I let Cedar be maimed."

"It couldn't be avoided," the Dominus said contemplatively.

"I never should have trusted Taryn. I let myself be led astray. These are not the qualities of a cleric."

"We can make decisions only with the information laid before us," he replied. His eyes grew distant, a haunted look crossing their gray depths before they snapped back to their piercing gaze. "The capacity to trust in others is not a failing." His tone brooked no argument.

"Even if that trust is abused?" Mia asked, disregarding his tone.

"Especially when it's abused. You may not feel that you have earned your place among us, my child, but the practical lessons that you've learned in the past thirteen months more than make up for, ah, let us call it, your independent nature." With that, he stood and stretched his back and grasped his cane from its resting place. Mia always wondered whether it served as more of an ornament than a support. "Now, my child"—he gestured his free hand toward the acolyte pin stuck to her sash—"will you be joining us then?"

"I suppose I don't have a choice," she said, sighing and rising to give him a bow and escort him to the doorway.

"Ah," he said, "but one always has a choice."

MIA PEERED THROUGH the large carved doors toward the assembly in the Great Hall. The last time she had entered here, it was to make amends. This time it was to be inducted as a cleric of the Order. Those gathered—which appeared to be almost everyone—chatted in hushed tones as they awaited the commencement of the ceremony. Mia's fellow acolytes occupied the space closest to the door. Iris's eyes were fixed upward as she pointed to the stonework and intricately carved skylights set into the ceiling. Another acolyte stared openmouthed at the delicately woven tapestries that hung along the walls of the chamber.

Where the floor was usually open and displaying the spectacularly inlaid design of an elder arboreal, today seats were arranged in neat rows facing the dais, with a central aisle between the rows. Gourds were placed all around, bathing the room in a soft, golden light, and bunches of curling vines bursting with flowering colors were placed along the dais and podium.

The clerics obviously had taken pains to arrange this ceremony. Cedar's thick hair and brown skin caught Mia's eye from a distance, and her breath caught in her chest at the patch strapped over his ruined eye. Part of her wanted to run to him and throw her arms around him, while another part wanted to run from him and hide from the damage she had wrought. He sat stiffly and nodded occasionally as others spoke to him. Mia looked away lest he feel her eyes boring a hole in the back of his head.

The Order wasn't an organization to make merry with music and dancing, and this event was no different. Dominus Nikola, Brother Cornelius, and Brother SainClair assumed their positions on the dais as a signal that the proceedings were about to begin. The other senior clerics seated themselves behind them. Mia cleared her throat nervously and wrung her hands in her robes. Sister Valencia had dropped off the darker, softer robes of a full cleric for her to wear to the ceremony, but Mia was currently without a sash or pin. She fingered the heavy egg shape of her mother's locket, turned the little tab at the top to expose the sigil within, and peered at the somber owl springing forth from the lotus flower. With Compendium gone, this was her only rendering of the SainClair family crest. She twisted the locket closed, tucked the delicate leafy chain back into her tunic, and patted it against her chest.

"Good morning to you all," Dominus Nikola called out to the assembly. "I trust we're all in good spirits as we welcome into our ranks a new cleric of the Order. We're gathered this morning to bestow upon Mia Jayne SainClair the rank of cleric. Is Ms. SainClair present among you?"

Mia entered the room upon this cue and stood at the threshold. This part of the ceremony was scripted.

"I, Mia Jayne SainClair, am present to receive the honor bestowed upon me," she said, wrestling with her voice to keep it steady and natural sounding.

"Then come forward, Ms. SainClair, to make your vow and take your place among us," the Dominus said.

His face appeared serious, but his gray eyes held a spark of warmth deep within. Mia straightened her back and walked deliberately and proudly to the front of the room. Any residual guilt that struggled to well up as she passed the faces staring intently at her was pushed into the depths. She would make this vow and do her part. The past was the past. When she arrived at the base of the dais, she turned.

"I have come now to make this vow to all of you," Mia stated.

Sitting in the front row, Cedar lifted his head, his face still ashen beneath his light-brown skin. His remaining eye, large and dark, was fixed on her, but his face was stony and unreadable. Her heart withered at the sight. She turned and climbed the stairs of the dais to stand before Dominus Nikola. He placed his hand on her right shoulder, where her sash and pin would lay.

"Do you, Mia Jayne SainClair, vow to serve the Order in all things from this moment until your last breath?"

"I do," she stated.

"And will you treat those here as your own brothers and sisters, your family for life, from this moment until your last breath?"

"I will."

"And do you now accept the responsibility to spend your life and time in this world in the preservation of Lumin and its flora through study, scholarship, reflection, ingenuity, and combat, if necessary?"

"I do."

"Now," he said, "will Brother Thaddeus SainClair step forward?"

SainClair rose from his chair to the left of Dominus Nikola's and proceeded to a nearby table. On the table was laid a sash and pin. Mia hadn't noticed it from the back of the room. SainClair lifted the sash and pin and strode over to stand next to the Dominus.

"Thaddeus SainClair, are you willing to vouch for this acolyte's character and fitness to ascend to the rank of full cleric among us?" Dominus Nikola asked.

"I am," replied SainClair, his icy-blue eyes resting on Mia's aqua ones. The corner of his mouth curved into a small smile, although he remained largely motionless before the Dominus.

"You may now bestow upon her the rank." Dominus Nikola took his hand from Mia's shoulder and gestured to the sash.

SainClair held up the sash and draped it around Mia's hip and up over her right shoulder. She was reminded of her first day here when Cedar similarly draped her sash for the first time. She stood motionless as he held the fabric in place with his right hand and deftly pinned it to the tunic with his left. Mia let her eyes wander to her shoulder even as her head pointed forward. Her acolyte pin had been replaced with a shiny gold pin bearing an elder tree filled with fruit.

"I had this one made specially for you," SainClair whispered near her ear. "Look."

Mia turned her head and looked down at her shoulder. Her uncle grasped the pin and tugged gently. The center, where the tree resided, flipped in an outer ring in which it was set. The other side was an engraving of the SainClair sigil, the owl and lotus gleaming in gold. Mia's eyes watered, and she took a deep breath, determined not to cry. She gave her uncle a tremulous smile, and he winked at her as he grasped his own pin and flipped it similarly.

"I love you," she mouthed silently. He winked again and stepped back next to Dominus Nikola.

"And so, Sister SainClair, you've made your vows and assumed your obligations to us, your family, and so we now vow to you as follows."

Then the whole room spoke as one, their voices resonating along the walls and filling Mia's ears and her heart.

"As you have given your vow to serve us, we vow to serve you. As you are now linked to us as family, we are now your family. As you now dedicate your life to service of the realm, you add your voice to ours, and we are one. Welcome, Sister SainClair!"

The room applauded and cheered. Hoots filled the air, and Mia broke out into a huge smile and blinked back the tears that continued to threaten. SainClair stepped forward and embraced her in a hug, and the warmth of his arms enclosed her. Dominus Nikola and Brother Cornelius clapped behind him, and the voices of the others clamored their congratulations. Mia was finally home among family.

ABOUT THE AUTHOR

Alia Luria lives in Orlando, Florida, with her partner and their two Pembroke Welsh Corgis, neither of which is named Hamish. When she isn't writing far-flung tales, she practices corporate and privacy law.

Visit alialuria.com or follow @alia on Twitter for information on and excerpts from *Ocularum*, the next book in the Artifacts of Lumin Series.

Made in the USA
Charleston, SC
08 June 2015